GODLESS

GODLESS

A Novel

DR. JAMES DOBSON
AND KURT BRUNER

New York Boston Nashville

Copyright © 2014 by James C. Dobson and Kurt Bruner

FaithWords
Hachette Book Group
1290 Avenue of the Americas
New York, NY 10104

www.faithwords.com

Printed in the United States of America

RRD-C

Originally published in hardcover by Hachette Book Group.
First trade edition: November 2014

10 9 8 7 6 5 4 3 2 1

FaithWords is a division of Hachette Book Group, Inc.
The FaithWords name and logo are trademarks of Hachette Book Group, Inc.

The Hachette Speakers Bureau provides a wide range of authors for speaking events. To find out more, go to www.hachettespeakersbureau.com or call (866) 376-6591.

The publisher is not responsible for websites (or their content) that are not owned by the publisher.

The Library of Congress has catalogued the hardcover edition as follows:

Dobson, James C., 1936-
  Godless : a novel / Dr. James Dobson and Kurt Bruner.—First edition.
      pages cm
  ISBN 978-1-4555-1318-5 (hardcover)—ISBN 978-1-4555-1316-1 (ebook)
  1. Population aging—Fiction. I. Bruner, Kurt D. II. Title.
  PS3604.O24G63 2014
  813'.6—dc23

                                    2013019841

  ISBN 978-1-4555-1317-8 (pbk.)

In memory of the late James Dobson Sr., who recognized the myth of a population bomb as both groundless and godless.

AUTHOR'S NOTE

When I first approached Dr. Dobson about partnering to author a series of novels he told me a story that seemed to confirm our chosen theme.

As a young man Jim Dobson became a professor of pediatrics at the University of Southern California School of Medicine and served on the attending staff at Children's Hospital in Los Angeles. Thrown into the influential world of academia, he zealously sought wisdom from a man he admired more than any other, his namesake, James Dobson Sr. He ran everything by his dad and mentor, relishing the opportunity to discuss the ideas he was encountering with a man who possessed both a formidable intellect and a heart for God.

In 1968 Jim Dobson wrapped a Christmas present to give to his father, a best-selling book written by Stanford University professor Paul R. Ehrlich. *The Population Bomb* warned of mass starvation during coming decades due to overpopulation. The book had begun shaping a widespread belief that we needed to limit population growth to avert a global catastrophe. Dr. Dobson handed the gift to his father anticipating yet another round of discussion about popular ideas. But to his surprise, after glancing at the cover and reading the book jacket, his father handed it back to his son. As Dr. Dobson explained years later, "That was one of only two books my father refused to read. He knew, intuitively, that it was more than just wrong. It was also evil."

The Population Bomb turned out to be groundless. Rather than mass starvation, the world experienced an agricultural explosion that has made food more plentiful and less expensive than was ever imagined possible. But the facts did not prevent Ehrlich's claims from continuing to shape modern assumptions and, tragically, choices.

All three books in this trilogy project what will happen three decades in the future when those choices come to sinister fruition. The economic pyramid will flip. Too few young will be forced to bear the financial burden of a rapidly aging population. Imagining what will transpire in such a world does not require a penchant for prophecy or speculation. One need only project current demographic and cultural trends. Decades of falling fertility have already created the future we depict.

In *Fatherless* we explored one of the causes, men neglecting the honor and responsibilities of paternity. In *Childless* we asked what happens when sex is severed from the life-giving joys of maternity. In the final installment, *Godless*, we confront the chilling implications of Dostoyevsky's claim that without God all things are permissible.

These books pull back the curtain from an assault on human thriving that began when our first parents believed a rebel's lie. As we've said earlier, a happy home is the highest expression of God's image on earth. And there are forces working to destroy that image, not all of them visible to human eyes. But there is also a resilient beauty and hope found in God's design for families, something the most ardent forces of hell cannot destroy.

Kurt Bruner

GODLESS

PROLOGUE

August 3, 2044

Veronica's eyes flew open as she felt the rising sun warm her face. Panic forced her upright. "Where are we?"

No response. *Louder.* "Mommy?"

A wordless, groggy moan came from the front passenger seat.

"Mommy!" Veronica insisted. "Are we almost there?"

Sleep's time warp had displaced the six-year-old. She looked out the window in search of clues while rebuking herself with a huff. She had broken a promise. Actually, three promises. "I will stay awake. I will stay awake...stay awake." They were the last words she could remember saying before losing her battle with the gravitational pull of a four a.m. departure.

A range of mountains on the horizon told her they had escaped the plains of Nebraska. They must be in Colorado, land of Grandpa's ticklish whiskers and Grandma's fresh-baked cookies.

The smile of anticipation was quickly replaced by a frown

when Veronica remembered that Grandma was gone. Grandpa lived alone now. And Grandpa didn't make cookies.

But he still wore Grandma's favorite aftershave. He still hugged Veronica tightly against his tummy whenever she came to visit. And his enclosed porch sheltered the rich aroma of expensive cigars whenever they played go fish while sipping soda.

Her grin returned. So did her impatience for details.

"Daddy?" she said toward the driver's side of the car. "Are we in Colorado yet?"

Another groggy moan.

Following his usual pattern, Veronica's father had pulled the car into the AutoDrive lane before dozing off. He always insisted they hit the road before sunrise because he wanted to take advantage of the two-and-a-half-hour stretch between North Platte and Denver. His daughter's question invaded the hypnotic hum of tires massaging the highway. He glanced at a dashboard screen.

"We'll be there soon, sweetheart," he mumbled. Then he repositioned his head against a propped pillow.

She huffed again, crossing her arms at the offense. Daddy still treated her like a five-year-old! Did he honestly think she would be satisfied with such a vague answer?

"*How* soon?" she demanded.

Her father sat up while rubbing the sleep out of his eyes. He looked through the rearview mirror, then gave a single chuckle toward her annoyed expression.

"Sorry, sweetheart." He looked more purposefully toward the dashboard. "We'll arrive in precisely thirty-seven minutes."

Another panic. Could she color a picture that fast? The best part of their monthly visit was when Grandpa escorted Veronica into what he called "the gallery," an empty bedroom where works by "my favorite granddaughter" were taped to the wall. They both knew she was his *only* granddaughter.

She had no siblings or cousins. But she loved hearing him say it anyway.

Unwilling to disappoint her grandfather, Veronica reached to tug on Mommy's blouse. It worked. Danielle Bentley sat up and faced her daughter. A confused gaze gradually morphed into attentive concern. "Good morning, sunshine."

Veronica waited while her mom relished a stretching yawn.

"I need my coloring book," she said urgently.

Twenty minutes later Veronica added a finishing touch to a picture she couldn't help admiring. Mrs. Angelina actually looked like a kitty cat thanks to careful attention to the shape of her ears. On the previous visit Grandpa had mistakenly assumed Veronica had colored him a bunny, embarrassing Veronica and humiliating his cat. Mrs. Angelina must have resented that picture whenever she walked through the gallery toward her litter box. No self-respecting kitty wants to be portrayed as a rabbit.

"Did you remember the form?" Veronica heard her father ask.

"On the tablet," answered Mommy.

"I mean the printed copy."

"In the suitcase," she reassured him.

"Dad hates digital records. He thinks anything you can't touch with your hands or sign with real ink will be manipulated by Big Brother."

"He doesn't have a brother," she said.

"I know that," her father said while frowning at the missed punch line. "I meant Big Brother from *1984*. You know, George Orwell."

Veronica's mother thought for a moment, then said, "My mom would have been in grade school in 1984."

"Never mind," said her husband. "My point is that we need both the digital and the hard copy. I don't want anything to prevent finalizing the change." His voice hushed. "I can think of much better ways to spend every fourth weekend than making this drive."

Overhearing the comment, Veronica tried to imagine how else they would get to Grandpa's house. "Are we gonna fly next time?" she asked excitedly.

Her father looked confused by the question. Mommy answered instead. "No, baby girl, we're not going to fly. Daddy is just tired from the trip."

Veronica wondered why sleeping made her daddy so tired, but she turned her attention to more immediate concerns.

"What do you think?" she said while handing her mother the picture.

"My goodness!" she said. "Grandpa will love this one."

"So will Mrs. Angelina," Veronica added proudly.

The girl's mother reached into a travel bag by her feet and pulled out a small tablet. She handed it to her daughter. "We have about ten or fifteen minutes to go," she said. "Why don't you play a game while Daddy and I talk?"

The mother turned toward her husband. "What if he's changed his mind again?"

"He hasn't," the man insisted.

"That's what you said last time."

"He can't. There's too much riding on this. He knows that."

"He knew it last time, but he still said no."

Veronica's father appeared to be biting the inside of his cheek while breathing deeply through his nose. "Don't remind me."

"Maybe we should wait a while. You know, give him some space to clear his head. He's probably still grieving."

"It's been almost five months, for Pete's sake!" he said impatiently. "He needs to move on with his life."

"I'm not sure talking about his death is the best way to do that."

"Nobody's talking about death. He's healthy as a horse. He'll probably live another ten years. Twenty maybe."

"How do you discuss a will without talking about death?" The mother glanced back at her daughter, then hushed her voice further still. It didn't help. Veronica could still hear every word. "And if he's so healthy, why not wait a few more months?"

Resentment squeezed through the man's clenching teeth. "Because the investors need a long-term guarantee now. One signature and they'll fund the expansion. Without it I'm sunk." He lowered his intensity to a whisper. "Besides, his current will isn't fair to us." A quick glance at the rearview mirror. "Or to Veronica."

The woman looked out the window. "We're coming up on the exit."

The man quickly tapped an icon to disengage AutoDrive, then pulled into the far right lane.

"He's your father," she said with a glib wave of her hand. "Do what you want. But I still think you're rushing things."

A dismissive *humph* ended the conversation.

—⁓—

As the car pulled into the long driveway, Veronica pressed her face against the window to find the spot where Grandpa normally stood whenever watering a stubborn patch of dry grass. No trace. He must be out back enjoying a morning coffee or cigar.

She took one last admiring look at Mrs. Angelina's ears before reaching for a handle that would only turn on Daddy's cue. Seconds later she bounced toward the house with the portrait in hand. She climbed the front steps and pressed a doorbell that she knew would release any of a dozen tunes Grandpa called "oldies but goodies." She didn't recognize today's selection.

"Pearl Jam!" her father shouted while approaching from behind. "Classic."

Veronica listened at the door, waited, then pressed again.

"Black Eyed Peas!" the man guessed while joining her on the porch. "No. Chili Peppers!"

Another wait.

"Did he know we were coming?" the mother asked her husband.

"I sent it to his schedule yesterday." He glanced at the time. "We're a bit early. He's probably out back."

Veronica leaped from the porch and raced around the side of the house to catch her unsuspecting grandfather by surprise. Midway, however, she came face-to-face with Mrs. Angelina. She fully expected the cat to act aloof in retaliation for her previous artistic flop. But Mrs. Angelina instead ran her body along Veronica's leg as if greeting a long-lost, deeply missed friend.

The girl picked up the kitty with one hand while carefully protecting her new and improved portrait with the other. She carried them both toward her parents who, by this time, had dialed a security code that unlocked the front door. She followed them into the house. Her mommy's face told her that something wasn't right.

"Dad?" Veronica's father called out. No response.

Mrs. Angelina's body seemed to tense, as if she was reacting to the same smell invading Veronica's nostrils.

"Something stinks," she said while holding her nose. It was a stark contrast from the cologne and cigar smoke that usually greeted her senses.

"The power must have gone out," suggested her mom. "Spoiled freezer meat?"

"Stay with Mommy, Veronica," her daddy said while inching toward the kitchen. Ever confident, even brash, he now appeared hesitant. Possibly even scared.

Just then Mrs. Angelina writhed violently to free herself from Veronica's embrace before scurrying up a winding staircase toward the bedrooms. In her effort to prevent Mrs. Angelina's escape Veronica tore the picture. Angry, she ran after the cat to scold her for ruining Grandpa's gift.

"Wait, Veronica!" her mother called out. But Veronica was too upset to listen. Mrs. Angelina needed a time-out!

The naughty feline ran through slightly ajar French doors into the master bedroom. Veronica followed, then crawled toward the bed and leaned her cheek against the floor, expecting to see Mrs. Angelina in the spot where she hid whenever trying to avoid a playful child. Or, in this case, escape a well-deserved rebuke.

No cat.

Then she heard two competing sounds: her mom ordering Veronica to come downstairs, and the faint meow of Mrs. Angelina in the adjoining bathroom.

Veronica moved toward the second, where she encountered a sight that would haunt her dreams for years to come.

——⁂——

Danielle sat on the lawn cradling her daughter while her husband spoke to the officer who was tapping details into a small tablet. The policeman had already questioned Danielle about the only clue either of them had found: an empty vial labeled PotassiPass. A serum, he had explained, commonly used by the transition industry.

"Wait. Transition?" Veronica's dad said. "At home?"

"The latest thing," said the officer. "But somebody messed up on this one. They're supposed to alert us in advance that it's happening. And they should have scheduled the post to occur within twenty-four hours."

"Post?"

"Post-transition processing. There are strict guidelines."

A moment passed. "So you think my father volunteered?"

The officer shrugged. "What else? Dressed for a funeral. Sitting in the bathtub. A vial of PotassiPass lying beside the body."

The officer swiped his tablet screen up and then down as if looking for a missing detail.

"But I must say, I've never seen anyone go it alone before. Is there anyone you can think of who might have assisted? A sibling perhaps? Or a close friend?"

Silence.

"Sir?" prodded the policeman.

"Yes. I'm sorry. You were saying?"

"Can you think of anyone who might have assisted your father?"

"Assisted? No. No one. He lived alone. My mother passed away a few months ago and…"

"I see," the officer interrupted as if hoping to sniff out an important clue. "May I ask how she died?"

"Cancer. A long battle."

"Oh." A brief pause. "I'm sorry for your loss. Both losses."

"Thank you," the man said mindlessly. "But I still don't understand."

"Understand what, sir?"

"If my father was planning to transition, why wasn't I told? I thought transitions required family co-approval."

"Used to," the officer explained. "That part of the law changed a few months back. I'm sure you remember the hubbub. It was all over the news for about ten days in March. Or was it April? I can't remember. Created a lot of noise at the time."

"I don't watch much news."

"Good for you. Depressing stuff."

"So my father could have scheduled himself for a transition without informing anyone?"

"Technically, no. The law requires that someone agree to assist and to ensure health-code compliance. But there's not much we can do to enforce that stipulation. Heck, we can't even hit the violators with a fine."

The officer chuckled, then quickly shifted to the more important issue at hand. He pointed to the girl, who was still clinging tightly to her mother's torso. "How is she?"

"Pretty shaken up," said the father.

"I bet."

They took a few steps toward mother and child. The officer put his hand gently on the little girl's head. His eyes met the mother's. "I suppose it's fortunate you showed up when you did. Take it from me, it would have been much worse after a few more days of decomposition."

Veronica's mom offered a slight nod of acknowledgment. It was true. Grandfather had looked mostly himself, albeit stiff, cold, and lifeless.

"It was Grandma's favorite," Veronica said between weepy sniffles.

"What's that, sweetheart?" asked her mom.

"Grandma said Grandpa looked very handsome in his black suit. It was her favorite."

"Is that so?" asked the officer. "I bet he wanted to look his best for her."

Veronica cheered slightly at the suggestion. She looked toward her parents. "You mean Grandpa went to see Grandma?"

Her parents appeared momentarily flustered. Neither answered.

"I'm sure of it," said the officer. "They're probably talking about you this very moment."

The hint of a smile appeared on Veronica's face. She looked at the policeman. "Really?"

"Really. And what's more..."

The officer halted when he noticed Veronica's father motioning him away from the scene. They stepped away, leaving Veronica and her mother alone on the grass.

The girl lowered her gaze, then settled back into her mommy's comforting embrace. "Mommy," she said softly. "Why did Grandpa go?"

"I don't know, baby girl," her mother whispered while wiping moisture from the girl's tear-stained cheek. "I don't know."

A stretch of silence passed between them.

"Mommy."

"Yes, sweetheart?"

"Do you think Grandpa is with Grandma?"

Danielle thought for a moment before responding. "I'd like to think so, Veronica. But I can't be sure."

Another moment of quiet grief.

"I m-m-miss them," Veronica quivered.

"I know you do, baby girl. I know you do."

PART ONE

PART ONE

CHAPTER ONE

Alex Ware held the doorknob to take one last deep breath before rejoining the meeting. His "quick break" had run long enough, even though he hadn't yet fully regained his composure. Not that anyone would have noticed, since he'd managed to excuse himself from the room before actually saying anything retaliatory. Good thing. Board members like their pastors calm and placid. His job was to model the Jesus who hugged innocent children, not the Jesus who chased money changers out of the temple.

He tried whispering a petition for the wisdom of Solomon and the patience of Job. But prayer felt out of reach. So he turned the handle, hoping God already understood the mess in which he found himself, and the land mines awaiting him on the other side of the door.

He entered a room divided into three distinct factions.

Phil Crawford and Kenny James were huddled near a touch screen, eyeing a diagram that hadn't been there before Alex's escape. It contained two overlapping circles with arrows pointing in several directions. Scribbled text read "Economic engine?"

Both men loved undecipherable charts and corporate lingo that invariably highlighted their pastor's lack of business acumen. Alex knew he had no interest in or capacity for running the church like a corporation. So did they.

Stephen Wilding stood by the window with Lydia Donovitz and Mary Sanchez. He appeared politely disinterested as the women sipped diet sodas and chatted about matters much more pressing than whatever appeared on the meeting's agenda: how well Mary's daughter was doing in her sophomore year of college, when Lydia's husband would return from Europe, or, Alex could only hope, how many volunteers they had recruited to fill vacancies in the preschool and third-grade classes.

The third faction, consisting of Roberto Wilson and Brandon Baxter, was seated at the table minding its own business. In their early thirties, both were slightly younger than the pastor. Each was fairly new to the church board. They represented an effort to bring "fresh eyes" and "new blood" to the leadership team.

Brandon had some connection to the founding pastor. His grandson? Or perhaps his nephew? But Alex had no idea whether the newcomer might help tip the balance of power slightly in the pastor's direction.

As it was, the most influential voice on the board was that of the chairman, Phil Crawford, who finally noticed Alex's return to the room. "Good," he said while tapping a SAVE icon on the board and returning to the table. "Ready to resume?"

"Ready. Sorry for the delay." The pastor's voice exuded a tone of grateful deference while his eyes moved quickly from person to person—a show of warmth that also helped him gauge positions. If they met his gaze or nodded it meant they understood his dilemma. Those who looked away probably sided with Phil. Downward glances implied wavering.

None of the seven looked him in the eyes. But only two looked away.

"I believe we were just about to vote on the question of whether…"

"Before we do that," Alex interrupted while pointing toward the digital board, "I wonder if you might explain the diagram."

He knew Phil wouldn't be able to resist the invitation—a clever distraction Alex would soon regret.

"Glad you asked," Phil said eagerly, returning to the drawing. "Kenny and I were just talking about the central question that frames everything on this evening's agenda."

Alex glanced down at his tablet. They had discussed four of six items.

Worship Attendance: A slight decline this month, but still better than it had been before Alex's arrival. During the prior three years, attendance at the worship services had plummeted from nearly two thousand to below eight hundred on campus, plus a few hundred online participants. Alex's youthful vigor and engaging teaching style had seemed to stabilize the situation by attracting a younger crowd. A fairly successful year, Alex thought. Not good enough, the board had concluded.

Giving: Unlike attendance, income had continued to fall. The Christ Community personnel committee had hired Alex, a progressive young man in his early forties, hoping he might bring new vision and passion to the congregation. And he had, some. But the growth had been largely offset by a continued departure of the elderly. Not his fault, the board agreed. But still a challenge, since young attendees tended to give less than the dwindling older crowd.

The Mortgage: The prior pastor had led the church through a capital campaign that had raised enough money for an impressive down payment on its new worship facility. The rest of the project had been funded through a low-interest loan it intended to renegotiate later. "Later" landed on Alex's watch. Unfortunately, thanks to the post-census meltdown of '42, banks were now charging exorbitant interest rates. The higher mortgage payment coupled with lower giving translated into increasingly tense meetings with the church finance committee that, it just so happened, was also chaired by Phil Crawford.

Outreach: Six months after Alex arrived the board realized a younger face with an engaging teaching style was not enough to restore the church's glory days. So they formed something they called the Dream Team: a committee that would solicit suggestions about how the church might more effectively reach the surrounding community. Every board meeting featured a new list of ideas gleaned from a variety of sources, including what Phil called "benchmarking" trips to larger, more successful area churches. Only a few of the suggestions ever got implemented, and none of those received the promised budget or volunteer support. But that didn't stop the flood of dreams from consuming an inordinate share of the pastor's schedule.

The fifth item carried the label *Bentley Donation*. It had triggered thirty minutes of disagreement just before Alex left the room.

"The circle on the right," Phil began while pointing to his diagram, "is the younger demographic of the church. They represent relevance and impact. To the degree this circle expands"—a wave of his hand caused the circle to grow—"we know we are accomplishing our core mission."

To his own surprise, Alex followed the point. He even felt himself nodding in agreement.

"The circle on the left represents our older members." Phil waved his hand across the shape, prompting it to shrink. A second wave shrank it further. "They represent our economic engine."

"Our what?" asked Brandon, the youngest member of the board.

"Our economic engine," Phil repeated, as if saying it louder would provide sufficient explanation.

Brandon's question gave Mary Sanchez confidence to speak. "I don't know what that means."

"That makes three of us," confessed Roberto Wilson.

"Four," Alex added, raising his hand.

Phil rolled his eyes toward Kenny James, who gladly accepted the hand-off.

"Every business and nonprofit entity must ask itself several strategic questions, including 'What drives our economic engine?' Or, in *layman's* terms," he said with a wink toward the pastor, "'How do we make money?'"

"But we don't make money. We receive donations," Alex reminded him.

"Semantics," Phil interjected. "We aren't that different from any other business. We provide a service, and people reward us by funding our product."

"Our product?" asked Brandon.

Phil edited himself. "Our ministry, then. The point is people pay the bills by transferring money from their pockets to ours. Whatever motivates or facilitates that transfer is, in short, our economic engine."

"I see," Alex said guardedly.

"An engine we need to do a better job of fueling."

"Because?" asked Alex.

"Because, *Pastor*, we can't turn on the lights or extend impact without cold, hard cash."

Alex folded his hands in front of himself on the table as he leaned forward, then back. "Of course," he said. "And the older donors give a higher portion of their income than younger donors."

"Exactly!" Kenny interjected as if to rescue the moment. "But they do so because they care about reaching the younger generation."

"I'd like to think they care about reaching everyone," Alex said.

The comment seemed to stall Phil's advance, but only for a moment.

"Well, yes, they do," he said. "But that's not the point."

"What is the point?" asked Mary, as if chiding Phil for his manners.

"Don't you see? If we announce Wayne Bentley's transition donation during the worship service we can send an important message to our older congregants, the fuel of our economic engine."

The wrenching knot in Alex's stomach intensified. So did the urge to overturn a money table.

"Wayne Bentley, God rest his soul, volunteered in order to help this church expand its impact," Phil continued. "He set an example for others to follow."

"Wayne Bentley didn't transition to help the church," Alex insisted. "He did it because he was depressed."

"I refuse to believe that!" snapped Phil. "Wayne was the happiest guy on the planet, not to mention a generous donor to the building fund."

"Wayne was grieving Wendy's death. The same Wendy, by the way, who made him promise to fulfill *her* pledge to the church." Alex realized he had said too much. "Forgive me. That information was supposed to be kept confidential." He blushed at the rare misstep. "I would appreciate everyone keeping what I just said in this room."

"Actually," said Lydia Donovitz, "I think it's pretty common knowledge. Wendy asked for prayer for her husband nearly every time she came to Tuesday Bible study. She said he came to church to network with potential clients more than to—"

Alex cut her off. "Thank you, Lydia. That's probably more information than we need at the moment."

"I'm just saying—" She halted in response to the pastor's rising hand.

"Can we get back to the point?" Phil asked adamantly.

Alex considered his next move. He knew much more than he should say.

It was Alex who had sat with Wendy Bentley after both procedures. The first, a double mastectomy, had stolen her feminine confidence. The second, a four-month checkup, had erased any hope of remission. He knew all too well that Wendy's greatest fear was not her own end, but her husband's future. Sure, he had a gregarious demeanor and a large network of "friends" at the Christ Community Church. But Wayne Bentley had more interest in Wall Street than in streets of gold.

"Another great message, Pastor!" he would bellow while pumping Alex's arm at the back of the sanctuary every Sunday.

"My husband doesn't know God," his wife had confided from her deathbed.

It was Alex who had handed Wayne Bentley a box of tissues while enduring a grief-laced attack. "She trusted you, Pastor," the widower had sobbed. "You should have encouraged her to transition. She didn't have to suffer!"

But it was Wayne, not Wendy, who had suffered. Pain management gave her ninety-two peaceful days—three months that had forced Wayne to abandon silly notions and face unpleasant realities. Death was not, as he had come to accept, a natural part of life. It was, as Wendy had believed, a cruel enemy. And that enemy had stolen his wife's beautiful, completing presence. Wayne's impressive net worth seemed a pittance absent the priceless prize of his life partner.

Wendy had never even raised the question of whether to let the cancer run its course. Alex had only affirmed a decision already made, a conviction purified in the crucible of her suffering. She took it for granted that life was a gift and death a foe. So she chose to face the end with quiet poise rather than defiant fear. Alex had never seen anyone die with more dignity.

It was also Alex who had comforted the little girl who had discovered her grandfather's lifeless body in the bathtub. Veronica Bentley had tugged on Alex's pant leg after Wayne's memorial service, a trembling chin posing a question with no simple answer.

"Is Grandpa with my grandma now?"

Alex couldn't recall meeting the girl or her parents before, even though Wayne's son, Luke, had said they'd attended the candlelight service on Christmas eve, his mother's last holiday in church. He'd told Alex that he had prepared a revised will "at Dad's direction" but that Wayne had failed to sign the changes "before he…um…left us." According to the son, he hadn't really wanted the church to receive such a large portion of the estate. Luke called to ask if Alex would be willing to "work with me to fix the error in light of my father's passing."

His father's *suicide*, Alex had thought.

"As I mentioned earlier…" Every eye turned toward the pastor's words. "I won't do it."

Feet shuffled. Throats cleared. Backsides shifted in seats.

"I can't do it," he added.

Phil huffed. "Then I will!" Attention shifted to the other end of the table. "Give me five minutes in the service this weekend," he commanded. "List it in the worship guide as 'A Word from the Board.'"

Alex's gut tightened further. He wanted to protest, to stand up to Phil Crawford now that a disagreement involved something more significant than website edits or the new janitorial contract. He could roll over when debating administrative details. But not when it came to asking his flock to volunteer.

He held his tongue while assessing each face now fixed in his direction. Why did no one speak? Surely others understood what was at stake. Would Mary condemn such an announcement? Or Brandon?

Silence.

"All in favor?" Phil asked with his arm held high.

Kenny's went up immediately. No surprise.

Stephen, as usual, followed their lead.

Lydia and Roberto each raised a single, apathetic finger, apparently more concerned about wrapping up the agenda than defending their pastor's convictions.

The other votes wouldn't matter. The majority had ruled.

"Done," Phil pronounced as if pounding a gavel.

Alex felt at once angry and nauseous. He tried to place the emotions. A normal reaction to his inability to turn a ship he had never received permission to steer? No. It was more than that. He sensed a line was being crossed. And it felt wrong. Very wrong.

He thought of his wife, Tamara. She had repeatedly reminded Alex that God had led them to Christ Community Church. "Do what you can and leave the results to him."

Good advice that had served him well. His first anniversary as pastor was just around the corner. As expected, the honeymoon period had lasted about six months. He'd received lots of accolades over his teaching and plenty of comments about his "darling wife" and "beautiful family." But his nearly twelve months in the pulpit seemed to have had little effect on what these people actually did after Sunday lunch, never mind Monday through Saturday.

Phil scribbled intently on a tablet. "How's this?" he asked with a self-satisfied expression before reading aloud. "The board of Christ Community Church extends our deepest sympathies to the family and friends of longtime member Wayne Bentley. Wayne was a pillar of this faith community who took his final breath on August third. We also wish to express our gratitude for the generous donation made possible by his transition. Both Wayne and his late wife, Wendy, loved this church and modeled what it means to give of themselves for the good of others."

Phil waited for reactions.

"Nice," said Lydia.

"Sounds good to me," added Kenny.

No one else spoke.

"Do you want to be a bit more specific?" asked Stephen. "Something like 'If you or a loved one wish to discuss including Christ Community among your transition beneficiaries, a member of our planned giving team would be happy to meet with you.' Seems a shame to waste the opportunity for a plug."

"A bit tacky if you ask me," said Lydia.

"I agree," added Phil. "But it would be good to remind people about planned giving in the wake of Wayne's example. How about the following Sunday?"

Alex realized the question had been directed to him. He shook his head slowly. No one pressed. They apparently wanted to throw him a scrap of say in the matter.

He glanced back at the agenda. One item remained. *A Concern*. That usually meant a complaint about the volume of the worship band's music or some equally monumental matter. Alex looked at the time. Twenty minutes past the scheduled end. "Would anyone object to tackling the final item in our next meeting?" he asked.

All eyes shifted back toward Phil, who, it seemed, had already discussed the matter with the group, probably before waxing eloquent about economic engines.

"Actually, I think it would be better to cover it tonight," Phil replied.

Not good.

Phil dove in as if reading from a teleprompter. "Let me start by saying how much we enjoy your teaching ministry, Pastor Alex."

"Thank you," he replied while bracing for impact.

"And far be it from me to tell you how to do your job. But what you said this past Sunday did not go unnoticed."

Alex's mind raced, trying to recall anything he might have said that could have created *A Concern*. Nothing came.

"What I said? Can you be more specific?"

Phil looked toward Kenny. Neither actually rolled his eyes.

"The part where you talked about the upcoming election."

"What? I didn't talk about the election on Sunday. Or ever for that matter."

Phil looked down while tapping his tablet. He began reading. "We live in a generation that's forgotten what it means to honor fathers and mothers. We see our seniors as a quick source of capital to solve our economic woes rather than what Proverbs calls them, a cherished source of wisdom..."

Alex waited for more, but Phil stopped to look up from his reading.

"Any of this sounding familiar?"

"Yes," said Alex. "I was teaching from Proverbs chapter one. Is that a problem?"

"Do you really think such blatantly political statements are appropriate from the pulpit? I mean, the Republican convention is later this month, for Pete's sake. Surely you knew that."

Alex did his best to connect the dots. No good. "I must be missing something."

"You can't be serious!" Phil said. "Criticizing the Youth Initiative is not only taking obvious sides between candidates, it also makes you...makes *us* sound insensitive to the economic troubles of our community."

Alex sat quietly trying to fit the square peg of political savvy into the round hole of applying Scripture to life.

"I'm just glad the Bentley kids weren't at the service," Phil added.

"The Bentleys?"

Phil continued. "Although I'm sure there were others in attendance who must have been offended."

"Offended? For saying we're supposed to respect our parents?"

"For implying it's a sin to volunteer!" Phil barked.

That's when Alex recalled a brief comment from Phil about his daughter. She had recently graduated from college "thanks to Mom's generosity."

The possibility of offending Phil and others in the congregation hadn't really crossed Alex's mind. He despised the growing pressure on the old and disabled to transition their assets to the young and productive by volunteering for self-extermination. Perhaps his disdain for the transition industry had indeed influenced his comments on Sunday. But politics?

"Listen, Phil," Alex said. "I didn't mean any offense. I know a lot of people have had to make some pretty difficult decisions since the collapse. And I didn't intend to tell people how to vote. I was honestly just trying to make the Scriptures relevant. You know, real-world application."

Alex intended to say more in his own defense when he noticed Stephen fidgeting with his empty paper cup and Mary squirming in her seat. The conversation was making everyone uncomfortable, Alex most of all. He lifted a single hand of surrender. "Never mind," he said. "I can see your point. I guess I wasn't thinking."

Phil, who had been crouched slightly forward as if preparing to pounce, eased himself back in the chair.

"Good." He inhaled soothingly. "Good."

Three seconds passed.

"I just thought it was my responsibility to raise the issue. You know, for the good of the congregation."

It was a phrase Alex mulled over in his head the entire drive home. Was it really for the good of the congregation? He understood why many of his parishioners had voted for candidates and policies that had backed the Youth Initiative. After all, it promised economic salvation after several brutal years. Something had to be done to turn things around.

He also knew that every family must decide such matters for itself. Alex had no right to add salt to their wounds or angst to their choices. No right, perhaps, to tell them how to live their lives. Or, more to the point, how to end them.

But did he have a responsibility to speak out against something he knew in his gut to be wrong? Shouldn't sermons be about more than inspiration and comfort? Weren't they supposed to persuade?

He thought of the old abolitionist movement in America two centuries past. It had been led by men like Frederick Douglass who challenged pastors to "agitate, agitate, agitate" in defense of human dignity. They had. And they had changed the world. But that was a different era, when people still believed ministers had a role to play in the public square.

Another outspoken minister came to mind. A hundred years earlier a young pastor named Dietrich Bonhoeffer had spoken out against the Nazi solution to what nice churchgoing citizens called "the Jewish problem." People listened to him also, right up until he was hanged as an enemy of the state.

Alex might not hang, but he could lose his job. Even if he did speak out against the Youth Initiative, would it make any difference? After all, as the meeting he had just left reinforced, no one seemed to be listening to him anyway.

CHAPTER TWO

Matthew Adams feared his string of successful closings was about to end. And it wasn't his fault. He had told his boss he would rather not take Mandy with him. Trainees had a way of throwing him off his game and distracting him from a process he had honed to near perfection. Especially trainees as cute and bubbly as Mandy Salinger. Cute and bubbly had no place in such an important line of work. Matthew was neither, part of the reason he had the highest client recruitment ratio of anyone at MedCom Associates.

"That's why I want you to train her," the boss had insisted. "She has great potential. But she needs to learn from the best."

Matthew's weakness for flattery had led to the present dilemma. To interrupt or not? Should he take back the reins or let Mandy steer the conversation into a ditch? He decided to wait, hoping his trainee would remember the coaching he had given during the drive over.

"Get right to the point," he had said. "Don't beat around the bush or make small talk to ease your way into the bad news. Say it as quickly and clearly as possible. It's the most compassionate way."

Mandy had been taking too long. She had also misfired on his second directive. "Don't become emotional. Your job is to explain their options, not give them a shoulder to cry on."

Matthew watched Mandy's eyes moisten in reaction to the woman's tears. *Hold it together, girl,* he thought in her direction. *Keep a professional distance!*

Too late. After a mere thirty seconds of silence Mandy wrapped her arms around the woman.

Despite his disappointment, however, Matthew understood. He had made similar mistakes while new to the job. He recalled trying to console his earliest clients. The first few minutes were the hardest. The look in their eyes. The questions on their faces. And knowing full well the difficult choice news of denial would require.

But helping them make the best decision was the whole purpose of these appointments, something unlikely to happen if Matthew let feminine empathy displace a well-crafted script.

"Place the options screen in front of them immediately, while the weight of the news is still settling on them," he had coached. He could tell that was not going to happen as long as he allowed Mandy to run point.

He quickly confirmed the name displayed at the top of the appointment summary. "As Ms. Salinger just explained, Mrs. Baxter, your situation falls outside the acceptable range for such a large outlay."

He tapped an icon and held his tablet where the woman could read the details for herself.

Like every other prospective client in Matthew's case load, Ellie Baxter did not fit the criteria established by the Youth Initiative for the funding of such an expensive medical procedure.

The woman exited Mandy's embrace. Then she held the

girl's hand while turning toward the screen to read the standard-template language of Medical Communications Associates' Client Response Form 309.

"What does this mean?" Ellie Baxter pointed to a phrase Matthew had explained to dozens of prospective clients before.

"Net-value ratio," he said matter-of-factly. "The estimated economic output of an individual compared to the cost associated with a given procedure or treatment."

She let go of Mandy's hand, then stood slowly. Facial muscles betrayed a feeling of offense Matthew had hoped to avoid. Mrs. Baxter, unlike many clients, understood the precise meaning his words were meant to obscure.

"So I'm not worth the expense of removing the tumor, is that it?"

Mandy reached toward the woman. "This has nothing to do with your worth…"

She stopped short at the cautionary glower from Matthew. He knew what he was doing. And she was about to mess it up.

"The Youth Initiative includes very specific guidelines about benefits available to citizens facing a variety of life-season dynamics," he replied. "Age, among others, is one of the determining factors."

"I see," she said, lowering herself back into the chair.

Matthew had come to expect such reactions. Few citizens had ever read the Youth Initiative's fine print, especially those most enamored of its promises. He allowed a moment of silence before continuing. "Part of our role, in addition to communicating the decision, is to help you consider options."

She looked up. "Options?" A tiny glimmer of hope invaded her eyes.

"Yes, ma'am," Matthew said, tapping the screen. A page appeared containing a list of follow-up services his company could provide. "MedCom Associates has helped thousands of clients in similar situations. We start by walking you through the potential benefits associated with volunteering, both to you and your loved ones."

"Volunteering?" Ellie repeated. "Volunteering for what?"

"To transition your assets. Do you have children or grandchildren, Mrs. Baxter?"

"I have a son. He lives in California."

"Great. Well, your son can be listed as a beneficiary to your estate. Any grandchildren?"

"No. His wife has a perfect figure."

Matthew sensed a trace of sarcasm. *A good sign.* "I understand," he said with a wink.

"But I do have a nephew, my brother's boy, Brandon. He has three: twin girls and a boy. I see them every weekend after church for Sunday dinner."

Religious, Matthew thought. *Even better.*

"Well then, you'll probably want to allocate part of your estate to your church or use it to establish a college fund for your great-nieces and -nephew. Unless, of course, you'd rather fund your daughter-in-law's next plastic surgery."

Matthew glanced toward Ellie. Humor was a tack he rarely risked. The look on her face confirmed his gut instinct. She would rather laugh than cry.

"But I still don't understand," Ellie responded. "I already have a will. Frederick, my late husband, insisted we update it every year."

"When was the last revision?"

She thought for a moment. "I guess about ten years back, the year before Frederick died." She appeared reflective. "My goodness. I can't believe it's been that long."

"The laws have changed since then. But we can help you with those details later. For now, I'd like to capture some information to initiate your client account."

"Of course," Ellie agreed, sorrow refilling her voice. "I'm sorry. This is a lot to take in."

Mandy squeezed the woman's hand, this time minus the non-verbal rebuke from Matthew. He had rescued the situation, making him more at ease with the girlish impulse. Prospects who allowed him to create an account usually also scheduled a pre-transition consultation. Sixty percent of those would go through with the full process, gleaning him a 1 percent commission on estates valued anywhere from a hundred thousand dollars to millions. Easy money, if you knew what you were doing. And based upon his recent string of closings, he should experience his best paycheck yet. Possibly enough to put him back in the black.

"I understand," Matthew said softly. "And don't worry. We will take care of every detail."

He retrieved the tablet to access the registration form before sliding it back in front of Mrs. Baxter. "We received this information from your primary physician. Would you mind confirming the details before I ask you a series of questions?"

She read. Then she nodded.

"Great. Now, let me scan the calendar for an opening."

"An opening for what?" Ellie asked.

"For your pre-transition consultation appointment. We will go over all the legal and procedural details so that you are comfortable with—"

"Transition?" she interrupted. "You mean at one of those death clinics?"

Matthew froze. He had only heard one other prospect use that phrase before. It hadn't led to a commission.

"I'm sorry," he fumbled to say. "I should have clarified that my company is on retainer with NEXT Incorporated. We provide advisory and processing services for clients interested in—"

"I'm not," she said curtly.

"Not ready?" Mandy asked.

"Not interested. I don't believe in that sort of thing."

"But you were denied treatment. You'll…" The trainee couldn't bring herself to say it.

"Die? We're all going to die, sweetheart."

Their roles suddenly reversed as the woman cradled the bewildered girl's hands. She looked Mandy in the eyes before turning to Matthew.

"I appreciate your concern, young man, but I don't want to schedule a consultation. Thank you."

The wind left Matthew's sails. He blushed at having misread the situation so badly. But he had been around the block enough times to know there was still a possibility, however slight.

"I understand," he began. "We certainly don't want to rush you into anything you aren't comfortable with. It can be scary facing these kinds of decisions."

"I didn't say I was scared…" She paused, looked toward the window, then wiped a tear as if overruling sorrow with something deeper. Perhaps faith?

The moment lit a fire within Matthew. He took his greatest pride in the occasions when he managed to turn a cold, economic choice into something more significant: something heroic, especially for those with religious sensibilities.

He glanced at Mandy. This was an opportunity to show her how it was done.

"You mentioned attending church," Matthew said. "Can I assume you are a spiritual person then?"

She nodded. "Christian. You?"

"Yes, ma'am," he lied. In truth, Matthew had abandoned two versions of the faith: his mother's Catholicism and his former mentor's Manichean substitute. Neither, he had come to believe, worked. But the latter remained useful when he was trying to inspire reluctant volunteers. "In fact, I've studied theology at the university level." True, if you counted informal coffee-shop conversations with a noted scholar like Dr. Thomas Vincent.

"Did you?" she asked politely, her mind probably still preoccupied with news of her treatment denial.

"I did. That's why I take inspiration from the example of Jesus. He would not only approve of volunteering, he modeled it."

"He what?" Ellie said as if she had misheard the statement.

Mandy appeared equally confused. She hadn't been trained on this part of Matthew's script.

"He modeled what it means to abandon this decaying, physical flesh for the transcendent existence of pure, untarnished spirit."

"You mean when he died for our sins?"

Matthew had navigated similar questions before. "That's a common misunderstanding about Jesus's death," he continued. "But it doesn't make much sense, does it? I mean, what does a man's crucifixion have to do with fixing my vices? It seems more likely, at least to my way of seeing things, that he showed us the way rather than paid our parking ticket. Don't you think?"

Ellie appeared momentarily intrigued by the thought. Then a bit dismayed.

"No," she retorted. "No. No. That can't be right."

"A lot of early Christians would beg to differ."

"Such as?" she asked.

"Ever hear of a guy called Saint Augustine?"

She nodded hesitantly, suggesting a vague recollection of the ancient Church father's name.

Matthew knew it was a partial truth. Yes, a young Augustine had embraced Manichean philosophy. But he had later submitted to church dogma about the incarnation. But Matthew, like his former professor, preferred the Manichean view.

"Anyway," Matthew continued, "to volunteer is about much

more than preserving assets for your beneficiaries. It is about fulfilling your ultimate destiny."

"To go to heaven?" Mandy asked eagerly.

Matthew shot her a piercing stare. "No," he said. "To transcend physical limitations. To free oneself from the pain and corruption of bodily existence." He looked directly in the woman's eyes. "And to cut short the process of suffering that will otherwise define your final days."

The woman felt the brutal thud of a harsh reality. Matthew had intended her to.

"We decay, Mrs. Baxter," he added in a gentler tone. "The sooner you decide to volunteer, the sooner you will snatch victory away from pain's cruel hand."

A long silence ensued.

"Young man," the woman finally said, "I think you misunderstand the real enemy."

Enemy? "How's that?" he asked.

"You seem to think pain and suffering are the worst things imaginable."

Aren't they? he wondered.

"I don't want to die," she continued, pausing to wipe a final stray tear. "And I certainly don't want to suffer."

"You don't have to," Mandy interjected.

The woman accepted the girl's extended hand with an appreciative grin. "But the real enemy has nothing to do with what happens to my body." She turned to look at Matthew directly. Confidently. "Our real enemy wants to devour the soul."

Matthew tried to decipher the look in Ellie Baxter's eyes.

Resignation, as with his mom?

No, not resignation. *Resolution.* She possessed the kind of calm surrender that emboldens rather than cowers in fear or pleads for mercy. He remembered something similar in Reverend Grandpa the night he died. The night the dreams began.

This woman seemed to be resting in a submission Matthew couldn't bear. Its presence made him angry, and a bit frightened, like hearing the howls of unseen wolves while huddled around a dying campfire. The fright must have shown on his face.

"Are you OK?" asked Mandy. "You look a bit pale."

"Fine," he said too quickly. "I'm fine."

"Young man," the woman said, "I think I'm supposed to give you something."

She stood and moved slowly to the adjoining kitchen, out of eyeshot. Matthew heard a drawer open, then a rustling noise, as if she was searching through a stack of forgotten notes or old photos.

"Here it is," she said before returning to the room. She placed something on the coffee table in front of Matthew. It contained an image about three inches square. He recognized a replica of an Expressionist painting called *The Scream*. He flipped it over to find an online address inviting the bearer to schedule a "Free Spiritual Dialogue Session."

"I hope you'll get in touch," the woman added, laying her hand gently on Matthew's forearm. "I sense you need to talk to someone."

Matthew's eyes shot up from the card. *How dare she*! It was *his* job to coach *her*, not the other way around. It was Ellie Baxter who faced the prospect of prolonged suffering, not *he*. If anyone needed someone to talk to it was this half-crazy debit who didn't know Saint Augustine from Saint Nick, not Matthew Adams, a promising scholar temporarily condescending to the needs of health-system flunkies.

He took the card, placing it in his back pocket to keep it safe until he could find a trash container. "Thanks," he grunted with a smirk.

"May I have one of those, too?" Mandy asked.

"Certainly, dear," the woman said as she began shuffling back toward the kitchen.

"I think our job is done here," Matthew said, excusing himself from the scene. "I'll let you wrap up. I'll be waiting in the car. Use your own password to verify the 309."

And with that Matthew walked out the front door, leaving his trainee to formalize a failure he had no intention of owning.

CHAPTER THREE

Four hours after dropping Mandy off in front of the house she shared with her partner, Matthew found himself still slumped over a half-finished drink. He had no interest in whatever games happened to be showing on the dozen or so screens throughout the sports bar. Nor did he much notice the usual attraction of Peak and Brew, an assortment of attractive college girls funding tuition by filling beer mugs and chip bowls. He usually finished his customary two beers in about thirty minutes before heading home. But tonight he had ordered a third to justify continued use of the table that would otherwise accommodate three or four rowdy frat boys eager to toast their favorite team's run or score.

He glanced around the packed house that stood a few blocks from the University of Denver campus. Peak and Brew was a favorite gathering place for students. But classes didn't start for another week. Matthew had continued to track such details even after abandoning his dream of graduating from the University of Colorado and his backup plan of attending classes in Denver. His dark days had killed both the possibility and the desire.

A chorus of voices groaned in unison. Matthew's eyes shot up to find the most convenient screen. That's when he remembered the Summer Olympics were in full swing. It seemed the USA men's volleyball team had just missed a match point. He tried to care, but instead lifted the glass to his mouth before placing it back on the table without taking a sip.

Four blocks away was a perfectly comfortable bed ever ready to console its owner. Matthew typically slept his way out of sudden fits of rage. But this one felt deeper and, he feared, would last longer. He only hoped it wouldn't turn into a funk like the one he had suffered the previous fall.

Why had the old woman's refusal bothered him so much? He told himself it was because she'd broken his winning streak. But he knew there was more to it. He knew it had something to do with the look in her eyes or her show of concern. Probably both. The frail, quiet Mrs. Baxter had shaken him to the core.

He'd felt something similar the day he heard his mom tell her transition specialist how much she wanted her son to become a professor. Was a transition less heroic when the volunteer didn't comprehend what was happening, when she blindly trusted her son to have her best interest at heart? But she must have understood, deep down, that it was for the best. Hers to avoid further deterioration and, he had convinced himself, misery; his to fund the dream of college, graduate school, and an eventual classroom of his own.

A renewed sense of anger rose within at the thought of what should have been. The kind of life that chance, fate, or God had stolen from him.

He recalled the humiliation that had spawned his dark days. The tuition that couldn't be paid. The trustee who refused to release money that rightfully belonged to him. Being forced to take an elder-care job working for a cantankerous old debit. Reverend Grandpa, as he had insisted on being called, had infuriated Matthew with a stubborn resistance to common sense.

He was old.

He was disabled.

He was an emotional and financial burden to his daughter and a debit in society's economic ledger.

He was trapped in a decaying body.

He should have volunteered for his own sake, and for his grandkids' sake.

But he refused. He even poked fun at Matthew for suggesting it.

Matthew had nearly convinced himself that both his mom and Reverend Grandpa were better off; that he had done the right thing. *Free those who suffer to thrive.* It had been a philosophy to live by and, someday, to teach. The perfect replacement for a catechism learned in childhood.

An explosion of cheers interrupted Matthew's reminiscence. His eyes darted from one screen to the next in search of what had prompted the outburst. They landed on the digital image of a baseball player's casual trot around third base on his way toward home plate. Celebratory high fives and kisses peppered the room as fans wearing caps that matched the player's relished what must have been a crucial home run in a tight game.

Matthew chuckled at the scene of grown men and women living vicariously through their favorite players. Die-hard fans. He had always been more fair-weathered himself, paying little attention to local teams unless they happened to make the play-offs. What was it like, he wondered, to follow a team through the ups and downs of the full season, to cheer them through the losing stretches, and to hold out hope that a winning streak might be just around the corner?

He missed being part of something, believing in something. But Matthew had outgrown both Father Tomberlin's creed and

Dr. Vincent's lectures. If an almighty being existed at all, he hadn't been playing well enough to deserve Matthew's attention.

Where had God been when the transition inheritance got tied up in a legal mess for so long it forced Matthew to drop out of college? When the money finally did arrive, half of it went to a criminal lawyer in order to get the police off his back. Such a waste! Especially since the detective had confirmed *three times* that Matthew couldn't possibly have committed the assassination.

And then there was the near miss with the breathtaking Maria Davidson. Against all hope, she'd seemed to find him attractive. A picture in the high school annual and a virtual connection had nearly blossomed into a real-world romance. That is, until a case of mistaken identity chased her out of his life forever.

Perhaps the most disturbing sign of God's absence had been the dark cloud that had overshadowed every fiber of Matthew's existence for seventy-three days he would rather forget. The trips to Reno had managed to numb some of the pain. But it had also drained what was left of his inheritance. So in the end, rather than funding his dream, his mother's estate had slipped into the hands of lawyers and casino owners.

He felt abandoned. Worse, rejected. He wanted to become an atheist. But then whom would he blame for all that had happened? So against his own will, Matthew still believed in God. And that, he realized, is what frightened him about the look in Mrs. Baxter's eyes. She seemed to know something about him Matthew hadn't figured out himself. Possibly saw through his honed script to perceive his lonely soul.

"I sense you need to talk to someone." She had been right. He had never felt so isolated in his life.

He had hoped the new job would help. Perhaps it had, a little. Everyone needed to feel successful at something. And he did, especially after receiving the associate-of-the-month award twice. But while success had funded a halfway decent apartment and paid down much of his gambling debt, it hadn't brought him what he missed most: a mentor like Dr. Vincent, whom he had vowed never to speak to again. Matthew had relished discussing philosophy, or religion, or even girls with his favorite professor. He now grieved the lost relationship almost as much as he resented the shocking betrayal. Why would Dr. Vincent name Matthew as Judge Santiago's potential assassin? Hadn't he known him better than that?

Matthew pulled the three-inch card Ellie Baxter had offered him from his back pocket. He flipped it from one side to the other and back again. Curious, he typed the online address into his tablet.

Confidential Spiritual Dialogue

Need a confidential ear? Someone with whom you can share your deepest pain or your most troubling questions? Or perhaps you need to get something off your chest but have no trustworthy confidant? We are here to help. Tap the icon below to schedule a confidential appointment with one of our trained team members. There is no charge. The cost has been covered by concerned donors who want to help you explore the next steps on your spiritual journey.

The offer reminded Matthew of what he had experienced as a child whenever his mother brought him to Father Tomberlin's confessional. He would reluctantly parrot the expected words, "Forgive me, Father, for I have sinned." Then he'd told the priest about every offense he could recall, and a few he made up for the fun of it. He had never taken the ritual seriously, but recalled feeling better afterward, especially whenever he had done something that left him feeling guilty.

Matthew smiled at the recollection. He would love to feel better now. Perhaps the Sacrament of Penance, or whatever they called the process these days, would do him some good. Not because he had done anything wrong, or because he believed in sin or absolution. But he did still consider himself a spiritual person. What harm could come of a confidential ear and a bit of perspective and advice?

Matthew's finger hovered momentarily over the calendar. He pressed it, then chose a convenient time and began entering the required details.

"Is this seat taken?"

Matthew looked toward the voice, which belonged to a man he didn't recognize. "Um, no," he muttered. "It's all yours." Matthew paid no attention to the stranger, who, he assumed, wanted to pull the chair to the edge of some crowded nearby table.

"Great," the man replied. "I hate to drink alone."

The chair hadn't moved. The man plopped himself down while extending a hand toward his unsuspecting host. "I'm Mori. Short for Bryan Quincy."

Matthew returned the gesture. "Matthew, short for Matthew Adams."

"Pleased to meet you, Matthew Adams." The man seemed to mean it. He appeared almost as lonely as Matthew. Not a solitary, reclusive lonely. The kind of lonely that talked to anyone and everyone to fill the silence.

The man had brown hair and a rich-looking beard containing much more gray than his crown or temples. Unlike Matthew's, his hair showed no trace of thinning. He appeared to have benefited from genetic screening. Impossible, of course, since blind conception would have been the norm at the time of the man's birth. Fifty years old? The estimate seemed plausible, especially in light of a rotund torso that suggested several decades of chatty beer-and-chip consumption.

"How did 'Mori' become short for Bryan Quincy?" Matthew asked, more from polite courtesy than burning curiosity.

"My middle name, Morrison, was my old man's surname," he said with a chuckle. "They called him Mori, so I became Little Mori. Then just Mori."

"Got it," Matthew said with an upward nod.

A cheer erupted around them, prompting both men to turn disinterestedly toward a screen. A replay, which seemed to delight the crowd, meant nothing to Matthew.

"'Little Mori' just didn't feel right in the classroom," the man added while lifting a mug to his lips.

"You teach?"

"If you can call it teaching." Another singular laugh.

"What do you mean?"

"I mean that teaching, by definition, ought to include learning. Which is something my students seem determined to avoid."

"High school?"

"College. University of Denver."

"What department?"

"Humanities."

"Philosophy?" Matthew asked, suddenly intrigued.

"Literature."

"Oh," Matthew said limply.

"Yeah," Mori sighed, "that's how most of my students respond when they discover mine is the only elective class that still has openings."

"Sorry. I didn't mean it like that. I was a philosophy major before…before I took a sabbatical."

"No need to apologize. I'm used to it. And I get it. Our generation was formed by Google and Facebook."

Matthew smiled at the mention of the classic brands. His thirty-seven years suddenly felt ancient.

"Why dive deeply into an ocean of words when you can skim along the surface on a Jet Ski?" Mori paused to reach for a source. "I think it was Nicholas Carr who said that."

Matthew didn't recognize the quote, or the author.

"Anyway," Mori continued, "this generation is light-years beyond where you and I were when we graduated from college."

Matthew didn't correct the misimpression.

"Or should I say, light-years behind. I can't remember the last student who had actually finished reading an entire classic novel. They don't know Melville, or Hugo, or even Dickens. You have no idea how irrelevant I feel teaching a literature appreciation course to kids who, for all practical purposes, are illiterate. At least when it comes to the greatest books ever written."

Matthew had always loved books. In addition to a tablet full of marked-up academic volumes, he had once owned a small supply of collector print editions. But he had read very few novels. Possibly none from start to finish.

"Pretty sad," he bluffed.

"You say you studied philosophy?" asked Mori.

"I did."

"So you've read Voltaire, Nietzsche, and the gang?"

Matthew smiled. "I have. You?"

"Of course. Like every other self-respecting atheist."

"Ever hear of Dr. Thomas Vincent?" Matthew asked.

"Sure. UC–Boulder?"

"That's right. He was my academic advisor during college."

"No kidding! I've read some of his stuff. Bright guy."

"Thanks," Matthew said as if deserving part of the praise. After another sip he came clean. "But I never got to finish the program. Had to drop out. Short on cash."

"Oh," Mori said with sympathy, "I'm sorry to hear that."

"Actually, I wanted to become a teacher myself. Religious studies."

"I bet you'd have been a good one." His eyes followed a passing waitress before he spoke again. "But teaching is only half the equation. You need willing pupils, something hard to find these days."

The men shared the silent communion of disappointment, lost dream sitting beside futile undertaking. Then, to his surprise, Matthew noticed a change in Mori's expression. Chilly cynicism dissipated, as on the face of a discarded coach suddenly assigned a fledgling team.

"Hey," the elder announced. "Can I suggest an author?"

"Fiction?" Matthew asked.

A nod. "Yeah. Something I think you'd like. Includes religious themes. But not like Moses or Milton. I'm not into that sort of thing. More like Nietzsche meets Sherlock Holmes."

Matthew recognized both names. A good sign. "I guess," he answered with a shrug.

"Dostoyevsky," Mori said before spelling the name. "The true Russian master."

Matthew tried to imagine enjoying any classic novel, let alone one from Russia.

"Trust me," Mori continued in reaction to the blank stare, "better than Tolstoy. Every bit as long, but worth the effort."

Matthew found himself entranced by Mori's rising enthusiasm.

"I promise you've never read more powerful philosophical dialogue than you'll find in *Crime and Punishment*. Or should you start with *The Brothers Karamazov*? More religious. Hard to say."

"Which is shorter?" Matthew asked.

"Wrong question," Mori chided. "You mean 'Which is better?'"

"OK. Which is better, then?"

"That's the problem!" Mori shouted. "After nearly twenty years teaching both books, it would be murder to choose one over the other." He laughed at an apparent irony Matthew didn't follow.

"Maybe I'll read them both," Matthew said to his own surprise. It seemed no accident, he thought, that Bryan "Mori" Quincy had approached this particular table. Perhaps a challenging reading regimen could help defend Matthew against another prolonged funk.

"Which one first?" he asked while readying his fingers over his digital device.

Mori rubbed his beard as his eyes rose upward in thought. "I'm not a spiritually oriented person myself," he finally said, "but I love a good debate about religion."

He looked toward Matthew out of the corner of one eye, as if the comment were a dipstick checking his new pupil's depth of conviction.

"Me, too," Matthew said, without specifying whether he meant *not spiritual* or *loves a good debate*.

"I relate more to Ivan Karamazov than to his brother Alyosha," Mori added.

Matthew stared blankly.

"Sorry," Mori said. "Ivan is the skeptic. His brother the believer."

"I see. Which book?"

"*The Brothers Karamazov.*"

Matthew tapped his pad several times, then paused. "Spelling?"

"K-A-R-A-M-A-Z-O-V. You'll never find more ruthless arguments against the goodness of God."

"Really?" Matthew said as he continued entering the title.

"Oh, yeah," Mori continued. "Ivan really makes Alyosha squirm. Even I cringe every time I read the part about the kid and the dog."

Curiosity piqued, Matthew tapped the DOWNLOAD icon. The

book instantly appeared on his screen. "Eight hundred pages?" he exclaimed.

"I told you it was long, but worth the effort." The professor jotted down a passage from the book. He handed it to Matthew. "Here you go. Read book five, chapters three through five. That should give you a taste. The section on the Grand Inquisitor will put you on the edge of your seat, I promise."

"Got it," Matthew said while making a mental note.

They chatted about this and that for about five minutes before Mori appeared to lose interest in his new protégé. A look of pleasant surprise came over his face while he waved to a fortysomething woman entering the front door. His partner? Or perhaps a colleague he could use to fill the next lonely silence?

"I need to give you back your chair," he said while standing. "It was nice to meet you, Matthew Adams. Maybe I'll see you around."

"I hope so," Matthew replied while accepting a firm farewell shake. He meant it.

Bryan "Mori" Quincy disappeared as suddenly as he had arrived.

Matthew glanced down at his tablet, eager to dive into his assigned reading. But a bouncing icon reminded him of his unfinished task. A single tap resurfaced the abandoned "spiritual dialogue" request form. He chose the first available morning appointment. Then he felt the threat of a yawn that reminded him why he usually stopped after two beers. Matthew waved toward the waitress. She winked an acknowledgment before tapping a device that sent him his tab. While entering his payment code Matthew heard the ping of an arriving confirmation message from Christ Community Church of Denver, Colorado.

A Protestant church? *Hmm*, he thought. *Could be interesting.*

CHAPTER FOUR

"Nice Of you to come," Mandy teased while closing the car door. "I was afraid you'd given up on me."

"Sorry I'm late." Matthew wiped the last bit of sleep from his eyes. "What've we got today?"

It was the trainee's role to review the string of assigned visits. MedCom provided a series of times and addresses.

"I figured we would start with the three addresses on the east side of town and then head north." Mandy waited, then smiled in response to Matthew's affirming nod.

He had trained her well. Matthew had been on the job long enough to discover a consistent glitch in the automated scheduling system. It was possible to disregard the scheduled appointment times; you could visit more prospects if you sequenced them by neighborhood. The less time spent driving the better. In Matthew's experience prospective clients were just as likely to be sitting anxiously at home whether he arrived early or late. What else did they have to do? Their lives had been put on hold until they received the news he had been assigned to deliver.

Of course, it would be much more efficient to send word of treatment denial directly from the attending physician's office via digital voice or text message. But MedCom had stumbled onto a huge opportunity to grow the transition market by offering a "high-touch service to patients receiving disheartening news." After successfully pioneering the service in Arizona and Florida, the company had been featured in the *Wall Street Journal* as a "model of best practices" that, if those practices were expanded, "might help the Youth Initiative come closer to hitting its overly optimistic volunteer recruitment targets."

Before MedCom came on the scene countless potential volunteers had slipped through the cracks. The process depended too heavily on physicians who had a hard time delivering bad news without going further. Dinosaurs from the era of the Hippocratic oath, many doctors suggested alternative treatment options or told patients they would perform the required procedure "under the radar" without compensation. Medical Communications Associates, later christened MedCom, had solved the problem and, in the process, generated significant revenues. As Matthew knew better than anyone, seniors were much more likely to volunteer in their moment of distress. The trick, he had tried to teach Mandy, was resisting the natural impulse to comfort.

"So," Matthew said while pulling away from the curb, "remind me of what we learned yesterday."

She blushed in self-rebuke while repeating her tutor's mantra. "Awkward silence is our friend."

"Exactly. And?"

"And I need to resist the urge to touch them." She sighed. "It seems so simple when we're reviewing prep summaries. I don't know what my problem is."

Your problem, Matthew thought, *is that you're a girl.*

Mandy was his sixth trainee. Of the prior five, all three female pupils had made the same mistakes. The guys, while less pleasant company, had found it much easier to maintain professional distance.

"You'll do better today," he said without conviction.

Mandy pointed her tablet toward the dashboard to set them on course to their first appointment. Then she asked if Matthew had watched the latest episode of a show he didn't recognize, then recounted a plot he didn't care to know.

He looked at his perky passenger. Did she admire him less today than she had twenty-four hours earlier? He had embarrassed himself by losing his composure and walking out of their final appointment. Very unprofessional.

"Oh," Mandy said after a brief pause in the whir of words, "you're supposed to call someone named Freddy."

He didn't recognize the name. "Freddy who?"

"Freddy Baxter. I guess he's pretty mad."

Matthew reached for any point of connection. "Baxter? As in Mrs. Baxter from yesterday?"

"Her son left a message last night. It came to us because Mrs. Baxter was in your case load."

Matthew groaned. He hated handling appointment follow-up calls, especially when they involved upset family members. The complaints were always the same. "What right do you have to pressure my dad into volunteering?" or "You really upset my mother!"

But it was part of the job.

"Let's hear it," he said, prompting Mandy to tap the PLAY icon on her tablet.

"This is Freddy Baxter. You sent some incompetent idiot to my mother's place yesterday to present the transition option. I spent half the evening talking to her last night. She was very upset."

Odd. Matthew remembered a calm refusal from a woman

who seemed more concerned about his depression than her own demise.

"You guys made me look like a fool!" the man's voice continued. "I called to console and reaffirm my mom's decision to volunteer, only to learn she had refused. Why the devil did I get an update notice saying she had said yes? Now she thinks the whole thing was my idea! Have someone call me tomorrow so we can get this mess straightened out."

The man cursed before the message ended abruptly. Matthew turned to look at his trainee. "Did you file the follow-up form like I asked?"

She had.

"And you selected the 'No thank you' option?"

The look on Mandy's face told him otherwise.

"We talked for a few minutes after you left," the trainee explained. "She asked me questions about how volunteering worked, where they carried out the procedures, stuff like that. I sensed she might be open to another try. I couldn't find a 'Maybe' option so I selected 'Follow-up advised.'"

Matthew groaned again. "'Follow-up advised' means they're ready for a pre-transition consultation."

"What?"

Matthew reviewed the process Mandy should have known. The system automatically alerted immediate family members whenever a prospective client agreed to move ahead. It even recommended language they might want to use to affirm the loved one's decision.

"I'm such a mess-up!" Mandy said.

"Well," Matthew replied, "I can assure you you'll never make this mistake again."

"Why's that?"

"Because I won't be calling Freddy Baxter to apologize." He smiled in her direction. "You will."

The day turned out to be more productive than Matthew had expected. They had managed to sign up four of five prospective clients, exactly the number needed to complete his commitment. Each trainee was required to observe ten successful closings before he or she could move up the food chain. Matthew could now go back to flying solo, at least until his boss hired another batch of rookies.

Opening a well-deserved can of beer, Matthew grabbed his tablet before plopping himself onto the only chair occupying his apartment's ten-by-twelve-foot living room, a leather-like recliner that still released the slight smell of cigarettes six months after he'd paid thirty dollars to haul it away from a garage sale.

He scanned a list of possible television programs. Then he remembered the assignment he had accepted from the teacher he had met at Peak and Brew. Matthew tapped the book icon to find *The Brothers Karamazov* by Fyodor Dostoyevsky. "Read book five, chapters three through five. That should give you a taste," Mori had urged. "Ruthless arguments against the goodness of God."

Matthew found the recommended section. He immediately recognized the names of the two characters speaking. Mori had called Ivan the skeptic and Alyosha, his brother, the believer.

At first Matthew felt as if he had stumbled into the second act of a longer drama; which, of course, he had. But he stuck with it, eventually grasping the thread of Ivan Karamazov's attacks that must have been the source of Alyosha's squirming.

"People speak sometimes about the 'animal' cruelty of man," Ivan was saying, "but that is terribly unjust and offensive to animals, no animal could ever be so cruel as a man, so artfully, so artistically cruel. A tiger simply gnaws and tears, that is all he can do. It would never occur to him to nail people by their ears overnight, even if he were able to do it."

It was an idea that had never occurred to Matthew. Man more vicious than beasts? Ivan expanded the claim with a series of stories, each more troubling than the last.

A soldier taking delight in torturing children, tossing them in the air and catching them on a bayonet before their mothers' eyes.

A trembling mother watching a man use the end of his gun to amuse her nursing infant.

"The baby laughs gleefully," Ivan explains, "reaches out its little hands to grab the pistol, and suddenly the artist pulls the trigger right in its face and shatters its little head...Artistic, isn't it?"

A five-year-old little girl tortured by parents who hate her for reasons unknown to themselves. They beat her, flog her, and kick her into a lump of bruised suffering. And then, angered by the child's mishap, they lock her all night in the freezing-cold outhouse after smearing her face and making her eat her own excrement. The mother goes back to sleep "while her poor little child was moaning all night in that vile place!"

Ivan asked Alyosha to picture a little girl in such a cruel dark, cold place; a child unable to comprehend what is being done to her, weeping an anguished prayer for "dear God" to protect her. Then he asked him to imagine another scene.

An eight-year-old boy, a house serf, throws a stone that accidentally hurts the paw of a dog, one of hundreds in the landowner's kennel. Noticing the limp, the landowner asks how the dog got hurt. Someone identifies the boy. "Take him!" commands the man. His servants force the child from the arms of his mother and lock him up for the night. At dawn the man rides out in full hunting attire, surrounded by dogs, handlers, and fellow huntsmen on horseback. Then the rest of the house serfs are assembled and ordered to watch, the boy's mother in front. The child is released and stripped naked. He shivers, not daring to make a sound, crazy with fear. "Drive him!" the landowner commands. "Run, run!" shout the others. He flees. "Sic him!" screams the man, loosing a pack of wolfhounds. Then the man hunts the child down before his mother's eyes until the animals tear the child to bits.

Matthew squeezed his eyelids tight at the suffering of innocence and the cruelty of men. Would a good God allow such things? It was the question Ivan was posing, to Alyosha's unease. Mori had been right: ruthless attacks.

He forced his eyes back onto Ivan's speech.

"Listen to me: I took children only so as to make it more obvious. About all the other human tears that have soaked the whole earth through, from crust to core, I don't say a word."

Matthew considered the tears that had soaked his own sliver of the planet. Certainly nothing as terrifying as what Ivan's afflicted children had endured. But, in their own ways, indictments against his mother's God. Not to mention Father Tomberlin's dogma.

Better no God, he mused, *than a cruel one.*

After finishing the second of the three recommended chapters, Matthew noticed the title of the last: "The Grand Inquisitor." He flipped quickly to count the pages. His sitcom-formed attention span protested at the length. But he overruled it, ordering it to brace itself for another disturbing scene. That's when he heard the ping of an arriving message. He gratefully accepted the distraction.

FROM: Serena Winthrop, NEXT Incorporated
Dear Mr. Adams:
I was given your name as one who might be interested in a unique opportunity. I am the director of research and de-

velopment with NEXT Inc. As you no doubt are aware, we are the leading provider of transition services in the United States through our network of affiliate clinics and physicians. The reason I am contacting you is that I have been asked to assemble a team of highly skilled professionals with a proven track record of success in the field of senior-care and/or volunteer recruitment services. We can provide a generous compensation and bonus package for those we select after a rigorous interview and testing process. I wonder if you would be open to a preliminary conversation? Next Monday perhaps? I have a long layover in the Denver airport and would love to meet if you are available between noon and 2:30 in the afternoon. Due to the confidential nature of our project I cannot share specific details here other than to say what we are doing will have a significant impact on this nation's ability to pull itself out of the present economic crisis. I'm confident you will find the investment of an hour well worth your time and effort. Please let me know if you are willing and available on Monday. I hope to see you then.

A surge of excitement lifted Matthew from the recliner. He walked five steps to the kitchen, then five steps back while rereading the message. His mind began to race.

Who would have given Serena Winthrop his name? Certainly not his boss; he depended too much on Matthew to train new recruits. *Unless.* What if MedCom stood to profit from whatever secret project NEXT was testing? Then his boss would suggest its best and brightest.

What kind of research or development did the project entail?

He could use a new challenge, but was he qualified for the job?

Matthew rebuked himself. Of course he was qualified. Why

else would a corporate big shot send him a personal invitation to apply?

He moved to the kitchen counter, where he carefully spoke to his tablet. The communication assistant typed a reply.

TO: Serena Winthrop
FROM: Matthew Adams
Thank you for your kind invitation to meet. I would love to speak with you at 12:30 on Monday. Let me know which gate and I will meet you there.
Regards.

He read the text on the screen three times before tapping the send icon. Too eager? Too casual? Should he change the appointment by half an hour to give her more time to unwind before meeting with a prospective colleague?

It was then that Matthew blushed at the realization that he would need to bring something to the interview that he didn't have: a professional résumé.

He walked to the refrigerator, swapping his beer for a different beverage. He poured a can of caffeine-laden Frappuccino mix over ice and took a sip. Then he positioned himself in front of the computer for what promised to be another late night.

CHAPTER FIVE

Alex woke early. Not from the alarm. He hadn't set it. He woke early because his wife's lips were tickling his right earlobe. By the time he realized what was happening the tickling had become nibbling, followed by her soft fingers caressing his bare chest.

"Good morning, Mr. Ware," she whispered. "Your first appointment has arrived."

He smiled mischievously.

"Hi, Daddy!"

He frowned, then opened his eyes while turning toward the chirpy voice.

"Good morning, sunshine," he said to his six-year-old with as much spunk as his groggy wits would allow.

"Do you like it?" Ginger was standing on Daddy's side of the bed, pointing to a bright-yellow barrette. He recognized the hairstyle it secured, two small strands of curl falling gently over each ear beneath the brunette bundle held neatly in the back; a miniature replica of Tamara's favorite hairdo.

"You look just like Mommy!"

His daughter beamed.

Alex slid his hand stealthily toward his wife's leg, which was still hidden beneath her side of the blanket. She giggled before kissing him on the cheek.

"Don't worry, Pastor," Tamara promised, "I might be able to fit you into my schedule…in a week or two."

He gave a retaliatory pinch before his wife fled the scene with their daughter in tow.

"See you at breakfast," she announced on her way out the door.

Alex sat up in the bed and reached reluctantly toward his dozing tablet, the first of nine steps in his weekday routine.

> Step One: Review the day's schedule.
> Step Two: Exercise. (Optional)
> Step Three: Shower and shave. (Mandatory)
> Step Four: Eat breakfast with the family. (Delightful)
> Step Five: Brush teeth and dress. (Also mandatory)
> Step Six: Kiss and tickle the baby.
> Step Seven: Kiss Tamara.
> Step Eight: Tickle Tamara. (Time and wife permitting)
> Step Nine: Drive Chris and Ginger to school.

The tablet came to life, revealing the time. Seven in the morning! Why was Ginger dressed and ready a full hour before they needed to leave? Then he remembered: field-trip day. Since Tamara was a designated driver she needed Alex to take the baby with him to the office. Mrs. Mayhew had said she would be delighted to have little Joey around for the day. "He'll be no trouble at all."

Alex knew Joey would create no trouble. And he might just manage to keep Mrs. Mayhew from *making* trouble. She was, bless her heart, a generous soul. No one else in the church had ever volunteered to spend eight hours per day "doing whatever Pastor needs done."

If only he had had the foresight to reject the offer. Not just because Mrs. Mayhew lacked any of the skills essential in a competent assistant, but also because she volunteered much more than her time. She volunteered confidential information to anyone who might ask, and to those who didn't.

"We can make the pastor's assistant a volunteer position," Phil Crawford had said, another brilliant strategy for solving the budget shortfall. "Mrs. Mayhew seems like a highly qualified candidate who would enjoy the opportunity to serve."

He had been right about one thing. She enjoyed serving. Which is why Mrs. Mayhew had no intention of leaving Alex in the lurch by ever, ever vacating the position. A reality that, for today, would prove helpful. Especially since he needed to get a good part of Sunday's sermon written using a four-hour block of time he had asked Mrs. Mayhew to protect. Tuesday was the one day of the week he had come to relish, because he could focus on the task he had been trained and, he'd once believed, hired to do.

"You've got to be kidding me!" Alex erupted after reviewing the day's agenda.

"What's wrong?" Tamara yelled from the hallway.

"Nothing," he lied. "Never mind."

How could Mrs. Mayhew put a counseling session on his schedule in the middle of his sermon prep time?

Then he looked closer. She hadn't. The appointment request had come through the church's "spiritual dialogue" outreach page.

Alex groaned.

The idea had been one of the earliest proposed by the outreach committee, something the members had seen at a nearby church that they considered "cutting-edge" and "outside the box." Alex had had to admit the concept sounded promising. Offer local residents a confidential session at a time of their choosing. Help them process emotions and sort through confusion triggered by life's inevitable pain. He'd imagined the invite cards and website facilitating on-demand evangelism by letting folks talk to a minister at the precise moment they needed comfort or, as the promotional label suggested, *spiritual guidance*.

Alex tapped the appointment. It included the phrase "Feeling down" in the space provided for specifics. The same as always. People never requested an appointment because they "Want to know more about God" or "Need to repent of sinful patterns." They just wanted someone to help them feel better. Not *become* better or even *do* better. Just *feel* better.

Alex agreed, in theory, that confession could be good for the soul. But so far it had done nothing but wreak havoc on his schedule. The board had originally approved the strategy because it would "cost the church nothing" while positioning it well in the community. "We'll share the load," Kenny Morrison had promised on behalf of the elders. Yet Alex had handled thirty-four of the thirty-seven appointments to date. Thirty-five after today's meeting with someone named "I'd like to remain anonymous."

~~~

Mrs. Mayhew lit up like a Christmas tree while straining to extract herself from a chair designed for someone of less generous proportions. "Come to Auntie Dimples!" she sang in little Joey's direction.

"Dimples," Alex puzzled aloud. "I still can't get over the fact your name is Dimples."

"A family nickname," she said proudly.

"To replace what?"

A disapproving scowl. "Your nine o'clock is waiting in your office," she said. "Just leave this little man with me."

Alex released Joey into Mrs. Mayhew's outstretched arms.

"Been waiting long?"

"Just arrived."

The pastor entered his office to find the man standing near a bookshelf, where he appeared to be admiring Alex's small collection of vintage print volumes. The man turned. Then he shuffled his feet as if unsure of protocol.

"Hello," Alex said, offering his hand. "I'm Pastor Alex."

After a brief hesitation the man returned the gesture. "Pleased to meet you, sir. I'm…" He thought for a moment. "I'm Frank. You can call me Frank."

Alex smiled at the suggestion. "Frank" had just moved up on his mental tally of assumed names. "John" remained the top pick among anonymous male counselees. "Bob" fell to third.

Frank pointed toward the bookshelf. "Have you read these?"

"I have."

"All of them?" The man looked back to reread titles he had apparently not expected on a minister's shelf. He mentioned three: *The Origin of Species* by Charles Darwin, *Beyond Good and Evil* by Friedrich Nietzsche, and *A Brief History of Time* by Stephen Hawking.

"All early editions," Alex explained with some satisfaction. "The first was a gift from my grandfather. I found the other two at garage sales." He moved to stand beside his guest for a closer look. "Believe it or not, most of these were found at garage sales. People have no idea how valuable these will be. Already are."

"I've collected a few myself," Frank said while turning toward Alex. "So you keep them as investments?"

"In part."

"But you've read them?"

"Yes. You sound surprised."

"Well, I guess I wouldn't have associated these volumes with a man of the cloth."

Alex chuckled at both the description and the presumption. "Well, that's one I've never been called before. As you can see, I don't wear a dog collar. I'm not a priest, just an ordinary guy like you."

The comment seemed to unsettle Alex's guest. "But...you *are* a minister?"

"Oh, yes."

"And our conversation will be strictly confidential?"

"Assuming you're not an ax murderer, whatever you say will remain between the two of us."

A nervous laugh. "No, no. Nothing like that."

"Shall we sit?"

It took Alex a few minutes to help his anonymous friend grasp the difference between the Sacrament of Penance and the goals of this appointment. "You can say anything you wish," he explained, "but I can't offer absolution, nor will I assign any acts of penance."

Frank appeared to like the notion of an informal chat instead of a structured ritual.

"I will listen and, if you wish, comment. But nothing I say should be perceived as a binding directive or as formal counseling. I'm licensed for neither."

Alex paused while the clarifications settled. "One more thing," he added. "I'd like to spend a few minutes at the end of our session asking you a few questions."

"About what?"

"About your spiritual journey."

The man thought for a moment. "Fair enough," he agreed.

Ground rules established, Alex asked what had led Frank to request an appointment.

"This." The man reached into his back pocket to retrieve a card.

Alex recognized it immediately. Hundreds had been mailed out to Christ Community members with a letter inviting them to use the cards as outreach tools. "Did you find it somewhere? Or did someone give it to you?"

"It was given to me."

"By a friend?"

"Not exactly," Frank replied.

"Someone at work?"

"Sort of," he said. "An older woman. She said I looked like I needed to talk to someone."

"Well then, I'm listening," said Alex.

The man appeared uneasy. He returned the minister's smile weakly before shifting his gaze toward the bookshelf.

"I went through a dark spell about a year back," he finally said. "It was pretty bad."

"Depression?"

"I guess. And nightmares. I found myself more angry than depressed, if that makes any sense."

"It does. Anger and sorrow are close relatives."

"Sure are," Frank said knowingly.

A brief silence.

"I've been reading this book," Frank continued as if trying to make small talk. "A Russian author. A famous novelist, actually."

"Tolstoy?"

"Dostoyevsky."

Alex smiled at the mention.

"You know of him?"

Alex walked to his bookshelf. "Let me see," he said while scanning his collection. "Ah, here we go." He walked back toward Frank and handed him a volume. The cover read *The*

Brothers Karamazov. "I got this one at an estate sale. A few bumps and bruises, but overall it's in excellent condition."

"So you've read it?"

"Twice. It's his greatest work."

The man appeared puzzled by Alex's affirmation.

"Didn't it make you squirm?"

"Which part?"

Frank thought for a moment. "The part with the kid and the dog, for example."

Alex reached into his memory, trying to connect the dots, until Frank offered more details.

"A boy accidentally hits his master's favorite dog with a rock—"

"Oh, yes," Alex interrupted. "And the master sends the hounds after him."

"That's it."

"I remember. Yes, that part does make me squirm, almost as much as the part when the soldier shoots the baby in the face."

Frank winced at the reminder while placing the volume on the coffee table.

"Definitely not a feel-good book," Alex continued. "But one of the most powerful depictions I've ever read of man's cruelty."

"Man's? Not God's?"

"Is that what you came to discuss, Frank, the problem of evil?"

The man hesitated. "No. Not really."

"Then what?" Alex asked.

Frank hesitated. "I'm starting to feel like I did at the start of my dark days."

"I see."

"My nightmares are back, for example."

"What kind of nightmares?" Alex asked.

"I don't remember details. Just the feelings."

"What kind of feelings, then?"

"Fear. Panic. More anger."

"Anger at whom?"

"Nobody. Everybody."

"Yourself?" Alex pressed.

The man offered the hint of a nod.

"What about God?" He perceived a tiny flinch. "Are you mad at God, Frank?"

The guest shifted in his chair without a word.

Alex had seen dozens of anonymous visitors in addition to consoling or counseling members of his flock. He always felt inadequate, as if fumbling for the right thing to say in response to their anxiety. But now, seated across from a man he had only just met and whose story he had barely heard, Alex sensed he knew what his curious visitor needed to hear.

"I had a seminary professor who used to say we can't love people, including ourselves, when we hate the one whose image we bear."

Their eyes met. Alex gazed deeply until the man looked away.

"I don't hate myself," Frank snapped. "And I'm not sure I even believe God exists."

"I know plenty of people who are mad at God for not existing. Or, put another way, for not showing up."

Another look of surprise, possibly fear, pinched the corners of Frank's eyes.

"Tell me about the dark period," Alex said. "You said it was a year ago?"

"A bit less."

"Do you remember what triggered it?"

"Not really," Frank said.

"Something that happened?"

A slight shrug.

"Something you did?"

Frank looked like a man covering cards he'd been dealt at the blackjack table. He leaned forward to pick up the thick novel. "Why do you like this?" he asked, apparently eager to redirect the conversation.

The question displaced Alex's train of thought.

"I mean, he makes a pretty good case against God."

"Does he?" asked Alex while watching his guest inspect the volume.

"You don't agree?" asked Frank.

"I don't. But more importantly, neither would the author. He was trying to make the case *for* God, not against him."

"A God who makes innocent kids suffer?"

"Is that what you took away from the novel?"

A hesitant nod.

"Then I'm afraid you may have missed the point."

A flush on Frank's neck told Alex the comment had wounded a fragile ego. He continued anyway.

"*The Brothers Karamazov* is about what happens when people reject belief in God. When we abandon the good that God is, all that's left is the evil that he isn't."

A long silence.

"Can I ask you another question?" asked Frank.

"Of course."

"What's your view on death?"

"I'm against it." Alex smiled at himself.

"I mean, do you consider it a good to embrace or an evil to avoid?"

Alex thought for a moment before answering. "I consider it a foe that's been defeated."

"So an enemy?"

"Of course. We were made for life, not death. That's why our Lord came, to defang the snake."

Frank appeared confused. Or perhaps disturbed. "You mean Jesus?"

"Yes. Jesus."

"The one who embraced death?"

"Not embraced it. Defeated it."

It suddenly dawned on Alex that his mysterious guest might be contemplating something drastic in response to his depression. But before the thought could fully form, a knocking sound invaded the moment. Alex spun toward the door to see a somewhat embarrassed Mrs. Mayhew peering in.

"I'm sorry to interrupt, Pastor," she said. "But I can't seem to find a diaper in little Joey's bag and, well, you know."

Alex blushed toward his guest. "My apologies," he said.

"Who's little Joey?"

"My youngest. Mrs. Mayhew is kind enough to watch him for the day. My wife is on a field trip with our daughter."

"Two kids. Wow!"

"Three, actually," Alex said while moving toward the door. He felt the rebuke of Tamara's final earlier instruction to "Pick up a pack of Huggies on the way."

"Listen," Frank said, standing, "I'll get out of your way. I appreciate your time and all, but…"

"No. Please." Alex raised his hand like a cop halting traffic. "There's something I need to ask you. I won't be long."

Five minutes later Mrs. Mayhew pulled away with little Joey strapped safely in his car seat, freeing Alex to return. The detour had given him a moment to consider how he might discover the real reason "Frank" had come.

CHAPTER SIX

His first impulse was to leave.

He had expected a kind, elderly gentleman nodding mindlessly at details of the dark days: the heavy drinking, the gambling losses, and even the girls. If that had gone well he might even have scheduled a second session to discuss Reverend Grandpa, his mom, and the rest. Matthew had scheduled the appointment in search of respite. But this Pastor Alex, whoever he was, seemed ready to attack.

But curiosity won the moment. What question would the minister ask? How, Matthew wondered, had a complete stranger perceived a secret Matthew hadn't fully realized until the moment he heard the pastor say the words? Matthew *was* mad at God. Not the God he had abandoned in childhood. Nor the one he had borrowed from Dr. Vincent's lectures. Matthew was angry with the real God. The one who, as Alex had put it, had failed to show up.

So he stayed. No harm in sticking around a few more minutes and then going on as if the conversation had never happened.

After all, Matthew had never mentioned his real name. He need never see Pastor Alex again.

"Please forgive me," the minister said, closing the door behind him and retaking his seat. "Thank you for sticking around."

Matthew nodded, an invitation for the invasion to begin.

Pastor Alex took a deep breath before restarting the conversation. "May I ask why you wanted to know my view on death?" he asked.

"No reason," Matthew said. "Just curious, you being a minister and all. I figure you must deal with death a lot."

"I do. I conducted a funeral just this past week for a longtime member of Christ Community." The minister paused to look directly into Matthew's eyes. "He committed suicide."

"I'm sorry to hear that." It was the thing to say.

"I had to try explaining why the man ended his own life to the four-year-old little girl who had discovered his corpse."

Matthew winced at the image.

"She asked me whether her grandpa was in heaven with her grandma."

"Sweet. What'd you say?"

"Probably the wrong thing," Alex confessed. "But I couldn't tell her the truth."

"Which is?"

"Which is that I'm not sure where her grandfather is right now."

"In a better place?" Matthew suggested. "I mean, don't all Christian ministers believe in an afterlife?"

"We do. But we also believe in an after-death. That little girl's grandfather could just as well be entering an eternity separated from God as the bliss of heaven."

"You told her that?"

"Of course not!"

It hadn't occurred to Matthew that ministers might doubt the eternal destiny of the faithful. Hadn't he just said the man was a longtime member of the church?

"What did you say when the girl asked if her grandpa was with her grandma?"

Alex inhaled regretfully. "I hope so. I told her that I hope so."

"Seems like a safe response. Harmless enough."

"Is it?" the minister asked. "Is it harmless to let a little girl believe her grandfather's transition has nothing to do with the state of his soul?"

"Wait," Matthew said. "You never said it was a transition. I thought you said the girl found the body."

"She did, when the family came down from Nebraska for a visit. His corpse was in the bathtub."

"Not in a clinic?"

"They're doing them in homes now."

"They leave the bodies?"

"Oh, no, that was a scheduling error. The man had mistyped the date when registering himself for disposal."

Matthew vaguely recalled his boss mentioning something about transitions taking place in homes, a practice that might reduce the number of potential MedCom clients. But he had dismissed the threat. Why would anyone choose a self-serve, low-cost option for such an important event?

Apparently, some already had.

Conflicting emotions played king of the hill in Matthew's mind.

First, a sense of diminishment, as if the end of some nameless stranger's life had somehow stolen a fraction of value from Matthew's own. He shook off the feeling in favor of a less troubling emotion, offense. How dare this minister equate a transition with suicide or suggest volunteering might damn an eternal soul! The girl's late grandfather, like Matthew's own mother, hadn't been a coward. They had been heroic. They had given a gift, not committed a sin.

"So you think the girl's grandfather went to hell?"

"I didn't say that," Alex said quickly. "I don't presume to know what was going on in his heart and mind. I prefer to think he was confused, or even deceived. But I know one thing for certain, Frank. No matter what you're facing or what you might have done, suicide is not the answer."

The statement stunned Matthew. *He thinks I'm planning to kill myself?*

"What did you say?" he asked.

"There are ways to treat depression, Matthew. Have you seen a doctor?"

Matthew felt a rising fury more intense than the one that had driven him from Mrs. Baxter's kitchen table. She had felt sorry for him. But that offense paled in comparison with this. Why on earth would he think Matthew so pathetic, so weak? Sure, he had gone through a dark spell. Who hadn't? But he had clawed his way back, no thanks to the God Pastor Alex Ware seemed so fond of. Matthew had a good job, one he did well. He was on track for the best month of commissions he had ever earned, which promised to put him back in the black.

He stood. "I need to go now."

"But…" Alex began.

"No!" Matthew shouted, surprising even himself. He took a deep breath while considering his next move. Flushed with embarrassment and wrath, he chose to walk toward the door.

The pastor didn't pursue. He remained seated, calmly looking toward the space Matthew had abruptly fled.

"Have you read the whole book?" he asked as if the outburst had never occurred.

"What whole book?" said Matthew, his voice trembling slightly.

"*The Brothers Karamazov.*"

"Of course," he lied.

The minister shifted in his chair, turning slowly toward the door, where Matthew stood eager to exit. "Then you know what happens to Ivan Karamazov." He approached Matthew while extending his hand. "I'd hate to see something similar happen to you."

They shook hands, silently, before Matthew slipped hastily out of the room.

CHAPTER SEVEN

Kevin recognized the outcropping of rocks. Just beyond the river's bend, the quietness of their scenic trip through Brown's Canyon was about to end. He braced himself—not for the rough water ahead, but for Angie's reaction when she realized he hadn't been *entirely* honest.

"Kevin?" she intoned, nervously gripping the paddle even tighter. "What's that?"

He cupped his ear toward the faint sound of the approaching rapids while glancing to Troy for fraternal support. He just shrugged.

Angie looked at Julia. She had nothing to offer since it was her first time on the river also.

Kevin returned his gaze to his wife and smiled, sheepishly. "Um. Just a bit of white water."

"But you said—"

"I know what I said. But…well…you should know better than to trust a politician!" He pointed to the breaking water ahead with the end of his paddle. "Time for a little fun!"

The raft drifted faster now, swaying slightly in the increased flow of the river. Angie gasped, pulling her paddle backward through the water in a futile attempt to stop moving. "If we get out of this alive, Mr. Politician—"

She paused long enough to shove her side of the raft away from one of the huge rocks.

"—I'm going to kill you!"

A moment after they had steered around a large series of boulders, the front half of the raft reared upward, nearly catapulting Kevin from his seat before slamming back down into a watery valley. The splash soaked Kevin's face, temporarily blinding him as he repositioned his legs to prevent being thrown. Julia screamed with delight from behind as Troy shoved his paddle into the rapids to keep them heading in some semblance of forward. The raft shifted again as the river began another series of drops.

"Hang on," Kevin shouted over the now-roaring rapids. He glanced at his wife, making sure she was OK. Even drenched from head to toe, with strands of hair stuck to her forehead in disarray, she was a lovely sight to behold. She brushed a clump from her face with the back of her paddling hand while tightening her grip with the other.

Ultimately, it had been Troy who'd convinced her to come along on this "little excursion," as he'd called it. "Water might get a little bumpy a few times, but nothing too bad." And of course, there had been Julia, all over the idea of a "little adventure." The word *little* had been used no fewer than six times to describe the outing. Of course, there was nothing little about it. At least that's how Angie would see it. Kevin, however, wasn't worried.

"What about the kids?" Angie had asked, figuring she had a definite out with that one. "Who's gonna watch them while we're off gallivanting?"

But then Julia's sister Maria had stepped in to salvage the plan. "I think Jared and I can manage the rug rats for a few hours," she had said.

Now the tiny boat spun halfway around before nose-diving into yet another valley, soaking everyone. Julia shrieked, then laughed wildly. She was having the time of her life, it seemed. Troy shared a satisfied grin with Kevin before digging his paddle into the water to help spin them back in the right direction.

Fifteen minutes later they were dragging their raft up onto the shoreline of a more peaceful stretch off the main river. Kevin thought that Angie might have actually enjoyed the white water for a few brief moments. Then he placed his hand on the small of her back affectionately. She just jerked away, giving him a rather cold shoulder. Now he was worried he'd made a mistake giving in to Troy's suggestion that they make their "relive our youth" trip through the canyon a double date.

Kevin sighed. At least they had made it safely through the roughest part of the trip. Now it was time to relax. Allow the sun to dry them off, refuel with food, and enjoy much-needed time away from Washington.

Angie and Julia unpacked their modest cooler while Troy unfolded the camping chairs. Kevin gathered fallen branches from some of the nearby trees and stoked a flame inside a makeshift fire pit.

"Whew!" Kevin said as he plopped onto the edge of the raft next to his wife. His excitement echoed off the surrounding rocky walls. "I gotta admit...I don't remember the river being quite that wild!"

Angie pulled her hair back into a sloppy ponytail, glaring at her husband. "Trying to make orphans out of the kids?"

Troy laughed—until Kevin reached across and slugged him in the shoulder.

"So, the two of you did this a lot?" Julia asked her husband.

Troy shrugged. "Maybe two or three times a year. Back in our college days."

"Men," Angie said disparagingly…although Kevin noted the glint in her expression. He knew that somewhere deep down she quietly admired Kevin's adventurous side. And he loved her all the more for her willingness to play along—especially when she'd clearly rather keep her feet planted firmly on dry ground.

"I don't know, Angie," Julia said. "I thought it was fun. Freeing. Like the rest of the world is a million miles away." She leaned in close to Troy, resting her head against his shoulder. His arm reached up around her. It was still a foreign sight to Kevin, but one that looked good on his best friend.

"I'm glad you guys could fly out," Troy said while pulling Julia closer. "We've seen less and less of you since the reelection campaign kicked into high gear."

Angie tore open a package of hot dogs and skewered one before handing it to Kevin. Truth was he needed some kind of break from all the stress of politicking. Coming out to visit his parents had been as good an excuse as any. And Angie needed the distraction even more than he did. While he was off hobnobbing with the rich and powerful, she was trying to juggle physical therapy appointments for little Leah while keeping the other three kids fed, clothed, and alive.

"A million miles away," Kevin said with a smile, Julia's words returning to him. He held his stick over the tiny flame. "It feels great. But I will say I'm starting to feel a bit like this hot dog out in D.C."

Julia looked toward Angie inquisitively.

"Not getting the promised support for the Bright Spots Initiative," Angie explained, repeating the very words her husband had said to her over the dinner table a dozen times in the prior month.

A million miles away, maybe, but Kevin still couldn't keep his mind from his work. Even here, away from it all, he'd managed to raise the subject.

"Sorry," he said. "I did it again. I promised Angie not to discuss work for at least twenty-four hours and there I go."

Angie grinned, then shrugged. "Well, you managed almost thirteen. I'll give you partial credit."

He leaned in and gave her a peck on the cheek. "Thanks, boss."

Angie slapped his chest, then accepted his overpowering squeeze.

Troy poked at the diminishing flames with a stick, then stood. "Fire's not gonna last very long without fuel. I'll go find some dry wood."

"Let me help," Kevin said, handing his wife his makeshift skewer.

"Oh, I get it," she said with mock offense. "Go on. I'll handle the cooking, as usual!"

Kevin laughed while planting a kiss on Angie's forehead.

They took their time wandering among the trees, away from the river's edge.

"So, what's *really* bothering you?" Troy prodded.

Kevin pursed his lips, glancing back to make sure Angie was out of earshot before answering flatly, "Franklin."

Troy nodded knowingly as his friend continued.

"He promised me the Youth Initiative Expansion Act would include the Bright Spots amendment I worked my tail off to incorporate into the House version."

"Cut from the Senate version. I know." Troy cleared his throat. "And I told you."

Kevin remembered his friend's warning. "Don't trust him. He'll sell you out." He should have listened.

Troy shoved a pile of kindling into Kevin's arms. "Which incidentally means I owe you a head rub."

Kevin smiled at the reminder of his friend's favorite retaliation. It had been too long. He missed their playful banter that had spanned decades, from debating the best way to attract freshman cheerleaders to which failing business to turn around. Even while serving as Kevin's chief of staff in Congress, Troy often stole a private moment to place his boss in a headlock until Kevin admitted the mistake of mistrusting his friend's instincts.

And this mistake, Kevin knew, deserved more than a mere head rub.

"Do you think it's too late to try your approach?"

Troy said nothing in response to the violation of tradition.

"Come on, Troy," Kevin said.

Troy waited without a word.

"OK," the congressman relented. "You were right. I was wrong."

"I know," Troy said with a rising grin.

"Now, will you answer the question?"

"Maybe. But maybe not."

"Let's go with the maybe not," Kevin prodded. "Best play?"

"Best play would be for you to tell Franklin you plan to walk."

Kevin dropped the pile of sticks. "Walk? Are you nuts? The convention is less than a month away."

"And?" Troy replied.

"And I represent an important voting bloc."

"And?"

"And I can't walk or I lose all influence in the platform debate."

"Oh. You mean the kind of influence that would prevent Franklin from cutting the Bright Spots amendment from the Youth Initiative Expansion?"

Kevin felt the rebuke.

"Don't kid yourself, Congressman. Franklin has no intention of letting your ideas shape the party's agenda. His biggest donors live and die by quarterly earnings reports, not generational demographic trends."

They had had this argument before. Kevin had won. But Troy had been right.

"Go on," Kevin said meekly.

"As soon as Franklin gets the nomination I expect him to abandon the Bright Spots proposal entirely."

It was a reality that Kevin had refused to accept. Until now.

"So I should walk away?"

"Of course not," Troy replied.

"But you just said..."

"I said you should tell Senator Franklin you *plan* to walk. I didn't say you should actually walk."

"Bluff?" Kevin asked indignantly.

"No. Mean it. And make sure he knows you mean it. Then you won't need to do it."

"I don't follow."

Troy rolled his eyes, then bent down to begin recovering the kindling Kevin had let fall. "Franklin keeps you close for one reason. He's probably been told he can't win the nomination, let alone the election, without breeder support."

Kevin winced. *Breeder* had been an offensive slur before it became a useful label among the political and media elite. Usually spoken with sneering disdain, the tag referred to the one segment of the population still growing. The segment Kevin, more than anyone else in D.C., embodied. It was the only real bright spot in an ever-darkening economy, and a source of long-term stability his Bright Spots amendment had been intended to defend.

"He won't let you walk. He can't. The bloc of votes you represent is too important to him," Troy observed. "As it is, he hopes you'll play along and be nice until after the election. Then he'll drop you and your proposal like a hot potato."

"You may be right," Kevin said, the words sticking in his craw.

"I'm definitely right," Troy corrected.

"But riding the Franklin wave seemed the best way to get my ideas out there."

"It was," Troy agreed. "But the only way to keep them out there is to play hardball. Make Franklin promise you he will publically support the Bright Spots agenda during the convention."

"Make him?"

"Threaten him, then. Tell him you need concrete assurances or he can kiss your smiling, vote-generating face goodbye."

Kevin sighed. "That would be bold."

"It would."

"But it would also be risky," Kevin added hesitantly. "What if he calls my bluff?"

"I already told you," Troy said sternly. "It wouldn't be a bluff. What's the point of everything we've done if we back down now? The fund-raising, the campaigning, even launching the Center for Economic Health would be for nothing if you don't hold your ground. Franklin is a fiscal conservative to the core. He's not going to change course on his support for the Youth Initiative without someone holding a gun to his head."

Kevin said nothing as the weight of Troy's words settled onto his shoulders.

"Come on, Congressman," Troy said, piling one final log on Kevin's burgeoning armload. "The girls are probably onto us by now. We have enough wood for a bonfire. Time to head back."

Back to his wife, yes. Back to the world, a million miles away...not yet.

CHAPTER EIGHT

"I **guess** we should go ahead and eat these," Angie said, examining a small stack of flame-charred hot dogs. "They might fossilize if we wait for the boys."

Julia laughed at the jab. "How long does it take to gather a few sticks?"

Angie pointed to a smattering of branches thirty feet away. "You mean like those?"

Julia shook her head in mock disapproval. "I guess they can't help themselves," she said, pulling herself away from the fire to join Angie near a large rock turned makeshift picnic table. It was their first real moment alone, finally finished roasting a meal neither cared to eat but that the husbands had included on the trip's list of required supplies.

"How are you?" Julia asked, preempting Angie's usual initiative in order to focus the conversation on the Tolbert family: Tommy's grades, Joy's swim lessons, little Ricky's teething and, of course, Leah's therapy. She hoped to keep Angie talking about her world until Troy and Kevin returned.

"Oh, no," Angie insisted, her eyes carrying a rebuke softened by her adorable grin. "You first." She took a sip of bottled water. "How is it?"

"How is what?"

Angie didn't say a word. She just waited, and glared.

Did she know? Julia wondered. Of course she knew. Way back in high school Angie had had a knack for detecting the least hint of distress in others. Seven years of motherhood had sharpened the instinct into an uncannily precise radar. It was one of the things Julia admired about her. Angie Tolbert was a patient friend, a supportive wife to Kevin, and a nurturing mom to their four kids. In short, everything Julia felt herself failing to become.

"Good," Julia finally said with an evasive smile. "Real good."

Angie's eyes narrowed.

"OK. And hard," Julia confessed. "I guess harder than I expected."

Her friend's pursed lips lifted into a warm smile of approval. Julia had done the right thing by coming clean.

"I bet it has," Angie said with a trace of admiration.

Julia looked back at the woman who, more than anyone she knew, embodied maternal success. Four young children. Four! And one of them disabled. Angie Tolbert was in an entirely different league from Julia, who, it seemed, could hardly handle one.

"I don't know how you do it," she said. A subtle plea. But for what? A secret weapon? A magic wand? A shoulder to cry on? Julia didn't request or receive comfort easily. Nor did she give it. Which, she feared, made her an unsuitable mother.

"What do you mean how *I* do it?" Angie asked. "I've never raised a preteen daughter."

"No, but you're raising four kids." Julia noticed Angie's shaking head. "What?" she asked.

"I still can't believe Kevin and I have four under eight years old."

Julia smiled at her friend's astonishment. "I know," she squeezed through the corner of her mouth. "What's up with that?"

They shared a laugh while Julia tried to imagine herself in Angie's shoes. No one had been surprised when the bouncy cheerleader inspired her husband's rise to the halls of Congress. As lovely as any trophy wife on Capitol Hill, Angie rarely visited the salon or shopped for glamorous dresses to wear to the next fund-raising event. She was far too busy changing diapers and cutting crusts off peanut-butter sandwiches. Did Angie ever resent the relative obscurity to which motherhood had confined her? She had even given up her part-time nursing job after Leah's birth, the sensible thing to do. No, the right thing to do. But it still must have been difficult. Julia wondered if she would have been able to make the same choices in Angie's shoes.

She would never know. Julia had never given birth. Never would.

But she had invited a twelve-year-old girl into her home. Amanda needed a family, something she and Troy could become to her. After everything Amanda had endured during her first twelve years, she deserved a real home. The kind of home Angie and Kevin had created for their kids. The kind Julia was discovering herself ill-equipped to give.

Angie's internal radar beeped. "Spill it, Julia," she commanded.

After a brief hesitation Julia decided to say what her friend probably already perceived.

"I'm having second thoughts."

"About the adoption?"

Julia nodded slowly. Shamefully.

Angie approached, placing her hand on Julia's arm.

"I'm not like you, Angie. I get so…" She paused.

"Tense?" Angie completed the thought.

Another embarrassed nod.

"And angry?"

Julia looked at her friend turned inquisitor. How did she know?

"And insecure, like you think you're doing everything wrong?"

"Exactly," Julia replied.

"Then you're just like every mother on the planet." Angie smiled reassuringly. "Go on."

"Like yesterday morning. I ran Amanda to the store to pick up a bottle of some shampoo her friends insist makes their hair smell like rose petals. New Aroma or New Fragrance. Something like that."

"NuScent?"

"That's it."

"Lilies," Angie said. "It makes your hair smell like lilies."

"Right, lilies. Anyway, I had no idea how expensive it would be until we got to the store, so I suggested a different brand."

Angie grinned. "I bet that didn't go over real well."

"Oh, my goodness!" Julia said. "You would have thought I had suggested shaving her head bald. She folded her arms tight like a temper-throwing child and stormed out of the store after calling me a stingy, selfish…" She paused, unwilling to quote the rest.

"Ouch," Angie said sympathetically.

"Can you believe it? After all I've given that girl."

Angie didn't appear to take up Julia's offense. "So what'd you do?" she asked.

"I bought a bottle of the stupid shampoo."

"Good girl," Angie said, to Julia's surprise. "Then what?"

"I was upset, so I took my time walking to the car in order to cool down."

Angie smiled like a teacher writing "A+" on a struggling student's test paper. "What did you say to Amanda?"

"Nothing. I just opened the door and handed her the bottle."

"Did she apologize?"

"No. We drove halfway home in silence."

"And then?"

"And then Amanda opened her window and tossed the bottle of NuScent into a ditch."

Angie winced.

"I nearly lost it," Julia continued, her head bowing slightly in self-condemnation. "I wanted to pull the car over and make her walk the rest of the way home. I wanted to ask her if she had any idea how much stress Troy and I have been under since she arrived, how much time and money we've spent trying to give her a better life, and how much sleep I've lost worrying about whether we made the right decision."

"You made the right decision, Julia. That girl needs you and Troy."

Julia nodded in hesitant agreement. "I know she does."

"And you need her."

Did she? During the countless hours she had rehearsed the decision in her mind, Julia had always landed in the same place. Troy wanted kids and would make a great father. Since they were unable to conceive their own, taking on a neglected transition-orphan seemed the right thing to do. At times Julia even felt as if God himself had orchestrated the union between infertile couple and parentless child. So why, she wondered, hadn't he endowed Julia with the kind of calm confidence and loving patience that overflowed effortlessly from her friend?

"You think I need temper tantrums and flying shampoo bottles?"

Angie laughed. "I guess, in a way, yeah. You do."

Julia gave a puzzled look.

"If motherhood has taught me anything," Angie continued, "it's that nothing gets us in better shape."

Julia imagined herself at the gym. "In shape?"

"Pushes us to become more than we want to be."

"I see," Julia bluffed.

"I don't think you do," said Angie. "You just described a situation that tells me you're becoming a wonderful mom."

"What?"

"You heard me, a wonderful mom."

Julia smiled condescendingly at her friend's effort to cheer.

"Don't give me that look," Angie scolded. "I'm not being nice. I'm being serious. Listen to yourself, Julia. You bought Amanda the shampoo. You cooled yourself down before getting in the car."

"And then I almost made her walk home and almost told her I regret initiating the adoption."

"Exactly. *Almost*. But you didn't. You swallowed your anger. You gave up the right to retaliate. You forgave. And as a result, you remained an agent of grace in that girl's life. You probably even moved her a step closer to feeling the kind of security she's never known but desperately needs. Secure enough, maybe, to start fighting who knows what emotional demons."

"I guess," Julia responded gratefully. It was true, the past year had brought more opportunities to back off, cool down, apologize, sacrifice, and give than she could have imagined. As difficult as the first year of marriage to Troy had been, adjusting to the expectations and needs of a wife, the year with Amanda had been infinitely more stretching. She had often reminded herself of Jesus's words Pastor Alex had mentioned in a sermon. "Learn from me, for I am gentle and lowly in heart."

She had been trying to learn. And perhaps, if she dared believe Angie, getting in slightly better shape.

"I'm very proud of you, girl."

The force of the words surprised Julia. Had her friend ever used them with her before? She tried to remember. Angie, like the rest of her friends, had expected Julia to graduate valedictorian from her high school class and then take full advantage of her Ivy League scholarship. They took it in stride when she received a Pulitzer Prize in journalism. No big surprise. Julia couldn't recall Angie offering the sentiment in response to her most impressive achievements. Why, after everything Julia had accomplished, would this put such admiration in Angie's eyes?

"And I promise you," her friend continued while a hand squeezed Julia's arm, "you're doing the right thing."

—◦—

Troy and Kevin arrived, finally, with what looked like "enough wood to build a small condominium."

Kevin reacted to Angie's playful wisecrack with a kiss on the forehead while Troy downed a bite of his now-cold hot dog.

"You might as well finish," Angie said, slapping her husband's behind as if punishing his concealed offense.

"Finish what?" he asked innocently, winking toward Troy.

"The conversation you were having about the Robin Hood tax."

"Robin Hood tax?" Troy asked inquisitively.

Angie looked toward Kevin, then Troy, then back to her husband.

"You mean that's not what you were talking about?"

Kevin shook his head. "You told us not to discuss work, remember." He suddenly looked eager to comply with her earlier, already violated rule.

"Wait," Troy said. "What's happening with the Robin Hood tax?"

"What *is* the Robin Hood tax?" Julia asked, apparently the only one in the dark.

"It's a distortion of an idea we floated a few months back," said Troy. "One Kevin assured me wouldn't see the light of day."

Kevin appeared sheepish. "I didn't want to ruin your trip."

Angie, apparently realizing her mistake, tried changing the subject. "How about if I warm up that dog?"

"Good idea," Kevin answered, still trapped in the line of Troy's threatening glare.

"What kind of idea?" Julia pressed.

Troy turned toward his wife. "I suggested proposing something called a 'fertility credit' that would allow seniors to receive a full tax credit when they donate toward conception and child-birth expenses for a married mom and dad."

"You specified married parents?" Julia asked.

"I know, it was a long shot," Troy said. "But we provided solid data showing the long-term impact of marriage on the economy and the kids."

Kevin chimed in. "I pitched it as a way to make the Youth Initiative slightly less offensive to my constituency. You know, give seniors an incentive for helping future bright spots. The older the donor, I suggested, the higher the allowable credit."

"Let me guess," Julia said. "Franklin rejected the idea because it might reduce the incentive to volunteer."

"Worse," Troy answered. "He loved the part about raising the allowable credit based upon the age of the donor. With one major adjustment."

"Rather than offer a new tax credit *to* seniors, he proposed a new tax *on* seniors. He called it the Robin Hood tax."

"As in stealing from the rich to give to the poor?" Julia asked.

"More like taxing the old to fund the young," Kevin explained. "He wants to add a five percent 'age-graduation tax' to every taxpayer over sixty-five to help offset the growing portion of the federal budget allocated to senior-care expenses."

"And it would increase an additional five percent every five years," Troy added angrily.

Julia ran a quick mental tabulation based upon the latest life-expectancy projections. "So by the time they turn ninety they would pay an additional thirty percent?"

"Only those who manage to resist every other strategy designed to pressure volunteers," Troy spat, as if a foul taste had suddenly invaded his mouth. He turned back toward Kevin. "How bad?"

Kevin picked up a small stone and tossed it toward the river. He waited for the splashing *splunk* before responding. "Anderson called me last week to say it would be best if I kept quiet about my opposition to the Robin Hood tax until after the election."

"Franklin is gonna include the projected revenue in his budget plan, isn't he?" Troy asked crossly.

Kevin said nothing, offering a single nod while attacking the river with another stone.

Troy grunted in disgust.

Julia felt her own anger rise with Troy's. Two years earlier she might have celebrated such a tax. She probably would have written a column hailing it as another innovative response to the growing financial crisis. Twelve months earlier she might have wondered what to think, torn between the expectations of her readers and a Christian faith she had only begun to nurture. But today she had no doubt or internal conflict. Such bullying of the elderly was just plain wrong.

"I wish I could help," Julia said.

Troy put an appreciative hand on his wife's sagging shoulder. They both knew it had been months since Julia received an assignment worthy of her reputation. The series of bright spot and dark zone stories written for RAP Syndicate had helped Kevin by creating a stir among readers. But it had also prompted questions from the editorial board that eventually led to the hushed departure of Paul Daugherty, the editor who had contracted Julia to pen the series. So her once-steady stream of work ran dry. All she had left was an occasional opinion column carried by syndicates too small to realize how far Julia's star had fallen.

"So do I, Julia," said Kevin. "So do I."

She sensed Kevin willing himself back into good spirits, a man determined to enjoy his brief but overdue break. Julia blushed at having burdened Angie with such minor worries as Amanda's tantrum.

"Listen, Troy," Kevin began, "I've got a few ideas brewing…" He hesitated, glancing toward Angie, who nodded permission to continue the thought.

But rather than continue, Kevin's eyes peered toward the food pouch lying open on the ground. "But we can talk about that after…"

A spark of recognition lit Troy's eyes as Kevin removed a small object from the bag. "I'm with you, buddy!" he said eagerly, as if suddenly transported to another time and place.

Julia looked curiously toward Kevin's hand. From it dangled a package she hadn't seen in decades.

"Moon pies!" Angie said with repulsion.

"Yeah, baby!" Kevin answered, winking away his wife's rebuke. "A Tolbert/Simmons tradition."

"Toss one of those beauties my way!" Troy said lustfully.

Angie moaned while flashing a mock gag in her friend's direction.

"Like I said," Julia winked. "They can't help themselves!"

CHAPTER NINE

Alex finished his usual Sunday morning greeting with a "special welcome for anyone visiting this weekend," then moved seamlessly into the few platform announcements. As usual, each had been scripted so he could emphasize key details with a quick glance at a tablet screen embedded in the pulpit. He had learned not to veer too far from the prepared comments, since the same text would arrive in every attendee's pocket device halfway into his message, another brilliant idea from the innovation committee. They knew that many of the people sitting through the sermon while looking at their digital tablets only pretended to fill in the open spaces in his notes. Why not reinforce the announcements by providing a scrolling script in the right column of their screens? Those actually listening to the pastor would benefit from reminders of upcoming church activities. Those playing a game or reading an article might instead tap the links and learn more about how to get involved.

The next item, however, had no scrolling text. Phil Crawford had decided to bypass the usual routine in order to "up the game" for his announcement.

"Thank you, Pastor," Phil began after approaching the microphone. As planned, Alex had explained that the chairman would be sharing "an important word from the elder board."

Phil paused before launching into his prepared remarks. That's when a digital image appeared on the platform screen. It took Alex a moment to recognize the couple, a much younger version than the one he had met.

"Those of us who have been around for some time fondly remember Wayne and Wendy Bentley." Phil paused while a different picture appeared, followed by a series of others, each showing the couple a bit older than the last. "The Bentleys modeled what it means to give sacrificially to the ministry of Christ Community Church."

Alex took a seat beside Tamara in the front row. As usual, she clasped his fingers with hers and gently pulled her husband's body close. Only this time her reassuring touch met the stiffness of bottled ire. He knew what was about to happen. Everything within him wanted to stand back up, walk onto the platform, and cut Phil off. But he instead sat silently in his usual spot waiting for the teaching portion of the service, the one part of his job still largely in his control.

"Ten days ago Wayne went to be with the Lord and his beloved bride, who had ended a long battle with cancer only six months before."

Alex recognized the next photograph. It included an image of his own daughter smiling broadly while presenting flowers to a weak but grateful Mrs. Bentley. Wendy loved it when Alex and Tamara brought the children with them on their visits to the hospital.

"Wendy loved children," Phil said with a smile. "Not to mention flowers," he added, prompting the congregation to chuckle on cue.

Tamara gave her husband a gentle squeeze as if inviting him to enjoy the moment. What his wife didn't know, and what infuriated Alex further, was that the image of their daughter had been included to increase the congregation's receptivity to a request Alex would never have made and that Wendy Bentley would have deeply resented.

"Do you know what else Wendy Bentley loved?" Phil Crawford continued. "She loved the work of the Lord. And it was that love that motivated her and Wayne to allocate a significant portion of their estate as a charitable gift to this church. So, on behalf of the elder board, I'd like to extend our deepest sympathies to the family of Wayne and Wendy Bentley as well as express appreciation to these longtime members for allocating a significant portion of their estate to Christ Community Church. Wendy. Wayne. If you can hear me now, know that we accept your donation with the utmost thanks and humility."

A spontaneous outpouring of applause came from the congregation in a show of obligatory solidarity while the chairman of the board appeared to gather notes. Alex held his breath. Had Phil decided to nix the rest of his script?

"A final word is in order," he began as the ovation waned. "I think Wayne would want you to know that he passed as a Youth Initiative volunteer..."

Alex sensed Tamara's eyes dart in his direction.

"...and that he made sure that his will specifically named Christ Community Church as a transition beneficiary, something I'm certain he would want us to encourage everyone over seventy years old to seriously consider as a way of giving their sacrifice even greater significance."

"Did you know about this?" Tamara whispered intensely into Alex's ear.

He responded with the slow nod of a beaten man.

"What are you going to say about it?"

"Nothing," he whispered back. "I can't."

His wife's fingers slipped out of his hand.

As Phil moved off the platform, the worship leader took his place. That's when Alex noticed something dancing on his tablet screen. On everyone's screen. It appeared in the service-flow window designed for those old enough to remember and prefer hymnals, most of them in the target demographic for Phil's appeal. The same worship words that appeared on the large platform screens could also be sized to fit in the palm of your hand. The bouncing icon read EXPLORE TRANSITION GIVING NOW and included the tiny image of a heart. Alex looked closer. The heart had a cross in the center.

He scowled in the general direction of Phil Crawford, who retook his seat. The chairman looked pleased with his demonstration of how to make an announcement stick.

———

For the next thirty-one minutes Alex presented a sermon that, he hoped, managed to avoid a single pitfall. Psalm 23 seemed like safe territory. Who could object to the Lord's being our shepherd or leading us beside still waters? It was the kind of message his board seemed to want. No controversy or guilt, flawlessly delivered and perfectly forgettable.

As he invited the congregation to pray, he scanned the sea of bowing heads. Actually, not a sea. More like a collection of ponds interrupting the landscape of empty seats. Despite a trickle of growth that had occurred on Alex's watch, it had been many Sundays since anyone had accused the sanctuary of reaching capacity.

As he began to voice a closing prayer, Alex noticed someone seated too far back to make out with any certainty. He was pretty good at noticing visitors, but this man looked vaguely familiar. Someone he had met recently. Anonymous Frank? Perhaps. But it could just as easily have been Mrs. Mayhew's nephew, who attended whenever he couldn't get tickets to a Rockies game, or some other middle-aged man sampling churches for a fresh crop of aging single gals.

"Amen," he said before glancing up quickly. No sign of the man, the back door settling itself closed after aiding a prayer-cloaked escape.

The next face Alex saw was Tamara's. A wink of approval told him she had forgiven his cowardice. He smiled gratefully, then readied himself for the second half of his Sunday role by walking to the back of the auditorium while the congregation sang a closing chorus. Members knew they could find their pastor standing at the exit door saying thanks for attending, meeting any visitors brave enough to identify themselves as such, and navigating requests for prayer or from-the-hip counseling on everything from aching joints to addicted children.

After shaking his seventy-third hand, Alex noticed Phil Crawford standing in the vestibule surrounded by a small group of middle-aged parishioners. Kenny James was standing by his side, nodding in agreement at whatever Phil was saying.

"Hello, Pastor."

Alex forced his eyes back. He saw Brandon Baxter standing before him. The newest member of the board had apparently waited for the usual stream of well-wishers and prayer-requesters to dissipate before approaching. Judging by the look on his face, he had something on his mind.

Maybe Psalm 23 hadn't been as harmless as Alex had assumed.

"Can I talk to you for a minute?" Brandon asked with a pitch and posture that seemed more penitent than hostile.

"Sure thing," Alex said. "What's up?"

Brandon scanned for listening ears. "Do you mind if we slip into your office for a moment?"

Odd. Brandon had never asked to meet privately before.

They walked fifty feet down the hallway, where Alex invited Brandon to sit.

"No need," he said. "I'll keep this brief. My wife and kids are out in the car."

Alex waited as the young man cleared his throat nervously.

"I wanted to apologize."

"Apologize?" Alex searched his memory. To his knowledge, Brandon Baxter had never done anything to cause him offense, or to offend anyone for that matter. His mild temperament had been a breath of fresh air to Alex in contrast to the opinionated and pushy crew who comprised the majority of the church board. "Apologize for what?"

"For sitting there like a bump on a log during the meeting this week."

Alex again searched for clues. It was true that Brandon Baxter hadn't said much. But he rarely did. Why the sudden regret?

"I should have spoken up when Phil started pushing the whole transition-donation thing. What he did today was awful. Just awful!"

Alex smiled warmly at his new ally. "I agree," he said cautiously. "My stomach is still in knots."

"Mine, too," said Brandon.

Alex placed his hand on Brandon's shoulder, sensing there was more to be said. "What else?"

"It's my aunt. She called me this week after receiving news she had been declined an essential surgery. She's pretty upset about what happened."

Alex couldn't recall ever meeting Brandon's aunt, something he didn't dare mention. "Does she want me to visit with her?"

"She does. She's never met you, but she watches the streamed service every weekend. She said you would understand why she's so agitated."

He did. Several other older members of the congregation had slipped into despair after being told a simple procedure that might have extended their lives would cost more than they were worth.

"Of course. Surgery is scary enough. Being denied treatment is even worse."

The look in Brandon's eyes told Alex he had missed something.

"Yes. But that's not what has upset her the most."

"I see," Alex said. "Then what did she want to talk about?"

"She received a visit this week from representatives from a company that tried to convince her to volunteer."

"Oh?"

"It gets worse. That same evening her son called to thank her."

"For volunteering?"

Brandon nodded. "He didn't know she had refused."

Alex sighed deeply, angrily.

"Exactly," Brandon added. "Anyway, she told me she wished her son could have heard what you said last weekend."

A blank expression told Brandon his pastor couldn't recall.

"You remember. Phil quoted you in the board meeting. You said we should treat the elderly as a source of wisdom rather than a source of capital to solve our economic problems."

Alex nodded at the recollection.

Brandon appeared contrite again. "I felt terrible."

"About what?"

"A day after I let Phil criticize you for playing politics my aunt quoted you as a source of hope. Until that moment I never connected the dots. Like the rest of the board, I was so concerned about your words offending some I never considered how they might sustain others."

A moment of silence passed.

"Again, I'm sorry."

"Forgiven," Alex said warmly. "And appreciated."

"Here's my aunt's number. I said I would ask you to call when you have time."

"I'll do it."

"Thanks, Pastor."

"No," Alex replied. "Thank you, Brandon. I can't tell you what this means."

They returned to the lobby, where Phil Crawford and Kenny James appeared to be waiting to corner their pastor.

Brandon lingered, apparently sensing an ambush.

The pair approached full of news.

"You won't believe what happened after the service!" Phil began. "Tell him, Kenny."

"A group of at least five couples circled Phil immediately after dismissal to ask about his announcement."

Alex had a bad feeling they hadn't done so to confront him.

"Yeah," Phil interjected. "I hadn't anticipated such positive response from the young. I thought my announcement would fly right past them."

"What did they say?" Alex asked flatly.

"Not say. Ask! They had all kinds of questions, mostly about how to approach the subject with their parents."

"What subject?"

"Volunteering. What else?"

"Yeah," Kenny added enthusiastically. "Three of them had been discussing the subject for months, trying to figure out how to encourage a mom or dad to transition without hurting their feelings."

"They said the way I framed it today would be helpful..."

"*Extremely* helpful!" Kenny corrected. "They said *extremely* helpful."

Phil appeared pleased by the clarification.

Brandon's eyes met Alex's. Neither said a word.

"What did I tell you, Pastor?" Phil said before turning to leave with his sidekick. "Before long I think we'll see more lump sum donations coming our way!"

Alex watched the two men walk toward the door, Kenny patting Phil on the back in congratulations for a job well done. They stopped their advance when Phil turned back toward Alex. "Oh, I almost forgot," he said, like a coach eager to motivate a promising rookie. "Great sermon today, Pastor."

CHAPTER TEN

Matthew had forgotten the massive size of the Denver International Airport. It had been nearly ten years since he last flew. He smiled at the recollection of a California vacation designed to help his mother get her mind off the bad news. The doctor had said her memory would only get worse, that she would eventually need continuous care. Matthew had offered to put his college plans on hold for another year so he could figure out a suitable arrangement. They couldn't afford an expensive nursing facility. Maybe they could find a part-time parent-sitter until he finished graduate school and accepted his first faculty post. Then came the first economic crash, shrinking his aspirations into a few community college classes that he took while working a coffee shop job.

As Matthew's approach parted the terminal doors he swallowed back a lump of grief. Or was it remorse? Either way, the moment reminded him of how much he missed his mother's nurturing presence.

He checked his appointment notes for the location of his meeting with Serena Winthrop of NEXT Incorporated.

"Where can I find the Admiral's Club?" he asked the holographic image of a man eager to offer assistance.

"You'll find the Admiral's Club located near Gate A-twenty-four. You can access Terminal A by train or through a two-hundred-yard bridge located one level above the main security lines."

Security! He had forgotten about that delay. Matthew glanced at the time.

"Which would be faster?" he asked the digital projection.

"I recommend taking the walking path because…"

Matthew didn't hear the rest as he ran toward the bridge. He continued his sprint before jumping onto a moving sidewalk, then pulling back to a rapid stroll. He didn't want to arrive with beads of sweat dripping from his forehead or soaking his newly pressed shirt.

He offered his driver's license to the security agent, who seemed slightly annoyed he had interrupted her reading.

She didn't accept it.

"Please," he said while extending his identification urgently, "I'm running late for an appointment."

"Aren't you forgetting something?" she asked with a smirk.

He tried to remember airport protocol. Nothing came.

"Your boarding pass," she said into the next page of her book.

"But I'm not flying today."

The woman gave an aggravated sigh while handing Matthew a card titled *Security Guidelines*. It included about fifteen bullet points printed in indecipherably tiny text.

"I can't read this," he said with rising panic. "Please, I have a very important meeting in four minutes. Can't you just tell me what I need to do?"

Fifteen minutes later Matthew reapproached the same security zone with a terminal access pass in hand. He cursed toward the line of fifteen travelers eager to make their flights.

Had Serena Winthrop given up waiting? He wouldn't blame her. Matthew had already violated the first rule of first impressions: show up early, never late.

After tying his shoes and re-buckling his belt Matthew noticed his own dark, expanding armpit stains.

Perfect, he thought. *Just perfect.*

Ms. Winthrop appeared every bit as put-together as Matthew felt disheveled.

"Thank you for agreeing to meet me," she said with more deference than he deserved. She had dismissed the transgression of a tardy arrival as par for the course when meeting colleagues in a busy airport.

He followed her toward a semiprivate corner of the room just past a row of corporate road warriors sipping drinks, some scanning messages about who knew what big deal awaiting input or review, while others read the latest edition of the *Wall Street Journal* or *New York Times* on their tablet screens. All of it seemed far removed from Matthew's dreary routine in one drab living room after another across the Denver metropolitan area. He relished the thought of his own life occupying such an energetic space.

"I've been looking forward to speaking to you in person, Ms. Winthrop," Matthew said after placing his drink on the side table positioned between the leather chairs.

"Serena, please," she insisted.

The name suited her. In her early thirties, she carried herself with an elegant grace that reminded him of Maria Davidson's older sister Julia: dark hair and long, slender legs that would distract less disciplined eyes. Ms. Winthrop, Serena, was someone Matthew might enjoy getting to know under less intimidating circumstances.

He glanced at the screen she had tapped while placing it on her lap. His newly crafted résumé.

"I was impressed by your range of experience," she said, the tone of her voice shifting from that of a cordial acquaintance to that of a potential employer.

He smiled, half expecting her to question the slightly embellished portions of his résumé. She instead zeroed in on the parts he considered least impressive, if most accurate.

"In fact," she continued, "I can see why you came so highly recommended."

"By whom?" he asked.

She looked surprised by the question and a bit embarrassed. "I'm afraid I can't answer that question," she said. "Our human resource team does the initial screening of candidates. By the time they reach me I assume such details have been confirmed and sources screened."

Of course. He blushed for having asked such a dumb question of such an important executive.

"I see that you have experience in two of the three categories we are seeking for this position. Ten years in senior care?"

He nodded silently. The span had required stretching eight years managing his mother's meds into nine and rounding the month spent with Reverend Grandpa up to twelve.

"And one with MedCom?"

Another nod. "I have one of the highest client acquisition rates in the company."

"I noticed that," she said, looking back at the page.

He wasn't sure whether boasting would suggest desperate anxiety or calm confidence.

"Any experience assisting a transition?"

He thought before responding. Did coaxing his mother count? He had walked through the entire process with her, even sitting on the other side of a two-way mirror to witness her final moments. But he couldn't actually claim to have assisted in the procedure.

Reverend Grandpa came to mind. Matthew knew what the authorities had never suspected. No, he hadn't injected his client with a needle or cut the oxygen tube. But he had aided the death by refusing to help the old man after his fall. It had been an act of compassion, lending his own courage to a man who should have volunteered, might have volunteered if not for a lingering religious disposition that would force a disabled dad onto an already stressed daughter.

"Twice," he said. "But I'm not a licensed transition specialist."

Even better, the woman's smile seemed to suggest.

"Our prescreening process discovered that your own mother volunteered. Is that correct?"

Another hesitation. "Yes," he confirmed on a technicality. "Two years ago."

"I prefer team members with personal experience on that front," she said coolly. "It helps them empathize with our clients."

"Clients?" he asked, realizing he had absolutely no idea what the job entailed. He knew it involved research and development. Nothing more.

Serena set her tablet aside to face Matthew squarely. "I'm sorry," she began. "I should probably tell you a little bit about the project."

"Yes, please," he said.

"What do you know about the wrongful death lawsuit against NEXT the courts finally wrapped up this past January?"

He probably knew more than Ms. Winthrop. It was the case that had kept his mom's estate out of reach for over a year, which in turn had forced him to drop out of college to work for Reverend Grandpa. By the time the case finally did end, releasing his inheritance, Matthew had already descended into the dark place.

"I know that it put us pretty far behind the targets established by the Youth Initiative," he said, echoing the drum fiscal conservatives had been beating for the prior six months.

"That's right," she said, "and put increased pressure on my department to come up with innovative ways to make up for lost ground."

Matthew suddenly understood why he had been recommended. Who better to help figure out how to grow the pool of volunteers than a top recruiter at MedCom Associates?

"We introduced a new home-based-transition kit several months back, something we had hoped to make available last year. The lawsuit kept us from taking it to market due to the usual oversight headaches. But now we are free and clear."

"How's that going?" he asked. "I mean, are many volunteers using the kits?"

"Not as many as hoped, which leads to our present situation. We expect whoever wins the upcoming election to ask for more aggressive strategies. Both parties know we've got a major problem on our hands. Other than the initial wave of transitions that included all of the low-hanging fruit, we've fallen behind on both projected revenue and savings in every quarter."

"Low-hanging fruit?" Matthew asked, unfamiliar with the phrase.

"Easy pickings. People who were eager for the Youth Initiative to pass because they were sick or depressed. They flooded into our clinics during the first few quarters. Most volunteers since have required a bit of convincing."

"Right," he said knowingly.

"Which leads to the project. We've learned that families need more than a self-serve kit. No matter how much they agree it's in everyone's best interest for a loved one to volunteer, very few family members seem willing to actually stick the needle into an arm in order to inject the serum."

"PotassiPass," Matthew added to suggest fluency.

"That's right," Serena said with a smile. "So we've decided to test a new service that is more hands-on. We believe families will be willing to spend part of their inheritance on something we are calling a *transition companion*."

She paused, watching Matthew's reaction to the label. "We think it sounds warm and supportive," she added.

"It does," he agreed.

"If we're right, the extra fee will more than cover the healthy bonus we intend to pay our client representatives. And if we're right, everyone wins. We should see a higher ratio of volunteers transitioning their resources to the young while reducing government entitlement outlays, all funded by family members willing to sacrifice a few thousand dollars for a service that makes the much less expensive at-home option seem more viable."

Matthew sat quietly, trying to imagine whether he would have used such a service when his mother volunteered. Would it have made the decision easier or not? His first reaction suggested not. There was something safely abstract about driving to a clinic where medical professionals handled the procedure and the disposal process. A highly trained *transition specialist* seemed professional and hygienic. *Transition companion* sounded cozy and slack.

"What about the organ donations and disposal process?" he wondered aloud.

"Nothing would change on that front. That process is already working well in most instances. Of course, the transition companion would handle scheduling disposal instead of relying on the family; another benefit to the service that will make the local authorities happy."

"Why's that?"

"People are only human, even volunteers. They forget to schedule the cleanup, or enter the wrong date. Officers seem to dislike calls about a decomposing corpse in the neighbor's bathtub."

"So the job doesn't include disposal?"

"Goodness no!" said Serena. "The process runs more like an assembly line. Just as the recruiter will hand off to a transition companion, the transition companion hands off to a member of our follow-up team. We actually have more follow-up personnel than we can keep busy. Our challenge has been finding candidates qualified for the earlier steps."

She took a sip of her drink before continuing.

"The time-consuming part will be spending time with clients who, on occasion, might get cold feet." Serena paused to retrieve Matthew's résumé, then eyed it briefly before looking back in his direction. "We need someone right away to cover the Front Range area. What do you say?"

Matthew realized he had been offered the job. "I'm flattered," he said, although *disappointed* would have been more accurate. He didn't know what he had expected a research and development job to look like. Certainly more prestigious than the role Ms. Winthrop had described. A comfortable office with a window view? Travel to and from New York, Los Angeles, or D.C.? Hardly realistic, he knew, for a man with such a thin résumé. But one could dream.

"You'll want compensation details," Serena was saying while handing him a slip of paper.

Twice his current monthly income plus a signing bonus!

"You'll also receive three percent of the transition estate value for each client served," she explained.

He mentally tabulated the possibilities. The job, while beneath the stature he had imagined, would provide the funds needed to get back to school twice as fast as his present path. He tried concealing his enthusiasm, but his face betrayed an eager acceptance.

"We would like you to start right away."

"Not a problem," he said.

"In fact," she continued, "I have your first assignment with me now."

Odd. A first assignment prepared in advance of his first interview?

She handed him a sealed envelope. "Inside you will find a series of confidential details required to access our Research and Development hub. Simply enter the pseudonym listed and then the pass-code. You'll find several training videos and the specifics needed to begin."

"Thank you," he said hesitantly. "But why a pseudonym?"

"This project is highly confidential, Mr. Adams," she explained. "The company asks that every member of my team use an alias."

"Why?"

"Plausible deniability."

"For whom?"

"For both the contractor and the company."

"Contractor?" Matthew asked. "Not employee?"

"Not technically," she said. "None of us is an actual employee of NEXT. Nor do we use our actual names."

"But..."

"Don't worry, Mr. Adams. This is how things are done when dealing with government contract work. Any disgruntled family member or religious nut case can initiate a frivolous lawsuit. We've found this approach protects everyone involved."

He felt more at ease. "Makes sense, I guess."

She stood, indicating the interview had ended. Matthew accepted her hand.

"Thank you, Serena," he said, suddenly curious about her real name.

"Thank you, Mr. Adams," she responded warmly. "And welcome to the team."

PART TWO

CHAPTER ELEVEN

Julia looked frantically toward the faint trace of light above the surface. Her lungs wanted to burst, desperate for a gulp of life-giving oxygen that might rescue her from a watery death. She looked down toward the darkness to see who, or what, clung to her ankle like an anchor pulling her deeper.

Then she remembered: the shadowy image of a man extending his hand toward her as she drifted farther away from his comforting presence, her desperate, angry plea for help in his direction, and the terrifying laughter of an evil presence summoning from beneath.

She sensed a sudden release as the young man beneath her loosened his grip and began sinking toward a shadowy grave. Her last glimpse was of his descending fist clenched in bitter defiance toward the masculine figure above, the one toward whom Julia now felt herself ascending.

Julia's head shot out of the water like a rocket launching toward the heavens. She inhaled urgently, gratefully, her arms flailing like unsynchronized paddles rowing in the direction of the man's extended hand. Her panic waned in rhythm with her strokes as she finally moved close enough to focus on the man's image, which had been a mere shadow in the distance. Her father? No. And yes.

If she had been able to see his face she knew it would offer a welcoming smile, his relief nearly matching her own. But she saw only his hand, fixed in the same posture of rescue it had held throughout her ordeal. With a last stretch of hope Julia felt him accept her fingers before engulfing them in his firm grasp of safety.

Then she felt her body jolt downward. She tightened her grip in reaction to the painful force. Julia had suddenly become the prize in a tug-of-war between competing destinies. Above, reunion. Below, despair.

She looked up toward the hand tightening itself around her own, giving her the confidence she needed to glance beneath.

A different face. Not the defiant boy's. A crazed man's, his eyes eager for adventure, yet filled with fear.

Julia extended her free hand toward him. But he refused it, instead jerking at her leg with greater intensity. He didn't want rescue. He wanted a companion.

Didn't he hear the diabolical laughter bellowing from the depths?

Couldn't he feel the biting chill of waters teeming with cruelty?

She kicked frantically in an effort to snub the mad invitation. The man pulled harder until her chin barely cleared the surface.

Julia turned her eyes back toward her rescuer as she felt an ever-so-slight loosening of her grip. Then she woke at the sudden glow of a bedside lamp.

"Shhh," Troy was saying, leaning on one elbow while gently caressing his wife's anxious cheek. "It's OK. You're here, with me, at home."

She looked into her husband's half-closed eyes, trying to place herself. "Home?" she said through the sound of her pounding heart.

Troy pulled back the covers while moving into a seated position on the edge of the bed. He lifted his leg to inspect the damage. "You kicked me something fierce!" he said while rubbing an abused shin.

"Kicked you?"

"And yelled at me," Troy added. "Or yelled at someone, anyway."

She whispered an apology in her husband's direction while reaching toward the nightstand drawer that had once held a pad and pencil for quick retrieval whenever ideas, or nightmares, invaded her sleep. Then she remembered. The dreams had stopped nearly two years prior, about the same time she met Troy. She recalled the relief after months of restless sleep and the countless mornings staring at a growing list of nocturnal echoes.

MAN
SHADOW
FEAR
ANGER
ABANDONED

"Not at all what I was expecting," Troy continued, confirming Julia's attack hadn't drawn blood.

Julia looked in his direction. "Expecting? What do you mean expecting?"

He flopped back onto his pillow. "Or rather hoping. I thought you wanted to…" he paused, then redirected. "I sort of woke up when you took my hand. I started to come in your direction to run my finger along your thigh, you know, the way you like. But before I could fully wake I felt your foot slamming into my leg. Then I heard you shouting something incoherent like 'I don't know' or 'Yellow snow.'"

"'Let me go,'" Julia remembered. "I was shouting 'Let me go.'"

He rolled back onto his side. "Hey, Jewel," he said with affection, "what is it? You look pretty shaken."

She calmed her breathing back to a near-normal pattern before forcing a harmless grin in Troy's direction. "It's nothing," she said. "Just a silly dream."

It was what she had always told herself back when the same nightmare dogged her night after night for nearly a year. Well, not really the same nightmare, but close enough to prompt the questions now invading her mind. Was it really possible for one person to inherit the dream of another? Was the similarity between her nightmare and that of Antonio Santos pure coincidence, or had it been a mysterious invitation toward the life she now inhabited? Back then she would have never even considered dating a man like Troy. Sure, he was handsome. Yes, he treated her like the "jewel" he called her. But he was also in the enemy's camp, or more precisely, defending ideas she'd once considered hostile to women. What a difference a few years could make. What difference, she wondered, might the dream have made?

The earlier dream, Julia eventually discovered, had begun on the last day of young Antonio Santos's life. He'd died in a nearby transition clinic after recording details of his own dream in a journal. But her earlier dream, unlike this one, ended before Julia could resurface, before she could flounder her way toward the mysterious man, and before the madman's hand tried pulling her back down.

"Go back to sleep," she said while patting her husband's chest. "I'm fine."

"You're sure?" Troy said while his head sunk back into a welcoming pillow. "I'll stay...up...if...you....want..."

She smiled at Troy's failed attempt at chivalry. He needed to rest after two grueling days on the river. So did Julia. But she knew that her mind wouldn't cooperate. Notepad or no notepad, she needed to sort her troubled thoughts.

—⁓—

Julia slipped gingerly out from under the sheets to avoid rewaking Troy. Circling the bed to tap off his lamp, she found her floral robe hanging on a chair. Troy preferred the sheer gowns she'd worn before Amanda's arrival, but she needed something a bit more practical now that they had accepted the promotion from newlywed lovers to respectable parents.

She stopped at the bedroom door and looked back toward the man whose admiring eyes and caressing fingers remained as thrilling as on the night they had wed. More so than those of any of the guys Julia dated before Troy. Men had always found Julia attractive, if a bit intimidating. They saw her as she intended to be seen: successful, articulate, and confident. But after a night or two in her bed they showed little interest in her mind or soul. Not that she could blame them. She didn't believe in the soul back then. But that didn't change the fact that she had one, and that it yearned for a completing opposite.

She knew immediately that Troy was different. He treated her like a prize to cherish rather than a toy to use. And he seemed sincerely proud of all she had accomplished. Or, rather, all that she had become: a loving wife who saw her husband as a partner to support rather than a competitor to beat, a caring mom doing her best to give Amanda the life she deserved, and a woman who courageously spent her journalistic reputation on a cause more important than popular prestige.

That's how Troy saw her, anyway. But it wasn't what Julia knew herself to be.

She knew herself as a wife who fought back the impulse to resent a growing dependence upon her husband's affirmation. She had once been the most independent woman imaginable: winner of the Pulitzer Prize, a celebrated columnist with twelve million weekly readers and a long line of editors eager to contract the next feature story by the famous Julia Davidson. She shouldn't need his approval or crave his affection. But she did.

Julia also knew how often she wanted to respond to Amanda's many tantrums by throwing the ungrateful girl out of the house. If not for a deep sense of pride that kept her from quitting anything, ever, Julia would have abandoned the whole motherhood gig long before now.

And Julia knew how much she missed the kind of professional recognition she had once enjoyed. How often she asked herself whether it had been a mistake to take up the bright spots cause with such abandon. Sure, it had helped Kevin gain his current level of influence on the national stage. But it had also lowered her several notches on a journalistic food chain on which the slightest pro-breeder sentiment was considered self-evidently idiotic.

It was Troy, not Julia, who had been the hero of their partnership. He had risked marrying a woman who barely believed in the concept of marriage, let alone Christian marriage.

It was Troy, not Julia, who had initiated their exploration of Christian faith. She'd meant it when she said she wanted to join him on the quest, assuming they would study a philosophy, not encounter a person. A Redeemer. A Lord. But they had. And she couldn't be more grateful, now. But then? It could have gone either way.

And it was Troy, not Julia, who had first modeled in his own life what he most admired in Jesus. "Lose your life to find it."

Troy had found meaning in his own life by giving himself away. First to Kevin. Then to Julia. And now to Amanda.

A vague sense of fear stabbed Julia's heart as she pulled the bedroom door quietly closed behind her. The returning dream had some ominous meaning, possibly tied to Amanda. If their enemy was indeed the kind of prowling lion Pastor Alex described, he must hate their desire to give the orphaned girl a proper home. What if Amanda's future depended upon Julia's ability to hold firmly to the mysterious man's hand, whoever he might be? What if the conflict she and Amanda had been experiencing was a warning, or a call to increased vigilance? And what if Julia, despite her best efforts, couldn't muster the kind of self-sacrifice required? Winning accolades from the journalistic elite had been easy compared to earning the trust and respect of a hurting adolescent girl.

Or was the dream about Troy? He'd been trying to garner support for Kevin's proposal out of a deep belief that opposing the Youth Initiative "strikes at the heart of our enemy's strategy." Maybe he was right. Perhaps the sadistic laughter rising from the dark depths meant that her husband was at risk.

Whatever the meaning, one thing was certain. The dream had brought a sense of dread, as if something dark and menacing was on the horizon. And it was up to her, if possible, to prevent it.

Julia walked to the kitchen and poured herself a glass of juice. She glanced at the logo on the front of the plastic carton. Two overlapping oranges smiled in her direction. Two, not one. Overlapping, not standing apart. What if this dream, like the last, was a twin? What if it suggested her life would once again overlap another's? She had inherited Antonio Santos's nightmare long before meeting his brother or reading his journals. Long before she would be hired to tell his story to the world, as if some unseen force had overlapped their dreams before connecting their lives.

She concentrated, trying to recall the face of the crazed man pulling at her ankle. Nothing came. What if his was the overlapping life, as Antonio's had been? And what, if anything, should she do about it?

Julia placed the carton of juice back in the refrigerator, then walked down the hallway toward Amanda's bedroom door. Placing her hand on the handle she turned and pushed gently inward to create a slim line of vision. She watched Amanda sleeping peacefully in her bed. Her chest moved up and down against the bedspread that had pink and green stripes, the one Amanda had selected while shopping with her foster guardian turned forever mom. A mom who knew she had much to learn about laying her life down for others. For Amanda.

"Dear God," Julia whispered, "please protect that little girl from whatever evil lurks."

She closed the door. Feeling the urge to voice a different prayer, Julia walked toward the sofa in the living room to the spot where she knelt beside Troy whenever he asked her to pray about matters beyond their daily bread, the kind of prayers she relied upon him to lead.

But Troy was asleep and knew nothing of her dream.

Julia sat on the edge of the sofa before folding her hands self-consciously against her chin. "Dear God," she began before stopping. She felt an urge to bend her knees in a posture of humility that lifted her troubled spirit. "Father, I don't know if you're trying to tell me something." She paused, turning her head upward toward the ceiling. "But I want you to know that I'm listening."

CHAPTER TWELVE

It was Kevin's favorite time of the day. In the stillness of early morning he stood in the dining room watching the pendulum of a vintage wall clock fill the house with a soothing, ordering rhythm: tick-tock, tick-tock, tick-tock. It was a soundtrack attached to warm boyhood memories: Mom fixing chocolate chip pancakes for Saturday breakfast while Dad read the news and sipped a mug of morning java.

The memory summoned Kevin toward the kitchen to pour himself a cup of coffee. But the coffee maker, like the sun, was still catching its final winks. He glanced at the time. Two hours earlier than his body clock insisted. No one else would be stirring for at least another hour. Maybe two.

He slid open the glass door to walk onto the deck, where he took a deep breath of still cool air while scanning the horizon. The sun remained beneath its distant blanket, revealing a faint trace of the brilliance it would soon bestow upon the nearby silhouette of the Rocky Mountains.

"You're up early."

The voice startled Kevin. Jim Tolbert was sitting in one of the two chairs that held memories of father-son chats after a successful soccer match or a "less than your best effort" geometry test.

"No java?" Kevin asked, pointing at his father's mug-free hands.

"The doctor said no more caffeine."

"And you obeyed?"

"He said it in your mother's presence."

They shared a knowing laugh.

His father began to stand. "I can fix you some worthless decaf if you want," he said.

"No thanks." Kevin waved his dad back into the chair. "You just relax. I'm fine."

He accepted his father's invitation to sit in the same chair he had occupied on countless earlier occasions, moments when he'd received advice from the wisest man he knew when facing some of life's toughest decisions.

About love: "Marry the girl."

About launching a business: "No risk, no reward."

About running for office: "We need good men in Washington. And you're a good man, Son."

Family friends described Kevin as the "spitting image" of his father. He liked hearing it. Mom had promised that "inheriting your father's good looks" would serve him well when the time came to find a bride. She always made the comment in Dad's presence, prompting a peck on her cheek and pat on her bottom. The ritual had embarrassed him as a boy. But the memory made him smile as a man, grateful for a model of playful intimacy he now shared with Angie. It was something he'd once taken for granted, considered normal. But he had since discovered how rare it was. None of his friends, including Troy Simmons, had grown up basking in the security that comes from parents who can't keep their hands off each other.

They sat side by side watching the gradual light of the rising sun. It was as if God were slowly turning up a dimmer knob to let their eyes adjust to the spectacular Colorado beauty garnishing the moment. As if God understood the import of father-son reunions.

"Angie still sleeping?"

"She is," Kevin replied.

"Still mad at you for the river plunge?"

Kevin chuckled. "Not really. But she's still pretending to be."

The elder Tolbert smiled knowingly. "I always loved it when your mom pretended to be mad."

Kevin flashed a grin in his father's direction. "I know you did."

Both men sighed at the recollection of Mom's feistier days, when she kept her man in line by threatening a pillow and blanket on the sofa rather than a cuddle in the bed. The threats were always empty, but worked nonetheless. Some things Dad refused to give up, most notably Mom's tender embrace.

"How's she been lately?" Kevin asked.

"Better."

A brief silence.

"I really think she's getting better," Mr. Tolbert added as if trying to convince himself.

"Any word on further treatment?"

He looked toward the question without reaction.

Kevin regretted asking. But he couldn't help himself. Ever the optimist, he thought the inquiry he had sent might have made a difference. Dad didn't know about the note. He had refused Kevin's offer to intervene, fearing it might come back to bite Kevin during the Youth Initiative debates.

"I can hear it now," he had warned. "'Congressman Tolbert, you claim to oppose the government's prioritizing elder-care expenses. Why, then, did you bring pressure to bear on the

Colorado Office of Medical Allocations on behalf of your mother, Gayle Tolbert? We have documentation proving you asked the COMA to approve your mother's treatment allocation despite the fact her case falls well below established net-value ratios.'"

But Kevin couldn't sit idly by and let them deny medications that might make a difference, no matter how slight. They had been helping relieve a lower back pain that microscopic surgery might cure. Mom had seemed more herself before turning seventy, the age at which a new Youth Initiative provision required an audit of her treatment allocation. The deeper the financial crisis, the lower the birthday for mandatory review: age eighty in 2040, dropping to seventy-five by '42 and plummeting to seventy earlier this year. He had even heard talk of yet another drop among some of his colleagues.

So Kevin had sent the note over his dad's objections. He received a form letter in reply. Not that he'd expected a specific acknowledgment. One congressional colleague had told Kevin not to lose hope, since he had received the same generic response before his loved one was approved. But the look on Kevin's dad's face now said no such provision had been made for his mom.

Kevin looked away to hide the anger in his eyes.

"Don't worry, Son," his father said, placing a hand on Kevin's forearm. "She'll be fine."

The squeeze of his dad's hand felt somehow different. Less engulfing. More frail. Come to think of it, so did his voice. Less commanding. More resigned.

"How about you, Dad?" Kevin asked. "Are you feeling OK?"

"Of course. Never better."

Kevin pieced disparate signs together in his mind: the slightly winded breathing; less vigor in his dad's walk, and sitting alone on the deck an hour before his usual rise. His father, the rock of his life, seemed weary. And frail.

"You don't look good," Kevin said.

"Thanks, Son." A glare of mock offense.

"You know what I mean. You seem, I don't know, more tired than usual. Have you been exercising?"

No reply.

"Eating right?"

Silence.

"Come on, Dad!" Kevin said. "What about the routine?"

The question prompted a chuckle. Jim Tolbert had always taught his son that a man's routine was sacred. Rise early. Work out. Read daily. Eat what your wife commands. And go to church every week to keep your head screwed on right. Apart from playing hooky from church during the years between getting his driver's license and meeting his future bride, Kevin had pretty much followed his elder's pattern of healthy, wholesome living.

"You're right, Son. Monday. I promise."

Both heads turned toward a sound inside the house.

"Mom?" Kevin asked his dad.

"Not likely. She usually sleeps for at least another hour."

That's when a pair of mischievous eyes peered around the partially open sliding door.

"Well now," came a voice that sounded more like the robust grandpa Kevin's kids had come to love, "who on earth could that be sneaking around the house so early in the morning?"

The question prompted a hushed giggle, then a second from behind. The prowler apparently had a stealthy accomplice.

"I couldn't say," Kevin played along.

Joy bounded onto the deck. "It's me!"

"Joy!" her brother scolded from behind. "I told you to stay quiet!"

"We were spying on you!" the five-year-old replica of Angie said, pointing in her grandfather's direction.

"Spying?" he said. "On me? Why would anyone want to spy on a harmless old man?"

"Because," seven-year-old Tommy replied, "we know your true identity!"

"Yeah," Joy echoed. "Your twue identity!"

The game was on. Ever since he was four years old Tommy had turned every trip to Grandpa's house into a secret mission. His goal, now shared by his equally determined younger sister, was to foil whatever scheme for world domination Grandma implied her husband might be weaving from the safe haven of their Littleton home, otherwise known as Alpha Command Center.

Jim Tolbert smiled toward Kevin. "Two against one," he said dreadfully. "I think I might be in real trouble this time."

<hr>

An hour later the secret agents sat on either side of their prisoner in self-satisfied delight while Angie placed a second chocolate chip pancake on Joy's paper plate. Kevin knew his daughter would likely only take a few bites, already stuffed from her first. But Joy insisted on receiving the same bounty-hunter prize as her brother. After all, she had helped break whatever secret code or uncover whatever evil plot Grandpa had intended to launch.

Kevin's mom was leaning against the kitchen counter beside the stovetop, the glow on her face as she turned back toward the skillet overpowering a grimace of pain. "Thanks, Grandma," he said in an effort to tip the first domino.

"Yeah," added Tommy. "Thank you, Grandma."

"Yummy!" Joy contributed to the chorus.

"You really didn't have to get up, Mom," Angie said for the third time in the past half an hour.

"Don't be silly," Kevin's mother replied. "It's tradition, right, kids?"

"Yeah!" Tommy said to second the motion. "Grandma always makes us chocolate chip pancakes."

"It's twadition," Joy added.

A whimpering grunt came from the high chair as little Ricky realized it had been nearly a minute since Daddy had landed the last spoonful of applesauce on his tongue's runway.

"Sorry, buddy," Kevin said while hastily filling the spoon.

Grandpa Villain had been sentenced to "hold Baby Leah" duty, a punishment he relished. Leah was no longer the baby of the family. But she still owned the title. Probably always would. Fragile X syndrome, a genetic disorder that impaired intellectual development, meant she might never fully care for herself. Kevin, Angie, and the kids would always consider her their baby. From all appearances, the three-year-old girl had smitten her grandfather almost as much as she had Daddy and big brother.

"Be careful, Grandpa!" Tommy noticed a chocolate smear on his youngest sister's cheek. "You need to do it like this." He reached to demonstrate the proper mouth-wiping procedure.

Kevin laughed at the look of bewilderment on his father's face. Breakfast had never been like this when Kevin was young. Like many of his peers, James Tolbert had raised one child. He had never juggled the competing demands of diapers, playing catch, helping with homework, driving to practice, scheduling doctor appointments, and wiping chocolate smears. The endless list of daily activities that defined Angie and Kevin's existence had been a gradually phased sequence for Kevin's parents, rather than a rapid-fire assault.

"Here, let me simplify the process." Kevin took Baby Leah from his father's arms and handed him the spoon in exchange. "You try feeding little Ricky and I'll clean up the mess you've made of my daughter's face."

"Respect the gray hair," the elder said threateningly, but also with a hint of relief.

"Finish what you were saying," Angie said in Kevin's direction.

"Saying? Oh, right." He positioned Leah on his lap and began the bouncing motion that experience told him made her feel secure. "I need to decide my next move. I think Franklin has the nomination in the bag. Maybe even the election. But he's still nervous."

"He wants Kevin to endorse his plan *before* the convention."

Jim Tolbert turned toward his son. "I thought you said his plan wasn't finalized yet."

"It isn't. He hasn't figured out how to word my Bright Spots proposal."

"But he plans to include it?"

"He says he does," Kevin explained. "But he seems to be dragging his feet."

"Of course he's dragging his feet," Angie seethed.

"He knows the press will bury him as soon as he includes it," Kevin said.

A slight growl came from the high chair. The senior Tolbert realized he had stalled the feeding spoon a few inches short of the runway. "Oh, sorry, little guy," he said while finishing the approach. "Here you go."

"Anyway," Kevin continued, "I feel like I'm between a rock and a hard place."

"Describe the hard place," his father said, assuming the role of clarity coach Kevin needed him to play.

"I can't support a plan that expands the Robin Hood tax strategy."

"He wants to hike my rates again?" Kevin's father asked.

"He's proposing a new wealth tax."

"Again?" Mr. Tolbert said as if recalling a past blunder. "Didn't they learn anything back in the twenties?"

"This time it's different. He only wants to tax the wealth of citizens who turn eighty."

Jim Tolbert placed the spoon in the half-empty bowl of apple-sauce before facing his son. "He wants to take assets away from seniors?"

A gloomy nod. "He does. But it's not just Franklin. Most fiscal conservatives agree. There simply isn't enough income available to tax to offset our deficits. They need to draw from national principal."

"They call it *national principal*?"

Another nod.

"So they are going to ask anyone who worked hard, paid their bills, and saved up for their old age to cough up their assets to cover the government's tab?"

"They won't just ask. They've tried that already. They haven't found enough volunteers."

"So they want to turn up the heat?" asked the elder. "They plan to smoke out the stubborn debits who've managed to resist the pressure to slit their own throats?"

"Exactly!" Angie interjected. "It makes me furious. There's no way Kevin can support that plan."

Kevin sensed his father inspecting the hard place. "So," his dad finally said, "what's the rock?"

Kevin's eyes met Angie's, then his mother's, then his father's.

"Well," he said hesitantly, "Franklin's right-hand man, Anderson, has hinted at a cabinet post."

Stunned silence.

"Labor?" his father prodded.

"Commerce."

More silence.

"Of course," the elder whispered. "You'd be perfect."

The comment surprised Kevin. Not that his father had said it, but that he also seemed to believe it.

"We're talking about the White House, Dad. Not a congressional committee chair. The big table. The center of national power."

"I understand," his father replied. "And you'd be perfect for the job."

Angie grinned. "I told you," she said.

"Told him what?" Kevin's mother asked from behind, still absorbing the shock of the news.

"I told him he's just what the nation needs. What better way to advance the Bright Spots agenda than as the secretary of commerce?"

"Come on, babe," Kevin said in self-deprecation. "You know as well as I do that will never happen."

"Why not?" his father asked. "You have the business skills and track record. You've made your mark in Congress. And you're nearly as smart as your old man!"

"And almost as handsome," Gayle chimed in while sliding the final pancake from her spatula onto her husband's plate. She winked after receiving his pat on her bottom.

"Anyway," Kevin continued after rolling his eyes in their direction as he had when he was a kid, "I think they're floating the cabinet post as a carrot, hoping I'll rally the breeders around Franklin's cause."

"Kevin!" his mother said, obviously embarrassed that her son would voice a slur in front of the children. "Watch your language."

"Sorry, Mom," he said. "But that's the commonly used term for folks like us now."

"It's not!"

"It is," Angie confirmed regretfully. "But we don't mind anymore. It's become a badge of honor. Especially now that other breeders consider Kevin their voice in Washington."

Jim Tolbert looked inquisitively at his son, prompting a full explanation.

Two years earlier Julia Davidson had published a scathing feature titled *Breeders* with the widely read RAP Syndicate. She had intended the story to disparage those of Kevin's ilk. But instead it had rallied a growing constituency to his cause. It made perfect sense in retrospect. For five decades a subculture of the nation had been bearing and raising what she once called "irresponsible broods of children." Kevin labeled them "bright spots" because they provided pockets of vitality and growth amid dark economic clouds. Clouds that had been created, they now realized, by a fertility rate far below the replacement level: too few children to create a thriving culture of long-term investment historically motivated by one generation's dreams for the next. Hidden well beneath the stratosphere of a world inhabited by the sophisticated class, breeders quietly earned a living, wiped runny noses, and created a bloc of voters that came of age just when Joshua Franklin needed their support. Support, many assumed, that would take its cues from the young congressman from Colorado who embodied their quirky subculture and religious sensibilities.

Kevin parroted the familiar chatter of aghast elites.

"More than one or two children? Are they out of their minds?"

"Opposed to the transition industry? You must be kidding!"

"Conceiving children in the bedroom instead of the clinic? No wonder they end up with so many debit kids!"

"Debit kids?" Kevin's mom said. "Do they say such things?"

"Not to our faces," Angie said. "At least not in words."

"Just with their eyes," Kevin added, holding Baby Leah closer as he spoke. "Bottom line," he continued, "Franklin wants me to nudge the breeders in his direction by going on the record in support of his economic plan."

"The rock," his father concluded.

"Exactly."

The sounds of boyish exasperation prompted Grandma to take the bowl and spoon Grandpa had abandoned so that little Ricky could finish his breakfast.

"Can we look for bugs now?" Tommy asked his mother, prompting an eager nod from Joy.

"Go ahead," Angie said. "But stay where we can see you."

The sliding door slammed seconds after her final word.

"Read him the letter, babe," Angie said to Kevin while removing Leah from his arms.

"What letter?" both parents asked in unison.

Kevin appeared reluctant to share evidence of what Angie considered his greatest triumph.

"He's been receiving letters from other parents with disabled children," Angie explained.

"Huh," Kevin's father said as if puzzled by the idea. "What do they want?"

"Nothing. They don't write me to ask for something. They write to say thanks."

"Read the one you got last Tuesday!" Angie prodded eagerly. "It's in your tablet."

A few moments later Kevin returned from the bedroom. "Here it is," he said after a few taps on the screen.

"Let me read it," Angie said hastily, trading Leah for a different treasure, the letter displayed on Kevin's device.

"'Dear Congressman Tolbert,'" she began. "'My name is Angelina Sanders. My husband and I have three children: a boy named Marcos and two daughters, Nicky and Bella.'"

Angie seemed to sing the second girl's name.

"'You probably know that Bella means beautiful. And that's what she is. Beautiful. I don't care who calls her a debit or how much time and money it takes to meet her special needs. She is every bit as precious and beautiful as our healthy daughter. As any daughter.'"

The letter went on to tell the family's story.

An excited couple shocked to learn their third child would be born with a rare disorder called Down syndrome. A genetic defect, the doctor had explained, that had been largely eradicated as more and more parents opted for genetic prescreening, something the couple believed was wrong.

Angie paused in her reading. She looked at Kevin in a moment of shared remembrance. They had known a similar moment. Had this family second-guessed themselves at the news? Had they fumbled to answer why they had opted for "blind conception" instead of screening out potential defects? Had they sensed the silent ridicule from those wondering what right they had to burden society with the long-term expense of a debit child?

They had, the letter went on to explain.

"'I want to thank you, Mr. Tolbert, for what you are doing to uphold the dignity and worth of my precious little girl,'" Angie continued through watering eyes and a wobbling voice. "'I can't tell you how much it means to know someone with your level of influence considers our child as beautiful as we know her to be.'"

Angie turned the tablet toward her audience of two. "They sent this picture."

Jim, Gayle, and Kevin admired the image on the screen. Then they looked at the child in Kevin's arms.

Kevin's father stood slowly and approached his boy to lay a hand of paternal approval on his shoulder. "Like I said, Son"— he paused to swallow back the lump rising in this throat— "you'd be perfect for the job."

CHAPTER THIRTEEN

Alex Ware stared intently at his schedule for any hint of a sign of a reminder of the appointment that Mrs. Mayhew had scheduled.

"I don't know why it isn't on my calendar, Mrs. Mayhew," he said into the phone, despite having a pretty good idea his volunteer assistant had something to do with it. "I just know that I see no appointment with Julia Simmons."

"Well she spoke to me about it yesterday and I told her you would meet with her today." Mrs. Mayhew sounded perturbed by her pastor's unwillingness to own the blame.

"I'm in the middle of having lunch with my son," he explained. "What time is the appointment?"

"She arrived a few minutes ago. I assumed you had slipped out to use the restroom or something and told her to wait in your office."

Alex groaned.

"Is everything OK, Dad?" Chris asked out of one side of his mouth over a partially chewed bite of sandwich.

Alex lifted a "just a second" finger toward his son across the table. "What about Tamara?" he asked into the phone.

"What about her?" Mrs. Mayhew asked in puzzled irritation.

He repeated a rule he had explained a dozen times before. "I only counsel women if Tamara joins me."

He knew Mrs. Mayhew considered it a silly policy. That might have had something to do with how often she "forgot" to honor it.

"Like I've told you before, Pastor, I'm perfectly willing to work quietly at your desk when you counsel women. No need to interrupt Tamara's day."

Just what he needed, the chief source of church gossip listening to parishioners sharing details of urgent pain or secret struggles. But he was not about to ask Tamara to drop everything, again, in order to rush over to his office.

"OK," he said reluctantly. "Offer her a soda and my apologies. I'll be there in a few minutes."

He ended the call to face his son's furrowed brow. It was the second time in a month Dad would need to bail on their guy-time outing. The prior week they had been lacing up bowling shoes when Mrs. Mayhew called to scold Alex for forgetting about his meeting with the flower committee chair who, she had reminded him, was one of the wealthiest women in the church. The woman had threatened to make a large donation toward the capital campaign, but Alex wasn't holding his breath, since she had barely given enough to cover the massive floral arrangements cluttering the front of the auditorium. But he'd gone anyway, giving his son a rain check he had yet to honor.

Chris wrapped his lips tightly around the straw protruding from a half-consumed milk shake.

"Sorry, buddy," Alex said sheepishly. "There's someone waiting in my office."

"But I'm not done with my fries," Chris protested over a mouthful of strawberry coldness.

"Tell you what," Alex offered. "I'll buy you an apple pie to go with your shake. You can eat it in the car."

A prolonged pause. "Two."

Alex's eyes widened. "Two apple pies?" He still remembered the days when his son could barely finish half of a kid's meal. At eight, he now routinely downed an adult-size burger, regular fries, and a large shake. "You think you can handle that much food?"

Chris nodded proudly while wiping a tiny stream of chilly pinkness from his chin.

"All right, then," Alex said. "Two pies it is."

After he had dropped his son at home and accepted Tamara's understanding peck on the cheek, Alex arrived twenty minutes after his "scheduled" appointment with Julia Simmons.

"Don't mention it," Julia said while standing to accept her pastor's unnecessary apology. "I'm just grateful you could see me on such short notice."

In Alex's experience, short notices usually accompanied bad news like a diagnosis or suspected infidelity.

"Would it be all right with you if Mrs. Mayhew uses my desk to work while we chat?" he asked with some hesitation.

The question seemed to unsettle Julia. Her eyes darted toward the door, where the woman who had been talking her ear off for the prior twenty minutes stood holding a small stack of unsealed envelopes.

"You won't even know I'm here," she insisted. "Just a busy bee. A busy, deaf, and mute bee."

"I suppose that would be all right," Julia said warily.

"I usually have my wife, Tamara, sit in on counseling sessions with women. But—"

"No need to explain," Julia interrupted, her smile suggesting admiration for the policy. "I would want Troy to do the same if he were a pastor."

Mrs. Mayhew scurried toward Alex's desk like a preteen girl sneaking into an R-rated movie. The pastor extended his hand in a gesture that invited Julia to return to the seat she had been occupying while awaiting his arrival. That's when he noticed which book she had removed from his shelf to kill time: a collection of quotations from a seventeenth-century philosopher named Blaise Pascal.

"Ah," he said with delight, "that's one of my favorites. The last edition ever printed in English. Fairly rare."

"How do you pronounce the title?" She pointed to a single word on the cover a few inches above the author's name.

"I'm pretty sure it sounds like connecting *pen* and *seas* with the roll of a tongue," he explained before demonstrating his pathetic French accent. "*Pensées.*"

"I always sensed from your sermons that you were well-read," Julia said while Alex took the seat opposite her. "But I didn't know you collected print editions."

He glanced toward his bookshelves with something resembling loving affection. "A bit of a weakness," he confessed.

"Tell her about the Lewis collection," Mrs. Mayhew said in violation of her promised silence.

Alex cringed at the interruption, then glowered in his assistant's direction.

"Sorry," she said. "I just thought—"

She stopped short when the pastor lifted his hand in silent rebuke.

"Tell you what," she continued. "I'll just listen to my music." She lifted two earbuds toward her ears before tapping a digital device sitting beside her pile of envelopes.

"Good idea," said Alex with relief as he turned back toward his guest. "She's never read anything by C. S. Lewis, but brags on my find anyway."

"Your find?"

"I found a collection of early-edition books by C. S. Lewis at a seminary liquidation sale."

"Isn't he the author you suggested Troy and I read last year?"

Alex tried to recall a context, then remembered the Simmonses attending his Exploring Christianity sessions. "That's right," he said. "I consider a bit of Lewis an essential part of every sampler plate."

"Sampler plate?" she said inquisitively.

"Sure. Anyone considering the Christian faith would do well to taste the Gospel of John, a bit of Paul's letter to the Romans, and a few gems from C. S. Lewis."

They shared a brief, polite chuckle.

"How's that coming for you?" he asked. "You were baptized, what, a year ago?"

"Nine months," she corrected.

"That's right. I baptized you and Amanda the same day, didn't I?"

A nod of happy recall. "Good memory," she said. "And it's going well. Although I think Amanda has had an easier time with the mind-set thing than me."

"Mind-set thing?"

"That's the wrong phrase, isn't it?"

"Mind shift?" he asked after recalling the title of a message series.

"That's it. The one about renewing your mind."

"Epistle to the Romans, chapter twelve," he said with a smile, pleased to realize someone was actually trying to put his sermons into practice.

Alex glanced quickly back toward Mrs. Mayhew to confirm her "deaf and mute" status before asking Julia what was on her mind.

"To be honest," she began, "I'm not sure where to start."

In Alex's experience, when they didn't know where to start

it meant there was much to be said. His mind raced through a mental checklist of typical possibilities.

Parenting struggles? He wouldn't be surprised. Adopting a preteen girl comes with a truckload of challenges.

Questions about the faith? Perhaps. Julia had already confessed the daughter was outpacing the mom.

But more often than not, short-notice appointments meant marriage problems.

"Why don't you begin by telling me what prompted your request for an appointment?"

She nodded. "Something happened the night before last."

She paused as if trying to muster the courage to continue. Her eyes seemed to be scanning a fear-filled memory. Julia looked toward the pastor's busy-bee assistant, then back at Alex. She seemed worried that describing the experience might expand its danger.

She finally spoke. "I had a dream."

In the years since his graduation from seminary Alex couldn't recall anyone ever coming to him to talk about a dream. But this week, out of the blue, there had been two.

"It's probably nothing," she continued. "I went back and forth on whether I should take up your valuable time talking about it."

"And yet here you are. So it must be more than nothing. Please, go on."

She had been looking at the floor, as if embarrassed by whatever confusion or insecurity had compelled her visit. But now, emboldened by the absence of condescension in her pastor's voice, she looked up. Her gaze seemed to possess a timid hope.

"Pastor Alex," she began, "do you think dreams carry meaning? Not repressed memories or anything like that. Actual meaning?"

He considered the question before responding. "Not most dreams, but certainly some."

The comment served as kindling to some flicker of possibility Julia had carried into the room. "Spiritual meaning?"

"Possibly. Or more."

Julia appeared puzzled. "More?"

"The Scriptures describe several occasions in which God used dreams to reveal a prophecy or give instructions."

"Prophecy? Is that like predicting the future?"

"I guess you could say that. Although from God's point of view they were more like movie trailers."

Another puzzled expression.

"Just a second," Alex said while standing. He walked to his bookshelf, where he found his stack of leather-bound Bibles, the kind used back in the days when people tracked the pastor's sermon text by looking down at an open copy of the Scriptures. He inspected the bindings before selecting the oldest of the pile and finding the table of contents. A quick scan carried his mind through a retrospective of God's blockbuster stories.

Jacob dreamed about a ladder to heaven shortly before a wrestling match with God that dislocated his hip.

Joseph dreamed he would be promoted above his older brothers right before they sold him into slavery.

Pharaoh dreamed about seven years of famine that would follow a period of plenty.

That's when it dawned on him. Dreams with meaning tend to hang out with trouble.

King Nebuchadnezzar's nightmare got a young Daniel promoted right before his friends got thrown into a fiery furnace.

Joseph dreamed he needed to flee to Egypt right before Herod killed every baby in Bethlehem.

Pilate's wife dreamed about Jesus right before her husband sent him to the cross.

"What's that?" Julia asked, interrupting Alex's attempt to put his thoughts into the right words.

He carried the treasure with him to his seat. "My grandfather's old Bible," he said. "Published way back in the seventies. King James."

"King who?"

"Sorry. It's an authorized King James Bible."

No reaction.

"Sort of like Shakespeare, old English words and phrases."

"I see," she said curiously, leaning forward to view the cherished artifact.

"I love the poetic language. It makes what we believe feel more…" He paused to let what he was trying to say catch up to what he felt. "It makes what we believe seem less clinical. More full of mystery, if you know what I mean."

The look on her face told him she didn't.

"Anyway," he said to get back to Julia's question, "I was just refreshing my memory about dreams in the Bible. They don't happen often, but when they do they typically occur just before something… significant."

"Significant to the person?"

"More like significant to God's redemptive purposes."

She waited for more.

"It's the main plot of the Bible: God restoring a fallen world to himself."

She released a sigh of relief. "So the dreams come from God?"

"You sound surprised."

"Were these dreams that came from God ever…" She paused. "Were they ever nightmares?"

"Is that what you had? A nightmare?"

She nodded slowly.

"Tell me what you remember about the dream."

She did.

A mysterious, shadowy man reaching toward her in the distance.

The descent into ever-darkening water toward a sadistic, ravenous laughter.

The face and fist vanishing below.

The ascent toward life and rescue.

And the second face, only vaguely familiar, trying to haul her
down again.

Julia sat in silence as if awaiting her pastor's verdict. Evil or
good? Warning or prophecy? Satan or God?

"Is that it?" Alex heard from behind. His face pinched in embarrassed anger as he turned back toward Mrs. Mayhew. She was
sitting on the edge of her chair with one earbud removed. "What
happened next? Did your fingers slip loose? Were you pulled
back under?"

She noticed the daggers coming from Alex's eyes. "Oh, sorry."
She placed the tiny speaker back in her ear canal. "Must have
fallen out. Don't mind me. Buzz, buzz, buzz," she sang while
grabbing another envelope from the pile.

"Forgive me," Alex said. A slight smile told him Julia found
the moment more humorous than mortifying. "Please, continue."

"That's when I woke up," she explained. "Or rather, when
Troy woke me. I spent the next few hours vacillating between
panic and prayer. And then I decided I needed to talk to someone."

Alex sensed there was more. "What else?" he asked.

"This isn't the first time I've had this dream. Well, most of it
anyway."

"Go on."

She explained that the first part of the dream had dogged her
two years earlier. Then it went away shortly after she met Troy.

"I was told the dreams probably had something to do with my
absent father. But that didn't explain the connection."

"Connection?"

"The first face, the young man who sank beneath me, was the face of Antonio Santos."

Alex didn't recognize the name.

"He was the minor who died in a NEXT transition clinic. It became a wrongful death lawsuit."

"That's right," Alex suddenly recalled.

She looked toward Mrs. Mayhew to confirm secrecy before leaning forward to whisper. "Antonio Santos died on the day those dreams began."

Alex felt a mild shiver. "Whoa." It was all he could think to say.

"What's more," she continued, "I received a copy of Antonio's journal from his older brother, the one who had initiated the lawsuit."

Julia reached toward the floor to retrieve a digital device from her purse. She tapped twice to call up a document before handing the tablet to Alex. "Read this portion. It's something the boy wrote to his mother."

If you ever hear from Dad again tell him I said goodbye. And that I hate him. I know he's the faceless man in my dreams, the one who never reaches back when I call for help. I'm glad I won't have any more nightmares. They scare me more than I've admitted. They feel like I'm drowning, getting sucked down away from the life I was supposed to live. But that's over now. I don't want to think about what should be or could be anymore. I'm ready to go.

Alex looked up in disbelief.

"That entry was posted on the last day of Antonio's life," Julia whispered eerily. "Which was also the first day I had the nightmare."

He sat quietly for several moments as his mind sifted through the implications. Nothing he had learned in seminary had prepared him for this. He knew that none of the vintage volumes on his bookshelf would provide the perfect quotation or explanation. Julia Simmons had inherited a dying boy's nightmare. Was such a thing biblical? Forget biblical, was it even possible? And if so, what could it mean?

"Do you think God is trying to tell me something about…" She reached for the words. "What did you call it, his redemptive purposes?"

Alex had no idea. "I do," he said anyway, opening the floodgates to Julia's other nagging questions.

"Why would God give Antonio the dream first?"

"Should I keep it secret or tell others?"

"Am I supposed to write about it? Is that why he chose a journalist?"

"If he wants me as some sort of mouthpiece, why would he let me lose my column with RAP Syndicate?"

"Who is the man trying to pull me under? Should I know him? Will I meet him? If so, should I approach him or run from him?"

Alex could only nod in solidarity at Julia's questions. She appeared disappointed but sympathetic to his baffled expression.

"Or am I just losing my mind?"

Finally, a question he could answer with certainty.

"This much I know," he reassured her, "your mind is in perfect working order."

Julia received the diagnosis gratefully.

"You didn't imagine Antonio's journal entry," he said, pointing back to the tablet. "And you seem perfectly clearheaded now."

She flashed an I'm-not-so-sure look in his direction.

"Trust me," he said. "I've seen lots of mentally disturbed people in my office through the years. You wouldn't fit in with that crowd."

"I don't know whether that makes me feel better or worse,"

she confessed. "At least if I were nuts Troy could have me committed."

The menace of dread dissipated as they shared a much-needed laugh.

Alex had a thought. "Julia," he began, "tell me your first impressions. You know, what you felt during the dream, or in the few moments right after you woke."

"I'm not real good at getting in touch with my feelings," she said with some embarrassment. "It drives my kid sister crazy."

"I didn't realize you had a sister," Alex said. "I guess I always assumed you were an only child."

"Maria. We lived together until I married Troy. Anyway, she calls me a high-control person because I use to-do lists instead of therapy to overcome my problems."

"I understand," Alex said. "But dreams contain more than images, they also convey emotion. What were your emotions telling you?"

She sat back in her chair, then closed her eyes as if trying to reenter a memory. The words finally came, each filled with potential significance to the mysterious meaning of the dream.

"I felt fear," she began. "No, terror."

Alex watched Julia's distressed face as she let herself relive the scene.

"Especially when I let go of the hand of the man on the surface."

"What did you *feel* about the man?" Hearing himself butcher the moment, Alex suddenly considered the barely passing grade he had received in Psychology 101 a gift of charity.

"Angry, at first," she explained. "I thought he had abandoned me. But then I saw his outstretched arm extending in my direction. He wanted me to swim toward him. Which I did, as soon as Antonio released my leg."

"And when you reached the man?"

"Relief. Gratitude. Security."

A brief pause.

"What else?" Alex prodded.

The answer seemed to stick in her throat on the way up. "Dependence." She opened her eyes. "That's another thing I've never been good at."

"Dependence?"

"I spent most of my life resisting the need for anyone else. Especially men."

"But then you met Troy."

"That's right."

"So do you think the dream has something to do with becoming dependent upon Troy?"

She appeared momentarily flustered by the question. "Maybe. In part."

"Go on," Alex suggested. "Any other feelings connected to what you saw?"

Julia closed her eyes again. "Just an overall impression that I'm being asked to cling to the mysterious man who seems to embody a calm, confident goodness."

"And the laughter? What overall impression do you have of the laughter?"

She shivered at the chilly reminder. "It comes from someone exactly the opposite of the mysterious man. Someone evil who craved a next meal. No, a next rape. And murder."

"You said you went back and forth between panic and prayer."

"I did," Julia confirmed.

"What did you pray?"

"What you might expect."

"No, tell me specifically. The same God who gives dreams also gives us the words to pray when we don't know what to ask. Do you remember what you said or what you felt when you prayed just after the nightmare?"

"I do," she said with visible relief. "I do. I recall asking God to protect Troy and Amanda and a few other people."

"What other people?" Alex pushed. "Your sister?"

"Actually, no," she said in what appeared to be surprised alarm. "For some reason I didn't feel like she was in danger."

"Then who?"

"I prayed for Kevin and Angie Tolbert and their kids."

Alex smiled at the mention, then showed concern. "Are they OK?"

She nodded. "We spent a day with them this past weekend. The usual headaches, you know, but nothing ominous as far as I could tell."

Alex noticed a second look of surprised realization overtaking Julia's face.

"What is it?" he asked.

"I just remembered something."

He waited.

"Now that I think about it, my most intense feelings came when I prayed for one of Angie's kids."

"Which one?"

"Baby Leah."

CHAPTER FOURTEEN

Matthew Adams took one last glance at the items in his bag. He was determined to handle his first assignment properly, which prompted him to confirm that everything was in order before ringing the doorbell.

The summer heat bore down on the back of his neck, adding a stream of sweat to the nervous perspiration Serena Winthrop's message had provoked ninety minutes earlier. As expected, service call details had been sent to his assigned message box with no advance warning. Ms. Winthrop had encouraged him to think like a fireman. "When the bell rings, be ready to slide down the pole and jump on the truck."

So that's what he did, tossing his carefully prepared collection of supplies into the car and driving to a somewhat dilapidated section of Castle Pines, a once-respectable neighborhood half an hour south of downtown Denver. He arrived ten minutes early, which gave him time to gather his thoughts, practice his script, and, most importantly, recheck his inventory:

- One small tube of sterilization cream to use before and, most importantly, after assisting the client
- A medium-size inhaler for volunteers who requested optional halothane vapor so they could sleep through the procedure
- One rubber tourniquet
- Two needle-capped syringes
- Three vials of PotassiPass
- A generous supply of towels and plastic bags

Matthew had expected more coaching than he had received. He had hoped to get specific answers to his lingering questions.

"What's the best way to calm the client's nerves?"

"Is it better to ask any family members to leave the room or let them stay?"

"Can I talk to them about spiritual matters, or is religion off-limits?"

But he was told the company considered him an experienced professional and trusted his instincts on such "soft-side" decisions. The only real training he got was a few video demonstrations of the formal procedure, a fairly simple process. Stick the needle in quickly; that's more comfortable for the client than if you hesitate.

"The most important thing," the trainer had explained, "is to remember all of your gear. We seriously frown upon the need to reschedule due to an oversight by one of our associates."

Everything appearing in order, Matthew reached for the doorbell.

The sun felt suddenly hotter on his neck.

He waited.

No sound.

He pushed the button again.

The silence prompted him to rap his moist knuckles on the hardwood door.

"Ms. Jackson?" Matthew said through a slight opening in the door. He could only see the left side of her pale face peering beyond the protection of a chain bolt lock. A curious posture, he thought, for a woman awaiting death. "My name is..." He almost gave his real name. That would have been his first blunder. He glanced back down at the digital screen to refresh his memory. "My name is Jed Smith."

The name meant even less to the woman than it did to Matthew.

"I'm here at your request."

Still no reaction.

"With your...procedure."

"Procedure?" she finally said. "I don't want any procedure. Go away."

She shut the door in his face. Matthew looked back at Ms. Winthrop's message, then at the address on the front of the house. He had the right place.

Another knock as Matthew half shouted through the wooden barrier.

"Ms. Jackson," he called. "I received notice that you requested a companion for your transition. My records indicate you confirmed the appointment last night."

He heard the sound of the small chain sliding free from its locked position. The door opened slowly, giving Matthew his first glimpse of the woman's unconcealed eyes. They did not, as he'd expected, betray sickness, depression, or even fear. They revealed something worse: apathy.

"You say I have an appointment?" she asked.

Odd, thought Matthew. "Yes, ma'am," he said. "I'm a transition companion from NEXT Transition Services. I'm here to help you with the procedure."

"I'm sorry," she said listlessly. "I forget things. Please, come in."

One glance around the front room of the house told

Matthew that Brianna Jackson lived alone. No other human being would have been able to tolerate such disordered stacks of everything imaginable: large cardboard boxes filled with old clothes, and piles and piles of disheveled papers suggesting Ms. Jackson had never converted to the digital age. Perhaps she believed her collection of handwritten notes, print magazines, paperback romance novels, photographs, insurance claim forms, check stubs, and a hundred other tree-killing keepsakes would one day prove valuable. At the moment, however, they merely blocked access to a sitting area that appeared to have been gathering dust since the days of telephone wires and cable television boxes.

Matthew followed the woman through a narrow pathway between the front door and the kitchen, where another mess awaited: fermenting leftovers stored conveniently on the counter, table, and stovetop rather than in the refrigerator. He shuddered to think what moldy heirlooms must reside there.

"Have a seat," she said after shoving aside a stack of flattened boxes that had once held frozen entrees and breakfast cereal.

He complied after a quick glance to make sure the chair contained no sticky residue or crawling parasites.

"Thank you," he said, careful to continue breathing through his mouth rather than risk a gag reflex from the pungent combination of moldering leftovers and prehistoric perfume.

Brianna didn't join him at the kitchen table. She instead walked out of the room.

Matthew waited for a moment before calling out, "Ms. Jackson?"

No response.

"May I call you Brianna?" he asked in an elevated voice. He had decided using the client's first name might help put her at ease. Less clinical. More sociable.

He waited again. No reply. He continued.

"Well, you can call me Ma—" A second close call. "You can call me Jed."

The procedure was supposed to take place in the bathroom, the client sitting comfortably in the tub while the transition companion handled what the registration form called "a painless sequence of three steps" that consisted of wrapping the tourniquet around the upper arm to make finding a plump vein easier, wiping a bit of sterilization cream on the forearm—which seemed an odd step in light of the purpose of the procedure—and injecting the PotassiPass serum into the bloodstream. Perhaps Ms. Jackson had gone to clear a small mountain of empty soap and shampoo containers out of the tub so that they could use the space as intended.

Matthew heard the faint sound of a flushing toilet. He sighed, then waited a few more minutes for Ms. Jackson to rejoin him in the kitchen. But she never came.

"Brianna?" he said while walking slowly toward the hallway down which Ms. Jackson had disappeared. "Is everything all right?"

He continued toward the back of the house, carefully navigating an obstacle course of tied-up plastic trash bags and mounds of clothes that had never made it to the washing machine.

He found the now-empty bathroom. The door was open, giving him a glimpse of a tub that had *not* been de-cluttered.

He walked farther to pass the open door to what looked as if it had once been the guest bedroom and then the storage facility for the first ten years of Ms. Jackson's clutter and junk fetish. No Brianna.

One more door remained. It was closed. He knocked. "Brianna? Are you OK?"

The door opened. Ms. Jackson appeared alarmed, as if suddenly confronted by a phantom. "Leave me alone!" she shouted while taking a backward step. "I don't have your money!"

Matthew recognized the look in Brianna's eyes. He had seen it before, during the final months of his mother's deterioration.

"It's OK," he said softly while extending a hand of reassurance toward her quivering arm. He touched her tenderly, just as he had done when trying to keep his mom from a tailspin of confused anxiety. "It's me, Jed Smith. You invited me into the house a few minutes ago."

Her eyes searched for the memory. Then she relaxed. "Oh, yes," she said with embarrassment. "I forgot."

She placed her hand on his gratefully.

"I forget things."

"I'm here at your request," he said in response, "to assist your transition."

The explanation seemed to calm her further.

Matthew escorted Ms. Jackson back to the kitchen, where he carefully explained her own recent history based upon the data points listed on the assignment form.

"It looks like you contacted our office last month to initiate the approval process. We contacted your next of kin to confirm sound mind." He paused to look at his client doubtfully before scanning the third entry. "And I see that we obtained both required digital signatures, yours and someone named Blake Jackson. Your brother?"

A thin smile crept onto Brianna's face. "How is Blake?" she asked. "I haven't seen him since…since…how long has it been?"

Matthew could only guess. "I would assume you saw him last week."

"Did I?" she asked with an edge of self-disgust. "Forgive me. I forget things."

Matthew looked at the next item. "And you decided to make Blake the sole beneficiary of your estate?" *Lucky guy*, Matthew thought, *inheriting the world's largest collection of useless rubbish.*

Brianna gave no response. She appeared distracted, as if temporarily visiting a different time and place. "I miss Blake. Did he ever get approved for treatment?" she finally asked.

"I'm afraid I wouldn't know," Matthew answered, feeling an impatience rise that reminded him of conversations he had had with his mother two years before. "I just need to confirm one last detail before we proceed."

Her glossy gaze returned to the present moment. "I'm sorry. You were saying?"

To meet the legal requirements, Matthew read word for word the next item, which she might or might not have understood whenever she'd decided to volunteer.

"Ms. Jackson," he began, "NEXT Inc. has reviewed and approved your request to participate in the beta-test phase of a new in-home transition assistance service. Despite the presence of a representative of our company, your transition will be categorized as a 'Self-Administered Termination,' described in Section 349 of the law commonly labeled the 'Youth Initiative.' My cooperation with your decision will be restricted to those services defined as 'Aiding Volunteers' and disposal of your remains will be handled in full compliance with the instructions detailed in Section 421 of the same statute. It is therefore understood that you assume complete responsibility to use the supplied kit as instructed and waive all right to hold NEXT Inc. liable for any unintended consequences of the procedure."

Matthew looked up from the tablet to visually check Brianna's comprehension. Then he tapped the first option on the screen: "Client Waives Liability."

Matthew placed the tablet in front of the woman. "Please press your left thumb onto this square section here."

She did.

"Perfect," he said, pleased to properly complete the legality. Nearly finished, and not a single mistake.

"So," he continued, "I suppose we should move to the bathroom."

"Oh," she said, as if suddenly remembering her manners. "Just down the hall. First door on the left."

He reached down to pick up the bag of supplies he had placed on the floor beside his chair, then stood. But she remained seated. He offered his arm, which she didn't accept. He knelt into position to look her in the eyes. Then he placed a hand on hers.

"It's perfectly normal to feel a bit scared," he said. "But it will be painless. I promise."

She returned his gaze. He didn't sense relief. He sensed bewilderment.

Matthew felt a fleeting hesitation. What if she had changed her mind? Was he supposed to pack up and leave? Suggest a new appointment time? Fail on his first assignment?

Then he remembered. Ms. Jackson forgets things.

"Listen to me, Brianna. You're doing the right thing. The heroic thing."

The attempt bounced off an apathy that ran deep. How long had she lived in solitary confinement? Even when such confinement was self-imposed, the absence of human interaction, human affection, could steal one's will to live. But a trace of that will remained in Ms. Brianna Jackson, it seemed, no matter how faint. She might not care to live, but she didn't want to die.

She pulled her hands away from Matthew's tender grasp. "Why are you here?" she asked brashly. "What do you want?"

"I told you, my name is Frank... I mean Jed. You scheduled me to come and help you..."

"I don't need your help," she barked. "I'm fine all by myself."

Matthew felt his heart pound with a sudden rush of panic, and anger. His first NEXT client was getting ready to hand him his first failure. His promising new career threatened to fizzle at the hands of a befuddled old woman who hadn't the sense to put leftover fish sticks in the refrigerator.

"Besides," she continued in a fit of foggy paranoia, "I don't have the kind of money you want."

"I'm not looking for money, Ms. Jackson. I'm here to…"

But it was no good. She shuffled hastily out of the room.

Matthew looked back and forth at nothing and everything. What to do now? Should he chase her down and force her into the tub? Did forgetting your transition appointment make your approval null and void? He had been given no instructions for this situation. Why would he have? Most volunteers probably served their transition companions cookies and milk before rolling up a sleeve to face the end with defiant resolve instead of running out of the room in reaction to a delusional mirage. What did she think he was, a hit man from the mob squeezing money out of pack rats? Or perhaps a crazed killer stalking harmless debits to steal a stack of old *Good Housekeeping* magazines?

You have a job to do, Matthew reminded himself. *And a mission to fulfill.*

If anyone needed to be freed from her misery, it was Brianna Jackson. Her forgetting that she had volunteered was proof enough that she needed to go. She hadn't changed her mind. She had simply misplaced it.

He knew what he needed to do.

A cold spike of adrenaline reached upward through Matthew's throat before descending down his limbs into hands suddenly quivering in dreadful anticipation of a task they were never meant to fulfill. Ignoring the rising fear, Matthew carried the bag of supplies in the direction of the bathroom he had passed while searching for his missing client. It took him less than a minute to empty out the tub and position the tourniquet, sterilization cream, and other items on the corner of the sink. Then he reached into his bag for something Brianna Jackson had not requested. He had decided to improvise, to make real-time decisions to deal with an unscripted scenario. He could cover the extra expense himself if needed, sort of a complimentary upgrade for an unusually anxious client.

He shook the container to confirm its status. Full.

A moment later he approached Brianna's bedroom door. He started to knock, but changed his mind. He instead turned the handle. Unlocked.

He didn't have time to plan how he would get her to breathe in the vapor. He nearly panicked when she turned toward his unexpected approach. But then he stopped.

"Brianna," he said gently. "I apologize. I can see that you're upset."

She softened a tad.

"I'd like to give you something to calm your nerves," he said while handing her the inhaler. "And then I'll leave you alone."

She looked at the label. Big words that meant nothing to her. "What is it?"

"It's what I came to sell you," he lied, assuming the role of door-to-door salesman. "But we're allowed to give free samples. No obligation. If it works, call in an order. If not, you'll never hear from us again."

She inspected the device. It looked like something asthmatic athletes used before a big run, only several times larger. "How many shots?" she asked.

"Whatever helps you relax. I inhale deeply three or four times. That usually does the trick."

She eyed it again, this time with more interest than the last. "So you use this stuff?"

"I do," he said. "Helps me fall asleep at night."

"And there's no charge?"

"A free sample, my compliments."

She lifted the inhaler toward her mouth. "Well, I have been feeling more nervous lately."

"I think this will help," Matthew said. "Go on, give it a try."

—◦◦◦—

Fifteen minutes later Matthew stood watching a single stream of perspiration flow down the side of his face. He reached down, tore a bit of bathroom tissue from the hanging roll, and wiped his face dry. All of his supplies had been carefully returned to the bag, with one exception. He forced his eyes back toward the tub. An arm dangled lifelessly, the rubber tourniquet still fastened securely above the elbow. He hadn't noticed he had been holding his breath until after the knot loosened and the item fell free. He exhaled, and then reached into the bag he had inspected before and, thanks to fast thinking, would likely inspect again. Removing a small tube he twisted loose the lid and released a large dab of cream to purify his hands.

He returned to the kitchen table to awaken his tablet and complete the final step in his assigned sequence: ALERT DISPOSAL SERVICES. He tapped the icon, informing some nameless colleague that he could remove the cadaver anytime in the next twenty-four hours.

Matthew walked out the front door and looked toward his car. He stood for a moment as the adrenaline that had fueled a dreadful improvisation waned. He inhaled deeply through his nostrils, eager for the fresh scent of the clean summer air. Then he turned toward the bushes, where he released a violent wave of nausea.

CHAPTER FIFTEEN

The shop offered a range of dresses that would look adorable on Amanda's slight frame, the perfect blend of modest chic and playful spunk. They were the kind of clothes Julia would have worn back when hints of pubescent transformation had begun to show themselves on her own figure. Amanda had recently graduated from training-bra-awkward to the petite-women's section of what must have been ten different stores in the past hour.

Julia displayed a blouse and matching skirt toward the twelve-year-old skeptic. "How about this?" she asked hopefully. "It would bring out your beautiful eyes."

The beautiful eyes rolled dismissively. "Too old!"

Julia glanced back at the set. "What do you mean, old? It's the latest fashion."

"Yeah, for someone in their forties."

The comment stung, as intended. Julia had recently celebrated her thirty-sixth birthday, tipping her officially closer to forty than thirty. Her taste in clothes, as in everything else on which she offered an opinion, was apparently out of date.

"I don't see what was wrong with what I tried on in the last shop," Amanda said.

That's when Julia rolled *her* eyes. Why had she even agreed to enter a store like Her Edge? "I told you," she replied, attempting to conceal exasperation with a maternal lilt. "It was way too low and way too short."

"It was cute," Amanda said. "Aunt Maria would love it."

Julia couldn't argue. Ever since her younger sister dominated the "most likely to turn heads" category back in high school, Maria had lived by the motto "If you've got it, flaunt it!" Julia, the valedictorian, could never compete with the fast-and-loose fashion sensibilities of Aunt Maria. Nor had she cared to. Elegant sophistication, not sassy allure, had served her well.

"I tell you what," Julia said, pulling out her trump card. "Let's go back to Her Edge and have you try it on again."

Amanda leaped. "Really?"

"You bet," Julia said, springing the trap. "I'll call Troy and have him meet us there. We'll let him decide."

The glow on Amanda's face dimmed.

"Or," Julia continued with a smug grin, "you can try this one on for size."

The girl took the outfit from Julia and slunk toward the dressing rooms with a pouty huff.

While scanning the store for other possible selections, Julia heard her phone chime. She skipped her usual glance at the screen, confident it would display an image of her husband's flirting grin. He probably wondered how much longer he needed to wander through the outdoor mall looking at nothing while Amanda tried on everything.

"I'm sorry, babe," she said after tapping the edge of her ear. "Amanda still can't decide…"

"Babe?" the voice answered. "I love when you call me that. Such a tease."

"Paul?" Julia asked with embarrassment. "Paul Daugherty?"

"The one and only," he said brashly. "How's my favorite journalist?"

Julia suppressed a groan. She had never liked Paul, even when she depended on him for her livelihood. How long had it been, nine months? A year?

"Favorite former journalist," she corrected. "Or have you forgotten?"

It was Paul who had sold Julia's last big series, a string of features in a weekend journal covering the real-life impact of the economic crisis. He didn't know she had pitched it in a stealth effort to help legitimize Kevin Tolbert's proposal by putting human faces on dark zone trends and bright spot choices. The stories created a mini-stir, especially once the editorial board realized the series cast a negative light on the former. The last thing RAP Syndicate wanted was for their readers to raise questions about what they considered "overwhelmingly successful" and "economically sound" policies that were finally tackling the mountainous budget deficit.

"I told you, Jewel," Paul said self-protectively, "I tried to defend you."

She knew Paul too well. He would have distanced himself from his "favorite journalist" the second he smelled the approaching witch-hunt. "The whole thing was Julia Davidson's idea," he would have backpedaled. "What was I supposed to do, censor her?"

Which is exactly what they would have expected him to do, although they would have resented the implication.

"I loved the series," he added. And he probably meant it. Paul had always admired Julia's talent as a writer, or at least envied it. "I told them it was a big mistake letting you go."

"I'm sure you did, Paul." It was more benefit of the doubt than he deserved.

"Besides, I got canned myself. So I'm no longer part of the evil empire."

The comment surprised Julia. Paul had become a fixture at RAP Syndicate, almost as well respected as she had been in her glory days. Julia had won a Pulitzer, but Paul had orchestrated one of the most aggressive acquisition strategies in the company's history. The company now described itself as home to the largest network of feature writers and opinion columnists on the Web. And, thanks to the sudden departure of one Julia Davidson Simmons, all of them safely antagonistic to debit-loving, religiously motivated breeders like Congressman Kevin Tolbert.

"You lost your job?"

"Two months back."

"I'm sorry to hear that." It was the expected thing to say.

"Don't be," he said glibly. "I'm glad to be out. In fact, that's why I called."

She waited for more.

"I just launched my own agency. Media and publicity, but mostly publicity."

"Really?" she said, distracted by the sudden realization Amanda was taking longer than she should to change.

"Yep. It's going great. I just landed a big contract with Trisha."

The name recaptured Julia's attention. "Trisha? As in Delisha?"

"That's right. Trisha Sayers."

Julia recalled the tour she had taken of the model turned fashion mogul's plush office complex two years earlier. Trisha Delisha, as she had been known in her curvy prime, had been a fan of Julia's popular column. "You're marketing clothes now?" Julia asked.

"Nah. Trisha chairs some new communications commission connected to the Youth Initiative. Nicole Florea gave me a heads-up after she heard about my demise. She suggested I shoot Trisha a proposal and, bingo, the Daugherty Communications Agency was born!"

Julia felt her stomach tighten at the thought of the mountain of federal cash pouring into agencies like Paul's to promote the same initiative her husband and Kevin had been working so hard to oppose.

"Congratulations," she said grudgingly.

"Thanks. So, how about you? Anyone snag you yet?"

"Snag me?"

"Come on, Jewel. You're probably crazy busy. Am I right?"

"Busy?" she muttered, eyeing a darling dress hanging slightly out of reach. "Oh, yes," she lied. "Busier than ever."

"I thought so," Paul replied. "So I imagine there's no hope for me."

"Hope for you to what?" she asked.

"To what? To hire you, what else?"

The question stunned Julia. And, to her surprise, gave her a slight surge of adrenaline. She hadn't realized how much her confidence had waned after a year of exile in journalistic Siberia.

"Hire me? To do what?"

"I told you, I landed a big contract. I need a writer who knows how to turn difficult concepts and controversial ideas into commonsense rhetoric."

Julia didn't know whether to take the statement as a compliment or a rebuke.

"You'd be perfect. And I can make it worth your while."

She said nothing while trying to absorb Paul's offer.

"Come on, Jewel," he said to fill the silence. "Don't play hard to get. I'm in a real bind."

"Well," she finally said. "I'll need to think it over, and discuss it with Troy."

"Who?" he asked before remembering. "Oh, right. Same partner?"

"Husband," she corrected. "Troy is my husband."

"Right, sorry. Still haven't adjusted to the idea, I guess."

"Can you send me something I can look over with specifics?" she asked hastily, eager to get off the phone to hurry Amanda along.

"Done!" he said triumphantly. "And don't worry about your day rate," he added. "I can double whatever you're making now."

Double? She must have misheard.

"Just do me a favor and look over the project summary document right away. I need to know who's in and who's out by tomorrow if I'm gonna have any hope of pulling off my first presentation."

"When is it?"

"Ten days," he said.

"And you're just hiring your project team now?"

"I know. Crazy, isn't it? But really fun. I'm on a deadline high like when we made our first big splash at RAP."

Julia resisted the urge to correct Paul's memory for the hundredth time. *She* had made the splash. *He* had merely taken the credit.

"What do you say?" he prodded. "Can I count you in?"

"I'll read the summary," she said. "No promises."

"I'll take it. Thanks, Jewel. I'll call you back in the morning."

"Fine."

"Bye, love," he said before ending the call.

Two seconds later she heard a ping. Paul's promised document had arrived.

Julia began reading the synopsis while standing just outside the dressing room waiting area. That's when she noticed Amanda's face peeking over the top edge of a partition door.

"There you are!" she said impatiently. "I've been waiting for five minutes."

"Why didn't you come find me?" Julia asked.

Amanda slipped out of the dressing room to model the perfect outfit. "Because I don't want anyone to see me in this!" she said with mortification. "I told you, it's too old!"

"Here," Julia said while shoving three other ensembles toward her foster daughter. "Try these."

Amanda glanced at the selections while shaking her head in obvious disbelief. "These are worse!"

"Just try them," Julia whispered intensely.

Amanda disappeared indignantly around the corner.

Julia found herself drawn into the text of Paul's project summary, her alarm escalating with each sentence. After reaching the end she quickly tapped her phone. Seconds later Troy answered.

"Hi, beautiful!"

Julia smiled at the voice of a man who considered her anything but old and out of style. "We have a situation," she said.

"What's wrong?"

"I need you to look at something I just received from Paul Daugherty."

"Paul Daugherty!" Troy said, understandably surprised to hear the name again.

"He just called me," Julia explained. "He's left RAP to launch his own publicity agency."

"I'm glad to hear it," Troy said, apparently pleased to have one fewer snake in an influential editorial position. "What did he want?"

"He's looking for help. Just landed a big contract with the federal government that…well…you need to read what he sent me. Where are you right now?" Julia asked.

"In Sports Authority looking at running shoes."

Where else? she thought. "Meet us just outside"—she glanced around the store to find the name—"Talbots. It's a few stores down from Macy's."

"How about in ten minutes?" he asked.

Before she could reply, Julia noticed a blur of preteen movement out of the corner of her eye. She turned to see Amanda, not modeling the next outfit, but storming toward the store exit.

"Amanda!" she called out. "Where are you going?"

The girl continued her escape without a word.

"You better come immediately," Julia said into the phone. "Amanda just bolted."

CHAPTER SIXTEEN

Five minutes later Julia was sitting beside her husband near a court-yard fountain. They had decided to wait rather than frantically chase Amanda in and out of the thousand possible hideouts the outdoor mall offered. Julia initiated the phone-tracking app on her phone to pinpoint Amanda's latest location.

"How far?" Troy asked.

"About three hundred yards that way," she said, pointing in the direction Julia already knew would become Amanda's likely destination. "She's in a store we visited earlier. Her Edge."

"You took her to Her Edge?"

"More like she took me," Julia said with exasperation.

He laughed knowingly. "I see."

Troy had always been more patient with Amanda's antics than Julia. And it made her mad; not that he modeled such loving per-severance, but that she hadn't figured out how to do the same.

"I'm not sure I'm cut out for this." Julia sighed.

He rubbed her slumped shoulders reassuringly. "You're doing just fine. It's a phase. She'll get through it."

"I'm sure she will. But I'm not so sure about me."

Troy chuckled dismissively. But Julia, she hated admitting to herself, was only half kidding. They had made the decision to foster-adopt very quickly, on the rebound from the bad news of learning they couldn't have children of their own. Troy wanted to be a dad and Julia, to her own surprise, had wanted to give him a child. They had envisioned steering a stroller and carrying a diaper bag at this stage, not checking call histories for secret boyfriends or enduring temper tantrums over fashion statements.

"To be honest," Julia began timidly, "I'm starting to wonder whether we should go through with it."

Troy swung his head toward his wife.

She looked away to finish what she probably shouldn't have started. "Maybe we're not the right parents for Amanda."

A long silence.

"Or rather, maybe I'm not the right mom."

She knew Troy wasn't part of the problem. Amanda practically worshipped him, drinking in every affirming word like a thirsty flower eager to blossom into the beauty God had made her to be. One wink or frown from Troy was all Amanda needed to direct her searching footsteps. She relished his paternal presence. Julia understood why. Little by little, Troy had made her feel what Amanda was starting to relish. Secure. Protected. Cherished. All gifts Julia had never received from her own absent father. Things Amanda craved and deserved.

Julia's fumbling attempts at maternal guidance, however, seemed far less useful. Perhaps her energies would be better spent turning editorial phrases than spinning in circles trying to do a job for which she was so poorly equipped.

Troy placed a single finger on Julia's cheek and gently forced her gaze back in his direction. "You're a wonderful mother," he said. "And it would kill Amanda to lose you."

She knew he was right. Amanda had come a very long way since they first met. Julia couldn't remember the last time Amanda had spewed profanity or any of the colorful language one might expect from an orphan girl living with a porn-obsessed half brother and his domineering girlfriend. She had even learned basic manners and a near-ladylike posture much more befitting to her natural beauty. Amanda retained an innocence that, thank heaven, had been nurtured rather than violated as it might have been had they not plucked her out from under her half brother's licentious guardianship.

"I know," she whispered while accepting Troy's refreshing embrace. "I guess I just didn't expect it to be so hard."

"I understand," he said, then extended his lips to her forehead. "Just give her some space. She'll be fine. You'll see."

She glanced at her phone to confirm Amanda's proximity. Still three hundred yards away, probably standing in front of the same mirror admiring the same outfit Julia had vetoed. The outfit, Julia relaxed to think, Troy would soon convince Amanda to abandon with a quiet, redirecting frown.

Julia suddenly remembered the document. "Oh," she said, "I almost forgot. You need to read the project summary Paul Daugherty sent me a few minutes ago."

She tapped the icon before handing Troy her phone, then waited for an outburst of angry abhorrence. Rather than transform into the Hulk as she expected, however, her husband lowered his head and closed his eyes in solemn resignation.

"Wait," she said. "You already knew about this, didn't you?"

"Not this specific project," he confessed. "But I knew a large marketing budget had been established to beef up recruitment. It's one of the points of contention between Kevin and Senator Franklin."

"So this is legit? They've hired a marketing agency to sell people on volunteering?"

"Not just one agency," he explained. "Paul Daugherty might be the first, but he won't be the only."

Julia grabbed the device from Troy's hand and began searching the document for a number. "Here it is," she said. "A one-hundred-million-dollar advertising campaign targeting second-tier markets. What's that?"

"First-tier volunteers were the low-hanging fruit. You know, the terminally ill or chronically disabled. They were easy recruits, enabling the Youth Initiative to hit initial targets without much effort. They had hoped early momentum from tier-one volunteers would inspire the second-tier market to do likewise."

"Second-tier?" Julia asked.

"Those with assets to transition but who don't face a terminal illness or protracted disability: the lonely, the depressed, and the potentially generous."

"Potentially generous?"

"Those who might feel badly for spending would-be inheritance assets even though they are perfectly healthy."

Julia nodded at the logic while squirming at the implication.

"Anyway, the Youth Initiative had projected significant growth in the second half of last year, but all of the bad press associated with the NEXT wrongful death appeal curtailed the rate of volunteers."

"But NEXT won that case," Julia said unnecessarily.

"They did. But they got a serious black eye in the process. Not to mention stealing all credibility from Franklin's 'signs of progress' convention speech."

Julia began to seethe at the snapshot of a deck stacked against every policy her husband and Kevin had been trying to advance. "Let me guess. They reallocated the Bright Spots funding to this marketing campaign."

"Some of it," Troy replied. "Until this moment, I didn't know how much."

The phone chimed.

"It's her," Julia said, extending the phone toward her husband. "You talk to her."

He didn't accept the offer. "I think it would be better if you answered."

She frowned in Troy's direction while tapping the answer button.

"Are you OK?" Julia asked rigidly, skipping her usual "Hello."

A brief silence on the line, then a sign of surrender. "I shouldn't have stormed off."

"No, you shouldn't have."

"And … well … I'm sorry."

Julia took a deep breath before saying what she didn't yet feel. "I forgive you."

"Can you meet me at—"

"I know where you are," Julia interrupted. "We'll be right over."

"We?" Amanda asked with some concern.

"Yes, we."

The call ended.

"Tell you what," Troy said. "How about if you stop off to get an iced coffee while I meet up with Amanda?"

Julia liked the sound of the offer.

"I'll see you at Peak Grinds in ten or twenty minutes?"

She nodded while receiving her husband's peck on the cheek.

———— ⁓⁓ ————

Julia looked up from the document on her phone. Something was gnawing at her instinct as an investigative journalist. The appalling nature of the entire marketing campaign, obviously. But there was more. Something about the fact that Paul Daugherty had landed the contract. She knew him well enough to distrust his explanation. A good word from Nicole Florea might have helped, but Paul would have been buried by Madison Avenue giants during the kind of competitive bid process tied to every federal contract.

She took another sip from her straw, only to hear the rattling emptiness of ice remnants.

"May I get a refill, please?" Julia asked after approaching the pimply-faced boy standing behind the counter.

"Tea?" he asked, shaking the cup as if listening for evidence of her selection.

"Iced coffee."

"Got it," he said before his eyes turned toward the sound of the opening coffee shop door. His gaze momentarily trumped Julia's request. She cleared her throat. "Oh, sorry," he said with a blush.

Julia turned toward the door to discover what had distracted the young man.

"Wow!" she said toward a beaming Amanda. "You look…" Julia tried to find the right words. *Adorable* might sound too young. *Lovely* too old. She recalled the teenage boy's dropped jaw. "Like a model!"

"Thanks, Mom!" Amanda said gratefully and with a hint of sincere repentance.

"She insisted on wearing it out of the store so you could see," Troy explained with a wink.

"Good choice," Julia replied. "Very good choice."

Amanda approached the admiring eyes of the much older boy behind the counter to order her favorite drink.

"I don't think I'll be getting my refill," Julia whispered toward Troy, who was watching the scene like a sheepdog smelling a nearby wolf.

"Did she select that outfit herself?"

"Sort of," Troy said slyly.

"Don't tell me how you did it," Julia said before kissing her husband's hand. "But well done."

While waiting for Amanda to finish flirting with the barista, Julia asked Troy whether he thought there was something suspicious about Paul Daugherty's call.

"Could be," he said. "What, exactly, did he want?"

"He offered me a job," she said dismissively, knowing she would never seriously consider the possibility.

"Really?" Troy said as if spotting a silver dollar on the sidewalk. "What did you say?"

Julia looked at her husband suspiciously. "I said to send me the project summary so that I could get him off the phone. You know how he is, never takes no for an answer. I figured 'Let me think about it' might help me escape."

Troy took a sip of ice water while staring out the window as if he were people watching. But Troy never watched people.

"Spill it," Julia insisted.

"Spill what?"

"Whatever's on your mind," she said. "I know that look, Mr. Simmons. You're mulling over some sort of strategy."

He smiled in her direction. "Well," he began, "I was just thinking about the Center for Economic Growth."

Of course he was. The CEG had consumed nearly every waking hour since their trip down the river. Kevin had thanked Troy for steering the policy think tank through a very difficult year. He had managed to grow the donor base and expand the network of policy wonks. The fledgling organization had accomplished more than either had dreamed possible in such short order. But Troy knew much more needed to be done if they had any hope of serious influence on the national stage. All they had done so far, he had said, was identify emerging innovations in bright spot regions. What they really needed was to demonstrate just how many constituents supported Kevin's proposal over Franklin's plan.

"What about it?" Julia asked, unsure she wanted to hear Troy's answer.

"Well," he said, "I was thinking about how hard it is to gain momentum. We're always playing defense. We spend so much time and energy correcting misleading characterizations of our vision that we can't seem to get on the proactive side of the debate."

She waited for the rest.

"We keep getting blindsided and caught flat-footed," he continued.

"And?" she asked warily.

"And it would be nice, for once, to know what's coming at us."

"Such as details of the Youth Initiative marketing message?"

"Exactly," he said. "I was thinking it would be helpful to have someone feeding us inside information so we can see the next salvo before watching it on television with the rest of the nation."

"You mean someone like a former award-winning journalist who's just been asked to work with the lead agency?"

Troy raised his eyebrows in mock surprise. "Great idea! I never would have thought of that."

Julia lightly slapped her husband's lying lips, then inspected the odd-shaped possibility from every angle. She asked the obvious question.

"Would that be ethical?"

"What's unethical about accepting a job offer?"

"You know what I mean," she said. "Is it right to say yes under false pretenses?"

He thought for a moment. "Think of it as undercover reporting. Only instead of working for RAP or Bing or some other syndicate, you'll be working on behalf of the citizens of the

United States making sure not a dime of taxpayer money is wasted on frivolous expenses."

She considered the suggestion. "Paul said he wanted my answer in the morning. I guess he's on a fast track to present initial creative concepts."

"Listen, babe," Troy said softly, apparently sensing her unease. "You have a lot on your mind with the adoption process and all."

They both looked toward the girl who would soon be their permanent daughter. She smiled back in their direction from the counter with an *Isn't he cute?* finger wave. Julia smiled at the sight while Troy growled.

"And I don't want you to do anything that would make you uncomfortable," he continued, easing his gaze back toward Julia. "But I would love to have your eyes and ears in the middle of this campaign to help us head off the enemy at the pass."

She squeezed her husband's hand. Did he really think she could help the cause? Or did he sense how much she missed being a player, how much she yearned to make a difference when the stakes were high?

"Let me sleep on it," she said.

But she knew full well that Mrs. Simmons, the woman formerly known as Julia Davidson, was heading back into the game.

CHAPTER SEVENTEEN

"Good morning, Mrs. Mayhew."

"Good morning, Pastor," she answered warily. "And what, may I ask, has you in such a chipper mood? You looked like the weight of the world was on your shoulders when you left the office last night."

It was true. He had felt pretty down, in part because he had been unable to help Julia Simmons unravel her mysterious dream. But it was mainly due to a call from Phil Crawford sharing "more good news" about the response to Sunday's announcement. "Two potential donors with sizable estates!" he had said in self-congratulation.

Of course, that was before Alex went home to Tamara and the kids. They had been fixing his favorite dinner, meatloaf and mashed potatoes. His wife had let six-year-old Ginger mash, so the potatoes contained more lumps than usual. But the look on Ginger's face when Alex gave the "Yummy" verdict transformed them into the best he had ever tasted.

After the meal, Chris offered to help Daddy with the dishes

while Tamara got the younger two down for the night. Alex knew Mom had made him volunteer. Eight-year-old boys don't do such things un-coaxed. But he enjoyed the time alone with his son anyway. They talked about things far removed from foreboding nightmares and overbearing board members. The really important stuff, like whether Superman could fly faster than the Flash could run and how tall Chris would be when he was Dad's age.

Then came the best part of the evening. While helping Chris button up his pajamas, Alex realized his wife had disappeared from their usual tag-team routine. "I'll get Mommy," he said, intending to pull Tamara into the room for Chris's traditional good-night hug.

"She already gave me a hug," Chris said. "She said you would read me a chapter and tuck me in yourself."

Odd, he thought. Had she said why?

"Tired," Chris said with a bounce.

Concerned something might be wrong, Alex handed Chris his chapter book while excusing himself for a moment. "Go ahead and start reading," he said. "I'll be back in a flash."

But he wasn't. After quietly slipping into the bedroom he did not, as expected, find Tamara sleeping. Alex instead noticed the glow of candlelight dancing out from a slight opening in the doorway to the master bath. He approached. There was just enough of a gap to peer inside with a single eye. There she stood, inspecting an outfit he had never seen, the kind meant for his eyes alone.

She turned toward the sound of her husband's gasp, revealing an even more enticing view of the gift she intended to give. A gift she had been giving for nine amazing years.

He tried to flee back to chapter book duty but Tamara whispered his name before he could reach the door. "Where are you going?" she asked with a welcoming smile.

That's when Alex turned to face the most beautiful woman in the world. He had intended to explain that Chris wasn't quite in bed yet. He wanted to lift a single finger, indicating he would be right back. But he couldn't bring himself to say anything to halt her approach.

Tamara kissed her husband's cheek while gliding her fingertips across his torso and letting him taste the scent of his favorite perfume.

"Wait," he said while taking a reluctant step back from her alluring invitation. "I didn't finish getting Chris to bed."

He recalled the mischievous smile on her face and the stretching yawn she pretended on his way out the door. "OK," she had whispered. "But I'm pretty tired. Better hurry or I might just fall asleep."

Both of them had remained wide awake for at least another hour creating intimate memories. Despite less sleep than he needed, Alex felt like a new man, a refreshed man, a completed man.

He looked at Mrs. Mayhew's doubtful glare, then said, "I guess I'm just eager to tackle whatever assignment God has in store for me on this *very* good morning." He returned a book to his shelf. "So, what's on the agenda for today?"

Mrs. Mayhew read off a list of duties that included approving the latest invoice from their cleaning supply vendor, calling a long-term children's ministry volunteer who, according to Mrs. Mayhew's confidential sources, probably wanted to complain about her exclusion from the new curriculum selection committee, and a preliminary review of the monthly budget report due to the finance committee by the end of the day.

"No lunch meeting?" he asked hopefully.

"Oh, for heaven's sake," she said, flustered, while rereading her list. "I can't believe I forgot to write that down."

He believed it.

"You have a lunch meeting with that board member." She

looked up as if trying to find a name written on the ceiling. "Oh, what's-his-face?"

"Phil Crawford?" Alex asked tentatively.

"I would remember Phil's name," she said with offense.

"Roberto?"

She shook her head back and forth slowly while closing her eyes tightly in search of the slip of mental paper on which she had jotted a detail too boring for gossip.

"Kenny? Stephen?"

Still no luck.

"Well, that only leaves Brandon," Alex said, somewhat relieved.

"Baxter!" Mrs. Mayhew hollered with self-satisfaction, as if the pastor's help had been unnecessary. "Mr. Baxter!"

"So I have lunch with Brandon Baxter?" Alex asked while raising a single eyebrow. "You're sure?"

The question agitated Mrs. Mayhew. "Of course I'm sure, Pastor. I just forgot to write it down." She walked toward the door indignantly.

"Where are we meeting?" Alex asked cautiously.

She turned back, the blank stare on her face providing the only answer he could expect.

Alex shot off a quick message to Brandon Baxter. He replied immediately, confirming they were meeting at Napoli's Italian Bistro, a place convenient neither to the church nor to the board member's office. *Oh, well*, he thought, *Brandon must be craving ravioli*.

Having completed his chores with time to spare before heading off to Napoli's, Alex decided to give his wife a quick call.

"Thank you," he said tenderly when she finished reminding him about Chris's after-school soccer game and telling him about a great new powder she'd found that seemed to be helping Joseph's diaper rash.

"For what?" she asked with a giggle, knowing full well what he meant.

"I love you," he added.

"I know."

"A lot."

"Me, too," she replied before ending the call.

—⁓—

"I'm sorry," Alex said while extending his hand to the woman seated beside Brandon. "I don't believe we've met."

"Pastor Ware," Brandon said, "let me introduce my aunt, Ellie Baxter."

The name had a familiar ring. Then he remembered. Brandon had asked Alex to call his aunt after the service on Sunday. Upset over Phil Crawford's transition announcement, however, he had let the request slip his mind. He and Mrs. Mayhew, it seemed, were a matching set.

"Of course," Alex said contritely. "I'm so sorry. I intended to call you." It was all he could say without crossing the thin line from slight prevarication to outright fib.

"Don't be silly," she replied, swatting away the apology. "I know something about what it's like to pastor a church."

The comment resurfaced another lost detail. Ellie Baxter had been married to the late Reverend Frederick Baxter, the founding pastor of the church Alex now led. Few in the congregation remembered the couple who had given so much to bring the fellowship into existence some forty years earlier. He vaguely recognized the eyes smiling toward him now. He had seen the same lively gleam in the photograph of three prior pastors and their wives hanging in Mrs. Mayhew's office.

"Of course," Alex replied gratefully. "Only I'm certain it was much harder in your husband's day."

"In some ways, I suppose," she answered. "But in other ways, nothing has changed."

"I hope you don't mind," Brandon said while inviting Alex to sit in the chair across from his aunt. "I took the liberty of ordering you the ravioli."

"Sounds good," Alex replied while taking a seat and looking toward Ellie compassionately. "I'm sorry about your treatment denial," he said. It had become a common sentiment when meeting with older members of Christ Community Church. "Brandon told me what happened."

"Oh, that." Her tone suggested a surprising disinterest. "I understand. They need to prioritize scarce medical resources."

Brandon appeared to seethe upon hearing the common mantra come from his aunt's lips.

"The reason I asked Brandon to arrange lunch," she continued, "was because I sensed the Lord wanted me to tell you something that I needed to say in person."

Alex had heard the same words on countless occasions in the past. Only this time it didn't raise his defenses. He knew that Ellie Baxter had not come to offer "constructive criticism" on his preaching style or to let him know that God wanted the church to go back to "good old fashioned rock tunes" instead of the more contemplative liturgical music that appealed to the younger crowd. Ellie Baxter, he knew, had something to say worth hearing.

"Please," he said. "Go on."

"I sense that the Lord wants me to tell you to stay the course."

He waited for the rest. Nothing came.

"Which course?" he asked.

She appeared confused by the question, as if she might need to check the status of her wireless connection. "Well," she answered, "I assume he means speaking out against the Youth Initiative."

The comment alarmed Alex. He *hadn't* spoken out against the Youth Initiative. Not in public, anyway. He hated it, sure, the way he hated cancer and hurricanes and traffic accidents. He considered it one more massive ricochet of shrapnel from Adam's and Eve's bites of the forbidden fruit. But not something he could change with mere words. His task was to affirm the goodness of God while comforting those afflicted by the harsh realities of a fallen world; or, in the words of his favorite seminary professor, to "shine a light instead of scream at the darkness."

"But," he stumbled, "I haven't said anything about political matters. In fact, the board has specifically cautioned me against doing so."

"Brandon has told me about conversations with the board," she interrupted. "And they're wrong."

Alex looked toward Brandon with concern. "Broad strokes," Brandon said while raising three Scout's-honor fingers. "No names or privileged information. I swear."

"Wrong about what?" Alex asked in Ellie's direction.

"About transition donations, for one thing."

Another glance toward Brandon.

"Don't look at me," he said defensively. "She heard Phil's announcement on Sunday."

Of course.

"Like I said," Ellie continued, "in some ways nothing has changed."

"What do you mean?" Alex asked.

"Let me ask you a question," she said as her answer. "Why didn't you make the announcement about Wayne Bentley's gift yourself?"

He sat in silence.

"Did you have knots in your stomach when that man celebrated Wayne's decision to volunteer?"

His gut tightened at the reminder. "Still do," he confessed.

She nodded in solidarity.

"How did you know?" he asked.

Ellic leaned toward Alex. "I know," she said sternly, "because that's exactly how my Frederick felt the entire year before he was asked to resign his pastorate."

Asked to resign? "But," Alex said, "I thought your husband retired on good terms with the church."

"Who told you that?" she asked.

He didn't know. "No one," he fumbled. "I just assumed."

"So did most of the members at the time," she explained. "Everything appeared to be going great on the surface. The church had grown from a small group of folks who could fit in our tiny living room to several thousand in weekly attendance. By 2007 we had launched a second campus, a third by 2012. I'm not sure how many people were coming by the time Frederick resigned, maybe seven or eight thousand."

"Actually, nine," Alex recalled. He remembered the number from an attendance chart the search committee had shown him, revealing rapid, expansive growth during the first decade of the church's history followed by a steady, gradual decline. It had reached the low point just before Alex arrived.

"So," Ellie was saying, "you can imagine why the board didn't want anyone to think Frederick had been pressured to leave."

"What happened?" Alex asked.

She sat back to receive a plate filled with steaming ravioli. "Thank you, young man," she said with a wink to the sixtysomething waiter.

Alex accepted Brandon's request that he say grace over the meal, then looked back at Ellie. She enjoyed a first taste of her lunch before finally responding to the pastor's question.

"We had a campus in downtown Denver that my husband launched in partnership with the homeless shelter. He raised enough money from our main campus folks to build a small chapel and a medical clinic where a few of our members who were doctors volunteered to help AIDS patients one day per week."

"A medical clinic?" Brandon said with surprise. "In a church?"

Alex was equally astonished. "What about the separation of church and state?" he asked.

"Neither of you are old enough to remember this, but medical treatment wasn't always considered the domain of the state. We couldn't pray in schools or place our hands on a Bible in court-rooms, but the church could still care for those without medical coverage."

A blank stare from both men. "Never mind that," she said as if feeling even older than she looked. "The point is, the church once provided medical services to hurting people in the city be-fore the incident."

"The incident?" asked Alex.

"That's what we called it. A member of our downtown congre-gation who got connected to the church through the homeless shelter approached Frederick after he finished his message one Wednesday evening." She paused. "The church hosted a mid-week Bible study. My husband tried to rotate into the teaching lineup at least once per month.

"Anyway," she continued. "This homeless man approached my husband as if he wanted to shake his hand or ask for prayer or something. But he instead walked right up to Fred-erick and spat in his face before calling him a pretty filthy name."

"Was the man drunk?" Alex asked, familiar with the rough re-alities of inner-city ministry.

"He might have been. But he was definitely angry."

"At something Uncle Fred said?" Brandon asked.

"At something he had done," she went on. "You see, it was the middle of a big brouhaha over whether the state should redefine marriage."

"Religious or civil?" Alex asked.

"That's just the thing," she explained. "We didn't distinguish the two back then. This was during a time when a religious marriage was the norm, or at least treated as every bit as legitimate as civil marriage."

Alex smiled at the thought of how much more satisfying it would have been to sign a license that described a couple as "husband and wife" rather than "legal domestic partners" or to live in a society that considered such unions a "covenant with God and each other" rather than a "nonbinding agreement of cooperation" on record with the state.

"What made that man so angry was that my husband signed a public affirmation. A network of pastors sent it to the governor asking him to defend their right to describe marriage as the union of one man and one woman."

Alex said nothing while considering the scene. How would he have reacted if asked to sign such a document? He agreed, certainly, that marriage was an institution ordained by God. But suggesting they restrict it to heterosexuals, while ideal, seemed almost naïve. Or worse, hateful.

"You can imagine what happened when the press got ahold of that story," Ellie continued. "'Homeless AIDS Patient Endures Hate Speech from Popular Pastor.' You wouldn't believe the vitriolic attacks that came against my Frederick after that incident."

"I'm sorry to hear that," Alex said, still trying to reconcile a man who would launch a medical clinic for AIDS patients while signing a public statement against gay marriage.

Ellie looked intently into Alex's eyes. "I think the Lord wanted me to tell you that story," she said as if suddenly remembering her point, "because you face a very similar danger."

"Danger?" he said. "What kind of danger?"

"My husband lost his ministry because he tried to affirm the sanctity of marriage." She paused as if trying to ignore a still-open, painful wound. "Offerings dipped after someone floated a ridiculous rumor that some of the money given for the AIDS clinic had found its way into Frederick's Christmas bonus. Young people stopped inviting people to our church, afraid their pastor might embarrass them by saying something homophobic." She shook her head in disbelief. "Frederick never said or did anything to hurt anyone in his life. But that didn't matter. He had the label."

"What label?"

"Hateful," she answered. "That's all it took for the board to disregard a decade of impact and quietly suggest he take a generous severance package. How did they put it? Oh, yes, 'So that both Frederick and the church can make a fresh start.'"

The trend lines returned to Alex's mind. Attendance and income had plummeted like a rock after Pastor Baxter's tenure. He wondered if Ellie and Frederick had endured a similar dip.

"How did you make out after that?" he asked.

"Frederick decided to leave the ministry to start a small business."

"Small?" Brandon interjected. "I'd hardly call FB Enterprises a small business!"

"I didn't say it stayed small."

"What's FB Enterprises?" Alex asked.

"A distributor of gluten-free snacks," she said modestly.

"The second largest distributor of gluten-free snacks west of the Mississippi!" Brandon added before turning to Alex. "He sold it for a boatload of cash about ten years back."

"Hush," Ellie said with a blush before feeling compelled to explain. "He got into the business just when it started to boom. We did quite well."

Brandon appeared suddenly angry. "That's why Freddy called to thank her."

"Now Brandon," Ellie said in gentle rebuke. "You don't know that."

"I do know it!"

"Freddy?" Alex asked when the conversation left him behind.

"Frederick Junior," Ellie explained. "Brandon thinks he arranged to have someone suggest I volunteer after learning my treatment had been denied."

"How else do you explain his sudden contact after…what… four months?"

The comment appeared to sting Ellie's maternal feelings. "Six," she said with embarrassment. "It had been six months since he last called."

"I'm telling you, Aunt Ellie, Freddy is up to something."

"You don't know that," she repeated.

The argument continued for a few minutes. It became clear that Brandon did not trust or like his cousin, who apparently lived on the West Coast with a partner who felt uncomfortable around the kind of religion embodied in the gentle, feminine soul sitting across from Alex now.

"May I pray for you?" the pastor felt compelled to ask, both to defuse Brandon's rising irritation and to bless a woman who had given him more than she knew.

"No," she said to Alex's surprise. No one had ever rejected the offer before.

"I beg your pardon?"

"I mean, yes, of course. But first I want to pray for you, if you don't mind." She reached over her partially eaten plate of food and touched Alex's hand. She began praying aloud before he could respond.

She thanked God for the young pastor's passion and asked him to protect Alex's beautiful wife and children.

She prayed that God would use her story to encourage Alex and to grant him the wisdom he would need to say what would need to be said in a manner that people could hear.

And she asked the Lord to open the eyes of the people of Christ Community Church to the reality of an enemy who wanted to disfigure and destroy God's image on earth.

Alex looked up from the prayer before Ellie had finished. He sensed this moment carried some mysterious importance, as if a mantle of divine grace was being passed and received. But what kind of grace?

The kind that enters the fray of a losing cause?

The kind that risks a family's livelihood to speak out against a system that, until this moment, Alex had considered well outside a simple pastor's scope?

Or, he hoped, the kind that shines a bright light in a darkening world?

"Amen," Ellie said with a slight squeeze of her pastor's hand.

"My turn," Alex said with a grateful wink in Ellie's direction. They bowed once again. "Father in heaven," he began, "thank you for sending Mrs. Baxter to me today. You know that I needed to hear what she has said. Thank you for her sensitivity to your leading, both now and during the years she and her husband gave of themselves to launch Christ Community Church. Please help me to not mess up the work you used them to begin…"

He stopped, suddenly aware that Ellie, too, needed a message from the Lord. He looked up and spoke her name.

She returned his gaze.

"Father, I know Ellie said the news of denied treatment didn't bother her. And I know that she wants to give her son the benefit of the doubt regarding his phone call."

She appeared both alarmed and touched by Alex's words.

"But I also know that she's feeling some anxiety and hurt."

Brandon looked up after realizing the prayer had become a conversation.

"Please give her your comfort and a peace that passes all understanding," he prayed.

The woman swallowed hard, then asked, "What should I say to my son?"

"Tell your son that your pastor told you all human life is sacred. And that yours, in particular, is precious."

A tear began forming in her eye as he continued.

"Tell him that volunteering isn't the act of a hero. It's the act of the deceived. Our enemy hates the image of God, which is exactly what you are."

"So I was right to refuse?" she asked, a single tear falling to the table.

"You were right to refuse," Alex said. "God is perfectly capable of taking you home when he's finished with you here."

He squeezed her hand gratefully.

"And I have a pretty good idea he's not done with you yet."

CHAPTER EIGHTEEN

Matthew continued staring at the back of his hand. It still ached. He didn't remember hitting it hard enough to bruise. The force of impact must have been buried in a pile of split-second clumsy decisions he had made during the brief moments afforded by the inhaler's magic mist. A burst of panicky strength helped him drag the deadweight woman from her bedroom to the tub. But it must also have drowned out whatever painful bumps and slams his body had endured.

"Another refill?"

Matthew looked toward the question to find a waitress dressed like a pro football cheerleader. He scanned her up and down. "What's your name?" he asked.

She rolled her eyes. "Sir," she said in a voice that sounded more like a chirpy girl's than a curvy woman's. "Can I get you another?"

Matthew must have seemed, to her eyes, a dirty old man hitting on a girl half his age. He blushed at the mistaken impression. He handed her his empty glass. "Yes, please," he said without thinking. He had planned to order something stronger. Perhaps a double scotch could calm his anxiety better than a second beer. But it was too late. The waitress had already scurried away, navigating her hips around a dozen half-empty tables back toward the bar.

He glanced up at the sea of flat-screen televisions to take his mind off the visual hiccups he hoped a few drinks might shake from his mind. But the images continued to flash in the same persistent sequence, as did the questions.

What if Brianna Jackson hadn't forgotten about her transition appointment?

What if she'd never made it?

Get a grip! He told himself again.

But no matter how much he argued with himself he couldn't shake the feeling he had done something wrong. Possibly even illegal. Why else would Serena Winthrop insist he use a fake name and a password-protected message box? Weren't transition requests part of the public record to protect volunteers from fraud?

"I've done nothing wrong!" he heard himself whisper. Even if he *had* bent a few laws, they were in the same category as those about double-parking or jaywalking. Certainly nothing that could get him into real trouble. After all, he had only done what thousands of transition specialists across the nation do every day. Just because he didn't have a sterilized room or slick brochure like the clinic his mother had used didn't make his actions any less respectable.

He had provided an essential service to the public good. And, he nearly believed, to Brianna Jackson. She was obviously too disoriented to think clearly. It had been Matthew's job, his moral obligation, to think for her. Just as it had been his job to think for his mother.

Brianna Jackson had been every bit as heroic as any other volunteer. So had his mother. Reluctance is not cowardice. Fear of dying and the will to live are deeply rooted impulses that were no longer useful to those in such a dilapidated condition. Perhaps Brianna had agreed to the procedure in a moment of weakness, caving to the subtle pressures to choose a nobler path. All the more reason Matthew needed to lend her his own courage, his own clarity of mind.

We decay. He still believed it. Rejecting the reality of God didn't require abandoning his mentor's entire point of view. Manichean philosophy had brought Matthew to the dance. And he would continue relying on its central tenet to combat irrational fear and unhelpful remorse.

Matthew had helped free his mother and his client from the prisons of deteriorating bodies. That had to be a good thing. A gift.

The jolt of recollection interrupted Matthew's train of thought as he remembered an unfinished item from the day's assignment. He tapped the screen sitting on the table. Up popped his private account, displaying two new messages. He read the first.

FROM: TRANSITION DISPOSAL SERVICES
RE: REMOVAL CONFIRMED

The time marker told him the body had been removed five hours after Matthew had sent the request. A sigh of relief came. Not just because Serena Winthrop had released payment for his first successfully completed assignment. But also at the reminder that his had been just one step in an overall process. The irrational fear subsided. Of course Ms. Jackson had scheduled the appointment. Why would Serena Winthrop, or anyone else for that matter, make up such a thing? He had done his job. Nothing more. Nothing less.

The cheerleader reappeared to place his refill on the table.

She said nothing, probably eager to slip away before Matthew could badger her further for her name.

"Thank you, miss," he said to her fleeing back.

He glanced into the glass mug, suddenly less thirsty.

Another mug settled onto the table. "Mind if I join you?"

He looked up. It was the man he had met a few days before in the same sports bar.

"Matthew Adams, right?"

"Good memory," Matthew replied. "Um, Morris?"

He gave Matthew a manly slap on the back. "Pretty close!" he said. "Mori."

"That's right, Mori. Short for...don't tell me...something Quincy."

"I'm impressed," the man said. "Bryan. Bryan Quincy. Not as easy to recall as Matthew Adams."

"Why is my name so easy to recall?" Matthew asked nervously while rubbing his bruised hand.

"Two firsts."

Matthew didn't follow.

"The first Gospel and the first man."

"First Gospel?"

"I forgot," Mori said with a laugh, "you don't read much."

"I read all the time."

"Not enough to recognize the first book of the New Testament."

The reference finally connected for Matthew. "Of course," he said with some embarrassment, "the first Gospel in the Bible."

"There you go," Mori said like a proud teacher.

Both strangers lifted a glass to seal the reunion.

"So," Mori said after swallowing, "did you complete your first assignment?"

Matthew's head darted anxiously toward the inquest. "What did you say?"

"Dostoyevsky. How's it coming?"

Matthew laughed nervously. "Oh, yeah." He tried to recall details. So much had happened since he had taste-tested the massive volume.

"What'd you think?" Mori pressed, as if trying to expose a lazy student's bluff.

"Like you said, it made me cringe."

Mori nodded knowingly. "But it made you want to read the rest, didn't it?"

Matthew said nothing while the man nodded in agreement with himself.

"I don't think you ever told me," Mori re-launched after swallowing a sip from his mug, "what is it you do for a living?"

He thought for a moment. "Sales."

"Sales? No kidding?"

"Why would I kid about working in sales?"

"You wouldn't, I suppose. I just never would have pegged you as a salesman. But then, I guess there's a bit of selling in every job."

"Even teaching?"

"Especially teaching! Every lecture I give is a sales pitch for something."

"Like what?" Matthew asked as if taking offense on the man's behalf.

"In a perfect world I'd be selling them on noble ideas."

"Of course," Matthew said.

"But in the real world I have less lofty ambitions."

"Such as?"

"Such as getting them to pause their gaming and social networking addictions long enough to read an actual book."

They both smiled at the truth of it.

"How about you?" Mori asked. "What does a former philosophy major end up selling?"

"I work with the transition industry," Matthew said with a hint of self-importance that was quickly dashed by Mori's burst of laughter.

"What's so funny?" he demanded.

"Forgive me," the man said while suppressing a few more chuckles. "I guess it was the timing."

"Timing of what?"

"I asked you what a philosophy student ends up selling." He paused to snigger. "And you say transitions."

Another burst of laughter.

Matthew clearly didn't get the joke.

"Don't you see?" Mori asked after taking a recovering breath. "Nietzsche taught the futility of life. Now Adams sells the merits of suicide."

Matthew winced at the jest. "Most people understand the difference between suicide and volunteering," he said crossly.

"Whoa," Mori said while lifting his hands in surrender. "Don't shoot. I didn't mean any offense. I just got tickled, that's all. Trust me, I'm a big fan."

"A fan of what?"

"The Youth Initiative. Thomas Malthus. Paul Ehrlich. Decrease the surplus population and all that." Mori lifted his glass as if offering a toast. "More power to them, and to you. It's guys like you who will dig us out of this economic ditch."

Matthew calmed himself, then offered a flimsy smile. "Well," he said, "I guess I'm a bit sensitive. I take my job pretty seriously."

"As well you should," Mori said. "And I'd be sensitive, too, if I had a bunch of religious nuts calling me a murderer." He thought for a moment. "But the way I see it, you're like a Boy Scout helping little old ladies. Only instead of escorting them across the street, you help them cross the threshold."

Matthew tried to discern whether the comparison was a compliment or another joke.

"In fact," Mori continued, "you would have loved the discussion I had with my students a few weeks back." He paused to wake his tablet. "I assigned them to read part one of *Crime and Punishment*."

"By Dostoyevsky?"

Mori appeared surprised. "You've read it?"

"No. But you mentioned it when you suggested I read *The Brothers Karamazov*."

"Oh, right, I forgot." He continued flipping pages in search of something. "Anyway, we were discussing one of the scenes when a student pointed out something I hadn't noticed before. Ah, here it is," he said while glancing toward Matthew as if confirming his student's attention. "This part happens just before Raskolnikov kills the old lady."

Matthew's eyes widened. He knew the novel had something to do with a crime. The title had told him as much. He now realized it involved killing an old woman. Just a coincidence, he wondered, or a sign? And if a sign, of what? And from whom?

"Oh, sorry," Mori said. "I've spoiled the plot for you."

Matthew shrugged.

"No matter," the teacher shouted while slapping his new protégé on the arm. "You probably weren't gonna read it anyway, just like my students."

He ignored Matthew's sheepish grin while transforming himself from lonely barfly to community college professor eager to enlighten anyone who would listen on the brilliance of the Russian master.

"Dostoyevsky gives the perfect rationale for the Youth Initiative."

"Really?" Matthew said curiously.

"You bet. In this scene a philosophy student argues why it would be more noble to kill the old woman than to let her live.

Here," he said while handing the tablet to Matthew. "Read for yourself."

Matthew flashed a puzzled expression. "What, you mean here? Now?"

"Of course," Mori said, pointing to the location on the screen. Matthew started reading aloud.

"Listen, I want to ask you a serious question," the student said hotly. "I was only joking of course, but look here; on one side we have a stupid, senseless, worthless, spiteful, ailing, horrid old woman who has not an idea what she is living for herself, and who will die in a day or two in any case. On the other side, fresh young lives thrown away for want of help and by thousands, on every side!"

Matthew looked up anxiously from the page toward his tutor. Why would he have chosen *this* paragraph from all the possible passages in all the possible scenes in all the possible novels ever written?

"Uncanny, isn't it? Mori said with a wink. "Almost like Dostoyevsky is speaking to us from the grave."

Matthew nodded quietly.

"Go on," the teacher urged. "It gets even better."

"A hundred thousand good deeds could be done and helped, on that old woman's money which will be buried in a monastery!"

Matthew's reading stumbled. He didn't follow. It must have showed.

"The old woman was going to leave her money to the church," Mori explained. "Keep reading. Now it gets really good."

"Hundreds, thousands perhaps, might be set on the right path; dozens of families saved from destitution, from ruin, from vice—and all with her money. Kill her, take her money and with the help of it devote oneself to the service of humanity and the good of all. What do you think, would not one tiny crime be wiped out by thousands of good deeds? For one life thousands would be saved from corruption and decay. One death, and a hundred lives in exchange—it's simple arithmetic! Besides, what value has the life of that sickly, stupid, ill-natured old woman in the balance of existence?"

He stopped. The words dripped with callous cruelty, the heartless philosophy of an envious man. But strangely, they also brought a mysterious sense of relief, as if the writer had anticipated Matthew's eyes reading them on this of all days.

"See what I mean?" Mori prodded, eager for his student to connect the dots. "It's like a more honest and direct version of one of President Lowman's flowery speeches. Only instead of all the fluff about heroic self-sacrifice and economic incentives he goes right to the heart of the matter."

"Which is?" Matthew asked hesitantly.

"Which is that we've got a bunch of selfish debits hoarding too many of the assets in this nation that could go to younger, worthwhile chaps like you!"

Matthew said nothing, at once buoyed and ashamed.

"So anyway," Mori added, "the protagonist, Raskolnikov, goes ahead and does the deed. He kills the old woman to get her money. But then there's a twist."

Matthew waited for more.

"Oh, no," Mori said, resisting the urge to continue. "I'm not about to tell you the whole tale. Read the rest for yourself. And not one of those micro-book recaps. The whole thing. Deal?"

Matthew nodded. "Deal."

"Dostoyevsky was way ahead of his time," Mori said while grabbing his mug for a post-lecture guzzle.

"Do you think he would have approved of the transition industry?" Matthew asked.

The professor peered over the rim of his tilting mug to indicate he was still listening, then plopped it back onto the table before wiping his mouth on his sleeve. "Who knows?"

"But you just said—"

"I said he was ahead of *his* time," Mori interrupted. "Not that he would agree with *ours*."

Matthew missed the distinction, prompting a frown from his self-appointed guru.

"Look," Mori said, "Dostoyevsky was part of the Russian Orthodox Church." He stopped, as if the comment had been enough.

"So he was religious?"

"It was the nineteenth century, for Pete's sake! Everybody was religious." He sighed at Matthew's expression before explaining the obvious. "Point being, I don't know what he'd have believed had he had a proper education. But I'd like to think he would agree with Ivan Karamazov." The professor cleared his throat for dramatic emphasis. "If there is no God, then all things are permissible."

Matthew waited while his mind absorbed the statement. "That makes sense, I guess," he said submissively.

"You guess? What other option is there?"

"Well," Matthew began, finally feeling the conversation shift to his own turf. "I think it's possible to be a good person without believing in God. I mean, I'm pretty sure I no longer believe in God. But I still try to do what's right."

"*I guess. Pretty sure.* What are you, Matthew Adams, a man or a Ping-Pong ball?"

Matthew chuckled at himself. "I guess I deserved that."

"I *know* I don't believe in a God," the professor announced. "So no one has the right to condemn my choices. Or anyone's for that matter. Like Ivan said, everything is permissible."

"Even murder?"

The question gave the professor pause. "I don't use that word. It carries judgment."

"Would you kill someone, then?"

"Depends."

"On what?"

"On simple arithmetic. If the death of one person can benefit many others, well, why not? Religious people, including Dostoyevsky, would call that murder."

"What do you call it?"

"Like I said, I'm not religious."

Mori appeared at ease with his viewpoint, as if its raw honesty gave it a sort of virtue. He affirmed simple ideals that were unencumbered by the thorny complexities and moral quandaries Matthew's own patchwork of beliefs had created.

Does God exist? If yes, life includes obligations and, probably, consequences. If no, then run the numbers and do what needs to be done. What *ought* to be done.

"Besides," he recalled from the scene Matthew had just read, "what value has the life of that sickly, stupid, ill-natured old woman in the balance of existence?"

"Makes sense, I guess."

"Again with the guessing?" Mori chided. "You should become a weatherman or an economist."

Matthew smiled. "Not I guess. It definitely makes sense."

The declaration felt right. Not because the man had made a convincing argument but because Matthew had made a necessary choice.

"Don't let the moralists get to you, Matthew Adams," Mori said. "Take pride in what you do."

Matthew accepted the affirmation with a grateful nod.

The conversation drifted into less lofty territory more fitting for guys in a sports bar, mindless chatter about the Rockies' chances at the pennant and whether Franklin had the Republican nomination locked. None of it was interesting enough for Matthew to accept Mori's offer of another round of drinks.

"Not for me, thanks," Matthew announced. "I'd better hit the road."

So he did, but not before tapping the screen to pay his tab. That's when he noticed the bouncing icon in the lower right corner, the second message he had never read.

FROM: SERENA WINTHROP, NEXT INC.
RE: ALL IN ORDER. PAYMENT IS ON THE WAY.

Matthew felt himself smile at the notification of a job well done.

CHAPTER NINETEEN

Julia quickened her pace to catch up with a euphoric Paul Daugherty as he hurried toward what he called the Launch Room.

"Not the *lunch*room," he explained. "The *Launch* Room."

"As in launching big ideas?" she guessed.

"Bingo!" he confirmed with a wink.

She had arrived, as promised, a few minutes before the brainstorm meeting that, she quickly learned, had started early.

"Genius doesn't keep a schedule," he explained before urging her to follow.

The editor turned entrepreneur paused outside the glass-walled room where a team of soldiers armed the first missile in his moneymaking arsenal, nearly all of them quite attractive soldiers. No surprise. Paul Daugherty had always insisted his employees possess two qualities: looks and talent, in that order.

He pointed toward the front of the room, where a manicured young man appeared to be leading the discussion. "He goes by Lancelot," Paul explained. "His real name is Lance Nordeman."

He paused dramatically as if Julia should recognize the name. She didn't.

"As in Carnes and Nordeman, the big Madison Avenue firm." Neither name meant anything to her. "Wow!" she bluffed.

"I know, right?" Paul said proudly. "Lancelot is the co-founder's son."

"Looks young," Julia observed. "What is he, twenty-five?"

"Twenty-three. Not much experience, but I'm betting he inherited his mother's creativity along with her beauty!" He chortled like a naughty child.

"Is Lance your creative director?"

"Lancelot," Paul corrected sternly. "He insists. And yes, he is. But Monica is the project leader."

Julia looked at the other faces in the room. "Monica Garcia?" Julia asked in disbelief. "You hired Monica Garcia?"

He smiled sheepishly. "The old gang together again!"

Julia stiffened. She had no interest in working alongside the woman who had once taken her job, not because she had a speck of talent, but because she had great legs. The woman who had "coauthored" a feature that had nearly destroyed Kevin Tolbert's reputation and happy home.

"Come on, Jewel!" Paul said playfully. "Water under the bridge. It's a new day. She'll behave, I promise."

Julia eyed Paul crossly.

"Please, Jewel, give it a chance. Monica has great instincts in the Launch Room."

Not to mention the bedroom, Julia thought to herself.

"Here we go," Paul said while opening the door.

She reminded herself of what she and Troy had discussed. Paul thought he was hiring Julia Davidson, the award-winning columnist who personified anti-breeder and pro-transition spin. He wasn't expecting the woman who had suddenly found religion and, worse, gotten married.

"Not just married," Julia had added. "But married to Kevin Tolbert's best friend, a man charging the evil Youth Initiative empire with a water pistol!"

She and Troy had shared a laugh before Julia pulled out of the driveway toward her top-secret assignment: undercover reporter investigating what she assumed had to be a crooked deal. Paul must have called in favors or, perhaps, blackmailed someone to win the contract. Her job, she reminded herself while entering the room, was to find whatever dirty little secret Paul had wrapped within the respectable veneer of a plush office suite.

"Everyone," Paul announced with his usual flair, "I'd like to introduce the newest member of Daugherty and Associates, the legendary Julia Davidson."

Five of the six people in the room joined Paul in offering a smattering of obligatory applause.

"As most of you know, I think the world of Julia. She and I go way back. You won't find anyone who knows how to connect better with our core audience."

"There, you see!" said a thirtyish man with a long, dark beard resting comfortably on his massive trunk. "He *does* have a target demographic in mind."

"I never said he didn't have one," Monica Garcia countered while sending an awkward, false, *lovely to see you again* wave in Julia's direction. "What I said," she continued, "is that it was evolving."

"We've been over this already."

Julia glanced toward the digital board, where the noble knight of Camelot stood trying to facilitate some sort of Round Table consensus. He looked toward Paul.

"Say it again."

Paul hesitated. "Say what again?"

"The target demo."

Silence.

"The center of the creative bull's-eye," Lancelot said while rolling exasperated eyes.

"Oh, right," Paul said clumsily, finally grasping the lingo.

"We have several targets—"

"See!" Blackbeard said.

"—but," Paul continued, "we want to speak most directly to fiftyish women who lean left."

"Exactly what I said!" Monica crossed her legs with self-satisfied emphasis, Lancelot's eyes following earnestly before he turned them toward Julia. She felt his gaze examining the merchandise while he flashed a licentious grin.

"How?" he asked in Paul's direction.

"How what?"

"How is the famous Julia Davidson supposed to reach our market? She is clearly too young to relate to fiftyish women." He winked in her direction as if to flirt. Julia took it otherwise.

"Well," she began while recalling the project summary Paul had sent. "If the goal is to recruit more seniors to volunteer, your best bet is to convince the person closest to them. The person likely managing their medications and trying to pay their escalating bills."

Paul smiled and took a step backward to give Julia the stage.

"That person," Julia continued, "is most likely a daughter who, up until now, has been reluctant to suggest the option to the mother who breast-fed her or the dad who still calls her sweetheart."

She paused. All eyes were fixed on to the newcomer who, she had made clear, hadn't been hired for her looks alone.

"Exactly!" Paul shouted. "Just the way I would have said it!"

"So would anyone who read the executive briefing," Lancelot said as if irked. Creative directors don't accept the final word. They give it.

Monica and the nubile blonde sitting beside Blackbeard both squirmed in their seats.

Julia and Paul slipped into open seats at the table while Lancelot refocused the team's attention on the question they had been tackling before the interruption.

"Let's keep going," he said. "We need at least a dozen more ideas before we break for lunch."

Julia pulled out her tablet to capture an image of the board on which earlier ideas had been posted. She tried to mentally fill in details behind four sketchy notes.

HEROIC CHOICE: They must have restated the existing mantra. To volunteer is to be heroic, part of the solution rather than the problem.

LASTING LEGACY: Possibly a reference to President Lowman's original argument that aging and disabled citizens would welcome the opportunity to leave an economic legacy to the next generation rather than become a burden.

DEBIT DEBT: This one included a parenthetical note: "Needs positive spin." But the suggestion, Julia imagined, had been anything but positive. Kevin had told Troy about Senator Franklin's idea to publicize the portion of the mounting national deficit linked to caring for seniors and the disabled. Insiders called it "debit debt" because the old and sick lose value. They are like depreciating assets rather than long-term investments.

FOR THE KIDS: Another familiar angle. Julia had used it herself in a column back when the president first floated the Youth Initiative concept. "What better way to show your love," she had parroted, "than to reallocate assets to your grandchildren rather than prolong the inevitable?" The memory filled her with shame. How many vulnerable readers had she nudged toward death through such careless prose?

"So far," Lancelot said while reviewing the same list of brainstorm droppings, "all we've got is overused clichés. We need something original!"

"I was thinking about beer ads," Blackbeard offered. "You know, spicy gals hanging all over beefy guys."

Monica rolled her eyes at the obvious jest while the blonde added her two cents. "Yeah. Sex sells!"

Paul chuckled at the thought. "I can see it now," he piled on, "geriatric geezers and cripples sipping the good life."

"Right!" Blackbeard bellowed. "Only instead of swigging bottles of beer we could show them injecting yellow toxins!"

The room exploded with laughter. Even the stern-faced Monica appeared to enjoy the moment. Julia smiled awkwardly in reaction to Paul's playful pat on the arm. She needed to play along despite a sudden mild nausea.

Lancelot retook control, tapping three fingers on the digital board before using his index finger to capture the suggestion. "Like I said, at this stage of the process there are no bad ideas."

He wrote two words, BEER PARTY.

The process had its intended effect. For the next several minutes ideas flowed, some of them silly, others deathly serious. None of them, Julia realized, touching upon the fundamental challenge advocates of the Youth Initiative faced. Given the choice, most people preferred to go on living. Studies had shown that a high percentage of the early recruits had been mentally ill or severely depressed. No matter how slick the marketing campaign, sane and sound people would not volunteer in anywhere close to the numbers recorded in the early days of the initiative.

Or would they? She recalled reading Antonio Santos's journals. He had been perfectly sane: a pretty optimistic outlook on life despite everything, a mother and brother who loved and cared for him. And yet he decided to choose death. He actually believed the rhetoric about heroic self-sacrifice. And he hated being on the debit side of the ledger. How had he said it? "I may be worthless, but I have my pride."

She felt a swell of anger at the playful banter occurring around her. At the risk of blowing her cover, Julia felt an irresistible urge to call attention to the insanity.

"Why not virgins?" she asked caustically.

Every eye stared blankly in her direction.

"I don't get it," Blackbeard finally said after straining to find the joke.

"Me, neither," said the blonde.

Julia bit her tongue at the realization that she had accidentally voiced her sarcasm.

"Ms. Davidson?" Lancelot prodded.

She looked around the room sheepishly, then decided to take the gamble. "I was thinking about what motivated the old suicide bombers in places like Palestine, Iraq, and Afghanistan," she explained.

The blank stares remained fixed in her direction.

"Think about it for a second," she continued mockingly. "How did leaders in those days motivate men, women, and children to strap on explosive vests to become human bombs?"

No reply.

"By offering them something better in the next life," she added. "Kill the infidels and earn a harem filled with virgins."

"Ah," Paul said, indicating he finally understood.

"Go back even further," Julia continued. "The emperor of Japan convinced pilots to crash themselves into targets. Again, human bombs."

Paul leaned slightly forward in his chair. "Listen, Jewel," he said, "I think you're taking my Launch Room analogy a bit too far. We aren't talking about recruiting suicide bombers or kamikaze pilots. We're trying to increase the number of old people volunteering to—"

"Wait," Blackbeard interrupted. "I think she's onto something."

Julia waited for a punch line that didn't come. She glanced toward the bearded man who, to her horror, looked serious. He must have misread her sarcasm. Rather than grasp the obvious parallel to manipulating people toward insanity, he appeared eager to use the examples as a springboard.

Blackbeard continued. "How would it look if we leveraged the power of religious belief to motivate volunteers?"

"Like promising rewards in the afterlife?" asked Paul.

"No go," Lancelot interjected while making a time-out sign with his hands. "This is a government-funded campaign."

"I don't mean literal religion," Blackbeard said, "just the idea of something better." He looked up while closing his eyes, as if entering his brilliance space in search of the right words. He started spouting off a sequence of possibilities. "Something more. Something greater. A better tomorrow…" He opened his eyes. "Come on, everyone, help me out here."

Different voices added creative dominos to the brainstorm while Lancelot rushed back toward the board to capture anything useful.

"A better place."

"No place like home."

"Where no one has gone before."

"Hold on," Lancelot said with a snap of his fingers. "Go back."

He scribbled on the board.

Paul read the solitary word aloud. "Home?"

Lancelot tapped his index finger against it and asked, "What can we do with this?"

The room fell silently into a moment of collective contemplation. Julia tried to think of a razor-sharp quip or caustic jab, anything to distract the group from whatever wicked stew they were cooking up in their minds.

"I've got it," said Monica. "'Going home.'"

While Lancelot began writing the phrase on the board, Paul leaned farther forward in his chair. "I like it," he said. "I like it a lot."

"Me, too," said Blackbeard. "It evokes a sense of comfort, sort of like heaven but without the religious overtones."

"I hadn't even thought of that," Monica replied. "I was thinking of the in-home transition process Congress recently approved. The idea of going to a clinic gives people the creeps. Doing it at home feels much more, more..."

"Peaceful," Paul said, completing Monica's thought.

"Right. Peaceful."

Lancelot drew everyone's attention back to the digital board, where he had been writing feverishly. "How about this?" he asked, pointing to the potential slogan.

GO HOME TO A MORE PEACEFUL TRANSITION

"Close," Paul said, standing and approaching the board. He replaced the final word. "There. That's more like it."

Julia read the final version with dismay.

GO HOME TO A MORE PEACEFUL PASSING

"Perfect!" Blackbeard announced, voicing the clear consensus of the group.

Paul looked in Julia's direction with a wink.

"Terrific work, Jewel," he said. "Absolutely terrific!"

CHAPTER TWENTY

Matthew pulled the damp sheets from his bed and placed them in a bundle on the floor. Then he felt the pillowcase. Soaked with perspiration. Even worse than last time. When was that, a week ago? No, three days earlier. The nightmares had become more frequent and more real.

Drifting away from the shadowy form of a man.

Sinking beneath the surface.

A hideous laughter prompting a frantic effort to resurface.

Then, just before losing all hope, envisioning a way to thwart his own demise. Or at least delay it. Drowning panic became dreadful resolve. He could offer others in his place.

And now, something new. Something darker. In prior dreams the vague "others" had been murky phantoms flailing their arms and legs near the surface, nameless ghosts he could offer as substitutes for himself. But this time they had faces. And the faces appeared asymmetrical, a bit like religious icons he had seen of Jesus or the Virgin Mary. Only they weren't the faces of saviors or saints. They were the faces of Matthew's first three transition clients: Brianna Jackson, his befuddled first, followed by Saul Weinstein and Josephine Green.

Tossing the wet pillowcase onto the pile, Matthew tried to shake the images. The nightmares would pass, he told himself. After all, he wasn't the only person on the planet providing transition assistance. He just needed to give it more time. Three clients was only the beginning of what Ms. Winthrop had promised would prove to be a lucrative career in a growth industry. He believed it based upon the first three commissions already earning interest in his bank account.

Brianna Jackson, the befuddled junk collector, had been worth more than her pigpen of a home had suggested. Based upon the amount deposited into his account, 3 percent of Ms. Jackson's total estate, Matthew figured her brother Blake must have done quite well.

Matthew's second and third clients had had even larger estates, all contributing to the highest balance he had seen in his savings account since before the dark days. Matthew was finally getting back on his feet. He shouldn't let a few silly dreams ruin a good thing.

But he knew they weren't silly. They carried a message. Perhaps even a warning. Of what? He could only guess.

Was God trying to say something? *Don't be ridiculous!* Matthew scolded himself. He no longer believed in God. And even if he did admit a faint inkling of possibility, Matthew had no intention of listening to the one who had ruined his life.

What about the devil? A sadistic, bellowing laughter in the dream had curdled Matthew's blood like that of a trapped fly sensing a thirsty spider's approach. "Satan wants to devour your soul," he had learned in catechism class. Fortunately Matthew no longer believed in such a person.

Perhaps his subconscious mind was trying to purge scenes it

had been forced to endure. After all, Matthew had only ever seen one dead body in his life before taking this job.

Then he remembered. There had been four faces, not three. Janet Adams, Matthew's mother, had been the first. Her eyes had held the same gaze of hesitant trust he recalled from the waiting room at Aspen House Transition Services two years back. Moments before her disappearance into the watery darkness he had recognized a look of betrayal, then terror, on her descending face.

Matthew's pulse quickened from a fear deeper than the one that had drenched his bed. Could the message have come from his mother? Had she haunted his bedroom as Marley had haunted Scrooge? Was she saying now what she hadn't been able to say then?

I was afraid.

I didn't want to die.

He remembered the question he had posed to Professor Vincent shortly before his mom's transition. "Do you consider it suicide if someone volunteers to transition?"

Matthew had been trying to determine whether helping his mother to transition would cause her to commit a mortal sin. He had had enough religious education to know suicide carried some pretty stiff penalties in the afterlife.

"Remember, Mr. Adams," the professor had said, "there's no such thing as a mortal sin. Just hard choices."

He sensed a different answer ricochet from his mother's terror-stricken gaze.

You sent me to hell!

"No!" Matthew shouted.

If a good God like the one Father Tomberlin described did exist, he certainly wouldn't send a woman suffering from dementia to hell just because she had put an end to her miserable existence.

But deep down Matthew knew what he had refused to let himself believe. His mother hadn't made the choice. Not really. Sure, she had technically approved the procedure. The decision, however, had been his.

Another thought invaded. What if the fear in his mother's eyes had not been about her own demise, but about Matthew's fate?

"Nonsense!" he said. Helping one's aging mother with "hard choices" was part of a son's role. She hadn't been able to make such a decision on her own. She needed his help. And his courage.

The other faces came to mind. They, too, had needed his help. His courage.

You killed me, Son.

"No!" Even if he had nudged her toward volunteering he had done nothing illegal or, he told himself, immoral. He had simply freed her to thrive outside the prison of a decaying body.

Volunteers deserved honor, not eternal damnation. And those who helped them transition should be celebrated, not haunted. That's what he believed. And that's what he would tell whatever God, devil, or ghostly aberration was behind his nightmare.

So why, he wondered, did he still feel a rising sense of dread?

CHAPTER TWENTY-ONE

Alex sat up with a start. He hadn't noticed Mrs. Mayhew's approach.

"I'm sorry," he said while moving the tablet away from her snooping gaze. "Did you say something?"

She frowned. "Must be pretty interesting. I knocked twice."

More like infuriating, he thought. An updated summary from Phil Crawford explained that three more families had decided to make Christ Community Church a transition beneficiary.

"What is it, Mrs. Mayhew?" Alex asked, eyes tightly closed. He hoped it was nothing that required mental engagement.

"Your appointment."

"Appointment?"

"The one I made for you this morning."

"You didn't tell me about any…" He stopped. "Let me guess, you put a note on my door."

"I did," she said with a self-satisfied grin.

He tapped an icon on his tablet to find an empty calendar. "But you didn't enter it into my schedule?"

"I didn't," she said just as proudly.

He pressed his eyes shut again. "May I ask why?"

"Because you told me to stick a note on your door whenever I scheduled a last-minute appointment."

"Yes. In addition to placing it on my calendar, put a note on the door."

She rolled her eyes. "That'd be redundant."

"When did you make the appointment?"

"An hour ago."

"I've been in my office for two."

She smiled vacantly, clearly missing the point.

"Never mind," he said. "Who am I seeing?"

"That young man who came before. Frank." She began to whisper. "If you ask me, he looks like he needs one of those mood enhancement implants, the kind they gave my sister-in-law. Made a world of difference in her general demeanor and—"

"Thank you, Mrs. Mayhew," Alex interrupted. "Please send him in."

She remained a moment longer, grabbing a pen and piece of scratch paper from Alex's desk.

"Mrs. Mayhew," he said.

She finished her scribbling. "Send him here," she said, handing him the scrap of paper. It had a clinic name written on it. "It'll do him a world of good."

Alex accepted the note while forcing a smile of gratitude.

———

"I'm glad to see you again, Frank," the pastor said after inviting his guest to sit. "Although a bit surprised."

The man shifted nervously in the chair. "Listen," he said. "About last time, I shouldn't have left so abruptly. I apologize."

"Accepted," Alex replied with a wink. "So, what brings you back?"

The man leaned slowly forward. Alex matched his guest's posture. Their eyes met.

Something had changed in the week since he'd last seen the man. He appeared more haggard, as if he hadn't eaten or slept.

Frank finally spoke. "I came here because I don't have anyone else I can talk to about spiritual stuff."

"Spiritual stuff?"

"Sorry," he said. "I don't mean any disrespect. It's just that, well, I used to talk to my mother's priest. But he's no longer an option."

"So you were Catholic?"

A single nod.

"What happened?"

Frank sat upright again. "I don't know. I guess I outgrew it or something."

"I see."

"Anyway, I can't talk to him anymore."

"So you came to me."

Another nod. Then silence.

"I'm listening," Alex prodded.

The man glanced to each side of the room as if to confirm privacy. "Do you remember when I told you I had been having nightmares?"

"I do."

"They've become worse," Frank continued. "Darker."

"I seem to recall you saying that you couldn't recall details from the dream," said Alex. "Just the fear and anger."

"That's why I wanted to talk to you. They've suddenly become more vivid. And they stay with me."

"Do you want to tell me about them?"

Frank slowly shook his head. There was fear in his eyes, and in his voice. "I don't think I should do that."

"But you said you wanted to talk about—"

"I want to ask some questions," Frank interrupted. "Like I said, about spiritual stuff."

"That's fine," Alex said, somewhat puzzled. "What do you want to know?"

"What can you tell me about icons?"

The question surprised Alex. "I know a little. We don't use them at Christ Community, but they're pretty common in certain Christian traditions. Why do you ask?"

Frank hesitated as if wrestling with how much detail to share. Then he glanced around the room. His eyes landed on an image. He pointed. "I saw something like that."

Alex's eyes tracked the man's finger until he spotted the book cover. "You saw Mary holding baby Jesus?"

"Not the actual image," he said. "But I saw faces in that same style."

Alex stood and approached the bookshelf. He picked up the large volume that had been a seminary graduation gift. "This is a book filled with Byzantine iconography," Alex explained.

The man waited for more.

"Byzantine icons were characterized by vivid colors," Alex continued while handing the book to his troubled guest. "Take a look."

He did, flipping quickly from page to page. "Why are they like this?" he asked.

"Like what?"

"I don't know how to describe it. Unnatural? Off-kilter?"

"Oh, you mean disproportionate?"

He nodded while continuing to turn pages.

"Eastern icons like these give you the feeling the person depicted is floating." Alex pointed to the jawline of a saint on the opened page. "And you'll notice they made the facial features longer than what we see in the present world."

"Why is that?" asked Frank.

"As I understand it, to create the impression we're peering into the unseen realm. Pagan religions made idols that people worshipped as false gods on earth. Christians, in contrast, made icons to depict angels and saints who worship the one true God in heaven."

Alex sensed Frank harden. "What is it?" he asked.

Frank closed the book and handed it back. "Nothing."

"Something from your dream?"

"No," he sighed. "Well, maybe."

"Frank, everything you say will be held in strict confidence."

He considered the offer.

"The faces I saw," he began. "They looked like the faces in that book."

"Do you mean the vivid colors?"

Frank shook his head.

"The floating sensation?"

He nodded. "And the disproportion."

"I see," said Alex. He offered the book again. "Which faces?"

"None of those."

"People you know?" asked Alex.

Frank hardened again. "I...I couldn't say." He began rubbing his hand.

Alex noticed the dark welt. "What happened there?"

The man quickly covered the bruise. "Just a clumsy accident."

The pastor waited while his guest tried to decide how much to say about whatever had been preventing sleep and stealing his appetite. Alex finally spoke out of compassion for a troubled soul. "You look tortured."

Frank appeared momentarily embarrassed, as if a weakness had been exposed. "I'm fine," he said firmly.

"Then why are you here?"

Frank's brow furrowed. "Let's say God did exist. How would you know he's good instead of evil?"

Alex smiled. "Well, your question, for starters."

A blank expression.

"You wouldn't ask that question," Alex continued, "unless you had a deep sense that there is such a thing as good and evil. You expect God to be good, right?"

"Don't you?"

"Of course. That's why evil makes me angry."

"Angry at God?" Frank asked.

"No. He hates evil more than I do."

"Then why does he allow it?"

"That's the first question I plan to ask him when we meet," Alex said with a smile. "But in the meantime, I know that something is wrong in our world. Something only a good God can fix."

A brief delay before Frank spoke again.

"I met this guy last week, a college professor named Mori. An atheist."

"A philosophy professor?" asked the pastor.

"Literature."

"I see."

"Anyway, he showed me a scene from this book called *Crime and Punishment*."

"Must have been the same guy who had you read *The Brothers Karamazov*."

Frank nodded. "He had me read the part about the Youth Initiative."

The comment puzzled Alex. "Really? I must have missed that part."

"Killing the useless old lady to use her money for the greater good."

The pastor thought for a moment. "Oh, yes," he finally said. "You must mean the part where the killer overhears the students' conversation in the bar." He paused while retrieving the scene from his long-term memory. "I guess I see a connection now that you mention it."

"So you agree?" Frank asked.

"Agree with what?"

"Transitions are for the greater good."

"Absolutely not!" Alex said with alarm.

"But you said Dostoyevsky was one of your favorites."

"Frank, have you read the book?"

"Some of it."

"Then you don't know the context of that scene?"

Frank seemed reluctant to admit ignorance.

"The author, Dostoyevsky, is saying exactly the opposite. He put the rationale for evil in the mouth of one character to help another character justify a wicked deed. Vintage Dostoyevsky. He did something similar in *The Brothers Karamazov*." Alex suddenly realized the conversation had taken a rabbit trail. He steered them back. "Tell me, why so much interest in the problem of evil?"

Frank shrugged.

"What did your friend, the professor, say about it?"

"I told you, he's an atheist."

"And if there's no God, then nothing can be called evil?"

Frank reacted with surprise. "That's almost exactly what he said."

"Of course it is." Alex smiled. "I imagine Mori sees himself as a modern Ivan."

"How'd you know?"

"Ivan Karamazov considered himself a brilliant philosopher brave enough to solve the problem of evil by killing God."

"I don't follow," said Frank. "How can killing God eliminate evil?"

"It can't," Alex answered. "That's why your earlier question points to the reality of a good God. We can only recognize what ought *not* be if we sense what ought *to* be. We know ourselves to be made for the true, the good, and the beautiful. Pain, suffering, hatred, ugliness, death, sorrow, these things are the opposite of what our deepest desires tell us ought to be. Like I said during your last visit, when we reject the good that God is, all that remains is the evil that he isn't."

The man sat quietly for a moment.

"Why don't you tell me what's really bothering you, Frank?"

The man appeared to fight back rising emotion. Then he put his head in his hands. "I killed them," he muttered.

Alex sat up with a start. What is a pastor supposed to do with a confession of murder? "Killed who?"

"The faces in my dream," Frank said to Alex's relief.

"You killed the faces?"

"I don't understand," he began. "I don't believe in God anymore. But if there's no God, why do I wake up from these dreams feeling like I did something, I don't know, something unholy?"

"Because there is a God," Alex answered. "And because you have done something unholy. We all have. The Bible tells us all have sinned. All have fallen short of the glory of God. In other words, we yearn for the good that God made us for even when drowning in the sea of our own sinfulness."

Frank looked up, distressed. "Did you say drowning?"

"The Apostle Paul wrote a letter to the church at Rome in which he said that the good he ought to do got repeatedly crowded out by the bad he shouldn't. It's like the undercurrent of our fallen nature keeps pulling us back into the deep water of wickedness."

"So you think the guy killing the worthless old woman was wicked?" Frank asked.

"The guy in *Crime and Punishment*?"

"Yes. Was that part of his drowning?"

"His. And ours. Every time we snuff out another human life we diminish the dignity of our own. We destroy something sacred."

"Like the icons?"

"I suppose," Alex said, suddenly making the possible connection. "Human beings were created to depict the image and likeness of God. That makes every one of us a living, breathing icon." He met the man's fretful eyes. "Frank," he said, "is there something more you want to tell me about your dreams?"

Frank blinked once. Then he pressed his eyes shut as if to summon courage. "Do you think..." He paused. "Do you believe dreams carry messages?"

Odd, thought Alex. *The very question Julia asked.*

"Yes," he answered, "sometimes."

"Warnings?"

"Perhaps."

The answer seemed to deepen Frank's unease.

"From the dead?"

"No. God doesn't send the dead to deliver messages. That's the job of angels."

"Angels?"

"Like the one who appeared to Joseph in a dream telling him to flee Bethlehem to protect Mary and Jesus."

"Always angels?"

"Not necessarily," Alex said. "Demons are fallen angels. I imagine they still carry messages, only from a very different source."

"The devil?"

"Among other names. I prefer *Father of Lies* because it captures the nature of our battle."

"What battle is that?"

"Satan is in an all-out war against the image of God on earth. The Bible tells us he seeks to devour, like a ravenous lion. But he's smart. That's why his favorite weapon is deception."

Frank's eyes invited further explanation.

"If you're oppressed, you know it. If you're tempted, you know it. But if you're deceived, you don't know it. If he can convince us of lies we will destroy ourselves. It makes his work easy."

"What lies?"

"There are so many."

"Such as?"

"Such as the lie that we are mere animals with no ultimate purpose. The man who sees himself as an animal will live like one. And he'll view other human beings as fellow animals. Or how about the lie that only the strong deserve to survive? Or that personal pleasure should trump personal responsibility? You get the idea. If we believe a lie we will live consistently with that lie.

"Evil is more real than we know," Alex continued. "And it's personal. Our enemy is not some mythical cartoon in red tights carrying a pitchfork. Jesus called him a liar, and the father of lies."

A brief silence lingered between them.

"But," Alex added, "Jesus described himself as the truth. And if you know the truth, the truth will set you free."

"Free from what?" Frank asked.

"From the power of deception. The only thing that can dispel darkness is the light. And, as it happens, light is Christ's other nickname." Alex smiled at his own comment while making a mental note to include it in an upcoming sermon. Then he noticed a look of dread on Frank's face. "What is it?" he asked.

"You really believe all of this? About God, angels…the devil?"

"Of course."

"So you think my nightmares are coming from hell?"

"I have no idea what's behind your dreams," Alex confessed.

"But I know that God exists and that evil is both real and personal." He leaned forward to look Frank directly in the eyes. "Something tells me you know the same."

The man looked away.

"That's what I meant when I said I don't want what happened to Ivan to happen to you."

"Why? What happened to Ivan?"

"You didn't really read the whole novel, did you, Frank?"

His head shook weakly.

"Then you wouldn't know that Ivan went mad," Alex continued. "Right after a bone-chilling conversation with the devil."

Frank's terror seemed palpable.

"Listen, Frank," Alex said grimly. "We either submit to the sanity of what's true or become ensnared by the madness of lies."

The man stood abruptly. "I need to go."

Alex rose with his guest. "What are you afraid of, Frank? Something has frightened you."

"I'm not afraid of anything," he said. "I just need to go."

Alex placed a hand gently on the man's shoulder. "Please, let me pray for you before you leave."

"No," he snapped, appearing irritated, then embarrassed. "I mean, no, thank you, I don't have time."

Alex removed his hand, releasing his guest to hurry toward the door.

CHAPTER TWENTY-TWO

"Thanks for coming so late," Matthew said while offering his guest the vacant leather chair.

Mori lit up a cigarette. "Don't mention it," he said, then took a single drag before releasing the toxins along with his words. "I had nothing better to do. Peak and Brew closes at midnight."

Matthew glanced at the clock and tried to make out the numbers through hazy vision. Woozy, probably from the third beer. Or was it the late hour? Either way, he wondered whether he could even carry on a coherent conversation at one or two o'clock in the morning. But he needed to talk to someone.

Mori glanced around the Spartan room. "Just move in?"

Matthew did his own assessment of the three pieces of furniture, adequate for a man living alone who never hosted a girlfriend. Or any friend. "A few months back," he replied. Or had it been a few years? He struggled to orient himself.

"Love what you've done with the place." Mori chuckled

while settling himself into the chair. "So, what's on your mind, Matthew Adams?"

"I met with a minister today. Or rather yesterday."

"Why on earth did you do that?"

Matthew offered a timid laugh in self-conscious rebuke. "I know. But I had questions."

"Then why not talk to me?" Mori asked sternly. Then he softened. "I mean, I thought we were pals."

Were they?

"Of course," said Matthew contritely. "I should have called you first. I know that now."

"He said something that upset you, didn't he?" asked Mori.

A single nod.

"Yep. I can sense it. You look like a tortured soul."

A tortured soul. Weren't those the same words Pastor Alex had used?

Matthew noticed a thin, condescending smile on Mori's lips, as if his diagnosis had been trite. Or amusing.

"Not tortured," Matthew said defensively. "More like conflicted."

"Conflicted, eh?" Mori exhaled another drag of smoke. "Over what?"

Matthew thought for a moment. "Over God, I guess."

"Not the 'I guess' nonsense again," said Mori.

"Sorry. I mean, I don't know who to believe."

"About what?"

"About God."

A disdainful snicker. "Does it matter?"

"You said it does."

"*I* said? When did I ever say such a thing? I told you, I don't believe in God."

"Exactly. You *don't* believe in God, so you *do* believe everything is permissible."

"Ah," said Mori, "so the real conflict is over what you've done."

The comment startled Matthew. Had he ever told Mori what he'd done?

"Feeling a tad guilty, are we, Matthew Adams?"

"About what?"

"How should I know? White lies. Dirty pictures. Illicit affairs. Unnatural acts. Whatever. I figure you've done something some minister considers sinful. So you called your old pal Mori to absolve you." He waved his hand in the shape of an inverted cross like a drunken priest.

Matthew winced. Once upon a time, as a boy, he had sought absolution from his confessor, Father Tomberlin. It had been decades since his last confession. But he still reserved a veneer of reverence for the sacrament, prompting a pang of offense at the mockery.

"Oh, that bothers you?" asked Mori, his waving hand repeating the sacrilege. "I don't mean anything by it. I just find the gesture amusing."

"You're doing it backwards," said Matthew, touching his own forehead. "The cross starts here, not at the belly."

Mori looked defiantly toward his host and repeated the inverted sequence. "I prefer it like this. And, as you said, I consider all things permissible."

A tense silence lingered between them.

"Enough playing around," Mori finally carried on. "Let's get started sorting out your conflict."

"Right, my conflict," Matthew said hesitantly.

"Let's go a round of devil's advocate. I'll be the devil." Another thin smile crossed Mori's lips.

"I don't follow."

Mori rolled his eyes. "Simple. You argue for the existence of naughtiness. I argue against."

"Naughtiness?"

"Sin, then. You make a case for the reality of some divine list of do's and don'ts. I'll push back."

"Why?"

"For Pete's sake! Have you never read Socrates? The best way to shoot holes in your assumptions is to carry them through to their logical conclusions."

"Makes sense, I guess."

"Again with the guessing! No more guessing. I'm gonna help you decide one way or the other. Right here. Right now."

Matthew considered the offer. He actually had grown tired of riding the fence. It would be nice to get to beyond his internal impasse, to feel proud of his accomplishments rather than ashamed. To decide, once and for all, whether helping volunteers was a noble task or a reprehensible deed.

"I'm listening," said Mori impatiently.

Matthew cleared his throat. "OK. The pastor I saw yesterday. He said that every person has sinned." He paused to search his memory for the precise words. "That 'we yearn for the good that God made us for even when drowning in the sea of our own sinfulness.'"

"Of course he did," Mori said with a sneer. "Preachers need sinners like dentists need bad teeth."

A polite chuckle. "I get that. But it makes sense, don't you think?"

"He said we yearn for good, did he?"

"Don't we? Don't you?"

"Depends. Good by whose definition?"

"I don't know. Your own?"

"Another guess?" Mori mocked.

"Your own sense of goodness, then."

The man thought for a moment. Then he grinned. "I enjoy no-strings-attached sex with beautiful women. But your minister friend would call that fornication because, in his rigid ethic, only married partners can indulge in the pleasures of the flesh. Given a choice, which definition of goodness would you rather embrace, mine or his?"

"Yours, I guess...er...I mean...yours."

"You're sure about that?"

Matthew scanned alluring images he had plastered onto the walls of his memory during decades of online lust. He nodded at the question. "Yes, I'm sure."

"There you have it. Mori's ethic, one. Christian morality, zero. What else?"

Matthew reached for another example. "The pastor said my reaction to evil suggests that, deep down, I know God is good."

"Oh, that's rich! So feeling irrational guilt over an occasional sexual tryst means you should believe in an almighty cosmic killjoy. Is that it?"

"That's not what we were talking about."

Mori flicked a patch of ash from his cigarette onto the floor. "What were you talking about, then?"

"The boy and the dogs," said Matthew, his eyes fixed on the glowing residue charring a small section of carpeting.

"The boy from *The Brothers Karamazov*?" asked Mori.

"That's right."

"My favorite scene."

Matthew looked back at his guest. "Not mine," he said. "Made me sad."

"Of course it made you sad! That's the whole point. Pushes your assumptions to their logical conclusion. If God is so good, why didn't he stop that landowner's cruelty?"

Matthew shrugged at the reminder of a question with no easy answer.

"Your minister friend believes in a God who allows little boys be torn to shreds by hunting dogs." God's accuser paused, as if contemplating whether to say more. "And"—he hesitated—"and in a God who would strike an old woman with dementia, forcing her son to abandon his dream of becoming a college professor to spend his time cleaning her soiled laundry and sorting her daily meds."

It took several seconds for Matthew's mind to absorb the comment. "What did you just say?" he finally asked.

"You heard me right. I know the real reason you wanted to talk. You still feel guilty about what you did for your mom. Don't."

Matthew felt rising anxiety. "How do you know about my mom?"

"And you've been worried about what happened with Reverend Grandpa, the old gasbag!"

Matthew's panic grew. He had never discussed his mom or Reverend Grandpa with Mori. Or had he?

"And when you freed Brianna Jackson from that trash bin of a prison she called home."

"Who told you about—"

"Excellent work on that one," he interrupted. "The old gal needed someone to push her past her confusion so she could finally do what was best for everyone."

Matthew stared at Mori for a long moment. Something wasn't right.

He had never mentioned his first client, Brianna Jackson, to his drinking pal. Nor could he recall inviting him to his home. In fact, the two had never exchanged contact information. They had only met a few times in passing while drowning their respective sorrows at the local sports bar.

"How did you find my house?"

Mori took a slow, final drag from his cigarette. "You invited me over to chat." He dropped the butt onto the floor and ground it into the carpeting with his shoe. "Don't you remember?"

"I didn't invite you...did I?"

"Why else would I be here?"

Matthew noticed a thin line of smoke rising from the crushed cigarette butt. "But you never gave me your number," he said, still trying to decipher the moment. "I couldn't have contacted you if I wanted to."

"You invited me nonetheless. Now, can we get back to the point of this conversation?"

"What is the point of this conversation?"

"I was about to absolve you, remember?" said Mori while waving his hand in another irreverent series of crosses. "All things are permissible, my son."

His voice became deeper, raspier.

"All things are permissible."

The pace of waving accelerated.

"All things are permissible. So go, and believe in sin no more!"

The man's voice broke into laughter that sounded like the low rumble of thunder mixed with a lion's threatening growl. Matthew felt the same streak of terror he'd last felt at his nightmare's cackling summons. His eyes darted to the clock, which was finally legible. It read 3:36 a.m. Then he glanced toward the leather chair. No Mori. Just vacant space formerly occupied by whatever phantom had invaded Matthew's dozing psyche.

He looked down at the bruise on his shaking hand. It hadn't faded. Nor, it seemed, had any of the jumbled memories and conversations that had formed themselves into a new, more troubling nightmare. What did it mean? Had his subconscious been trying to resolve needless remorse, or perhaps help him cut the religious strings that had been restraining his evolving scruples?

Or had the dream, if that's what it was, been a warning, as Pastor Alex had implied?

"It was just a dream!" Matthew shouted at the empty leather chair before whispering to himself, "It was just a stupid dream."

Five minutes later Matthew found himself leaning against the kitchen counter washing down an oatmeal raisin cookie with a tall glass of milk, the perfect antidote to beer-enhanced night-mares. He had propped up his tablet and begun flipping through a series of pages summarizing hotel amenities. A quick trip to Reno was just what he needed to distract his anxious mind. And he could easily cover the cost out of his share of the Brianna Jackson estate. Just twelve restful hours in the AutoDrive lane could take him back to his favorite distractions; to pleasures that had anesthetized his pain during the dark days. But those trips dripped with caution and remorse. How would it be, he wondered, to try out his newfound realization? All things were, after all, permissible.

Before reserving a room Matthew decided to alert Serena Winthrop that he would be unavailable for a few days. He searched his foggy memory to retrieve the correct user identi-fication name. Then he remembered: the name of a renowned transition pioneer and the number of clients he had served: KEVORKIAN130.

The page opened, prompting Matthew to curse at the sight of another assignment message from Ms. Winthrop, the last thing he wanted to see.

"No!" he said to the screen while typing a quick reply.

I NEED TO HEAD OUT OF TOWN ON PERSONAL BUSINESS. I WON'T BE ABLE TO ACCEPT THIS PARTICULAR ASSIGNMENT. I HOPE YOU UNDERSTAND.

His finger lingered before tapping the send icon. How would Serena Winthrop react? Would she understand, recognizing that he needed a break after facilitating three transitions in his first week on the job? Pretty impressive, Matthew thought, for a rookie. But it had taken a toll.

Should he mention his anxiety? Had Ms. Winthrop encountered similar feelings among other new hires? Wouldn't it be wise to take a short break to avoid burnout from a process that, regardless of how lucrative or noble, included a healthy dose of stress?

Or would such a note suggest Matthew Adams was weak, unreliable, or perhaps squeamish?

I guess I could wait and go to Reno over the weekend, he thought with a sigh.

He looked at the assignment more closely to grab the key details.

APPOINTMENT TIME: <u>11 A.M.</u>

That's less than eight hours from now!

APPOINTMENT LOCATION: <u>700 MONTEREY COURT, LOVELAND, COLORADO</u>

Nearly an hour's drive.

CLIENT NAME: <u>CHARITY RANDALL</u>
CLIENT AGE: <u>27 YEARS OLD</u>

Matthew glanced back at the age. Someone must have made a mistake, put a two in place of a seven or an eight. Charity Randall, whoever she was, couldn't possibly be ten years his junior. Or could she? He continued reading the summary.

IMPORTANT DETAILS: <u>MS. RANDALL MAY NEED ADDITIONAL ASSISTANCE INTO THE TUB DUE TO IMMOBILE LOWER EXTREMITIES.</u>

He read the line twice before his still-fuzzy brain grasped the meaning. Charity Randall, it seemed, was paralyzed from the waist down. Was that why someone so young had volunteered? Perhaps she had become obese, making it difficult for an aging parent to lift her increasingly heavy form. Or maybe she had simply grown tired of the debit label commonly attached to disabled citizens. What was it like, he wondered, viewing oneself as a negative entry in a sinking economy's ledger? Would she view Matthew, or whatever pseudonym he received for this assignment, as a hero rescuing her from a lifetime of condemning stares? Or would she see him as a man who, under different circumstances, might have carried her over a honeymoon threshold rather than lifting her into a tub-shaped coffin?

He didn't want to know. Even if the girl considered herself worthless, Matthew could not imagine himself mustering the fortitude necessary to complete the assignment. He began retyping a refusal message but halted when he noticed the final assignment detail.

PROJECT ALIAS: A MANICHEAN

A rush of panic. *A Manichean* was the name Matthew had invented for himself a year before when signing letters to Judge Victor Santiago, the man who had died in a murder that had never been solved, and for which Matthew Adams had been the prime suspect.

CHAPTER TWENTY-THREE

"Stop fiddling with that thing," Angie said to Kevin as soon as she entered the bedroom. He was adjusting his bow tie for the sixth time in the five minutes it had taken her to slip into her new evening gown.

"Wow!" he said in her direction. "You look amazing."

"Really?" she said doubtfully. "You aren't just saying that?"

Kevin continued to stare.

"What's wrong?" she asked while trying to inspect her dress.

"Not a thing," he exclaimed. "You look stunning. Absolutely stunning."

She blushed at his enthusiastic eyes.

"Kevin Tolbert!" she said playfully. "Wipe that hungry look off of your face. We have to leave for the fund-raiser. The senator's limo will be here any minute."

He winked. "Can't we stay here instead?"

She gently patted his chest. "You have to go, silly: you're giving the keynote address."

Angie handed Kevin her necklace before spinning around to face the mirror. "Now, help me with the finishing touch."

He took his time with the latch while relishing the aroma of Angie's perfume. Their eyes met through the mirror. Then she shifted her weight just enough for their bodies to touch.

"You're killing me, babe," he whispered into her ear. "Absolutely killing me."

She giggled. "Come on. Let's say goodbye to the kids."

Ten minutes later Kevin was standing outside a limousine introducing his wife to Joshua Franklin, the man likely to receive their party's nomination to the highest office in the land.

"Why, Congressman Tolbert," Franklin said while accepting Angie's extended hand, "you never told me you were married to a model."

Angie took the flattery in stride. "Actually," she said, "I'm pretty sure Kevin is just about the only man in this town *not* married to a model."

Polite laughter accompanied the trio's movement into the vehicle. A Secret Service officer closed the door behind them and patted the roof twice to signal "all clear" to the driver. They were off.

"Thanks for letting us join you in the limo, Senator," Kevin said while feeling the soft leather seats.

"Of course. Anderson told me you had something important to discuss before I introduce you tonight. I hope you don't mind if we chat en route, this is the only opening I had." He glanced at the time. "I'm all yours for about ten minutes, eleven if we hit traffic."

Kevin looked into his wife's eyes. He accepted her reassurance gratefully. "It's about the Bright Spots proposal. I need to know—"

"Listen, Kevin," Franklin interrupted. "I've been meaning to touch base with you on that. I imagine you were pretty disappointed in the latest revision to my plan."

"Well, actually, yes. I was."

"I don't blame you," Franklin continued. "And I don't like it any better than you do. But these daily polls are a real shackle. You know how it is. Timing is everything. We can sell the American people on anything as long as we don't get too specific."

"And my proposal is too specific?"

"Only this early in the process."

"Well, it seems it wasn't too early for other specifics. You included the Robin Hood tax penalties." Kevin paused to consider whether to say more. "And you backed the transition marketing project to the tune of a hundred million dollars."

Franklin shuffled in his seat. "I did," he said, "but only as part of a larger deal."

"So you felt it was appropriate to support a project designed to grow the transition industry just before announcing my plan to shrink it?"

"That's a mischaracterization," Franklin said.

"Is it?" Kevin pulled out his tablet and tapped the screen. He handed it to the senator. "Take a look at this."

Franklin read through the list of marketing slogans that Julia had sent to Kevin right after the Launch Room session with Lancelot, Blackbeard, and the others.

"That's a first-draft list of ideas in development at the lead agency. But then, you've probably already seen these."

"No, I haven't," said Franklin. "What agency?"

"Daugherty and Associates."

"How did you get this?"

"A friend works for them. They're on a fast track. Apparently someone insisted they launch the first phase of the marketing campaign during the convention."

"During the convention. Really?" Franklin said. "I'll need to have someone look into that."

Kevin glanced at a frowning Angie, then back toward Franklin. "You supported this project in a pretty public way before the convention. Why not do the same with my proposal?"

"I will back your proposal, Congressman," said Franklin as if swatting away an annoying fly. "At the right time."

"But the convention is only a few weeks away," Angie said to Kevin's surprise.

"Yes, it is," replied Franklin.

They waited for more. Nothing came, so Angie continued. "Don't you need the support of the Bright Spot's delegates?"

The senator's eyes shot in Kevin's direction. "Is she suggesting...?" He didn't need to finish. Both men knew what Angie had unwittingly implied.

As recently as July, political pundits had been speculating on the remote possibility of a brokered convention. While Franklin remained the clear favorite among fiscal conservatives, a growing number of delegates considered him too soft on tax reform. Support among some had shifted to the second-place candidate, Governor Wesley LaCalli. Franklin's cronies had tried to convince the governor to drop out of the race "for the good of the party." Rather than comply, however, LaCalli appeared to be holding out for a spot on the ticket.

So the senator's team had identified a different strategy for securing the nomination. They suggested Franklin woo fans of Congresswoman Mary Ortega. The mother of three, including one disabled child, Ortega had dropped out of the race a month earlier. But not before accumulating the third-highest number of delegates, most of them fellow breeders. When Ortega ended her campaign, many of her supporters began taking cues from the young congressman from Colorado, Kevin Tolbert. The man who, until this moment, Franklin had assumed firmly in his camp.

"Angie's not suggesting anything, Senator," Kevin said to break the awkward silence. "She's just asking a question. The same question I've been trying to ask you, but I haven't been able to get time on your schedule."

"So you ask me now, on the way to an event where I plan to introduce you to my biggest supporters? What is this, last-minute posturing?"

"There's nothing last-minute about it, Senator," Kevin replied. "You promised to include the Bright Spots proposal in your plan. But here we are, a few weeks before the convention, and I find out you've completely removed it."

Franklin's demeanor softened. "Look, Kevin," he said, "I made a promise, and I'll abide by it. I need you to trust me on that. But I won't be able to advance any plan if I don't lock up the nomination. And doing that requires a bit of…nuanced messaging."

Kevin heard Troy's caution ringing in his ears. *"Don't trust him. He'll sell you out. Franklin has no intention of letting your ideas shape the party's agenda. His biggest donors live and die by quarterly earnings reports, not generational demographic trends."*

He looked at Angie. Her eyes seemed to be shouting the same.

"I can't do that," Kevin finally said.

Franklin's face chilled as quickly as it had warmed. "Can't do what?" he asked through a clenching jaw.

"How do I know you'll defend my proposals later if you aren't even willing to mention them now?"

A brief silence.

"What is it you want, Kevin?" Franklin asked warily.

"What I've wanted all along, to see this nation back policies that will make it easier for families to thrive and to give the old and disabled dignity instead of treating them like useless debits."

"There, you see!"

"See what?" asked Kevin.

"That's exactly what I'm talking about. You can't use words like *families* and hope to garner the kind of support we'll need to win the White House. Nuance, Kevin, your proposal needs more nuance."

"How else do you describe husbands and wives raising children together?"

"First, by calling them partners instead of husbands and wives. Your language excludes same-sex couples, the childless by choice, and a whole range of alternative options that have no interest in becoming breeders."

Franklin appeared suddenly embarrassed, as if remembering to whom he was speaking. "Sorry," he said in Angie's direction. "I didn't mean to offend."

"We aren't asking them to become breeders," said Kevin, squeezing his wife's hand. "But we are asking the government to acknowledge what the research clearly shows: it's in everyone's best interest to encourage stable families and to curtail transitions. Whether we like the choices they are making or not, breeders drive our long-term economic growth engine. You've seen the research, Senator. Forget about the social or cultural implications. You can easily defend it as sound economic policy."

The senator chuckled to himself. "That's what I like about you, Tolbert. You're an idealist. A bit naïve at times, but you have a good heart."

"Naïve? What do you mean naïve?"

"You don't really think voters are going to suddenly embrace breeders just because they represent economic stability, do you? No offense, but the majority of this nation sees you as…as…"

Angie offered assistance. "As religious zealots polluting the planet by spawning a bunch of crib-lizards who consume more than their share of resources and then have the audacity to keep their old and disabled loved ones around as pets when that money could have gone to younger, healthier citizens?"

Both men looked at Angie as if shocked that such a lovely

mouth would repeat such raw, if common, depictions of her own subculture.

"Is that what you were trying to say, Senator?"

Franklin appeared flustered. Apparently Kevin and Angie Tolbert were less naïve than he had assumed.

Kevin smiled at his wife. Then he turned to grin at the senator. "Apparently not everyone sees a need for nuance."

Franklin glanced at the time. "We'll arrive in a few minutes. Skip to the bottom line, Kevin. What do you want from me?"

"I want you to come out publicly in support of the Bright Spots proposal. Now."

Franklin thought for a moment. "Even though it could kill my chances in the general election?"

"You don't know you can even secure the nomination without Ortega's delegates. And they want assurances the nominee cares about their concerns."

"Assurances from you," the senator added.

"Well, yes."

Franklin looked askew at Kevin. "Assurances you won't give unless I give you what you want, is that it? Are you threatening to walk, Kevin, after all I've done to put you on the map?"

Kevin swallowed hard. To further agitate the prospective presidential nominee could sap whatever influence he still had with the party. But to cower would, he knew, undercut the whole reason he had run for office in the first place. Not to mention dishearten his watching bride.

"I'm not making a threat," he said with a slight tremble in his voice. "But I am making a request. I'm asking you to do the right thing, to fulfill your promise so that I can fulfill mine."

"Yours? What promise did you make?"

He swallowed again. "I made a promise... to God."

A puzzled stare.

Kevin's wife took her husband's hand. "Angie and I had a

good life in Colorado, Senator. We didn't need to run for office
or endure the headaches and sacrifices these past several years
have required. Believe me, I would have made a whole lot more
money had I continued minding my own business instead of in-
vesting in campaigns and launching the Center for Economic
Health."

Kevin returned Angie's squeeze before continuing.

"But we believe to whom much is given, much is required.
God gave me a wonderful wife and four great kids. He gave me
a healthy body and mind. And he gave me a terrific partner with
whom I was able to build a successful business. So I promised
to leverage those blessings to make the world a better place. Or,
more specifically, a less antagonistic place."

"Less antagonistic to whom?" asked Franklin.

"To use your label, breeders," Kevin answered. "Young couples who consider children a blessing rather than a burden.
People who love and honor their aging parents rather than trade
them in for cash. And those who serve disabled loved ones as
fellow creatures who reflect the image of God rather than discard them as accidental genetic blunders. I made a promise to
God, Senator Franklin. He always keeps his end of a bargain. So
I fully intend to keep mine."

The senator appeared speechless. "I can respect that," he finally said clumsily.

"Can you?" Kevin asked. "Enough to publicly support my
proposal?"

A brief silence. "Tell you what, Kevin, I'll show you how serious I am about my promise tonight."

"Tonight? Why, what are you going to do?"

Franklin winked. "You'll find out soon enough." He pointed
out the car window. "Looks like we've arrived."

CHAPTER TWENTY-FOUR

A sea of tuxedos and evening gowns reminded Kevin of a scene from one of Joy's bedtime fairy-tale books. He could just imagine Angie running out of the room at the stroke of midnight, her elegant dress morphing back into shorts and a "World's Greatest Mom" T-shirt while a glass slipper fell from her elegant foot for Kevin to rescue. At this moment, however, she needed no rescuing. His lovely bride had become the center of attention at their table. No surprise. The grace that infused life into his heart and children had been put on display.

The wealthy insiders surrounding them seemed mesmerized by Angie's beauty and sophistication. They had probably expected someone else: a frumpy gal with sunken eyes who displayed the wear and tear of her unbearable breeder existence. A woman suffering the humiliation of marriage to a patriarchal dinosaur like Kevin Tolbert who kept her barefoot and pregnant. Four kids! And one of them a debit! None of them could have imagined such a charming, intelligent woman exuding such wholesome radiance. Kevin admired his bride, an authentic white rose situated amid a collection of plastic flowers. Call him biased, but no other woman in the room could hold a candle to Angie. She possessed the distinctive beauty that comes from relishing one's place in the world, a stark contrast to the surgically enhanced woman seated to her left.

"You must be proud of your husband," the Barbie doll said while positioning herself between Angie and the eyes of her slightly intoxicated date.

"I am," said Angie, grateful the woman had finally noticed and blocked the man's flirtatious stare. The couple must have been worth a fortune if they could afford the ten-thousand-dollar-per-plate price tag of tonight's dinner on top of whatever they must spend for hair and skin enhancements that, from a distance, made them look in their mid-thirties rather than early fifties.

The ogling man leaned forward to enter the conversation. "You seemed caught off guard by the senator's announcement," he said in Kevin's direction.

He had been. Both Kevin and Angie remained surprised, and annoyed, by Franklin's ploy.

"I'd like to introduce the latest addition to the lineup of up-and-coming young Republican stars who will be speaking at the convention," Franklin had said while welcoming Kevin to the stage.

Surprise number one. Party leaders had hinted, but never confirmed, that Kevin would be speaking at the convention. They first wanted assurances he would indeed support Franklin's nomination. He had given no such promise. But that hadn't prevented Franklin from implying he had.

The second surprise came after Kevin's speech. He had intentionally kept his remarks about Franklin obscure, careful to avoid any hint of an endorsement that might end up in the news. The last thing he needed was for the Bright Spots coalition to perceive that he supported the man who, as yet, had shown no affection for their agenda. Of course, Kevin couldn't have anticipated Franklin's next move. Before Kevin left the podium the senator jumped back onto the stage and threw an arm around Kevin to create a perfect photo op. "I think you can see," he said with a chummy grin, "why I've asked Congressman Tolbert to join the Franklin team."

Franklin had made no such invitation. Sure, Brent Anderson had hinted at the possibility of a cabinet post. But Kevin had known it to be a dangling carrot he would ignore until Franklin backed the Bright Spots amendment.

"Yes," Kevin responded to Barbie's escort, "it was a bit of a shock."

The man appeared skeptical.

"And an honor," Angie said while tapping her foot against her agitated husband's leg.

"Yes, of course, and an honor," he added quickly.

The couple looked away from the Tolberts when a waiter offered to refill their champagne glasses.

Kevin leaned toward Angie to whisper. "I'm going to confront him," he said while glancing toward the table where Senator Franklin sat surrounded by the fifty-thousand-dollar-per-plate donors. "He crossed the line."

"Yes, he did," Angie whispered through a contrived smile. "But I don't think this is the time or place to make a scene. Play along for tonight so you don't end up saying something you'll regret."

Wise advice Kevin couldn't heed. Some reporter was probably already crafting the morning's headline: "Tolbert Joins Franklin Team" or "Franklin Offers First Cabinet Post." Troy would kill him if he let the distortion go unchallenged.

Kevin kissed his wife's cheek before excusing himself from the table. "I'll be right back," he said as Angie offered a cautionary frown.

The senator noticed Kevin's approach. "Ah," he said to his admiring entourage, "here he is now. The man of the hour."

Kevin greeted the circle warmly before turning to the senator. "I wonder if we might have a brief word?"

"We were actually just talking about you, Congressman Tolbert," said a man seated on the opposite side of the table. "The senator says you're one of the best and brightest on Capitol Hill."

"Is that right?" Kevin forced a grin.

"That Center for Economic Health of yours," the stranger continued. "Brilliant stuff. Absolutely brilliant."

Kevin looked toward Franklin. What had he told them about the CEH?

"How many?" asked the woman seated beside Franklin.

"Excuse me?"

"How many supporters do you have so far?"

"We're approaching one hundred thousand," Kevin said, rounding up to the nearest impressive figure.

"And all of them motivated by this bright spots thing of yours?"

"Well," Kevin replied, "it's not exactly my bright spots thing. More like a growing consensus on the best way to improve our long-term economic prospects."

"Why haven't I heard of it?" asked a man Kevin vaguely recognized as the owner of a conservative news syndicate.

"Well," Kevin replied while flashing a confident smile, "because they accidentally sat you at the wrong table this evening."

A glower from Franklin told Kevin to tread lightly.

"But then," he continued, "I'm sure you'll be hearing more about the Bright Spots proposal from Senator Franklin during the convention."

Franklin stood, tossing his napkin onto the table. "If you'll excuse us," he said to his guests, "the congressman and I need a moment to chat." He looked toward a lovely woman seated on his left. "Please, Paula, tell them about the yacht you just purchased." He turned to the other guests. "She hosted a fundraiser for us on it last month. Very plush!"

The two men walked fifty feet away and positioned themselves near a large display of carved ice. Franklin's gregarious smile sank as he assumed a scowl. "Do you have any idea who you were just talking to?"

Kevin looked back toward the table. "Not exactly. No."

"Most of them are on the board of the Saratoga Foundation."

"Really?"

"Yes, really. And I don't appreciate you putting words in my mouth in front of my most generous donors. I'll decide what I say at the convention when the time comes."

"That goes both ways, Senator," Kevin said, incensed. "What was that stunt you pulled on the stage?"

"It wasn't a stunt."

"You created the impression I'm fully on your team, completely ignoring our conversation in the limo."

"On the contrary, Congressman. I did exactly what I said I would do."

A blank stare from Kevin as the senator continued.

"I told you I would show you how serious I am about my promise. And that's what I did."

"You promised to come out in favor of the Bright Spots proposal," said Kevin.

"What do you think I just did? I gave you a spot on the convention stage. Who better to make your case than you?"

Kevin felt as if a yellow light was beginning to flash.

"And I just told my most generous donors that I want you on my team. How much more supportive could I have been?"

Yellow turned red as Kevin's mind seesawed between significant opportunity and serious trouble. Speaking at the convention would let Kevin articulate his ideas to a national audience. If he did well, Franklin would be forced to embrace the Bright Spots proposal. An opportunity. But if Kevin's ideas fell flat with the party's base, Franklin would distance himself from the misguided breeder before Kevin could say hot potato. Either way, Franklin would win. Breeder delegates would read Kevin's visibility as a clear sign of support. Their votes would help Franklin lock up the nomination, after which he would bury the Bright Spots proposal for good.

Before Kevin could decide how to play the moment he felt the senator's arm easing him back toward the table. "Relax, Kevin. You made a very good impression on my friends. They want to see you succeed." A paternal pat on the back. "We all do."

Kevin noticed a familiar face approaching. He felt an immediate knot in his gut.

"Evan!" said Franklin, extending his hand. "Glad you could make it. You remember Kevin Tolbert."

Evan Dimitri offered a single disinterested nod in Kevin's direction before growling at the senator, "I thought you said Trisha was giving the keynote tonight."

Franklin laughed nervously. "That was the original plan," he said. "But we were fortunate enough to land Kevin instead."

Dimitri looked the congressman up and down. "Humph," he grumbled. "Why'd Trisha back out?"

"She didn't back out," said Franklin. "We decided this would be the best time and place to introduce Congressman Tolbert."

"Be careful, Josh," said Dimitri. "I hear Trisha's getting nervous about your...new friends. And Governor LaCalli has been winking in her direction."

Kevin translated the conversation in his mind. Trisha Sayers, the pop star turned fashion icon, remained one of the most admired fiscal conservatives in the party. But she hated the Bright Spots proposal almost as much as she hated Kevin Tolbert. And

Governor LaCalli would give his right arm to steal her away from Franklin's coalition.

"I hope you know what you're doing," Dimitri continued. "This thing is by no means locked up. And I don't like spending good money on losing candidates."

"Come on, Evan," Franklin said as forcefully as he dared. "The numbers look good. I don't think we need to worry about that."

A dismissive snort.

"And what about you?" Dimitri said to Kevin as if talking to a fly in his soup. "Still have the Youth Initiative in your cross hairs?"

Kevin glanced at Franklin. He appeared uneasy about what Kevin might say.

"I'm not shooting at anything, Mr. Dimitri. I'm just trying to help improve the economy."

"This is what I'm talking about, Josh," Dimitri said as if Kevin had left the room. "It makes our base nervous when you start criticizing the transition industry. A whole lot of the people in this room are donating to your campaign out of money inherited from volunteering parents."

Franklin reacted defensively. "I've never criticized the transition industry," he said. "I practically coauthored the Youth Initiative Expansion Act, for Pete's sake!"

Dimitri waved a dismissive hand. "You know this game: 'What have you done for me lately?' You can bet the likes of Trisha Sayers don't want reminders that you pandered to them yesterday. They want to know you'll support them tomorrow."

The thick-necked bully turned toward Kevin. "And you're not helping matters," he said. "I've told you before, I like the feel-good aspects of your proposal. People like the whole 'hope for the future' thing, optimism about a brighter tomorrow and all that. You send all the right messages. Celebrate the young.

Invest in the future. Play with your grandkids. Who wouldn't resonate with that vision?"

"My thoughts exactly," said Franklin in an attempt to salvage the moment.

Dimitri shoved a finger into Kevin's chest. "But you need to quit the moralizing."

"What are you talking about?" Kevin said while stepping back from the jab. "I'm not moralizing. I'm just telling the truth. The brightest economic pockets have lower transition rates and higher fertility rates. Right or wrong, good or bad, those are the facts."

"I'll tell you the facts, Mr. Tolbert," said Dimitri.

"Fact number one: Senator Franklin here hopes to get into the White House.

"Fact number two: He needs the support of fiscal conservatives.

"Fact number three: We have no hope of improving this messed-up economy of ours if we lose the savings and revenue generated by the Youth Initiative.

"Fact number four: You are perceived as a self-righteous blowhard every time you disparage the reputation and memory of millions of volunteers.

"And finally, fact number five: Josh here takes a big risk every time he is seen with you in public, or gives you a place at the table, or gets cozy with your so-called Center for Economic Health."

Kevin could feel his neck throb. He took a deep breath to avoid calling Dimitri any of the names bouncing around in his head. This conversation, as far as he was concerned, was over.

Apparently, so were his chances of influencing Franklin's plan. Neither Dimitri nor Franklin would listen to reason. They cared nothing for the facts. Perceptions, not realities, would drive every move made between now and the election.

"Gentlemen," Kevin said. "I think the time has come for me to rejoin my wife."

"You do that," spat Dimitri.

"Yes," said Franklin with all the charm he could muster, "enjoy the rest of the evening. We can discuss the best steps for moving forward tomorrow. I'll have my assistant arrange a time."

Kevin smiled, doubtfully, at the offer. Then he began to walk away.

Dimitri put his open palm on Kevin's chest, halting his advance. "Wait," he said gruffly. "One last thing."

Kevin braced for impact.

"A word of advice."

"What's that?" Kevin asked.

"You would do well in this town to remember people elect politicians, not preachers. I suggest you focus your efforts on the economy and leave moralizing to the clergy."

Kevin nodded indifferently at the comment before returning to his table. Angie leaned in close to ask how it had gone. "I could see the steam coming out of your ears all the way over here. Who was that man poking you in the chest?"

"His name is Dimitri."

"What did he want?"

"To give me a bit of advice."

She waited.

"He said I should talk about the economy and leave moralizing to the clergy."

Angie shrugged dismissively. Kevin had received similar "advice" before.

That's when it struck him. *The clergy. Of course!*

"I'll be right back," he said while getting up from the table like a battered athlete limping back onto the field.

"Where are you going now?"

"I need to call Troy immediately."

CHAPTER TWENTY-FIVE

Alex was starved. That's why he had suggested Troy Simmons meet him at a hot-dog stand located about three blocks from the church. They sat at his usual table, adjacent to the small grill owned by Hakim, a first-generation American. Hakim's parents had fled Egypt shortly after what many labeled the "Arab Spring," which had turned into a dangerous winter for devout Christians in the region. Hakim's mother, still alive, was so proud that her son operated his own small business and that their pastor frequented the stand whenever he could find an excuse.

As usual, Alex ordered the kosher brat. As usual, he smothered it with mustard and washed his first bite down with a swig of orange soda. But this time he felt a gurgling sensation in his gut thanks to Troy's unexpected request.

"Why me?" he asked after swallowing hard.

"First, because I trust you," Troy began. "I'd still be keeping Christ at a safe distance if not for the time you invested in Julia and me last year."

Alex smiled at the recollection of a hesitant couple entering his home to join his weekly Exploring Christianity chats. Troy had participated more enthusiastically than Julia at first. But both had eventually come around.

"Second, because you're good with words. We've been sitting under your teaching long enough to know that you have a keen intellect and the ability to make difficult ideas accessible."

Alex accepted the compliment with a slight bow of the head. "You're kind," he said. It was nice to know someone in the congregation appreciated his effort to craft sermons of substance.

"And, perhaps most important of all, you understand the urgency and difficulty of what we're trying to do."

He did. Alex admired Troy Simmons and his partner, Kevin Tolbert. But he didn't envy their task. To take on the transition industry was no small feat even for men with a proven track record in business and, more recently, politics. Alex knew himself unqualified for the first. He felt uneasy with the second.

"So you want me to write up the document?"

"We do," said Troy. "We're calling it 'An Open Letter to Our Elected Officials.'"

Two faces came to Alex's mind. His wife, Tamara, would smile proudly when she found out her husband had been asked to play a small part in opposing the transition industry. His chairman, Phil Crawford, would not. But then, he didn't need to know about it. What harm could possibly come from spending a few hours crafting a letter for Troy and Kevin to use in their efforts?

"And that's all? You just want me to write the letter?"

"Well," added Troy, "we'd also like you to persuade other ministers, priests, and rabbis in the area to join you in signing the letter. Julia thinks we can get a national media agency to pick up the story. You know, a group of Denver-area ministers holding Washington accountable."

Alex's stomach clenched. He examined his partially eaten brat. He placed it on the plastic table.

"Is there a problem, Pastor?" asked the ever-attentive Hakim while wiping his hands on a grease-splattered apron. "I can make you another if you wish."

"No, thank you, Hakim," said Alex while forcing himself to nibble and grin. "Excellent as always."

Alex turned back toward Troy, the real source of his indigestion. He recalled the conversation with Ellie Baxter. Her husband had paid a price after entering the fray of the most contentious issue of their day. It still made him mad: a pastor who, despite years of faithful service and effective impact, was forced from his position just because he took seriously what the Scriptures said about marriage. He could just imagine his own board's reaction should he make such a public statement on the Youth Initiative.

"Why not ask ministers in the Washington, D.C., area instead of Denver?" asked Alex.

Troy chuckled at the suggestion. "I could probably count on one hand the number of D.C. ministers who oppose the Youth Initiative."

"Of course," Alex said weakly.

"Besides, Denver has two advantages. First, the convention is happening here. And second, I love the idea of Kevin giving his bright spots speech in the same city where he grew up as a boy, a city where pastors like you challenge national leaders to support parents and respect seniors: a one-two punch that might catch the attention of a national news outlet. Julia calls it *earned media* because we could never buy the kind of coverage we might garner from a story they consider controversial. We can't compete with a hundred-million-dollar ad campaign, but we can build momentum among those who are, by and large, religiously active. You know," Troy said with a wink, "the breeders."

Hakim, overhearing the comment, scowled in Troy's direction.

"Pardon my language," Troy said. "I guess I no longer consider the label *breeder* offensive. It's sort of become a badge of honor."

Alex smiled in Hakim's direction. He had always wondered how the young father of four managed to support his own brood plus an aging mom by selling hot dogs and brats. Hakim was one of the bright spots Kevin Tolbert wanted to help. He was also one of the breeders scorned by the cultural elite.

Alex looked back at Troy. "What was that advertising slogan again? 'Come home'?"

"'Go home,'" Troy corrected. "Actually, 'Go home to a more peaceful passing.' Julia said the agency hopes the ads will drive an increase in volunteers among two target demographic groups."

"Which groups?"

"What they would call debits who are reluctant to die in a clinic, and people with religious sensibilities."

"What do they think 'religious sensibilities' means?"

"You'd have to see the storyboards," said Troy. Alex didn't follow. "They're sort of like pencil drawings of the final production. Julia took shots of them for me."

Troy pulled out his pocket tablet. "Here, take a look." He tapped a few times and extended it toward Alex with one hand while blocking the sun with the other. "They plan to float beautiful images of family togetherness and rainbows behind the words *home* and *peaceful passing* as if advertising a religious experience instead of mass suicide."

Alex thought for a moment. "Drink the Kool-Aid," he finally whispered in disgust.

"What's that?"

"Oh, it just reminds me of something that happened last

century. A cult leader named Jim Jones led a group of disen-franchised down-and-outers to leave the country and create a commune he called Jonestown. They moved to Guyana, South America. He eventually convinced his congregation to kill their own kids, about two hundred of them, by forcing them to drink Kool-Aid laced with cyanide. Then the adults did the same. It was one of the largest mass suicides in history. The parallels to what's happening now are nauseating."

Troy took a bite of his hot dog while waiting for more.

"Jones convinced hundreds of his followers that they should all die together as part of a mass 'translation.'"

"Wait," said Troy. "He called their suicides 'translation'?"

Alex nodded soberly. "Believed it would free them to all live together on another planet. I can just imagine him using the same ad strategy: 'Join me to go home to a more peaceful place.'"

A long silence before Troy spoke, angrily. "But this Jones guy only convinced hundreds. So far the Youth Initiative has con-vinced, or rather coerced, millions."

He paused.

"Please, Pastor, will you help us counter this ad campaign?"

Alex weighed the request in his mind. It would feel good to help mobilize pastors to speak out against a practice he had come to hate. He had always wanted to condemn the transition industry. But ministers were supposed to reach people with the good news of the gospel, not alienate them by addressing divi-sive issues. At least that's what he had always been told.

We can't force our beliefs onto unbelievers.

We should win their hearts and let the Spirit of God change their minds.

But this wasn't about imposing Christianity onto unbelievers. It was about exposing a lie that had begun to ensnare his own congregation.

"A simple declaration of what you believe about human dignity," Troy was saying, "that's all we're looking for. Nothing negative or attacking. We want to entice people toward the beauty of thriving families. I have the stats to make a no-nonsense, pragmatic argument for our proposal. But we need someone to make the moral case. If you write the document and arrange meetings with some of the more influential pastors in town I know we can make this work."

Alex knew he wouldn't refuse even as he searched for an excuse to say no.

"I'll do it," he finally said.

"Great!" Troy pounced, rattling off a list of ideas the pastor might consider incorporating into the document.

"Listen, Troy," Alex interrupted while inconspicuously wrapping his half-eaten brat in a napkin. "Why don't you just send me your thoughts and let me look them over before I draft the letter."

"Of course."

"I'll try to carve out some time this afternoon to get started."

"Thank you, Pastor. I really appreciate your help on this." Troy stood to leave, but sat back down when he realized Alex hadn't moved. "What is it?" he asked.

"I need to tell you something in complete confidence."

Troy appeared concerned as he nodded consent.

"I'll need to navigate this thing carefully with the church board," he explained. "I'm pretty sure I'll face some intense opposition."

"To what?"

"They won't like me saying anything that might offend those with loved ones who've volunteered or those willing to include the church as a transition beneficiary."

Troy's jaw dropped.

"I know," Alex continued. "But that's the reality I face."

Troy thought silently, then snapped his fingers. "What if I speak to them?"

Alex began examining the possibility in his mind.

"When's the next board meeting?" asked Troy.

"This coming Tuesday night, but—"

"Then let me attend," said Troy. "I'll explain what we want you to do and why."

Alex considered the suggestion. A successful, respected businessman like Troy Simmons could easily field objections from the bullying Phil Crawford. Risky, perhaps, but no more risky than moving ahead without board approval. Alex would not, after all, be speaking as a private individual, but as a representative of Christ Community Church. He needed their support. Or, at the very least, their reluctant consent.

"That might be a good idea," answered Alex. "Can you come to my office at eight o'clock Tuesday evening?"

"I'll be there," Troy said while bounding up from the table. "And don't worry about a thing." He rapped his knuckles against the table as if to promise good fortune. "I'm sure they'll support your role in this effort."

Alex wasn't so sure. He stood up, carefully concealing the uneaten portion of his lunch in his palm until he could find a discreet trash container.

"Here you go, Pastor!" said Hakim, enthusiastically offering Alex a second brat.

"Oh, um, thank you, Hakim," he fumbled. "But I better say no this time."

"I'd love a second," Troy intercepted, clearly in the mood to celebrate.

One man's triumph, thought Alex, is another man's anxious stomach.

CHAPTER TWENTY-SIX

Matthew had barely slept a wink in the thirty-six hours since receiving and ignoring the assignment. His mind remained fixed on a mystery. How had Serena Winthrop known his former alias, *A Manichean*? Even more troubling, what did she know about its history? *His* history?

It had been a year since Matthew had sat in a chilly jail cell after being falsely accused of the assassination of Judge Victor Santiago. The charge hadn't stuck. The police knew Matthew had been elsewhere at the time of the murder. But they never stopped suspecting his involvement as a possible coconspirator. Santiago had been the presiding judge in an appeal involving a wrongful death decision against NEXT Transition Services. The case, it turned out, had had enormous economic and political importance. But it had also affected Matthew's inheritance, which was why he had been so eager to correspond with the judge. He wanted to explain the real-world impact Santiago's ruling would have on lives such as Matthew's. Harmless enough, especially since he never signed his actual name. But some-

how, someone had learned of the letters and used them to frame
Matthew for a crime he hadn't committed. That someone, he re-
alized, must have been the woman now calling herself Serena
Winthrop.

"This project is highly confidential, Mr. Adams," she had
explained during the hiring process. "The company asks that
every member of my team use an alias."

She had told Matthew they would need the utmost confidentiality in order to achieve "plausible deniability for both the
contractor and the company." That's why Ms. Winthrop had
given Matthew different names for each assignment.

Jed Smith.

Randy Collins.

Chris Marlow.

And finally, A Manichean, the name he had used when writing
to the judge.

Matthew assembled the pieces in his mind. Ms. Winthrop
worked for NEXT Inc., the company that had had the most to
lose, or gain, from the court's ruling.

After Santiago's death the case had been reassigned to a new
panel of judges that later decided in favor of NEXT.

The police never found the actual killer. And Matthew never
learned who had sent the final, threatening note.

Fast-forward one year. Ms. Winthrop recruits Matthew to help
NEXT test a new at-home transition service. She never reveals
who recommended him for the job. Like a fool, he never insists,
too flattered by the offer.

It appeared the person who had framed him for murder had
also hired him to kill.

Matthew suddenly felt like a blind kitten stalked by a ravenous dog. He could hear the growling and smell the lust. But he
couldn't see the menace or path of escape.

He reluctantly clicked the bouncing image on his tablet, the third message from Serena Winthrop in the past twenty-four hours. The first had rejected his request that she give the assignment to another associate. The second had requested an explanation for his negligence. The third would probably threaten to dock his pay or, he could only hope, fire him.

MR. ADAMS:
IT HAS BEEN NEARLY EIGHT HOURS SINCE I LEARNED OF YOUR FAILURE TO CARRY OUT YOUR MOST RECENT ASSIGNMENT. I NEED TO SPEAK WITH YOU AS SOON AS POSSIBLE. PLEASE CALL ME WHEN YOU RECEIVE THIS MESSAGE.
SERENA WINTHROP

He dialed the number. After a single ring he ended the call. Typing a short reply would require less courage.

DEAR MS. WINTHROP: I QUIT.

Ten seconds after tapping the send icon Matthew heard the ping of an arriving message.

PLEASE, DON'T DO THAT. CALL ME.

Everything inside Matthew wanted to ignore the request. But he knew escaping would not be so easy. He swallowed hard while tapping REDIAL.

"Thank you for calling, Mr. Adams."

"Who are you?" he asked irritably. "And what part did you play in the death of Judge Santiago?"

"I beg your pardon?"

"You heard me. What part did you play in Judge Victor Santiago's death?"

"I have no idea what you're talking about," she said indignantly. "Was he a client? You know I don't handle such things myself. I told you, I head up research and development, not field services."

"Don't play dumb with me, Ms. Winthrop. You know what I'm talking about."

"No, I don't know what you're talking about," she said. "But I do know that you dropped the ball on a very important assignment yesterday. The cleanup crew arrived two hours after the scheduled transition for Charity Randall only to discover her still very much alive."

"I sent you a message asking you to reassign the case to someone else."

"And I rejected that request. We need more than eight hours' notice for that kind of change." Oddly, she sounded more like a boss correcting a delinquent employee than a predator licking its chops. "I didn't hear back from you so I ended up reassigning Ms. Randall's case to a different associate who took care of it this morning."

"Did you?"

"I did. Which is unfortunate for you, Mr. Adams, since the woman had a rather large estate. Your commission would have been substantial."

Matthew couldn't decipher whether Ms. Winthrop was toying with him.

"That's why I encourage you to take some time to reflect on your decision before walking away. I realize it can be stressful, especially lately since we've been trying to work through a backlog of cases. Under normal circumstances we like to give our associates a day in between assignments. We haven't been able to do that lately, for which I apologize."

Is this for real? Matthew wondered.

"I've been very pleased by your work to date, Mr. Adams,"

she continued. "And you're on the ground floor of what we believe will be a substantial growth industry in the years to come. Please, for your own sake, I hope you'll take a few days to reflect before jumping ship."

"Ms. Winthrop," Matthew said in the most professional voice he could muster. "I appreciate your concern and apologize for the difficulty I created yesterday, but we both know the real reason I decided to quit."

"Do we?"

"A Manichean," Matthew answered.

A moment of silence.

"Ms. Winthrop?"

"I'm here. Go on."

"Where did you get that name?"

"I thought I explained that earlier. We always assign an alias to protect the company and the associate."

"Please, Ms. Winthrop, I need a straight answer."

"I'm giving you a straight answer, Mr. Adams. The company insists that we use pseudonyms in order to—"

"What do you know about this specific pseudonym?" he interrupted.

"Nothing. It came with the assignment form like all the others."

"So you didn't choose it?"

"I never select the names."

"Who does?"

Silence.

"Ms. Winthrop, I need to know who gave you that name."

"I can't say," she answered.

"Can't, or won't?"

"Can't. I receive the assignment documents from the central office. Alias names are already included. I just pass them along." She sounded embarrassed. Apparently Serena Winthrop held a less elevated post than she had led Matthew to believe. She was, it seemed, a lovely go-between rather than a serious decision-maker. But a go-between for whom? And for what?

"Does that name mean something to you?" she asked. "I must admit it's one of the most unique I've seen."

"Listen," said Matthew. "I think I'll take your advice. You know, spend some time thinking about my decision."

"I'm glad," she said warmly.

"In the meantime, I'd appreciate you removing me from the list of active associates. I'll get in touch with you if and when I decide to take another assignment."

Matthew ended the call while breathing a hesitant sigh of relief. Serena Winthrop was not, as he had feared, a prowling animal stalking its next victim. But that only meant the real peril remained somewhere out of sight.

CHAPTER TWENTY-SEVEN

Julia examined each of the vaguely familiar faces around her listening to their pastor read. Apart from her husband and Alex she didn't know anyone's name. A relative newcomer to the church, Julia hadn't given much thought to which of her fellow worshippers served on the board of directors.

The meeting was already under way by the time she and Troy arrived. Pastor Alex skipped formal introductions. Julia nodded briefly at the collection of welcoming grins, her only connection to the individuals who would decide whether "An Open Letter to Our Elected Officials" would see the light of day. It read:

An Open Letter to Our Elected Officials:

We, the undersigned, wish to express our gratitude for your service to this nation. You play a crucial role in the God-ordained institution of government and we pray that you will be given strength for the task and wisdom for the challenges that lie ahead. As members of the clergy from a variety of religious traditions we, like you, seek to ease the suffering of hurting people and to nurture health in an ailing society. The Hebrew Scriptures state that when the righteous rule, the people rejoice. As spokesmen and spokeswomen for many of the people under your authority, we pledge our support and assistance in your effort to do what's right for this great nation. Toward that end we feel compelled to bring to your attention a growing concern over how some of the policies enacted in recent years are affecting the communities we serve.

First, difficult economic times have accelerated the already alarming decline in birthrates, further strangling off the only trickle of life capable of nourishing a rich garden of human thriving. All of our religious traditions uphold the beauty and priority of parenthood. And, despite the technological, social, and political pressures that make it increasingly difficult to do so, the most devout among us make the sacrifices necessary to bear and rear a new generation. We consider these families to be bright spots in an ever-darkening society. Will you join us in the effort to encourage and support those willing and able to shine the light of hope that radiates from the face of every newborn child?

Our second concern is directly related to the first. A shrinking pool of natural families has created an equally pressing crisis on the other end of the demographic continuum. Too few young and healthy bear the burden of a rapidly aging population. This state of affairs has created an economic strain on the entire society. Cultural elites derisively label the weak and vulnerable "debits" unworthy of life. The younger generation has come to resent rather than honor the old. But all of our faith traditions consider every human being worthy of dignity and protection, including those with graying hair and waning memories. Will you join us in the effort to defend the dignity of the aging and disabled among us?

"I'm sorry to interrupt," said the man wearing an agitated frown. "Would you read that last line again?"

The pastor paused and looked up from the document. "Of course," he replied while shifting nervously in his chair. "It says, 'Will you join us in the effort to defend the dignity of the aging and disabled among us?'"

The gentleman shot a glance toward a fellow skeptic, then back in Pastor Alex's direction. "What, may I ask, do you mean by *defend their dignity*?"

"I'd be happy to answer that," interjected Troy, prompting Alex to breathe a sigh of relief. "I'm not sure how much you know about the Youth Initiative, Mr.—?"

"Crawford. Phil Crawford."

"Pleased to meet you, sir," said Troy warmly. "You see, there's been an increasingly overt effort to pressure our older citizens to kill themselves."

The man winced. "Volunteer," he said as if correcting a mischaracterization.

"Right," Troy said, missing or ignoring the intimation. "Something those of us in this room know to be wrong."

"Not so fast," said another man. "We can't assume every member of Christ Community Church views transitions as immoral in all circumstances."

"I didn't say every member of Christ Community, I said those of us in this room." A brief silence while Troy scanned the faces around the table. Julia sensed her husband gauging reactions the way he did when sitting in on one of Kevin's presentations.

"Hang on just a second," Phil Crawford said, his neck turning red. Not because he was embarrassed, Julia realized, but because he was angry.

"Now, Phil," the pastor interjected in an apparent effort to quell an eruption, "why don't you let Mr. Simmons finish his explanation of the strategy before we discuss any concerns?"

The man ignored his pastor's comment. "Not everyone in this room agrees with your assumption, Mr. Simmons."

Julia noticed a glimmer in her husband's eye. He had smoked out the pastor's chief nemesis.

"I see," said Troy. "Please explain."

"There are a good number of people attending this church with loved ones who have volunteered. How do you think it would make them feel if their pastor was to sign a letter like this? Worse, if they found out their pastor wrote it?"

Troy took a moment to consider the question. "Well, I would hope they'd be proud of him for having the moral fortitude to—"

"Condemned," Phil interrupted. "They would feel judged and condemned, Mr. Simmons."

"Perhaps," Troy said calmly. "But I imagine they would also feel relieved."

The comment appeared to surprise the pastor. "Why relieved?" he asked.

"Well, if what you've taught us about the moral law is true, then every human being has an intuitive knowledge of right and wrong," said Troy. "So that must mean a whole lot of our people carry an unspoken guilt over a parent's transition they either encouraged or affirmed through silence. Wouldn't it be a relief to hear you diagnose their symptoms? To realize that the lingering remorse they feel is more than normal grieving? It's the shrapnel of a lie believed and acted upon."

"What lie?" asked the second skeptic.

"The lie that suicide is some kind of noble act. The lie that it's better to send spoiled kids to an elite university than to honor one's father and mother. And the lie that we can choose our own expiration date rather than accept every moment of life as a precious gift from God."

All eyes turned from Troy to Phil, seated at the opposite end of the table. Guns had been drawn. A showdown was about to begin.

"Hold it right there," Phil said with a halting gesture. "There's no need to get on a soapbox. I'm sure we all agree that life is a gift."

Do they? Julia wondered.

"And none of us like the transition industry per se. But this isn't about what's moral and what's immoral. It's about roles."

Troy appeared confused. "I don't follow. What do you mean by roles?"

"It's not our place as a board to tell Pastor Alex how to vote. He's perfectly free to support whatever candidate or public referendum he likes, just like the rest of us. But when he decides to speak or write as the pastor of Christ Community Church, we do have a say in that."

"Which is why I asked Mr. and Mrs. Simmons to join us this evening," said Alex. "I wanted to consult the board before taking any further steps."

Phil half nodded at the pastor's comment. "And it's a good thing you did," he said threateningly.

"So you mean it isn't Pastor Alex's role to speak or write on behalf of the church?" asked Troy.

"When it comes to something this divisive, absolutely not."

"Divisive? You consider affirming Christian beliefs on family and human dignity divisive?"

The second skeptic drew his weapon. "Like I started to say earlier, not everyone at Christ Community believes transitions are always wrong."

"But they are always wrong," Julia heard herself say. She looked at her husband before continuing. "I know what it is to blindly support the popular lies of our generation. I was one of the public voices cheering the Youth Initiative when President Lowman introduced the idea. I would use derisive terms like *debits* without a second thought. I even parroted all of the common arguments about wasting public funds keeping half-comatose seniors on a life-support machine. Two years ago the letter Pastor Alex wrote would have insulted me. But I would have been wrong."

"What changed your mind?" asked a woman two seats to Julia's left.

"To be honest, I'm not sure," she said while reaching for her husband's hand. "But I suppose part of it had to do with confronting the reality of what's going on. I met a young man named Jeremy Santos who let me read a journal written by his teenage brother, Antonio, a person I used to call a debit because he cost society more than he could possibly produce. But Antonio wasn't a half-comatose vegetable with a feeding tube. He was a bright, articulate kid who loved robotics and art and food. He also loved his mother and his brother." She paused. "And they loved him."

Julia's voice cracked as a swell of emotion overtook her composure. The moment surprised her. It had been nearly two years since she had read Antonio's journals. Why did they still prompt such raw emotion?

"I'm sorry," she continued after receiving a tissue from one of the other ladies. "But I'm one of the people who helped throw that young man onto the bonfire of human dignity. I helped make him hate his own life. I wrote well-crafted columns shoveling mindless rhetoric that made him feel guilty every time he took another breath."

The room fell momentarily silent as the group absorbed Julia's regret.

Phil cleared his throat awkwardly. "Well, I'm sure we all appreciate Mrs. Simmons's feelings," he began, "but we're not discussing whether transitions are good or bad. We're discussing whether it's a minister's role to get involved in politics. *Our* minister's role, to be specific." He looked at Alex. "With all of the problems already on your plate, why would you want to take on yet another distraction?"

"Because I don't consider it a distraction," the pastor replied. "I consider it an obligation."

"To whom?" Phil asked, pointing at Troy. "Him? No offense to Mr. Simmons, I'm sure he's a great guy, but why would you put the church at risk just because a random member asked you to do some politician a favor?"

"Because some of us think it would be a good idea," a hesitant voice answered. Julia looked for the source: a young man seated to Troy's right. "Hello, Mr. and Mrs. Simmons." He nodded in the couple's direction. "My name is Brandon Baxter. I'm the newest member of the board, so I'm not sure how much my opinion matters"—he looked back toward the other attendees— "but I like the idea."

Phil glared in the young man's direction like a third-grade bully suddenly challenged by a first-grade twerp. "You can't be serious," he snapped. "I can name at least a dozen members of this congregation who've listed Christ Community as a primary beneficiary to their transition inheritance. If Alex sends that…that…declaration, some of them might find out. I mean, this thing could get picked up by the news, for Pete's sake. What if that happened?"

"Actually," said Troy, "that's exactly what we hope will happen. The government is getting ready to launch a huge marketing effort to encourage more transitions. We can't compete with that. But we can create enough of a stir to get the attention of the press. Who knows, with a little help from some old friends"—he winked in Julia's direction—"we might get a few million fellow religious types to join the cause."

Phil's eyes turned to saucers. "You plan to release the document to the press?"

"If there's one thing I learned during my time in Washington," answered Troy, "it's that politicians only respond to one thing: public pressure."

The second skeptic spoke up. "I'm with Phil," he said. "I mean, it's bad enough you want our pastor to send a letter to politicians, but going to the press is crossing the line."

"What line?" asked Troy. "Can you be specific? Exactly what line does it cross?"

"The separation of church and state, for one."

"Oh, really."

"Yes, really!" snapped Phil.

"So you think a letter from a group of religious leaders affirming the value of parenthood and the dignity of the elderly will establish a state religion?"

"Don't be ridiculous. I didn't say that."

"You said this letter crosses the line separating church and state. Read the Constitution. That refers to Congress establishing a state religion, not religion holding the state accountable."

"I just mean that the letter feels wrong. The Church shouldn't meddle in state affairs."

"So the abolitionists were out of line?"

Silence.

"And the civil rights leaders? They should have kept their big mouths shut. Is that right?"

"I never said—"

"Dr. Martin Luther King Jr. was, I believe, the pastor of a church," Troy continued. "Or am I mistaken?"

Phil appeared flustered by the line of questioning. "I don't mean it would be illegal for Alex to send the letter. Just unwise."

"Because it upholds Christian ideals?"

"Yes…er…no."

"Perhaps because it might make people angry?"

"In a way, yeah," said Phil. "I mean, why create unnecessary obstacles to reaching people?"

"We didn't create the obstacle. The Youth Initiative did.

We're just responding by clarifying a Christian belief that killing the weak and elderly is wrong."

"Not our job!" said the second skeptic. "Our job is to shine a light, not scream at the darkness."

The verbal joust continued for several more minutes until Alex interrupted by leaning forward in his chair and raising a single hand that halted the debate.

"Phil," he said while looking into the skeptic's eyes. Then he turned toward the rest. "Everyone. Let me try to help us reach consensus, or at least clarify differences."

Phil leaned back and folded his arms across his chest while rolling his eyes in condescending deference to the pastor's request.

Alex began. "Imagine you see a little girl skipping across the sidewalk on the other side of the street. She's six years old and on the way home from a friend's birthday party wearing an adorable frilly dress and a matching ribbon in her hair that her mommy bought for the occasion. You notice that the girl is clutching a party-favor bag in her hand. She can't wait to get home to tell her mommy and daddy that she won a prize during the game of pin the tail on the donkey."

Julia joined most of the others in smiling at the thought. She loved the way Pastor Alex told stories.

"Then you notice a large man hiding behind a bush watching the little girl approach. You stare intently at his face. You've met the man before. He has visited our church. You give him the benefit of the doubt, but you keep watching until the girl reaches his location. That's when you see the man slip out from his hiding place to grab her. He covers the frightened girl's mouth to prevent screaming and drags her into the woods while her legs flail wildly in silent protest."

The room fell quiet.

"Let me ask you this. In that moment, what is your responsibility as a Christian?"

"Protect the girl," said a woman seated beside Brandon, a look of anxious dread in her eyes.

Alex turned in her direction. Then he scanned the others. "Does everyone agree with Lydia?"

Unanimous nods.

"The man is bigger than you. And the girl isn't your daughter," continued Alex. "Does that alter anyone's opinion?"

No takers.

"What if I told you that the man is hurting and lonely, and that he visited our church in search of something that might bring meaning to his life? If you confront him you might drive him away. Wouldn't it be better to ignore the situation so that you can preserve the opportunity to win that man to Christ?"

A few sniggers punctuated the nonsense.

He answered himself with a wink. "Of course not. In that situation the proper response for a Christian is to do whatever he can to protect the innocent little girl, including risking his own life if necessary."

Phil uncrossed his arms with an impatient huff. "What's your point, Alex?"

"My point, Phil, is that circumstances often dictate the proper Christian response. If you saw that same man sitting alone in a fast-food restaurant your responsibility might be to strike up a friendly conversation, perhaps share your faith over a meal. But when he tries to abuse a little girl, your desire to win him is trumped by your duty to fight him."

He paused, letting the comment settle.

"I've come to view the Youth Initiative as a very big man abusing God's beloved children. All I'm asking you to do is let me confront the abuser."

Phil pounded his fist on the table like a judge's gavel. "No," he barked decisively.

Every head turned in his direction.

"I beg your pardon?" said Alex.

"I won't allow it."

Brandon spoke next. "Excuse me, Phil, but I don't believe that's your decision to make." He leaned forward in a show of bold assertion. "I move that we approve the pastor's request for permission to send the letter."

"I second the motion," announced Lydia, flashing two fingers.

"All in favor?" Brandon asked.

Four hands shot up immediately.

"Just a minute," interjected Phil. "If we're going to do this we need to follow the official rules. It's the chairman's job to call for a vote."

"Then I suggest you do it," said Brandon impatiently.

The bully looked at the raised hands around the room. It was too late. The question had already been decided.

CHAPTER TWENTY-EIGHT

Kevin accepted Angie's congratulatory kiss.

"This is wonderful, sweetheart," she said while handing back the tablet. "Clear, positive, and respectful."

He leaned in for a second peck. Angie didn't notice, distracted by the demanding whimper of little Ricky, who had been holding his mouth open for a next spoonful of applesauce.

"Troy was right about his pastor," Kevin added. "Definitely the right man for the job."

"So what's next?"

"Well, now that they have approval from the church board, Troy and Pastor Ware plan to recruit additional clergy. We hope to get about a hundred signatures before sending the letter to every member of Congress and distributing it at the convention. Julia plans to call in a few favors to convince RAP Syndicate to cover the story."

The phone rang.

"I'll get it!" they heard Tommy shout over the thud of feet galloping down the stairs.

"Anyway," Kevin continued, "I think this could work."

"I hope so," said Angie while wiping a mushy glob from the side of Ricky's grin.

"But that's not the best of it," he said.

"What else?"

"Daddy!" shouted Tommy from the living room. "It's Grandpa Tolbert."

Kevin kissed Angie on the head on his way out of the kitchen. "Hold that thought."

Moments later Kevin overheard Tommy's side of a conversation.

"Little Ricky's doing great," he said before pausing for Grandpa's next question.

"She's still not talking," Tommy answered. "But I'm doing what you said every single day."

Kevin smiled at the reminder of the "therapy" his dad had assigned. Tommy was to give Baby Leah a daily dose of the same medicine Grandpa administered for Grandma's back pain. "One kiss and a hug twice a day will help a whole lot," he had instructed his seven-year-old grandson.

In truth, no amount of kisses and hugs could cure a genetic disorder. Kevin had learned to accept a very different set of hopes for Leah from the ones he held for his other three children. Reluctantly at first. He, like Angie, had only gradually settled into the realization that their second daughter might never live on her own. Leah would likely always require the loving attention of her mommy, daddy, and, someday, siblings. Grandpa's prescription was not intended to cure Leah. It was intended to groom Tommy for the highest calling any person can receive.

"Hey, Dad," Kevin said after accepting the phone from Tommy.

"Hi, Son."

"How's Mom doing?"

"Oh, you know how it is. Her back has been acting up again."

"So the kisses and hugs aren't helping?"

His dad chuckled. "Not as much as I'd like."

Kevin hesitated, then said, "Let me make a few calls, Dad. I might be able to—"

"No," interrupted his father. "Your mother insists. No special intervention. What you're doing is too important to risk a scandal."

"It shouldn't be a scandal to ask that my mother receive the medical attention she needs."

"No, it shouldn't. But we don't manage what ought to be. We manage what is."

Kevin groaned at the truth of it.

"How you holding up?" Kevin asked. His father hadn't looked so good during their recent trip to Denver. He had seemed a bit tired, and frail. "Have you seen a doctor like I asked you to?"

"I did. Actually, that's why I called."

A brief silence.

"Dad? Are you still there?"

"I'm still here," he said. "And I plan to be here for some time."

An odd reply. "What does that mean?" Kevin asked with concern.

"I don't want you to worry," he said.

"Worry about what? Dad, what's going on?"

"An elevated PSA," he said as if mentioning the time of day.

"Which means?"

"Nothing." A brief silence. "Or prostate cancer."

"Cancer?" Kevin shouted. "You tell me not to worry and then say you have cancer!"

"Prostate cancer," Mr. Tolbert answered as if correcting the statement. "And it might be nothing. And even if confirmed, it's not like lung or bone cancer. They have procedures for these things. No big deal."

"*These things*? You make it sound like a hangnail. It is a big deal."

"They'll send in a few nanobots and I'll be good as new. I'm not worried."

"What about Mom? Is she worried?"

"Of course she is." A brief pause. "So I want you to talk to her."

Kevin frowned. "You want me to tell her it's nothing, don't you?"

"Exactly. I tried, but she doesn't believe me."

"She doesn't believe you because it *isn't* nothing, Dad."

"Please, Son, do me this favor. She has enough on her mind as it is."

Kevin sighed. "All right," he said. "I'll talk to her. But I'm not gonna lie to her."

"Of course not. I just want you to tell her what the doctor told me."

"Which is?"

"Which is that almost nobody dies of prostate cancer."

"*Almost* is a pretty nebulous qualifier," Kevin objected. "How serious is it?"

Another silence.

"How serious, Dad?"

"If the procedure gets approved, my chances are excellent."

If?

"The doctor submitted my case for review and expects an answer any day now."

"Why doesn't that make me feel better?" Kevin asked. "And no wonder Mom is worried. They denied her pain medications, for Pete's sake, and she's two years younger than you."

"That's what she said."

Kevin thought for a moment. "I'll make you a deal."

"What kind of deal?"

"I'll talk to Mom if you let me make some calls."

"No, Kevin. You can't risk it. I'm sure I'll be fine. And even if I'm not, I won't let you jeopardize everything you've worked for."

"But—"

"No buts, Kevin. Promise you won't try to intervene for either of us, at least until after your speech."

Kevin agreed, reluctantly.

"Don't tell your mother I coached you," said his father.

"Of course not."

"Call her later tonight. Tell her you heard about my condition and that you did some research to find out—"

"Dad," Kevin interrupted. "I've got it. I'll call her later tonight, OK?"

"Great. Thanks, Son."

They ended the call and Kevin walked back into the kitchen to tell Angie the news. She must have sensed his unease, reaching across the table to hold her husband's hand.

"Do you want to pray?" she asked.

He did.

Angie lifted her sweet voice to heaven on behalf of Kevin's parents. She asked God to lessen the pain in her mother-in-law's back and protect Kevin's dad. She prayed that the procedure would be approved and successful.

"Thanks, babe," said Kevin.

"What was it you were going to tell me earlier?" she asked, suddenly recalling their unfinished conversation.

"Oh," he said, less eager to share the news. "I got a message from Franklin's office. They decided to give me a prime spot at the convention: Wednesday evening at eight o'clock."

"Wednesday night!" she said. "I can't believe it."

Kevin shrugged, suddenly less impressed with the placement than he had been a few minutes before.

Angie lifted a finger to Kevin's cheek to force his eyes toward her own. "And Father," she prayed with her gaze fixed on Kevin's, "I pray that you will use my husband to restore respect and dignity to those considered unworthy of medical attention. Unworthy of life."

She paused at the sound of three-year-old Baby Leah waking from her nap. Then they heard the thump, thump, thump of Tommy's feet running toward his baby sister's room, where Kevin knew he intended to administer another dose of Grandpa's therapy.

CHAPTER TWENTY-NINE

The young woman remained on her knees with hands folded and head still bowed. She glanced out the corner of one eye toward Mrs. Mayhew's beaming face and her pastor's affirming smile. She looked up. "Is that all? We're done?"

"That's all, sweetheart," said a sniffling Mrs. Mayhew.

"Wow," said the girl, "I thought it would be more, I don't know, complicated."

Alex chuckled. He loved watching the reaction of new believers after he guided them through the prayer of salvation. Sometimes they wept. Sometimes they grinned. And sometimes, like now, they questioned the procedure.

"Like I said," he explained, "Jesus has already done the hard part. All you have to do is accept his free gift." The pastor looked at his assistant. "How about it, Mrs. Mayhew? Did it sound like she got it right to you?"

"Of course she got it right," Mrs. Mayhew said while engulfing the girl in a maternal embrace.

Alex glanced at the time. He was scheduled for another lunch with area pastors in twenty minutes, this time at one of the largest churches in southern Colorado. Skip Gregory was hosting the meeting at the Chapel's main campus, the largest of five facilities housing a combined weekend attendance of over four thousand members.

"Listen, Paula," he said while the girl attempted to free herself from Mrs. Mayhew's suffocating squeeze, "I'm afraid I need to head out for a meeting across town."

He gently tapped his assistant's arm, prompting Mrs. Mayhew to finally release her victim.

"Mrs. Mayhew here will give you a Bible and a booklet to guide you through a few baby steps as you begin your walk with Christ."

"Thank you, Pastor," the girl said while offering her hand. "I really appreciate your taking time for me."

"Believe me, Paula, the honor was all mine." He meant it. For once, a Spiritual Dialogue appointment had actually accomplished the stated goal of welcoming a searching soul into the open arms of a saving God.

On his way to The Chapel, Alex used the glow of Paula's decision to brighten his outlook on the upcoming meeting. *Maybe things will go better this time*, he thought. Of the roughly seventy ministers he had invited to breakfast, lunch, or dinner during the past week, only fifteen had shown up, most of them more interested in the free meal than the topic of discussion. Troy had asked Alex to recruit a hundred area clergy to cosign the open letter. But all his messages, calls, and invitations had only garnered six: two Catholic priests, one Orthodox rabbi, two Baptist pastors, and one Presbyterian elder.

But today would be different, he insisted. Every minster in town knew Skip Gregory. Most had attended one of his evangelism conferences. That's why it had been such a triumph getting Skip to host today's gathering. Or rather, getting Skip's assistant to finagle a *yes* out of the popular minister. Alex's wife Tamara had met the woman, Nancy, at the hair salon. It turned out they lived only a few blocks apart so they exchanged contact information to begin a morning walk routine that fizzled after about two weeks. But they remained friendly, enjoying brief chats whenever they ran into one another around town. It had been the connection needed to get a foot in the door. Alex smiled, recalling the message that "Pastor Gregory would be delighted to host a bright spots lunch."

Alex pulled into the massive parking lot five minutes before the scheduled start time. It took another three minutes to read the campus map, locate the right building, and trot up a flight of stairs to the second-floor office complex.

"Hello, Nancy," Alex said warmly when he finally found the lead pastor's office.

"Hi, Alex," Nancy said with a smile. "How's that sweet wife of yours?"

"Very well, thanks. She sends her love. And thank you for making this happen today," he added. "I really appreciate all you've done."

"Don't mention it," she replied while standing. "I only wish there had been a better turnout."

Alex's heart sank. "How many?"

"I don't have an exact count." She began escorting Alex toward the gathering room. "We only ended up ordering fifty boxed lunches."

"Fifty?" he half shouted. "You had fifty RSVP?"

"A bit less," she explained. "We added a few lunches to be safe. There are always last-minute stragglers."

Alex breathed a sigh of grateful relief upon entering the room filled with mingling ministers. He recognized a few faces, pastors from some of the larger congregations in town. As he expected, an invitation from Skip Gregory's office carried weight.

"Where's Skip?" he asked.

"On his way," said Nancy. "He's wrapping up another obliga-tion."

"Counseling?" Alex guessed.

"Heavens no," she said with a laugh. "Ninth hole."

<hr>

A solitary boxed lunch remained on the serving table as Alex took a final glance toward the door: still no sign of the man who had promised a few opening remarks. Most of the attendees had already finished eating their sandwiches and chips. A few had even removed the walnut chocolate chip cookie from its plastic wrapping to start nibbling on dessert while glancing impatiently at a watch or checking messages. If Alex waited any longer, he feared, some of the pastors might leave.

He walked to the makeshift lectern Nancy had arranged in the corner of the room: a music stand positioned so as to be visi-ble from every table.

"Well, it appears our host has run into a bit of a scheduling challenge," Alex began apologetically. "But I want to honor your time, so, with your indulgence, I think I'll begin."

The ministers shifted in their seats to face a man few had ever met but who, it seemed, would be pinch-hitting for the one they had come to hear.

"My name is Alex Ware. I'm the pastor of Christ Community Church, where I've served for nearly a year."

He could just imagine what the seasoned pastors facing him were thinking: *A rookie pastor from a small church.*

"I want to begin by thanking each of you for attending. We're all busy, and it means a great deal that you carved out the time to support what I hope will—"

The door flew open. "Sorry, guys," Skip Gregory said with

short breath. Every face lifted at his arrival, skeptical yawns transforming into looks of eager anticipation as the successful pastor they both admired and—truth be known—envied moved toward the podium. Skip shot a playful glare at a rotund pastor seated near the remaining boxed lunch. "Sorry to disappoint you, Brother Zane," he said. "But I *will* be needing that lunch after all."

The room erupted into overdone laughter as the man wagged a reproachful finger at the jab. Alex stepped back to offer their tardy host the stage.

"Thanks, Alan," Skip said while patting Alex on the shoulder. He faced the crowd of fellow ministers. "I apologize for my late arrival, especially in light of the priority I place on what we've gathered here to discuss today."

A sudden pause while Skip retrieved a small tablet from his pocket and tapped the screen to call up whatever notes he had received from his assistant. Alex read the screen from over Skip's shoulder: BRIGHT SPOTS PETITION.

"Listen, guys," he began, "I consider the Bright Spots Petition an important initiative that I hope you will sign. I don't pretend to understand the details, but I stand behind the spirit of what Alan here is trying to do."

Alex leaned close to whisper, "My name is *Alex*. Alex Ware."

Skip blushed at the mistake while offering a slight nod. Then he turned back to his audience.

"Gentlemen, you are all bright spots, shining the light of the gospel to a lost world. And some of you remember the days when churches could do that important work as tax-exempt organizations."

Tax-exempt organizations? Alex felt a sudden panic. Had Skip even read his letter?

"Imagine how much brighter our light could shine if the federal government acknowledged the significance of what we do

by restoring the charitable donation write-off for religious insti-
tutions."

Affirming nods peppered the room while Alex reached for a
way to graciously correct his host.

"The fiscal crisis is likely to get worse, not better. It will
be more and more difficult for church members to give in the
months and years to come. They need the kind of tax relief a
bright spots strategy would give."

Alex couldn't let the confusion continue. "Excuse me, Skip,"
he said gingerly.

The minister smiled at the interruption. "But I've rambled
on long enough," he said. "I'll just rescue my boxed lunch from
Zane over there and let Alex unpack the details." Another round
of chuckles accompanied Skip as he moved from the lectern toward the serving table.

"Thanks, Pastor Gregory," Alex began before clearing his
throat. "I need to start with an apology. I should have commu-
nicated more clearly that the Bright Spots Petition is not about
a charitable gift write-off for donations, although I'd love to sign
that petition myself if and when it ever exists."

All eyes turned toward Skip. He appeared momentarily embarrassed, then flippant. He shrugged. "So much for announcement cue cards!"

Nervous laughter filled the room in solidarity with a mistake
every pastor had made at one time or another.

Alex continued. "Perhaps the best way to help you understand what we hope to accomplish is to read an open letter to
our elected officials that I drafted. Several area clergy have already signed it." He handed a stack of one-page documents to a
man seated in the front row, who jumped to his feet to distribute
them to the group.

By the time Alex finished reading aloud the room had become
more subdued than a funeral parlor. He waited as the group ab-

sorbed the words. No reaction for several minutes. Then Alex noticed a single hand slowly rising in the back of the room. "Yes, sir," he said eagerly, relieved at any sign of life.

"Am I to understand that you are asking us to sign this?"

Wasn't that clear from the beginning?

"Well, yes," Alex responded. "We plan to release it at a press conference on the first day of the upcoming convention in Denver. The idea is to generate conversation among the party delegates who will frame the platform and, more importantly, to create buzz in the media."

A stiff silence. Skip Gregory leaped to his feet as if reaching to catch a falling vase.

"Forgive me, gentlemen," he said while approaching the podium. He put an arm around Alex's shoulder, "but it appears we have experienced what they call a failure to communicate."

"I certainly hope so," someone said from the back of the room.

"You see," Skip said in Alex's general direction, "this particular alliance of ministers is committed to political neutrality."

"Of course," said Alex. "So am I."

"Well," continued Skip, "I would hardly call this document neutral."

"But it targets both parties," responded Alex. "It isn't partisan in the least—"

"And we agree," Skip interrupted, "that Christians should be good citizens by voting and, at times, getting involved in the political process."

A collective nod around the room told Alex that Skip was speaking on behalf of most, if not all, in attendance.

"But we aren't ordinary citizens, are we? Every one of us in this room is a minister. A leader. What we say in public carries greater weight. And greater risk for misunderstanding."

"Which is why we need to speak boldly and clearly," Alex

said, the elevated pitch of his voice betraying rising intensity. "Our national leaders need to hear from those of us called to speak for God."

A disapproving murmur around the tables.

"Speak for God?" said the rotund man, his mouth half full of crumbled cookie. He swallowed the final remnants before speaking again. "Who says it's our job to speak for God?"

Alex was sure he had misheard the question. "Excuse me?"

"Our job is to preach the gospel to a lost world," the man continued.

Skip retook the floor. "Listen, Brother Alex, we appreciate what you're trying to do here. We really do." More deferential nods. "But getting involved in controversial matters like this will do nothing to help us reach people who need Jesus."

"But you just said you would sign a petition to restore tax exemption for church donations. Isn't that controversial?"

"Apples and oranges, my friend. Apples and oranges."

Alex tried grasping what was, apparently, a clear difference. "All I know," he finally said, "is that the people in my congregation are starting to reflect the same trends as the rest of society, especially when it comes to transitions. We need to do something. Or, at the very least, say something."

Another stiff silence.

"I don't know about the rest of you, but I'm tired of consoling elderly members who feel a growing pressure to volunteer. Even their grown children, some of them believers who attend our church, have begun to nudge Mom or Dad toward crafting a transition will." Alex looked at Skip directly. "Don't you get tired of bodiless funerals where the grief of loss includes the shame of a guilty conscience?"

"Actually," Skip replied, "I don't do many funerals these days. My associate handles pastoral care matters."

"Well, I do," said Alex. "And I can tell you that both the old and the young are being victimized by this tidal wave of death called the Youth Initiative. Someone needs to stand up and say it isn't right."

Something in Skip's eyes told Alex he had just lost his platform. And his battle.

"I'll tell you what," said his host with a tone of gracious condescension. "Why don't we all agree to take this letter home and prayerfully consider whether we can, in good conscience, lend our names—and the names of our churches—to such an effort?"

A swell of affirmation followed. Alex knew it would result in a quick exit for all, and the signatures of none.

Fifteen minutes later Alex drove back to the office trying to sort through conflicting feelings. He blamed himself for failing to make a compelling case. Why else would so few join a cause clearly in the right?

Or had the entire effort been a mistake? Who was he, after all, to question the philosophy of a man who had built one of the largest, most influential churches in the state? What had Alex done besides barely keeping Christ Community from shrinking into irrelevance? Maybe the more seasoned leader had a point. Perhaps Alex should focus more on sharing the good news of the gospel than on condemning evil.

The conversation with the young woman in his office came to mind. It had felt so good inviting a lonely soul to accept God's welcoming grace. Calling national leaders to repentance, on the other hand, had done nothing but put a knot in his gut and, he feared, a label on his chest: Pastor Alex Ware had become "too political."

CHAPTER THIRTY

Kevin eased himself out of bed before the alarm could sound. He tapped the MUTE icon to protect Angie from disturbance. It had been a rough night for both of them thanks to Joy's two o'clock calamity. Kevin had stripped their daughter's wet sheets from the bed while Angie soothed her mini-trauma. Joy's accident had been Daddy's fault, they agreed. Deep in thought preparing for his upcoming convention speech, Kevin had forgotten to tell Joy to use the toilet before climbing into bed.

He checked the time while tiptoeing around the mattress. As expected, he found Joy lying beside the bed. She had spent much of the night nestled between Kevin and Angie, preventing either from getting any rest. At about five in the morning he had tossed a pillow onto the carpet and moved Joy gently to the floor, where she continued sleeping now. With any luck he could keep the household quiet while Angie and Joy caught a few more winks.

Moving to the kitchen, Kevin poured himself a cup of morning verve before positioning himself in front of the computer. He reopened a document that he had finally abandoned around midnight. Then he frowned at the words on the screen. In one week Kevin would deliver the most important talk of his life. This, he knew, was not it.

He reviewed the key points.

THE PROBLEM: The nation, like most of the developed world, finds itself in a financial tailspin thanks to a century of falling fertility rates. Too few young bear the burden of a rapidly aging population.

MAKING MATTERS WORSE: Rather than solve the problem, President Lowman's Youth Initiative has deepened the crisis by fostering a culture that devalues human life and dignity.

BRIGHT SPOTS: There are many "bright spot" communities that share the same two characteristics: lots of children and few transition volunteers.

PROPOSAL: First, we need to advance policies that will ease the burden on those trying to form families so they can raise up a new generation of innovators, business owners, consumers, and taxpayers. Second, we need to restore a sense of dignity and respect to our elderly and disabled citizens.

INVITATION: Help us make it a little easier for bright spots to shine. They are the hope of our future.

He had intentionally omitted an overt endorsement of the prospective nominee. Kevin still didn't trust Senator Franklin. So he limited his comments to motivating delegates to consider the positive impact of bright spot communities.

But something is missing, Kevin thought.

He took another sip of coffee while staring at the screen. Then he tapped an image of Troy Simmons, his most trusted advisor. After one ring Kevin remembered the time zone difference. It would be four o'clock in the morning in Colorado. He hit CANCEL.

Kevin sighed at his inability to focus. He had crafted hundreds of speeches before. Why, all of a sudden, such a struggle? Was it because this would be his first in front of a nationally televised audience? Or was it that he, and he alone, could give voice to ideas that ran diametrically opposite to his party's current trajectory? What's more, opposite to Franklin's own agenda?

Kevin felt the familiar tingle of his wife's fingers sliding around his chest from behind. "Morning, babe," she yawned into his ear before planting a peck on his whiskered cheek.

He spun in the chair to invite Angie onto his lap. She accepted.

"Joy?" he asked.

"Still asleep."

"Good. Sorry about last night. I've been a bit distracted."

"Of course you're distracted," said Angie. "This is only the biggest speech of your life."

"Thanks for the reminder," he said with a nervous chuckle.

She offered an affirming squeeze. "I'm not worried a bit. You'll be wonderful."

He suddenly believed it. If...

"Would you take a look?"

"At what?" she asked.

"My speech."

"You already read it to me, silly. I said it was very good. Don't you remember?"

"I know, but you lied."

She slapped his chest playfully. "I didn't lie!"

He laughed. "Well, maybe you didn't lie. But you didn't tell the whole truth."

She said nothing.

"Fess up," he said, positioning his hand over the ticklish spot on Angie's thigh. Her brow threatened retaliation for any attempt. "Now," he said, "are you going to help me make this speech better or do I need to squeeze?"

She waited. Kevin's tickles usually ended up prompting a different sort of play. A mischievous smile and a wink told him she might welcome the attack.

"Joy is still sleeping in our bedroom," he reminded her.

"Oh, yeah," Angie said while gently pushing his hand away from her leg. "In that case, show me what you've got."

They both turned toward the screen.

"It's all there," she said after reading the entire document. "But I see what you mean. It's positive, forward-looking, and clear, yet seems to be missing your usual charm."

"My charm?" he said in surprise.

She kissed him briefly on the lips. "Yes, Kevin Tolbert, your charm."

How, he wondered, was he supposed to add charm to a nationally televised speech?

A sound came from the computer. Kevin tapped the screen.

"Well, well," said an obviously groggy Troy Simmons. "It looks like you two are having a good morning!"

"Hi, Troy," said Angie while leaping up from Kevin's lap to move toward the pantry. "How are Julia and Amanda?"

"Sound asleep," he said. "So was I." He looked at Kevin. "Did you call me on purpose? I heard a ping and saw your icon."

"Sorry about that," said Kevin. "I ended the call when I remembered the time difference. Go back to bed. It can wait."

"I'm up now," he said while wiping sleep from his eyes. "What'd you need?"

Kevin explained his dilemma before sending a copy of the draft to Troy. Then he waited.

"I see what you mean," Troy finally said.

"Angie says I lack charm."

Angie huffed while placing a bowl of cereal on the table.

"I didn't say *you* lacked charm! I said the speech needs your charm."

"She's right," said Troy. "As it is, the content comes across fine. But it needs to connect skeptical listeners to the beauty it implies."

"I guess I was kind of hoping that message would come from your pastor's letter. I figured it was my job to make the economic case for bright spots and let the ministers give my proposal a human face."

Troy said nothing. Kevin tried to read the look in his friend's eyes. Disagreement? No. More like disappointment.

"What's wrong?"

"About the clergy letter," he began. "The process hasn't gone as well as we had hoped."

"Meaning?"

"Meaning Alex has only managed to recruit a handful of signers."

"How many?"

"Not enough."

"How many, Troy?"

"Nine."

"Nine? That's it?"

"Afraid so."

"I thought you said Pastor Ware was the man for the job."

"I did. And he is. I couldn't have asked anyone to try harder. He contacted practically every minister in the state, including a very influential alliance of pastors from the largest congregations in Denver. None of them signed on."

"None?"

"Not one. In fact, Alex says he's been catching heat from several of them."

"For what?"

Troy appeared embarrassed to say. "They've accused Alex of hurting the cause of the gospel by stirring up controversy."

"You're kidding me!"

"I wish I were," said Troy.

"Did he explain that millions of people are being pressured to die in the name of heroic self-sacrifice?"

"They know."

"Doesn't it make them angry?"

"Not angry enough, it seems."

"And he showed them the letter?"

"Of course he showed them the letter."

"Then how can they call it divisive? You couldn't write a more affirming, non-controversial statement about human dignity."

"Most of them agreed with the content of the letter," Troy explained. "They just didn't want to sign it."

"Why?" asked Angie over Kevin's shoulder.

"They don't want to become political," said Troy.

"Political?" Angie said. "How is defending human dignity political?"

"I'm still trying to figure that out myself. Apparently they don't understand the difference between the public square and partisan politics."

"But they're pastors!" shouted Kevin. "They *should* know the difference."

"Shhh," warned Angie. "You'll wake the kids."

Kevin willed himself calm while attempting to make sense of what he had just heard. Why would anyone consider such a simple action out of bounds, especially those called to teach the truth? Why would men and women who spoke for God silence themselves on such a foundational subject as human dignity?

The three said nothing as Kevin absorbed a disheartening realization. "It's no wonder we live in a godless world," he finally said.

For the past several years Kevin had sacrificed his family's financial stability in order to run for public office. He had endured false accusations that had nearly destroyed his marriage and reputation, and had put it all on the line in order to make a difference in the public square. Despite everything, however, he had taken strength from the knowledge that other believers, and especially ministers, stood shoulder to shoulder with him in the effort to defend God's image on earth.

But the truth, it appeared, was that Kevin's tiny band of comrades stood exposed in the cross hairs of enemy fire. And reinforcements were nowhere in sight.

CHAPTER THIRTY-ONE

"Now?" Alex said to Mrs. Mayhew's image on a flat screen on the wall. "But I just walked in the door. We're sitting down for dinner."

His assistant offered a sympathetically tortured frown. "I know. I'm so sorry. I told Mr. Crawford it wasn't a good time to meet since you had several hospital visits late this afternoon. How is Mrs. Bingham feeling, by the way? The poor dear."

"The doctor said she'll be fine once they zap the kidney stone," Alex said impatiently. "So Phil is waiting for me at the church right now?"

"Oh, not just Mr. Crawford. Most of the board."

"What? He called a board meeting without my knowledge?"

"They started at six o'clock."

Alex glanced at the time. In session for over an hour. Not good. "Why didn't you call me earlier?"

"Mr. Crawford said to wait because they had a sensitive matter to discuss before you arrived."

Alex looked at Tamara. Her eyes asked what it could mean.

Alex shrugged dismissively. No point in upsetting her with paranoid speculation. "OK, Mrs. Mayhew," he said nonchalantly, "I'm on my way."

He decided to finish his meal before rushing out the door.

After forcing Chris to finish his green beans and skimming "the icky stuff" from the bottom of Ginger's meatloaf, Tamara leaned close. "What are they meeting about?" she asked.

"Not sure," he said. "Probably the budget."

"Why would they call an unscheduled, last-minute meeting about 'sensitive matters' just to discuss the budget?"

He flashed an awkward grin. "They want to give me a raise?"

—◦◦◦—

By the time Alex arrived, whatever conversation had prompted the meeting had run its course. And, judging from the uncomfortable stiffness in the room, had led to unpleasant conclusions.

As usual, Phil Crawford was seated at the head of the conference table. He looked impatient, as if the fifteen minutes Alex had spent eating had inconvenienced some perfectly sequenced timeline. Kenny James sat to Phil's right, his eyes fixed to a tablet screen. Like everyone else in the room he seemed to intentionally avoid eye contact. Clearly this was not about bumping up the pastor's salary.

"Sorry I'm late," Alex began. "Mrs. Mayhew just called me thirty minutes ago. I didn't realize we would be meeting this evening."

"Please, Alex, have a seat," said Phil.

Brandon Baxter was missing from the room. *Unavailable or never invited?* he wondered.

"We've spent the past ninety minutes discussing our dilemma," Phil began while Alex settled into a chair.

"What dilemma is that?"

Phil glanced at Kenny, who accepted the hand-off with a hesitant nod.

"'Pastor Ware,'" Kenny began reading, "'we wish to bring to your attention several recent incidents that require resolution if we hope to restore stability and unity to this congregation.'"

Alex looked at Phil. "A letter? Really? You're going to read me a letter? Please, just tell me what's going on."

"I'll tell you what's going on," Phil said eagerly. Apparently the letter had been someone else's idea. "You've put us in quite a fix."

Mary Sanchez, seated to Phil's left, placed a hand on the chairman's arm as if to offer a gentle reminder of an agreed-upon approach.

Phil sucked in air before pursing his lips. Then he waved his hand in surrender to the will of the board. That's when Kenny continued reading.

"'Two specific concerns have been brought to the board's attention, both related to what could be described as a lack of wisdom in handling matters that affect the financial health of Christ Community Church.'"

Financial health? Had someone accused him of squandering church resources, or perhaps embezzling funds?

"I don't understand," said Alex. "Every expenditure is cosigned by—"

"This isn't about the budget," Phil interrupted. "It's about meddling in politics."

"Please, Phil," said Stephen Wilding, "let's not jump ahead of—"

"The man can read the official letter after the meeting," Phil barked. "I don't want to waste any more time beating around the bush." He looked directly at Alex. "The bottom line is that you've placed this church at serious risk."

"And how, specifically, have I done that?" asked Alex.

"First, by condemning family members of those in the congregation who made the difficult choice to volunteer. Some of them, I might add, who have been very generous to this church."

"But I've never condemned anyone," Alex said. "I haven't mentioned transitions in a single worship service."

"Come on, Alex!" Phil said. "You know what I'm talking about."

"No, I don't."

The chairman snatched the tablet out of Kenny James's hand and began scrolling. "Here it is," he said after scanning a document. "Christ Community Church has been named in a lawsuit filed by a Mr. Frederick Baxter Jr., son of longtime member Ellie Baxter."

"Wait. Freddy Baxter is suing the church?"

"Filed two days ago," said Kenny.

"For what?"

Phil continued reading. Apparently Freddy Baxter had been anticipating a large transition inheritance after the death of his mother. She had been denied approval for a surgery necessary to remove her tumor. The son had expected Mom to transition rather than suffer.

Alex recalled the meeting with Mrs. Baxter. "I sense that the Lord wants me to tell you to stay the course," she had said while encouraging him to oppose the Youth Initiative. Despite her courage, however, Ellie Baxter had also seemed sad. No, hurt. Her son clearly desired his mother's wealth more than her presence.

The lawsuit, Phil went on to explain, claimed that the leadership of Christ Community Church had intervened in a family matter by convincing Mrs. Baxter that volunteering would be a sin against God.

"That's not true," Alex objected. "If anything, Ellie Baxter convinced *me*. In fact, she's the one who suggested I take a stand against the Youth Initiative."

"I'm glad you brought that up," said Phil. "It raises the other purpose of this meeting."

Alex braced himself for more.

"As I feared, your letter to elected officials has come back to bite us."

"But it hasn't been sent yet," Alex explained. "It's not scheduled for release until next week."

"Word gets around. And in this case, word reached Freddy Baxter's lawyer. He has a copy of the draft with your signature on it. He says it's all the proof needed to substantiate Freddy's claim that the leadership of Christ Community has a vendetta against the transition industry and, therefore, heaped guilt on a vulnerable old woman."

"That's nonsense."

"Which part?" asked Phil.

"Ellie Baxter is no vulnerable old lady. She has spunk, and more courage than anyone in this room, myself included."

"That may be," answered Phil, "but it doesn't change the fact that we have a serious problem on our hands."

A prolonged silence.

"So, what do you want me to do?" Alex finally asked. "Should I meet with Freddy Baxter?"

"Absolutely not!" said Phil. "The last thing we need is for you to mess this up more than you already have."

"But I—"

Phil raised his hand to halt the pastor's objection. "We don't want to hear it, Alex. The board has already decided that I should handle this directly. I deal with tough negotiations every day in my profession. I don't have the time for this mess, but I'll make it a priority in order to avoid escalating tensions."

Alex scanned the room. Every eye was staring at the floor. "I see," he said. "If that's what the board has decided."

"It has," snapped Phil.

"But, if I may make one suggestion." All eyes moved back toward Alex. "I think you should speak to Mrs. Baxter before you respond to her son's claim."

"That's a good idea," braved an otherwise docile Lydia Donovitz. But she pulled back into her shell when Phil frowned at the comment.

"It's too late for that. I'm set to meet the lawyer over lunch tomorrow. Our goal tonight," he said toward Alex, "was to inform you of the situation and ask you to cease and desist this political nonsense until after I've settled the case."

Alex swallowed hard. "I understand. I'll lift you in prayer."

Phil appeared to squirm at the sentiment. "Uh, thanks. I could use it," he said. "For now, however, I need to ask you to leave while the board handles one other item of business."

"Of course," said Alex. He rose from the conference table and turned toward the door.

"Thank you, Pastor," he heard from behind. He looked back toward the voice of Mary Sanchez.

"For what?" he asked.

"For trying," she said, like a mother hoping to cheer a child who hadn't made the cut.

Alex nodded gratefully before walking out of the room.

"Mrs. Mayhew?" he said after bumping into his assistant, who had, it appeared, been listening through the door. "I thought you went home."

"Oh, sorry, Pastor," she said sheepishly. "I just had a few more details to handle before heading out."

Great, he thought. The entire gossip network probably already knew what Alex clearly sensed: his days as pastor of Christ Community Church were numbered.

CHAPTER THIRTY-TWO

"More wings?" asked the perky waitress.

Matthew looked in her direction, this time noticing a face. Cute. She reminded him a bit of Maria Davidson back in their high school days. He let his eyes move down to enjoy the rest of the view. There was a time when he would have been timid about such blatant ogling, a carry-over from catechism classes and a once-intact chivalry. But the girl's skimpy uniform had made an offer he couldn't refuse.

She didn't seem to mind, offering a playful smile in response.

Must be new, thought Matthew. Every other waitress at Peak and Brew had become callused to lonely-guy advances.

"It's all-you-can-eat night," she added. "What do you say?"

He winked, hopefully. "Why not? How could I say no to such a lovely…face?"

She patted his shoulder with one hand while removing his bone-filled basket with the other. "Be right back!"

Matthew relished an echo of the girl's scent while watching her dart toward the kitchen.

"Pretty nice, eh?" came a familiar voice, accompanied by the sound of a beer mug settling onto the table. Matthew turned toward a man he had last seen crushing a cigarette butt into his living room carpet while irreverently waving a priestly hand. "I think she'd say yes," Mori added while slapping Matthew's slumped shoulder.

"Say yes to what?" he reluctantly asked the barstool buddy who had turned into a midnight phantom.

"I'll give you two to one that lovely piece of femininity would accept an invitation to your place after her shift ends."

The suggestion both bothered and enticed. Matthew had never been so bold with women. But then, he had never truly believed all things were permissible. How had Mori worded his living room absolution? "Go and believe in sin no more," Matthew recalled. "Is that it?"

The man chuckled. "I like the sound of that," he said. "Makes it much less complicated to pick the forbidden fruit."

Both men took a sip of beer.

"Speaking of which…" said Mori in the approaching girl's direction.

A fresh basket of spicy wings arrived. Matthew offered Mori the first pick. He accepted gratefully, giving Matthew a moment to think.

Mori's midnight visit *had* been a dream, hadn't it? Surely the alcohol had clouded Matthew's mind before he dozed off. There had been no cigarette burn in the carpet the next morning. His barstool pal had never actually spoken the blasphemous mockery beguiling Matthew's mind. Nor had he been the source of insidious laughter behind Matthew's lingering dread. Stress from the new job, he decided, had caused the frightening episode. And tonight was free of such pressures. No new clients awaited his assistance.

"So," said Mori, "how've you been?"

"Truthfully, a bit frazzled."

"Work?"

Matthew nodded. He needed a willing ear, yet doubted the wisdom of confiding in a man prone to transformation into a smoking, cackling demon. But, sadly, he had no one else. Bryan "Mori" Quincy had become, for better or worse, Matthew's sole confidant.

"I'm thinking about quitting," he explained.

"Over your head?"

Matthew took offense. "It's not that," he said. "I just... well... let's just say it's complicated."

"Remind me of your job."

"I work with the transition industry."

"That's right! I remember now. You sell suicide to old ladies."

Matthew frowned. "Actually, I moved out of the sales side of things into research and development. A pretty big deal, actually."

"Well, now, that sounds more like something a former philosophy major should do for a living." He paused. "Wait. You said you're thinking about quitting?"

A sheepish nod. "Like I said, it's complicated."

"Feeling guilty?" asked Mori.

"For what?"

"How should I know? I've just been around long enough to connect the dots between 'It's complicated' and 'I'm thinking about quitting.'"

Matthew nodded at the truth of it.

"Let me guess," continued Mori. "Whatever this research and development job entails carries certain... how shall I say it... ethical dilemmas."

Matthew said nothing. Of course helping volunteers carried ethical dilemmas. Each assignment had created a knot in his gut and each death had included a moment of inexplicable grief.

Matthew felt as if chunks of his own humanity fell away with each final gasp of life. But it was the price someone had to pay for a greater good. Not to mention a bigger paycheck.

"No," he finally said. "It isn't guilt."

"Good," Mori reaffirmed. "Pesky thing, that guilt. Especially, I imagine, when conducting research and development in your line of work. Sort of like the old Nazi experiments."

The comment stunned Matthew. "Why do you say that?" he asked. "What do Nazi experiments have to do with research and development?"

"That's what they were doing," Mori replied. "Hitler's Germans weren't mindless fools with a fetish for killing Jews, Gypsies, and homosexuals. They were on a quest to move us up the evolutionary ladder."

"By exterminating an entire race?"

"Oh, that came later: collateral damage of the war. Although even that fit their philosophy, don't you think?"

Matthew reached for a wing and a fresh napkin. "What philosophy is that?" he asked before taking a bite.

"The belief in the greater good of a purified human race. They started by sterilizing the infirm to avoid the spread of weak genes. Then they progressed to euthanizing debits, those incapable of contributing to society."

"Doing what to debits?"

"Euthanizing them."

"Meaning?"

"The same thing as the Youth Initiative," Mori explained. "Funny, until this moment I never realized how similar they sound. Anyway, the other killings came later as a way of ethnic purging. Basic Darwinian philosophy: survival of the fittest and all that."

Mori reached for another wing, pausing his hand over the basket while shooting a glance toward Matthew.

"Go ahead, I've had my fill," said Matthew. He cooled his tongue with a long swig before placing the empty mug back on the table. "But I still don't see the connection to research and development."

"Surely you know about the experiments," said Mori.

A blank stare.

"Fascinating bit of history," Mori continued. "The Nazis conducted a series of medical experiments on prisoners, mainly Jews and disabled non-Jews. After the war the experiments were labeled torture, so the findings were suppressed. But I imagine they learned quite a bit that might otherwise have proven useful."

"Like?"

"Couldn't say. They experimented on twins to try to understand genetics. They studied bone, muscle, and nerve regeneration by removing them from one person and grafting them into another, all without anesthesia. Imagine that! They even tried to find ways to treat hypothermia since so many soldiers died on chilly front lines. If I remember correctly, they stuck Jewish prisoners in ice water for hours and made others stand naked outside in sub-zero temperatures. And that's just a few of the experiments. The poor souls who survived were either killed or left to linger with a mutilated, fragile body."

Matthew cringed at the sound of it.

"I know. And all of that agonizing disfigurement would have been wasted had the Allies destroyed the findings. That's what some medical ethicists wanted to do. They disagreed with how the information was obtained, so wanted to deprive the world of useful knowledge. Like I've said a thousand times before, the world would be much better off if we completely abandoned the notion of sin. I would never do something like that to prisoners myself," he said as if in self-congratulation. "But if the Germans had the courage to make it happen, why shouldn't someone reap the benefits?"

"Courage?"

"Insanity, then. Either way, why waste potentially useful research. Am I right?"

Mori began downing his own drink as Matthew considered the question. This same man had introduced Matthew to the notion that a world without God was a world without limitations, something well and good for the strong, but rather hard on the weak. It took audacity of mind to believe as Mori did. And a callous heart, something Matthew had not sufficiently formed.

"I guess you're right," he finally answered. "I *have* struggled with ethical considerations. But that's not the main reason I'm thinking about quitting."

"What is, then?"

He wanted to tell Mori the whole story, seek his advice on a dilemma he still had no idea how to resolve. Someone out there was in a position to frame Matthew for a murder he hadn't committed. Someone was toying with him, using his former alias to threaten retaliation should Matthew decide to walk away from…from what? Had Matthew accepted a legitimate job advancing an important innovation in transition services? Or had he been a petty hit man doing the dirty work for some invisible power broker? Either way, Matthew felt trapped in a quandary no drinking buddy could help him escape.

"Matthew Adams?" Mori was saying while snapping his fingers in Matthew's direction. "Still with us, my friend?"

"Sorry," Matthew said self-consciously. "Listen, I need to scram."

"So soon?"

"Early morning," he lied. "Lots to do."

"Then do you mind if I cut in on the waitress? I mean, if you aren't going to ask her…"

Both men looked at the girl. She was leaning against the bar, chatting with yet another lonely guy.

"She's all yours," said Matthew while waving his tablet over the bill. He stood to leave.

Mori put a hand on Matthew's chest. "Hang on a second," he said. "Looks like I'm too late. She's heading this way. Like I said, I think you made an impression."

Matthew watched the girl approach, her spunky trot slowing to an alluring saunter. She began running her fingertips up and down her plunging neckline. Frozen with anticipation, Matthew looked into her eyes to confirm he was, indeed, her intended prey.

Then he nearly let out a scream of terror.

CHAPTER THIRTY-THREE

It was a face from a nightmare.

No fresh, rosy cheeks.

No bright, penetrating eyes.

No soft, pleasing smile.

Rotting flesh clung limply to a skull peppered with sparse strands of filthy grayish-blond hair. Her body, still vivacious, now carried a head more suited to a cemetery haunt than a one-night stand.

Matthew looked at Mori. He flicked a bit of ash from a half-burned cigarette before slowly returning his friend's gaze. He seemed amused by the fear in Matthew's eyes.

"Surprise!" he said with an insidious grin.

Matthew turned back. No girl.

"Who are you?" Matthew asked in a voice fraught with fear.

The man leaned in close. "Keep it together now, Matthew Adams. You can take a little joke, can't you?"

Matthew began rubbing clenched fists over his eyes. "I'm losing my mind!" he whispered while trying to ignore the voice distorting itself into a devilish baritone of laughter. He covered his ears fiercely, but the sound continued.

"You're not going to quit that job. Do you understand me, Matthew Adams?"

Matthew pressed his ears even harder. No use.

"Our research isn't quite finished yet," continued the invasion. "And you have a very important part to play."

The laughter resumed as Matthew felt a tug at his leg like the one he had experienced in the nightmare. Something, someone, was trying to pull him into ever-darkening depths. He kicked at the sensation while forcing his eyes open.

"Matthew?" said Mori, who was standing beside the waitress. Both of them looked worried, and confused.

"Should I call someone?" asked the girl, her lovely face restored.

"That's probably a good idea," said Mori, clearly at a loss as to what would have prompted such a bizarre reaction. "You OK, buddy?"

Matthew didn't know how to answer. No, he wasn't OK.

"I need to go," he said urgently.

"I can call you a cab if you want," said the girl.

"No, thank you. I'll be fine," he said while weaving himself around crowded tables in a mad dash toward the exit.

Two minutes later he pulled out of the Peak and Brew parking lot. He just needed to get home to sleep off whatever delusion was messing with his mind. Then he remembered that the same presence, real or imagined, had already visited his living room.

He glanced in the rearview mirror and noticed a pair of headlights following closely behind. Still breathing heavily with justifiable paranoia, he turned left, then right, then left again. He found himself on a street that went who knew where, trying to escape who knew what.

The headlights remained a hundred yards behind.

Fear turned to anger. "I won't let you hunt me like an animal!" he shouted at the mirror while making an obscene gesture. He turned again in hopes of finding a public parking lot where he might force the shadowy menace into the light. A brightly lit grocery store sign stood just up the road. He accelerated toward the haven of twenty-four-hour shopping convenience.

Matthew raced into a parking space just outside the sliding entrance doors. A mistake, he realized, when the other car, a stretch limo, pulled up immediately behind. He was blocked.

Tempted to run into the store, he thought again. If this was another ghostly apparition, what good would come of that? If a phantom had found its way into Matthew's living room and favorite sports bar, it could just as easily chase him through the vegetable aisle of a grocery store. He stepped out of the car, determined to stand his ground.

"Good evening, Mr. Adams," came an unexpectedly pleasant voice. A voice he recognized immediately.

"Ms. Winthrop?"

The limousine door opened. "Won't you join us?"

Matthew braced himself for another morphing face. Then he bent slightly to peer inside the vehicle. A shadowy figure sat beside Serena Winthrop. He was smoking a cigar. Another demon eager to haunt, or a flesh-and-blood human being planning something worse? There was only one way to find out.

He accepted the invitation to enter.

"I'd like to introduce you to my boss," said Ms. Winthrop.

Matthew felt himself in the presence of wealth and power.

The feel of leather as his fingers touched the limousine seat.

A tailored suit that lay in perfect symmetry across the man's broad shoulders, and a deep blue tie adding just the right hint of authority to his white French-cuffed shirt.

Despite a posh package, however, the man seemed gruff. His stern eyes and solid jawline reminded Matthew of an annoyed pit bull groomed for show.

Matthew settled into the seat across from the man. He took a deep breath, determined to display strength he didn't possess.

The man removed the cigar from his lips. "Do you know who I am?"

"No, sir," Matthew answered respectfully. Weakly.

"Allow me to introduce you to Mr. Evan Dimitri," said Ms. Winthrop with a reverence that suggested fame, power, or both.

But the name meant nothing to Matthew. "Pleased to meet you, sir." He extended a hand. "Matthew Adams."

Dimitri waved off the gesture. "I know who you are," he said before repeating the names Matthew had received for each assignment: Mr. Smith. Mr. Collins. Mr. Marlow. And finally, accusingly, "Mr. Manichean."

Panic choked Matthew's speech as he realized he was facing the man behind Judge Santiago's assassination. Unspoken questions shot in rapid sequence.

Why did you kill the judge?

Who gave you copies of my letters?

Why did you frame me?

How did you track me down to hire me?

Why did you hire me?

What do you plan to do with me now?

"Serena here tells me you refused your last assignment," said Dimitri, reaching toward the woman's thigh.

Matthew swallowed back enough fear to answer. "Like I told Ms. Winthrop, I need a break. Things have been pretty stressful and, well, to be honest, I'm not sure this is the right line of work for me."

"Would you like to quit?"

Matthew inspected the question. To say no might avert immediate danger, but at what long-term cost? To say yes could end his ordeal, but it might also land his name on some transition companion's assignment list. If other transition companions even existed.

"You can resign at any time," continued Dimitri. "Although, of course, we would need you to sign a confidentiality agreement stating you won't disclose details of this project to anyone, ever."

"Not a problem," Matthew said enthusiastically. "I won't tell a soul."

Dimitri looked at his lovely sidekick. Both nodded, as if Matthew's reaction had confirmed their assumption.

Ms. Winthrop spoke next. "The reason Mr. Dimitri and I wanted to meet with you this evening is because we were concerned about your possible resignation."

"Concerned?" Matthew asked warily. "Why concerned?"

"You've done a good job for us, and we'd hate to lose you. We want to make sure you consider all aspects of this decision. Where else, for example, could you make such a good income in this economy?"

Matthew felt a hint of relief. "Oh, the money has been helpful"—he turned to Dimitri—"and appreciated. But I've never cared about money all that much."

"There are also risks to consider," she added.

He spoke slowly. "What...kind...of risks?"

"As you know, we've managed this project in such a way as to create distance between the actions of contract employees and ED Enterprises."

"Don't you mean NEXT Incorporated?"

"We are not, technically, part of NEXT. Research and development operates as a distinct legal entity. An entity that is able to protect you as long as you remain under our umbrella. The moment you walk away, however, we would no longer be able to intervene should anyone take legal action against you."

"What kind of legal action?"

"Well, as one example, the police are currently investigating a recent at-home transition due to concerns it may have been a murder. The volunteer, or victim, depending on your perspective, had a rather large estate. The money was supposed to go to distant relatives. But in the final week of her life the woman changed her will, leaving the money to a suspicious beneficiary."

Matthew didn't follow. What did any of this have to do with the threat of legal action against transition companions? "I'll take my chances," he said.

"I understand," she said. "But please, before you make a decision, I'd like you to look at something." She pulled a tablet from her purse, then tapped an icon on the screen.

"What's this?" he asked.

"Just watch it," barked the pit bull.

A video began. The first image was a woman Matthew recognized immediately: Brianna Jackson. He recalled the moment, her peering out the front door at Matthew while failing to remember she had requested his assistance. Scenes moved quickly to condense the prolonged ordeal into a fast-paced episode of a hidden-camera comedy.

- Unsuspecting transition companion enters cluttered home of eccentric old lady
- Old lady claims she never made an appointment, but confesses she "forgets things"
- Woman wanders into the back of the house, then hides in her bedroom shouting "Leave me alone!" and "I don't have your money!"
- Transition companion coaxes her to the bedroom where

he explains that it's normal to feel scared and promises a painless death
- Old lady dies in the tub
- Transition companion vomits into the bushes

The video ended. "It's Ms. Jackson's death that is being investigated," said Ms. Winthrop. "So, as you can see, it might be a good idea for you to remain under our protection."

Matthew felt his own throbbing pulse.

"Relax, Mr. Adams," said Dimitri with a snort. "Our cleanup crew made sure to remove every possible clue that would link you to Ms. Jackson's death. And I can personally guarantee that the police will never see this footage."

"But," said Matthew, un-consoled by the promise, "this means I committed murder."

They were words he had never imagined himself speaking. A deed he had never imagined doing. He looked at Dimitri. "And so did you!"

"True, technically," he replied. "But the woman should have volunteered years ago. We just gave her the shove she needed."

Matthew felt the sting of his own earlier rationale.

He hadn't pressured his mother to transition. He had merely helped her think it through.

He hadn't caused Reverend Grandpa's death. He had simply loaned him a courage he lacked.

He hadn't killed Brianna Jackson or Saul Weinstein or Josephine Green. He had simply lent them a helping hand. A hand, he now realized, that had been manipulated like a marionette's on a string.

"They didn't want to die," Matthew said angrily.

"Maybe not," answered Dimitri. "But they needed to die. Our entire economy will collapse if we wait for every debit in this country to muster enough courage to volunteer. That's why this test is so vital, and so secret. We're part of something important, Mr. Adams. This is no time for any of us to become skittish over 'ethical concerns.'"

Matthew sat up with a start. "What did you just say?"

"You heard me," he said while pointing toward the front of the limousine. "I'm well aware of your chats about philosophy and ethics with the professor here." A power window lowered to reveal the driver, Mori, smiling in Matthew's direction.

"I believe you've met our colleague," said Ms. Winthrop.

"It was Mr. Quincy here who aided Judge Santiago's transition," added Dimitri. "The one you so kindly helped us achieve."

"I had nothing to do with the judge's death!" insisted Matthew, his mind racing at a thousand miles per hour.

"Didn't you?" said Dimitri while tossing a small pile of letters onto the floor. "Then how on earth do you explain these?"

They were copies of the letters Matthew had sent to the judge, requesting an audience. Letters he had last seen sitting in the police station. Letters signed with the alias A Manichean.

Matthew's head sank in defeat. "So it was you who wrote the final letter," he said.

Dimitri neither confirmed nor denied the statement. He instead handed Matthew a document. "So, shall we discuss your next assignment?"

He glanced at the page. Two unfamiliar names. "Husband and wife?" he asked.

"Yes," answered Ms. Winthrop. "Both pretty depressed after being denied treatment."

"A dual transition?"

"That's right," she said. "But don't worry, Mr. Quincy here will assist you."

Matthew looked at his drinking pal, then back toward Dimitri. "When's the appointment?"

"We need it handled tonight."

"Tonight?"

A nod.

Matthew reread the assigned names. "And who are they?" he asked.

"The parents of someone you've probably heard of," said Ms. Winthrop.

"Who's that?"

"Congressman Kevin Tolbert."

PART THREE

CHAPTER THIRTY-FOUR

A rattling sound stunned Kevin out of a deep sleep. Dazed, he squinted at the clock: 5:33 in the morning. He heard the noise again, prompting him to quickly grab and answer the phone vibrating annoyingly on the bed stand.

He didn't recognize the caller's voice. "Who?"

"Cain, sir," the man repeated. "Detective Tyler Cain. Denver Police."

Kevin shot up with a start.

"I'm calling about your parents."

"What about them?"

"They're gonna be fine," said the detective reassuringly. "But they're both pretty shaken up."

"Why? What happened?"

Angie's hand touched her husband's shoulder. He turned to look in her blearily anxious eyes, then tapped a speaker icon so that she could hear the officer's reply.

"There was an altercation with two men who came to the house last evening."

"A robbery?"

"No, sir. Said they came at your dad's request. Showed your mother an official-looking document before she invited them inside."

"What time did this happen?"

"It was around eleven o'clock. She told me she couldn't sleep. Back pain or something like that."

"What was the official-looking document?"

"I have it here. Says your father scheduled an at-home transition." A brief silence. "Do you know anything about that possibility?"

Kevin felt a cold shiver of alarm. *Mom and Dad transition? Impossible!*

"No, I don't. And no, they wouldn't."

"That's what I thought. Anyway, your dad had already gone to bed. Woke up when he heard your mother scream."

"Scream?" said Angie.

The feminine voice apparently confused the officer. "Excuse me?"

"That's my wife, Angie. She's listening on speaker."

"Oh, of course. Hello, Mrs. Tolbert. I'm sorry to disturb you with such upsetting news."

"Why did she scream?" Angie pressed.

"She told me she screamed when she realized what the men intended. One forced her onto a chair and started to tie her arms, while the other moved toward the bedroom. But your dad was ready for him."

Kevin felt a fury rise. "Did they hurt her?"

"No, sir. Like I said, just shook her up. Your dad stopped them."

"Where is my father now?"

"At University Hospital."

"The hospital!" Angie cried.

"Yes, ma'am," he explained. "The officer who responded to their call thought someone should look at Mr. Tolbert's injury. He took a blow to the head during the struggle, quite a bit of blood, but nothing serious. Your dad fought off two grown men with nothing but a hiking boot. Must be a tough old guy. Still, the doctors said they want to monitor him for twenty-four hours in case of a concussion. Both of your parents are resting comfortably now."

Kevin took his first effortless breath since the call began. "Thank God," he said.

"Yes, sir. Based upon the evidence I've found we could have been having a very different conversation."

Angie squeezed her husband's arm tightly.

"What kind of evidence?" asked Kevin.

"I've been investigating a string of similar incidents for the past year," Tyler explained. "The first was a pretty high-profile case. A federal judge was found dead in his chamber."

"I remember that," said Kevin. "It was tied to the wrongful death claim against NEXT."

"That's right. I was a private detective at the time. I got called in after Judge Santiago received a series of suspicious letters. I tracked down a suspect who, it turned out, didn't commit the crime. But whoever did appears to have expanded his or her scope."

"I don't follow," said Kevin.

"Well, sir, there have been at least eight other deaths in the past year that appear to be linked. In each case the alleged volunteer had loved ones who claimed no knowledge of a scheduled transition. We've suspected the family members themselves, since most of the deceased left large estates to a child or some other close relative. Until now, however, we've been unable to speak to any of the victims themselves. All of them were found dead in a bathtub just like any other at-home transition."

"How awful," whispered Angie.

"Yes, ma'am. Frankly, we would have suspected you, Congressman, if your parents had been found dead."

"I understand."

"I'm not sure you do. You see, a letter was found on the coffee table in your parents' living room. It appears to have been written by your father, explaining that he'd decided to volunteer so that the house could be sold and donated to...let me find it...here it is. He wanted the proceeds given to something called the Center for Economic Health. Mean anything to you?"

"It's a think tank I founded with my business partner—" Kevin stopped short, his mind suddenly connecting the dots.

"Sir?"

"I'm leading an effort to garner support for something we call the Bright Spots proposal."

"I've heard of that," said the officer. "Part of the anti–Youth Initiative movement, right?"

"You could say that. Although we prefer to emphasize what we're for rather than what we're against."

"Such as?"

"Such as the priority of bearing and raising children and respect for aging and disabled citizens."

"Hmm," said the detective suspiciously. "So the money from your parents' transition would have been used against the transition industry?"

"His parents' murder, not transition," said Angie indignantly.

"Right, murder. But the money would have helped you fight the Youth Initiative?"

"Theoretically, yes. But like I said, my parents would never volunteer. They're vehemently against suicide, no matter how noble the motivation."

The officer said nothing for several moments.

"Detective?" asked Kevin. "Are you still there?"

"Sorry," he finally said. "I was just thinking. You may have helped fill in a missing piece of the puzzle."

They waited for more.

"The intruders fled so quickly from your father's boot that one of them left behind a box filled with supplies. It contains a vial of PotassiPass, the serum used in NEXT clinics."

"Isn't that what you would expect?" asked Angie.

"Actually, no. This particular serum has only been approved for use in clinics. Typical home-based volunteers use a different brand, one that's pretty tightly controlled. Every ounce is tracked to make sure none of it gets into the hands of curious kids or homicidal maniacs."

Kevin considered the implications. "So the men who tried to kill my parents work for NEXT?"

"Not likely. I've spoken to the inventory control team at NEXT. They've had no incidents of stolen serum. Ever. Like I said, tight controls."

Angie spoke next. "So what gap in the puzzle did this fill?"

"Not sure yet," said the detective. "But I doubt it's a coincidence this happened to the parents of the politician spearheading an effort against the transition industry. Especially since the string of deaths began with Judge Santiago. The common wisdom was that he intended to rule against NEXT. Obviously he never had the chance. His death got the case reassigned."

Kevin's face fell into his hands at the realization that his battle against the Youth Initiative had put his parents at risk. And for what? The Bright Spots proposal had been losing momentum, not gaining. Franklin's invitation to speak had been his way of throwing the movement a bone. The senator wanted breeders' votes, not their values. And he knew Kevin could deliver those votes better than anyone else in Washington.

Angie wrapped her arms around Kevin's deflated frame. "I'm so sorry, sweetheart," she whispered into his ear.

"I've been so naïve," he said regretfully.

"This isn't your fault. And your parents are all right."

Kevin accepted Angie's embrace before turning back toward the phone. "I'll be on a plane later today," he said. "Tell them I'm on my way."

"I will," said the detective. "Please let me know when you arrive. I'd like to ask you a few more questions once I look a bit closer at what we've discovered here."

"Certainly," said Kevin before ending the call.

CHAPTER THIRTY-FIVE

Alex waited for his wife's reaction.

"They're firing you?" she asked with quivering fury.

"They never said that," he corrected.

"Then what did they say?"

"That it would be best for everyone concerned if I resigned."

Tamara stared blankly at the words. Alex had done the same ten hours earlier when Phil Crawford and an attorney gave the verdict: the board had decided to settle the Baxter lawsuit. It was, they had determined, the only practical course of action, since going to court would cost a fortune in legal expenses with no assurance of victory. A settlement could help them prevent a prolonged, unproductive distraction from the mission of Christ Community Church.

Tamara appeared unconvinced by his explanation, and slightly confused. "Okaaay," she said warily. "So why ask you to resign?"

A good question Alex hadn't been able to answer for himself despite a sleepless night.

"Is everything all right?" Tamara had mumbled groggily when Alex finally arrived home around midnight.

He hadn't been ready to talk about it. "Fine," he had lied, "go back to sleep."

Now, with his wife sitting in front of him dazed by the news, he reached for an explanation.

In truth, the church could settle a bogus lawsuit without asking the pastor to leave. But Phil Crawford wanted retribution for Alex's roundabout insubordination.

Never mind that the pastor reported to the entire board, not just the chairman.

Never mind that the board had backed his decision to draft the letter.

And never mind that every word of the accusation against Alex had been false.

Phil Crawford had decided that Alex needed to go.

"Our members will want to know who's responsible for such a sizable financial hit," Phil had said. "Sooner or later they'll learn that your activism ended up costing this church more than we can afford to lose."

Alex had a pretty good idea who would inform them.

Tears filled Tamara's eyes. Alex moved close to wrap his arms around his best friend and lover. She smothered herself in his embrace.

"It isn't right. You know it isn't right."

Tension melted into sobbing. Alex felt himself succumb to the same emotion. The jarring shock of injustice had transformed their youthful optimism into wounded betrayal. What was worse, he couldn't fulfill a husband's role. He ached to shield Tamara from the shrapnel the board's decision would bring. But he couldn't protect her. He felt as if his manhood had been stolen away.

He tried anyway.

"Listen," he said, gently cradling his bride's moist face in his hands, "there's no need for us to panic. God will use this for good, I know it."

Or at least he hoped it.

"We have three months to figure things out."

"Three months?" Tamara asked. "What do you mean?"

"The board said that if I resign they'll give me a three-month severance package, possibly more."

She repositioned herself within Alex's embrace. "You should demand six months. No, a year."

That would be a stretch. But Alex did have some leverage.

"Of course," Phil had said, "we'd like to handle your resignation in a manner that will protect you and your family from unwarranted speculation and damaging rumors. That's why I've agreed to explain the reason for your resignation to the congregation myself."

"And what reason would that be?"

"Simple. Your love for the people of Christ Community Church motivated you to avert a damaging scandal."

"And that's supposed to prevent speculation and rumors?"

"Don't worry," Phil had said while placing a paternal hand on his pastor's shoulder. "I'll be sure to give the announcement a positive spin. Some of the younger families at Christ Community really like you, Alex. I see no reason to disillusion them or cause them to question your integrity."

It had been a not-so-veiled threat, one that tortured Alex during the six hours he had spent staring at the ceiling while waiting for Tamara to wake.

If he refused the severance offer he would risk destroying his own reputation, not to mention the church's. The look in Phil's eyes had made it clear that he wasn't bluffing: one way or another Alex needed to go. He should probably accept the offer to sidestep a battle he would no doubt lose.

He recalled the story Ellie Baxter had shared about her husband. Reverend Baxter had lost his ministry even though he had done absolutely nothing wrong. Sure, he'd landed on his feet. The Lord had even opened doors for them to launch a successful business. But Alex knew himself incapable of similar fortune. He wasn't wired to become an entrepreneur. He was called to be a pastor.

Tamara reached for a tissue and dried her tears. She took a determined breath. "So," she said, "what's our next move?"

Not *your* next move. *Our* next move. The question buoyed Alex's spirit. He and Tamara were in this together, come what might.

"I'm not sure," he said while inviting her back into his arms. "Phil wanted an immediate answer, but I told him I would let him know next week."

"I bet he loved that," she said sardonically.

The sound of a different cry wafted from the adjoining bedroom. Baby Joseph was ready for his early-morning feeding.

Kevin chuckled at the reminder.

"What's so funny?" asked Tamara.

"Perfect timing," he said. "At the precise moment you ask what's next you get a summons."

Tamara sat up to look in her husband's eyes. He offered a wink.

"I may not know how we'll make a living," he began. "But I know our most important work is nowhere near done."

"I love you, Mr. Breeder," she said while squeezing her husband's torso.

"And I love you, Mrs. Bright Spot."

CHAPTER THIRTY-SIX

Mrs. Mayhew appeared distraught. "Where have you been?" she asked while nervously fidgeting with one earring.

"What's wrong?" Alex asked while closing the front office door.

"Did you lose your phone?" she asked urgently.

He felt his pocket. "Nope. Right here. Why?"

"I've been calling and messaging for nearly an hour."

He glanced at the screen. "Oh," he said with surprise, "I'm sorry. I must have forgotten to turn it back on this morning. I had kind of a rough night."

She glowered at the oversight. "Well you certainly had me worried."

Alex could only think of one thing that would have put Mrs. Mayhew so on edge. "Phil Crawford?"

A puzzled look. "What about him?"

"Does he want to speak to me?"

"How on earth should I know?"

"Isn't that what has you so upset?"

"I didn't say I was upset," she insisted. "I said I was *worried*."

"Worried about what?"

"About what that young man might do."

"What young man?" asked Alex.

"The one who came before." She raised a hand to one side of her mouth and began to whisper. "And if you ask me, he looks even more disturbed than he did the last time. "

"You mean he's here? Now?"

"He's waiting in your office."

"When did he get here?" Alex glanced at the time.

"He was standing outside the office door when I arrived, waiting for someone to let him in." She whispered again. "I've been a nervous wreck. You never know what a man like that might do to a helpless woman who can't track down the pastor. I told him you would arrive no later than eight thirty. That was fifteen minutes ago."

Alex placed his hand gently on her shoulder. "I'm sorry, Mrs. Mayhew."

Her arms crossed and her brow furrowed like an angry child's. Forgiveness would need to wait.

He found the man bowing his head in prayer, or perhaps despair. Alex reached into his memory to recall a name. "Frank?"

His guest shot up from the chair and lifted his eyes. "Um, yes, that's right." He turned to face the pastor self-consciously. "I hope you don't mind. I really need to talk."

"Please, sit," Alex insisted, waving the troubled soul back toward the sofa. "Can I get you something? A bottled water perhaps?"

"Nothing, thanks."

That's when Alex noticed an inflamed welt on the man's left

ear and a large stream of what looked like blood on his sleeve. "Good heavens, are you injured?"

Frank glanced down at the stain, then shook his head. "I'm fine. It's nothing."

Alex recalled their last visit. Frank had run out of the room when pressed. He decided not to push for details about the blood. "OK," he said while taking the seat across from his anxious guest, "I'm listening."

"When I came before you said everything I say would be kept confidential."

"Within limits, that's true."

"What limits?"

"Well, I would alert the authorities if I knew you had molested a child, as one example."

"I would never do that!" Frank said crossly.

"I'm glad to hear it," said Alex. "How about telling me what's on your mind?"

The man closed his eyes while massaging forehead and temples. He appeared to be weighing the risk of talking against the torture of silence. "OK," he finally said. "But I'm going to speak hypothetically."

Alex considered the idea. "Fine," he said.

The man inhaled deeply. "If a person did something illegal because someone else tricked him, would he be guilty of the crime?"

"You'll need to be more specific. What kind of crime?"

Frank looked like a man scanning a mental map to find an indirect route to his intended destination. "Well, not a crime, actually."

"Then what?"

"A medical procedure. Something perfectly legal in one instance but potentially criminal in another."

"I don't follow," said Alex, staring at the blood on his guest's sleeve. "Are you saying you've carried out an unlawful medical procedure?"

The man's head dropped again. "Not exactly. And sort of."

Alex sensed the man needed a nudge toward courage. "Listen to me, Frank. I can't offer any advice if you don't tell me why you came. You said you needed to talk. So talk."

A brief silence.

"All right. But I need you to promise you won't repeat it to anyone."

"Does it involve child abuse or murder?"

He hesitated as if weighing his answer. "No, it doesn't."

"Then what you say will remain between the two of us."

The promise loosened Frank's tongue. "I need to confess."

"Like I said before, I'm not a priest, but—"

"Not that kind of confession. I'm not after forgiveness for sin. I want protection from danger."

"What kind of danger?"

"Someone framed me for a murder I didn't commit. Then he tricked me into doing something that looks really bad. But I didn't break any laws."

"Why not alert the authorities?"

"No police!" the man snapped. "Like I said, I haven't done anything illegal. But the person framing me has. I want him exposed."

"If you've done nothing illegal why not go to the police?"

"Because they won't believe me," said Frank.

"What makes you say that?"

"I just know, OK?"

Alex met the man's eyes. "Does this have anything to do with your nightmares, Frank?"

The question seemed to surprise, and alarm.

"You told me you were destroying icons in your dreams. Still?"

He nodded. "Yes, but they've gotten worse."

"The dreams?"

A slow, tormented sigh. "If they are dreams."

Alex waited.

"Do you remember what you said last time?" asked Frank. "About Ivan?"

"In *The Brothers Karamazov*?"

"That's right. The atheist."

Alex reached for the memory. "I believe I said Ivan went mad."

"You said he went mad *after* a conversation with the devil."

"Have you had conversations with the devil, Frank?" Alex wondered what he would say if the answer was yes.

Frank's eyes darted back and forth as if scanning for an intruder. "I don't know about the devil," he confessed, "but I've seen some pretty scary stuff."

Alex felt a sudden chill. Perhaps Mrs. Mayhew's alarm had been justified after all. Something, he sensed, had been tormenting his guest that could not be perceived with mortal eyes.

An apparition? Possibly.

Madness? Perhaps.

Both manifestations of the same age-old disorder.

"Listen to me, Frank," Alex began. "Regardless of what you've seen or heard, there is only one way to escape what's behind the dread I see in your eyes."

The man fixed his gaze on the pastor as he continued.

"Like I told you before, the devil is a liar. That's what makes him even more dangerous than whoever you think is trying to frame you."

"I *know* someone's trying to frame me!"

"Fine. Someone *is* trying to frame you, then. It doesn't change the fact that the enemy of your soul is the greater threat. The first can get you thrown in jail. But the second can make you lose both your mind and your soul."

The man's body tensed.

"I have no idea what you've done, Frank. But no matter what it is, it's never too late to repent."

"I told you before," said Frank crossly, "I don't believe in sin."

"Yes, you told me that. But you also said you don't believe in God or the devil. Yet here you are, scared to death that one or both of them is on your heels."

"I never said that!"

"No, but it's why you came, isn't it, Frank? You're trying to decide which is worse: submitting to a holy God or falling prey to a ravenous devil. Trust me, Frank, you don't want the second. Admit your sin. Accept God's grace. Embrace sanity rather than madness!"

"I'm not going mad!" Frank shouted as if drowning out the possibility. "And I haven't committed any sin."

"All have sinned, Frank. Every single one of us is infected with a disease that drives us away from goodness, health, love, and joy. But Jesus Christ dealt a death blow to evil so that we could find freedom from sin's bondage."

"Stop using that word!" Frank pressed his hands over his ears like a child frightened by the sound of thunder. "I haven't done anything wrong," he shouted as if trying to convince himself. "I serve the greater good! I end suffering. I free people from decay!"

The room fell silent. Frank uncovered his ears. He looked embarrassed. "I have to go."

"Please," said Alex, "don't. Let me help."

He remained in the room. A good sign, thought Alex.

"Tell me who you freed, Frank. Whose suffering did you end? Someone you loved?"

No response.

"Please, tell me what's going on."

"I will," he said. "But I need to take care of something first. Can we talk again?"

"Of course," said Alex. "When?"

"I'll let you know. But I need your promise. Complete confidentiality, like confessing to a priest."

Alex thought for a moment. What choice did he have? "OK. Complete confidentiality."

"Then I'll talk to you soon," Frank said before rushing out the door.

CHAPTER THIRTY-SEVEN

Julia felt the man's hand pulling her up out of the water. She noticed his feet, then her own. Both of them were walking on the surface toward a white, sandy beach basking in the warmth of a rising sun. The abrupt sense of security mixed with anticipation dispelled what she had been feeling moments before.

The ache of grief, not for herself but for those sinking into the shadowy depths below.

The horror of sacrilege as she witnessed stunning beauty thrashed beyond recognition, majestic icons horribly disfigured.

And the helplessness of watching other victims shake angry fists at the man's outstretched hand.

Like her, they could have been lifted toward the tender grace of light rather than sinking into a bleak cruelty. Their lungs, like hers, could have filled with the fresh air of hope instead of the dark water of despair. And their faces, like hers, could have beamed at the smiling acceptance of a father rather than recoiling from the profane caress of a killer.

She woke at the chilly exposure of a vanishing blanket and the urgent sound of Amanda's voice. "Hurry up, Mom!"

"What time is it?" she asked as a spear of panic forced her head from the pillow.

"Ten past nine," came her daughter's urgent reply. "I'm gonna be late for tryouts!"

That's when Julia remembered. Despite Troy's resistance to the idea, Amanda had signed up to become a cheerleader thanks to Julia's willingness to second the motion.

Three minutes later the two raced away from the driveway toward Littleton Middle School. Julia had thrown on a pair of ugly sweats before running out the door. Amanda had managed to find a clean pair of shorts and slip into her most flattering yellow T-shirt.

"Great!" she groaned in horror while inspecting the visor mirror. "I *would* get a zit on the day of tryouts!"

Julia smiled sympathetically. "Don't worry about it, sweetheart," she said. "You look fine."

Something felt off.

"No," she corrected. "You look beautiful."

Amanda extended her hand toward Julia's disheveled hair, the same hair Amanda had admired since the day they met. "Thanks, Mom," she said. "So do you."

Julia glanced at her makeup-deprived face in the rearview mirror, then accepted the embellished compliment with a peck on Amanda's hand.

"What was that for?" Amanda asked while cradling the echo of a kiss.

"For accepting me as your mom," said Julia.

Amanda grinned.

They pulled onto the campus parking lot before Julia thought of Troy. "Wait," she said, "I thought your father said he would drive you to tryouts on his way to work."

"He left before I got up," Amanda explained.

It wasn't like Troy to forget a commitment, especially one that involved Amanda.

"He left a note," Amanda continued. "Didn't you see it?"

"What did it say?"

Amanda shrugged. "Something about an emergency and that he had to run off to the hospital."

"The hospital!"

But Amanda was already out the door, rushing toward a horde of adolescent girls in search of sideline glory.

"Troy?" she said after tapping his smiling image on her phone. "What's going on?"

"Hi, babe. I didn't want to wake you. Did you get my note?"

"Amanda read it. What emergency?"

"Kevin called this morning. His parents are at University Hospital and he wanted me to keep an eye on them until his plane arrives."

"What happened?"

Troy explained. Julia became more and more furious with each detail of the story.

"Someone accidentally scheduled them for an at-home transition?"

"It's more likely someone was targeting them."

"Why would anyone want to kill Jim and Gayle? And why make it look like a transition?"

"Think about it, babe. Kevin is about to offer alternatives to the Youth Initiative. I can think of a lot of people who would like to stop that from happening."

It hadn't been that long since Julia had aided such an effort herself. In pursuit of journalistic prestige she had nearly ruined Kevin's reputation and destroyed his happy home. It wasn't hard to imagine someone with far more to gain going to much greater lengths. She suddenly felt an overwhelming urge to pray.

For Mr. and Mrs. Tolbert.

For Kevin and Angie.

And, as before, for someone else.

"Are the kids all right?" she asked.

"Fine, as far as I know."

"Baby Leah?"

"Why do you ask?"

"I don't know," she said. "I just...I had another dream."

"I see. Was Baby Leah one of the faces?"

"No. But I can't shake the feeling she's in danger."

"Should I call Angie?"

Julia thought for a moment. "No, don't do that."

"But you just said—"

"I see no use in getting her worked up over a feeling I can't decipher, let alone explain."

"You're sure?"

"Yes. I'm sure."

Troy promised to keep her informed before ending the call.

Julia drove back to the house, where she showered and got dressed for the day. Then she retrieved the blanket Amanda had yanked onto the floor and covered her naked bed before sitting on the edge to think. She realized that no to-do list demanded obedience: she had no deadlines to hit, memos to write, or meetings to attend. She had, thankfully, resigned from Daugherty and Associates after obtaining the needed information about the ad campaign.

She glanced at a small notepad resting on the nightstand. It was the same notepad that had been her midnight companion back when she lived in an apartment with her sister Maria and nephew Jared. The same notepad onto which she had captured countless middle-of-the-night sparks of brilliance that might become another Pulitzer-winning feature. And the same notepad that contained her frantic notes from scenes that had once terrorized her restless sleep. She flipped open the pad to read the familiar words.

MAN
SHADOW
FEAR
ANGER
ABANDONED

An hour earlier she had been shaken out of the same progressing dream. Years before it had prompted panic as she felt the downward summons of sadistic laughter. A few days earlier it had frightened her with the vile destruction of iconic beauty in faces she didn't recognize and, perhaps, would never know. But now, sitting in the quiet of a home she shared with a once-lonely man and a once-orphaned girl, Julia sensed a greater meaning to the nocturnal tale.

She slid a small pencil from the notepad and positioned it over the page to receive whatever ideas might present themselves. But she wasn't prepared to receive what actually came. Despite an overwhelming urge to use the power of the pen, her greatest strength, to engage the enemy, she felt an overwhelming impulse toward a different kind of action. It was as if someone was assigning a task that, unlike writing, she felt ill equipped to perform. And so, setting aside her journalistic prowess, Julia engaged a very different front of the battle.

She turned around, bent her knees, and bowed at the side of the bed.

"Dear God," she whispered, "I sense you want me to pray. You know I'm not very good at this. But here I am, asking you to protect my friends, the Tolbert family. Especially Baby Leah."

The words broke as emotion overtook Julia's voice. She felt as if she had been given a tiny fragment of a sorrow that no mortal could possibly bear, the sorrow of one who had created a masterpiece beyond words only to see it thrown onto a trash heap of discarded human dignity.

"Father in heaven," she continued, "I don't know what to do. Someone hates what the Tolbert family represents. What *every* family represents."

A memory flooded Julia's mind. One of the first sermons she and Troy had ever heard by Pastor Ware described God creating man and woman and inviting them to become fruitful and fill the earth. The union of man and woman, the pastor had said, reflected the very image of a God who is, himself, a communion of persons.

"Father," she continued, "someone clearly hates what Kevin and Troy are doing. The same someone who, in my dreams, is pulling men, women, and children into darkness."

She paused.

"You gave me this dream for a reason, I know it. Please, God, tell me what you want me to do."

She waited in silence. But for what? A voice? A clap of thunder? Surely something that would tell her what to do next. Nothing came, so she said the prayer again, clasping her hands more tightly than before. Still no answer.

Unfamiliar with the protocol of fervent prayer, Julia remained on her knees for several more minutes. A sharp pain in her left leg finally compelled her to open one eye, then the other. She stood and walked toward the kitchen to fix herself some breakfast. Surely a bowl of cereal wouldn't stand in the way should God finally decide to say something.

She heard a single ping come from a tablet that was sitting on the kitchen table, where, she surmised, Troy had been reading the morning headlines before receiving Kevin's urgent call.

Julia tapped the bouncing icon to open a message. Anonymous.

DEAR MS. DAVIDSON:
I HAVE RELIABLE DETAILS FOR A MAJOR NEWS STORY. I

TRUST YOU TO TELL IT PROPERLY. ARE YOU INTERESTED IN SCOOPING EVERY OTHER JOURNALIST?

An annoying bit of spam, Julia wondered, or the answer to her prayer? She decided to find out.

DEAR ANONYMOUS:
I DON'T WRITE ANONYMOUS STORIES. WHO ARE YOU?
JULIA DAVIDSON SIMMONS

A reply came just as fast.

I WILL GIVE YOU EVERYTHING YOU NEED IN TWO HOURS. WILL YOU MEET ME?

Julia considered the offer.

MEET WHERE? AND WHAT IS THE STORY ABOUT? HOW DO I KNOW IT WILL BE WORTH MY TIME?

She waited.

WHERE: CHRIST COMMUNITY CHURCH
STORY: WHO KILLED JUDGE VICTOR SANTIAGO

CHAPTER THIRTY-EIGHT

"Oh, hello." Mrs. Mayhew appeared startled and a bit embarrassed by Julia's approach. She quickly lowered the sealed envelope she had been holding toward the light as if trying to make out the contents. "I'm sorry, dear. I wasn't expecting anyone. Do you have an appointment?"

"I think I do," said Julia. "But I'm not exactly sure where or with whom."

Mrs. Mayhew stared blankly.

"I received an odd message asking me to meet someone at Christ Community Church. But there was no indication of who I'm meeting."

"That *is* odd," muttered the pastor's assistant.

A moment of perplexed silence.

"Wait. I wonder if your appointment has anything to do with this." She handed Julia the envelope marked "Urgent and Confidential: For the Pastor's Eyes Only."

Julia handed it back. "But I'm not the pastor."

Mrs. Mayhew frowned at the comment. "I realize that. But

someone put this envelope on my desk while I was rearranging the flowers in the sanctuary twenty minutes ago. And now, here you are. Hardly seems like chance to me."

"So Pastor Ware is out?"

"Oh, no, he's in his office."

Julia glanced toward the closed door. "With someone?"

"Alone," said Mrs. Mayhew.

"And that envelope arrived twenty minutes ago?"

A nod.

"Do you think it might be a good idea to show it to him?"

"What, now?"

"Well, it is marked urgent."

A look of annoyance swept over Mrs. Mayhew's face, as if delivering the envelope would thwart her effort to learn what was inside. "Of course," she said weakly while raising an index finger. "Excuse me for just a moment, will you, dear?"

While Mrs. Mayhew slipped into the pastor's office, Julia checked her tablet for another update from Troy. All good news: Mr. and Mrs. Tolbert were doing fine, Kevin's plane had arrived and he was en route to the hospital, and the police had gathered clues linking the incident to a series of other spurious transitions that appeared unrelated to Kevin's activities.

She breathed a sigh of relief while typing a quick message to Angie.

GOT THE GOOD NEWS. TROY IS WITH KEVIN'S FOLKS.
THEY'RE DOING WELL.
PRAYING FOR YOU.

As usual, she reviewed the message before tapping send. Something was missing. She added one additional line.

HUG THE KIDS FOR ME. ESPECIALLY BABY LEAH.

The door to the pastor's office swung open.

"Hello, Julia," said Alex with some urgency. "Please, come in."

She followed him into the office.

"Please, have a seat," he offered, his eyes still fixed on the handwritten letter in his hand.

"I received a strange message a few hours ago asking me to meet someone here," Julia began. "Something about getting the scoop on an important story."

"Yes, I know. I just received this." He handed her the note.

Dear Pastor Ware:

Thank you for promising to protect the confidentiality of my confession. I hope you don't mind that I intend to confess over the phone. Two reasons.

First, my childhood priest, Father Tomberlin, listened from the other side of a thin veil hanging between us in the confessional. That made it easier for me. I'd prefer letting the phone conceal our faces.

Second, and more to the point, I have asked someone to join you. Her name is Julia Davidson, a journalist. I want her to expose the person who framed me by reporting what I say as if I'm a confidential informant. You will serve as a corroborating witness, her second source. Unorthodox, I realize, but confirmation from a minister will provide credibility to her story without exposing my identity.

Please call me if and when Ms. Davidson arrives.

Thank you, again, for your concern and help in this matter.

Frank

Julia looked up from the page. "Is this legitimate?"

Alex nodded slowly. "He was in my office this morning. There was blood on his sleeve and he said he wanted to confess something. But he left before explaining further."

Julia glanced apprehensively at the pastor's assistant, who, it appeared, had no intention of leaving the room.

"You may as well sit down, Mrs. Mayhew," the pastor finally said. "I think we'll want a third witness to whatever we're about to hear."

The woman quivered like a little girl accepting a bright-red balloon. "How exciting," she said, quickly planting herself on the sofa.

Julia joined her and Alex around the coffee table. The pastor placed his tablet in front of them and tapped in the contact code that appeared at the bottom of the note.

"Here goes," he sighed while bowing his head as if offering a silent prayer.

They heard a click on the line. "Thank you for calling Confidential Conferencing." Julia had heard the same woman's inflection every time she booked an airline ticket, pressed two for her credit card balance, or waited on hold for a government official. "Please hold while I connect you to your party."

Mrs. Mayhew sat up on the edge of her seat as if anticipating a roller coaster's dip.

"Hello," said a male voice.

"Frank? This is Pastor Alex. I received your note and I'm here with Julia and, I hope you don't mind, my assistant. I thought it might be a good idea to have a third witness."

"Fine," came a tense reply. "Thank you for honoring my request."

Julia leaned in closer to the phone. "This is Julia," she said. "Before you begin, can I ask a question?" She took silence as consent. "Why me?"

"Sorry?" said the voice.

"Why did you specifically ask me to hear your confession out of the countless possible journalists?"

"Why not you?"

"Well, I'm not currently part of a syndicate, for one thing. There's no guarantee I'll be able to convince someone to run the story."

"They'll run the story," he said dismissively. "And you'll tell it as it should be told."

"What makes you say that?" she asked.

"Because you understand me."

Julia felt alarm. "Have we met?"

"Not directly. But I know you pretty well."

She swallowed hard. "How?"

Several seconds passed. "I dated your sister."

Julia rushed through a mental checklist of Maria's flings. Then she remembered. A year earlier the police had used Maria in a sting operation to catch a man suspected of threatening Judge Victor Santiago.

"Matthew? Matthew Adams?"

A prolonged silence. "I can't tell you my name," he replied nervously. "Nor can I allow you to speculate. I'm an anonymous source. Understood?"

Julia nodded toward the voice. "Yes, I understand."

"Pastor Ware?" the voice insisted.

"I understand also," said Alex.

"Me, too," added Mrs. Mayhew eagerly.

The man continued. "The main reason I chose you, Ms. Davidson, is that I know you'll understand why I made the choices I did."

"How do you know that?" Julia asked warily.

"You were part of my inspiration, for one thing."

"Was I?"

"Does the title 'Free to Thrive' ring a bell, Ms. Davidson?"

Regretfully, it did. It had been one of the more popular columns from her RAP Syndicate days, advocating genetic pre-screening over blind conception. It was something she had written before meeting Troy, before discovering their infertility, and before viewing children as gifts to be received rather than products to be manufactured to match picky customer specifications.

"You said we should give babies the freedom to thrive by eliminating the risk of unnecessary disease and disability," he continued.

Julia thought of Baby Leah.

"The last words of that article helped me make a very difficult decision. You said we should give the same freedom to those of us already burdened by both."

Julia looked toward Alex with embarrassed eyes.

"What kind of decision?" the pastor asked.

"Excuse me?"

"You said the article helped you make a difficult decision."

"My mother was doing poorly," the man explained. "It was costing us a fortune, too much for me to pursue her dream that I become a college professor."

"I see," said Alex. "So you 'set her free'?"

"Well, not me specifically. But yes, we chose a transition."

"Who chose?" Julia asked.

"She did!" the man snapped with offense. "My mother chose to transition so that I could afford tuition."

"I don't follow. How did my column help?"

"I was reluctant to go through with it," he explained. "I guess I never fully recovered from my Catholicism." A pensive chuckle. "My old priest even told me it would be a sin for her to volunteer. But your column helped open my mind to a less rigid religious view. Long story short, I came to believe that our bodies and minds decay so we should free those who suffer from unnecessary anguish."

"Was your mother suffering?" asked Alex.

No reply.

"Frank? Was your mother in pain?"

"That's not the point," the man said. "My point is that you, Ms. Davidson, will understand why I went down this path."

"What path is that?" she asked.

"A path that got me in trouble with the law."

He told his story. A wrongful death lawsuit against NEXT Transition Services had held up the man's transition inheritance money. The case had gone to a federal appeals court. It had hung on the opinion of presiding judge Victor Santiago. The man had written to the judge, hoping to open a dialogue. Somehow, someone had gotten copies of the letters and forged a final, threatening note. When the police found the judge dead in his chambers they had naturally assumed the man had been the culprit.

"But I know who the real killer is," the voice insisted. "And I know who hired him to do it."

"We're listening," said Alex.

"The killer goes by the name Mori. He works for a lady who calls herself Serena Winthrop and a man named Dimitri."

"Evan Dimitri?" asked Julia with alarm.

"You know him?" asked Alex.

"Not personally. But my husband has met him. A power player behind Franklin's campaign."

Mrs. Mayhew's eyes became saucers. "Joshua Franklin?" she shouted. "The senator?"

Julia nodded. Then she remembered. Pastor Alex had mentioned blood on the sleeve of the man she now knew for certain to be Matthew Adams. "Did you...kill Dimitri?" she asked.

"If only I had."

"Then what did you do, Frank?" asked Alex. "You arrived in my office this morning clearly distraught about something. You had blood on your shirt. Whose blood was it?"

"He threatened to turn me in to the police if I didn't accept another assignment."

"What kind of assignment?" asked Julia, feeling the same dread that had pervaded her dreams.

"They hired me to help with at-home transitions," Matthew confessed. "Everything appeared to be aboveboard. I had no idea…"

He stopped short as if realizing he had said more than he should. Then he continued through a breaking voice, "I can't forget their faces."

"What faces?" asked Alex. "The ones that look like religious icons?"

"Yes," he admitted.

"Can you give me names?"

"Brianna Jackson. Saul Weinstein. Josephine Green."

A pause.

"Jim and Gayle Tolbert."

Julia leaped to her feet. "Is that whose blood was on your shirt?" she shouted.

"I didn't kill them," Matthew was saying. "I promise. The old man attacked us. That's when I realized the assignment was a sham. I ran. Mori, he's the killer, not me. I did nothing wrong. I'm a victim. I just did as I was told."

Julia felt a rising nausea. "That's what the Nazis said." She sneered at horrendous evil once again hiding behind complicit weakness.

The room fell silent. The man's story had been heard.

"Listen to me, Frank," Alex finally said. "You need to turn yourself in to the police."

"I told you, I did nothing wrong. Dimitri, he's the guy they want."

"Of course," the pastor continued. "But it seems you've been a pawn in something far more ominous than you may realize. Something beyond what we can see with our eyes."

Julia, sensing the same, looked at her pastor. He returned her gaze.

"I don't believe it's an accident that the two of you have been brought to this moment," he began. "Frank, you told me you have been having dreams. Julia, so have you."

She nodded in unison with the sound of Matthew's sigh.

"You both asked me whether dreams carry meaning. Perhaps even a message. Well, here we are, together, receiving a message that couldn't be clearer."

"What message?" asked Matthew.

"Julia," said Alex, inviting her to explain what she only now, only vaguely, perceived.

"I was wrong," she began. "Life is a gift to receive and protect, not select and discard."

"Then why did you write—"

"Forget what I wrote, Matthew," she interrupted. "That was before I realized."

"Realized what?" he asked skeptically.

She couldn't find the words.

Alex intervened. "Julia has been growing in her understanding of what I said to you earlier today, Frank. Something the Bible calls repentance. Acknowledging you've been heading in the wrong direction, and turning around."

"I told you before, I don't believe in sin."

"But you know yourself to be a sinner, don't you, Frank?" He looked toward Julia. "Or should I say Matthew?"

The phone went silent.

"I can't explain why, but I sense it's no accident two people with similar dreams have been brought to this moment. God wants to save us from our own rebellion. He extends his hand, offering the grace of rescue. Julia took that hand. You can do the same, Matthew. Turn yourself in and start fresh."

"I can't do that."

"Can't, or won't?"

"I haven't done anything wrong."

"All of us have sinned. All fall short of the glory of God."

"I told you, I don't believe in God," Matthew said severely. "And you won't call me Matthew. I'm an anonymous source. You promised."

"I'll honor our agreement," said Julia. "But I need more details if I'm going to write a complete story. Can we meet face-to-face?"

"I've told you everything I can. Now please, do what I've asked."

"But—"

The call ended.

"Oh, my," said Mrs. Mayhew as if clicking off the television, "that certainly was exciting, wasn't it?"

Julia met the pastor's eyes. "What do you think he'll do?"

"I don't know," he said, rubbing his temples. "All I know is that from the first time we met I sensed that man had a tortured soul, as if he had begun sliding toward madness. Now I fear something even worse."

A brief silence.

"What was it he said?" Alex continued. "That he freed his mother to thrive?"

"That's right," Julia said with lamentation at her part in Matthew Adams's descent.

"And then he mentioned the names of others he helped to transition, or, in his words, 'free.'"

The pastor reached toward the coffee table, placing his hand on a large book. He rubbed the cover's iconic image of the Madonna and child.

"I worry he now intends to 'free' someone else."

"Such as?" Julia asked with alarm.

A tentative shrug. "Himself, perhaps?"

A cloud of heaviness settled over Julia. She reached one hand toward Mrs. Mayhew and the other toward Alex. "Please, Pastor," she said, "will you pray?"

CHAPTER THIRTY-NINE

Kevin jumped out of the taxi as it approached the front door of University Hospital. His best friend stood waiting just inside. They embraced.

"How are they?" asked Kevin as they rushed toward the elevator.

"They're fine," said Troy. "Although your dad is a bit upset that you got on a plane so fast. He kept ordering me to call you off."

"Let me guess. He said there's no need to make a fuss."

Troy smiled while pressing the elevator call button. "Exactly. Although your mom was glad to know you were on your way."

"I wish I could have come sooner. It's been, what, twelve hours since the attack? Any suspects yet?"

"You can ask the detective. He's still here."

They stepped onto the open elevator.

"Still here?" Kevin growled. "Why on earth isn't he tracking down whoever did this to my parents?"

"Whoa, pal," said Troy, placing a paw on his friend's tense shoulder. "Take it easy. I told you, they're going to be fine. They've been gathering clues. In fact, he's interviewing Julia right now."

"Why interview Julia?"

A single ding followed by opening elevator doors.

"Let's just say she had an interesting morning." He waved his hand to insist Kevin exit first. "But I'll let you hear it from her directly."

They turned left and walked about fifty steps.

"This is it," said Troy as they approached the room. "You go ahead. They'll want you all to themselves for a few minutes. I'll be around the corner with Julia and the detective."

Kevin eased the door open. He saw his mother sitting beside his father's bed. They were holding hands, eyes fixed on a television screen mounted on the wall. Kevin smiled when he realized they were watching an episode of his mom's favorite classic program, *I Love Lucy*. His dad had never even liked, let alone loved, Lucy. He had apparently lost the battle over programming preference, as usual.

With two raps on the door Kevin drew their attention away from the screen. His mother's eyes instantly welled up with tears. She tried to stand but Kevin waved her back into her chair. He approached quickly, entering her outstretched arms while placing a firm hand on his dad's shoulder.

"Are you two all right?" he asked.

"Fine," said his father with a manly snort that betrayed tender emotion. "You shouldn't have come. A bunch of fuss, that's all."

"I'm glad you're here, Son," overruled Kevin's mom. She squeezed his neck tighter. "Very glad."

"I got here as quick as I could." He sat in the other chair.

"You shouldn't have come at all," his dad repeated.

"So you said." Kevin winked toward his mom. "You look like an underdressed mummy," he added while pointing at his father's head bandage. "I'd hate to see the other guy."

"Nailed him right in the ear with my old hiking boot. Your mother wanted me to get rid of those boots years ago." He looked at his wife. "Good thing I didn't listen, right, doll?"

She slapped his outstretched hand. "Hush," she scolded. "Nobody cares about your crusty old boot."

He turned back to Kevin. "Find a guy walking around with a size-ten boot print indented into the side of his head and you'll find the culprit."

They shared a chuckle.

"The police officer who called me this morning said there were two intruders."

"That's right. But I only nailed the one. The other guy was in the living room tying your mother to a chair. I'd have given him a full-facial whack if he hadn't run so fast."

"It's a good thing he did run," said Kevin's mom. "You were lying on the ground bleeding. I thought you were dead." A distraught sigh. "It was terrible. Just terrible!"

"It was just a little blood," barked Kevin's dad. "That wouldn't have stopped me. There was no way I was going to let them harm my sweet bride. I wanted to kill someone when I saw her strapped down with those plastic zippy things like some kind of animal!"

Kevin felt his father's anger fueling his own.

"Where is that detective anyway?" the elder continued. "We need to catch those guys before they try to invade some other home."

Kevin stood and moved toward the door. "Let me check. He was talking to Julia Simmons."

"Great!" said his dad with displeasure. "The detective is sipping coffee and chatting instead of chasing criminals."

Kevin's thoughts exactly.

He rounded the corner to find Julia, Troy, and a man he didn't recognize. He had a shadow of dark stubble on his head and a small beard on his chin. He wore plain clothes with a badge that read "Denver Police" hanging from his belt.

The man leaped to his feet at Kevin's approach while Julia rushed in for a consoling embrace.

"Oh, Kevin," she said, "I'm so sorry."

He patted her back. "Thanks for coming, Julia."

The stranger extended his hand toward Kevin. "Congressman Tolbert, I'm Tyler Cain. We spoke earlier this morning."

"Yes, of course," he said while measuring the man's grip. "My father and I would appreciate a briefing on what you know."

"Certainly."

The four moved into the hospital room for a consultation.

"Excuse me," said a stern-looking nurse who had apparently slipped into the room to check her patient's blood pressure. "We only allow three visitors at a time."

Tyler removed the badge from his belt. "Police business," he said assertively.

The nurse reached for a laminated plastic name tag hanging from her neck. "Hospital rules."

"Please," said Troy, "won't you just give us a few minutes? The congressman's parents were attacked in their home this morning. We need to figure out who was behind it and why."

The nurse's eyes widened, then she glanced at the name on his father's chart. "Congressman... Tolbert?"

"That's right," said Kevin.

She smiled admiringly. "I voted for you."

He quickly peered at her tag, "Thank you for that, Ms. Sledge, is it?"

"Please, call me Jill."

"Jill then," he said warmly.

The nurse looked at the others, then back at Kevin. "I just had my third baby," she said, as if making a generous contribution to the congressman's cause. The emotion in her voice caught Kevin by surprise.

"Thank you for that, also," he replied.

She removed the blood pressure device from the senior Tolbert's arm. "Let me just get this out of your way," she said before scurrying out the door.

"Well," said Kevin, taking command of the ensemble gathering around his father's bed. "Tell us what you know."

"We didn't know much more than what I shared with you on the phone this morning until Mrs. Simmons here told me about a meeting she had with her pastor about an hour ago."

Kevin looked at Julia. "Pastor Ware?" he asked, struggling to make a connection.

She relayed the odd story.

A mysterious message inviting her to meet at the church.

An anonymous note asking the pastor to hear the writer's confession over the phone.

The hope that Julia would use the confession to expose an alleged assassin.

"Mrs. Simmons believes the anonymous confessor to be a man named Matthew Adams," said Tyler.

Kevin tried unsuccessfully to place the name.

The detective continued. "We had him in custody last year for a while, but let him go when we learned he couldn't have committed the murder."

"Wait," interrupted Kevin. "I don't understand what any of this has to do with the attack on my parents."

The detective pulled out his tablet and tapped the screen before handing it to the couple. "Do either of you recognize—"

"That's him," shouted Mr. Tolbert. "The guy I whacked with my boot!"

"Thank the Lord," said Mrs. Tolbert. "You found him."

"Not exactly," explained Tyler. "This picture is about a year old, from when Mr. Adams was being held under house arrest until we could officially confirm his innocence."

Mr. Tolbert frowned. "Great! You set him loose to continue the killing spree?"

"No, sir," said the detective. "He didn't kill the judge. I know that for a fact."

"How?" asked Kevin.

"He was with me at the time of the murder. I had tracked him using what appeared to be threatening letters he had written to the judge. In fact, that's when I first met Mrs. Simmons."

Julia nodded at the mention. "Matthew is a former high school acquaintance who had a crush on my sister," she explained. "Mr. Cain used Maria as the bait to reel him in."

"But he was innocent then," said Tyler.

"Well, he isn't innocent now," barked Mr. Tolbert. "That is definitely the man who attacked me."

"Why would he want to kill my parents?"

"That's what I've been trying to figure out," said Tyler. "Like I said this morning, I've been investigating a string of similar incidents ever since I rejoined the force about a year back. But until now I've had no survivors who could provide positive identification."

"But you just said this guy didn't kill the judge. So how is he connected?"

The detective turned toward Julia. "That's what Mrs. Simmons was about to explain when you walked up."

CHAPTER FORTY

Julia cleared her throat. "Well, during his phone confession this morning the anonymous voice claimed he had been framed for Santiago's murder. He also said he had been tricked into doing something bad."

"What kind of bad?" Tyler asked.

"He didn't say. But he insisted it wasn't anything illegal."

The congressman spoke next. "Like a scheduled transition?"

"That would fit the other cases," said Tyler. "All apparent volunteers."

"So that's why they claimed my husband made an appointment," said Mrs. Tolbert.

"Well, what are you waiting for?" asked Kevin's father assertively. "Go after the fool!"

"We would," said Tyler, "if we knew where he was." He looked at Julia. "Did you pick up any indications of where he might be heading next?"

"No. Nothing," she said. "But he sounded pretty distraught. I got a very bad feeling. So did Pastor Ware. He's afraid Matthew plans to do something dramatic."

"Like?"

"Like take his own life, or possibly the life of the man he believes is behind all of this."

"Who's that?" asked Tyler.

Silence.

"Did he mention a name?" he pressed.

Julia hesitated. "I'm reluctant to say."

He waited for more.

"You need to understand. I nearly destroyed a man's reputation once before." Julia looked toward Kevin with eyes full of regret. "I swore I wouldn't let that happen again. All I know is what an anonymous source, a man desperate to pin the blame on someone else, has alleged. I need confirmation before I accuse anyone."

"What about the pastor?" asked Tyler. "Do you think he might tell us?"

"He swore to keep the conversation confidential. All he agreed to do is confirm hearing the confession I report, which I intend to do as soon as I can substantiate details of the accusation."

"What kind of details?" Tyler insisted.

"He claimed that the person who framed him did so by mimicking letters Matthew wrote."

"I have those letters," said Tyler. "They matched the alias of the letters your sister received. Remember?"

She thought for a moment. "Who else saw those letters?"

"The assistant chief," said Tyler. "Judge Santiago's assistant. Oh, and Mrs. Santiago, of course, since the final letter came to her at the house."

Julia shook her head thoughtfully. "The confession didn't include any of those. He pinned it on someone pretty influential."

A sudden realization pierced Tyler's memory, a remote possibility he had tried to forget. There was one other name that he'd hoped would never cross his lips, that of a man he'd convinced himself had nothing whatsoever to do with the judge's assassination. Because if he had, Tyler shuddered to think, Tyler himself would share the blame.

"He didn't by chance mention a man named...Evan Dimitri?"

The room fell silent. Kevin and Troy appeared stunned while Julia simply nodded.

Tyler sighed deeply. "I was afraid of that," he began. "But it fits."

"Evan Dimitri of the Saratoga Foundation?" asked Troy.

More nodding.

Kevin spoke next. "Didn't Dimitri write a large check to my reelection fund?"

"He did," said Troy uneasily. "But more to the point, Dimitri is the big money behind Franklin's run for the White House."

"Do either of you know a reason Dimitri would want to see Judge Santiago dead?" Tyler asked.

"You bet," said Troy. "Dimitri has a vested interest in protecting and expanding the Youth Initiative."

"What kind of interest?"

"He controls the serum of choice used by NEXT Transition clinics."

"He owns PotassiPass?" Tyler asked as if finding another piece of the puzzle.

"And a dozen other related businesses, I'd bet."

That's when Tyler noticed Kevin Tolbert's head fall into his hands. "I'm so sorry," he said.

"What do you have to be sorry for?" asked Mr. Tolbert.

"I think I know what's going on. And it means I put the two of you at risk."

"How?" asked his mother.

"Dimitri hates my Bright Spots proposal, or at least the parts that run counter to the Youth Initiative. He knows I'm speaking at the convention next week. He knows a large bloc of voters like my message."

"Of course they do," said Mrs. Tolbert. "But—"

"Listen, Mom," he interrupted. "There are billions of dollars at stake in this debate. Every potential volunteer is a potential source of revenue for a man like Dimitri, not to mention a potential life preserver for a federal budget drowning in debt. I should have realized…" He stopped.

"What's wrong?" Tyler asked in reaction to the congressman's face.

"Imagine the headlines. 'Parents of Youth Initiative Critic Volunteer for Transition to Support His Cause.' What better way to discredit me?" He turned toward his parents. "Mom, Dad, I'm so, so sorry."

"Don't be ridiculous," said the elder Tolbert. "You've done nothing wrong." Then the old man looked straight into Tyler's eyes. "Am I right?" he demanded.

More right than he knows, thought Tyler. How much to say? It was Julia who had originally suggested someone like Evan Dimitri might provide clues in the Santiago case. Innocent enough, he had thought. Float the letters by Dimitri to glean a scrap of information, no matter how remote. Instead of leading him to the killer, however, Dimitri had shut him down right after seeing copies of the letters written by Matthew Adams.

"Julia," Tyler said, "I think I can provide the confirmation you need for part of Matthew Adams's confession."

She appeared confused by the comment. "How?"

He hesitated. "Can't say. I can only say that Evan Dimitri had access to Matthew Adams's letters."

"Which would have given him what he needed to frame Matthew!" she said, connecting the dots. "So he was telling the truth. Matthew has been nothing more than a pawn."

"So it would appear."

"I don't care if he's a pawn, a knight, a bishop, or a rook," said Mr. Tolbert, "I want that man arrested for what he tried to do to my wife."

"Of course," said Tyler. "Don't worry. We'll track him down."

"He could be anywhere by now," said Julia, glancing at a clock beside Mr. Tolbert's bed. "It's been nearly four hours since he left Pastor Ware's office this morning."

"Alone?" asked Tyler.

A blank stare.

"Did Matthew visit the pastor's office alone this morning or was the other attacker with him?"

"I believe he was alone." Julia appeared to think for a moment. "Why do you ask?"

"Because it's been over twelve hours since the other man fled the Tolberts' house. He could be anywhere in or out of the country by now."

"Dear Lord!" said Mrs. Tolbert. "That means he could be in Washington. Angie! The kids!"

Tyler felt a swell of panic in the room. "Congressman Tolbert," he asked intently, "are your wife and children in a safe place?"

"They're at home," came the urgent reply.

"Baby Leah," whispered Julia.

"What about her?" asked Tyler.

"I can't say for sure," Julia said with confusion and alarm.

"Can't say what?" Mr. Tolbert demanded.

"I've felt a need to pray for Leah, as if something was about to happen. I hadn't thought it might be connected to this incident until now."

Kevin was already activating his phone.

So was Tyler. "This is Detective Cain," he said to the dispatcher. "I need you to contact the D.C. police immediately.

I want a patrolman sent to the home of Congressman Kevin Tolbert right away." He looked toward Troy, who gave him the address. He repeated it into the phone.

The congressman appeared distraught, and suddenly pale. "No answer," he said. "I'll try my backup phone." He pressed another icon. One second later he reached into a vibrating pocket, then grimaced at the realization he had brought both phones with him.

"Is there any other way to reach her?" asked Tyler. "A neighbor perhaps?"

Tyler noticed Julia kneeling beside Mrs. Tolbert in an apparent fit of prayer.

That's when the congressman's phone rang again. Tyler glanced at the screen to make out what appeared to be a photo identifying the caller.

Kevin's fingers shook as he accepted the call.

"Angie?" he pled. "Is that you, babe? Are you all right?"

A brief silence as all eyes tried reading the congressman's face. Features frozen in fear quickly melted into a warm, relieved grin.

"Hi, buddy!" he sang while tossing a wink toward Mrs. Tolbert and Julia. Their prayers, it seemed, had been unnecessary. Or perhaps answered. "I'm with Grandma and Grandpa," he was saying. "Uncle Troy and Aunt Julia are here, too."

He paused to listen. "Now?" he asked before adding, "you got it!"

Kevin tapped an icon before pointing the device at the television screen mounted on the wall. "Tommy says we all need to see something."

The screen came alive. They waited a few seconds for the big event. "Ready, Daddy?" said a boy who, to Tyler's eyes and ears, seemed seven or eight years old.

"We're ready, buddy!" Kevin replied.

Tyler positioned himself at just the right angle to see what was on the screen. A lovely woman, the congressman's wife, sat on a sofa holding a toddler on her lap.

"Hi there, Leah," said Grandma, returning the child's Mommy-induced wave.

"Hi, Angie," added Julia.

"I'm so glad you're all together," said the mommy to her relieved audience. "You won't believe what just happened."

The screen zoomed closer to the toddler.

"Here we go," came her big brother's voice.

The lovely woman leaned close to whisper something into the little girl's ear. Whatever she said prompted a smile of delight. All eyes remained fixed on the scene.

Then they heard it: a single, indecipherable syllable, followed by another.

The room erupted with elation as if the kid had hit a grand slam in the World Series.

"Did you hear that?" shouted the congressman while accepting a kiss on the cheek from Julia and a high five from Troy.

Tyler looked at the elder Tolbert, who sat beaming with pride in his hospital bed. "What just happened?" he asked.

"This is a big day for the Tolbert family," the old man explained. "Our granddaughter, whom we feared might never speak, just said her very first word."

"Not just any word," added the congressman. "She said, 'Daddy'!"

CHAPTER FORTY-ONE

Tyler woke to a smell he barely recognized. He glanced at the clock: eight a.m., too early to rise on a Saturday morning. But the aroma of sizzling bacon teased his appetite and his curiosity. Renee had expunged all fat and flavor from his diet shortly after the honeymoon. Why, all of a sudden, had she decided to fry up a skillet of breakfast heaven?

"Hey you," he yawned after finding his way to the kitchen.

"Hey back at ya," she said with a wink.

"What's this?"

"Oh, just a little surprise."

Tyler had been a detective long enough to recognize a decoy when he saw one. Renee had something up her sleeve. Under normal circumstances he would have resisted the temptation to take the bait. But Renee, unlike the criminal class, knew his greatest weakness.

"Smells terrific!" he said while taking a chair at the kitchen table. Renee's parents, Gerry and Katherine, were already seated, casually sipping their usual grapefruit juice. The two had become another part of the marriage package. With no place else to go they had ended up moving in with their daughter and her reluctant boyfriend turned devoted husband. They were, at times, a pain in the neck. But they were Renee's family. *His* family. And the inconvenience of their presence came with a sense of satisfaction he had never known before asking for her hand.

Renee used a fork to remove a piece of bacon from the pan. Tyler frowned at the sight of a turkey strip. He had expected the good stuff.

"Smitty called," said Renee casually.

He couldn't remember the last time the assistant chief had called on a weekend. "What'd he say?"

"Wanted to know if you had seen the weekend journal this morning." She delivered a piece of dry toast and bacon to Tyler's plate. "Here you go," she said while kissing his cheek. "Enjoy!"

He offered an appreciative grin while nibbling. "I'll take a look," he said. "Seen the tablet?"

"Next to your plate."

But it wasn't.

"Daddy!" scolded Renee. "I put that there for Tyler to read the news, not for you to play Pac-Man."

"Tetris!" he insisted before sliding the device toward his son-in-law. "Pac-Man was for kids."

Renee rolled her eyes while Tyler tapped the screen twice. A headline appeared.

FRANKLIN SUPPORTER LINKED TO SANTIAGO ASSASSINATION

He glanced at the byline. It read "Julia Davidson Simmons."

"She did it!" Tyler said.

"Did what?" asked Renee.

He held a "wait one second" gesture toward his wife while scanning the article. It included nearly every important detail.

The unsolved mystery of Judge Santiago's assassination.

The anonymous confession from a transition industry worker.

A string of "volunteers" at odds with Saratoga Foundation chairman Evan Dimitri.

Large donations to Josh Franklin's campaign in conjunction with efforts to expand Youth Initiative policies.

A series of allegations against Franklin that, of course, he denied.

"She doesn't say anything about Matthew Adams," Tyler mumbled to himself.

"What's that?" asked Renee, who, it seemed, hadn't really been listening.

"The suspect I tracked down last year, the one who wrote those letters to the judge; she doesn't mention his name." He thought for a moment. "No, I suppose she wouldn't. Revealing an anonymous source would destroy her credibility as a journalist."

"More bacon?" asked his wife, oblivious to the conversation her husband was having with himself.

"No, thank you," he said, waving off the offer.

Gerry nodded eagerly while lifting his plate.

"What did Smitty say, exactly?"

"Like I said, he asked whether you had seen the weekend journal."

"Anything else?"

"Don't think so."

"Excuse me for a moment," he said before moving toward the bedroom to make a call.

"Oh, no you don't," Renee insisted. She patted the chair in a summoning motion. "I have another little surprise for you." She paused. "Well, a big surprise actually."

As he suspected, the bacon had been a ploy. He obediently positioned his body back at the kitchen table while his mind scripted the conversation with his boss.

Dimitri will have seen the article by now. He might already be on a private jet leaving the country. Or hunting down Matthew Adams.

"I said, close your eyes!" sang Renee.

He did.

"Now give me your hand."

"Why?"

"You'll see." He sensed his wife holding her breath while placing a tiny object in his palm.

He opened his eyes and glanced at the gift. A white thermometer-like device displayed two solid lines.

"Does this mean . . . ?" he began.

She continued holding her breath while her head nodded at a feverish pace.

"So we're gonna have a baby?"

She exhaled. "Can you believe it?"

"But they said our chances were—"

She finished his sentence. "—terrible! I know."

A year earlier Tyler would have been mortified at the news. That's when he was trying to figure out how to escape yet another clingy girlfriend. The thought of becoming a father would have been the only thing unpleasant enough to scare him away from sex. But now, thanks to Smitty, he had a whole new perspective on marriage and kids. A whole new purpose to his once-empty life.

"I didn't think we could do this!" Tyler said into her moist, forty-year-old eyes. "I mean, our age."

"You mean my age," she corrected.

"Well, yeah, they said—"

"I guess God had other plans," she cut him off before pressing her lips against his.

Exactly what Smitty would say, thought Tyler.

"Congratulations, my boy!" said Gerry while Katherine pressed both hands excitedly over her own mouth.

"OK," said Renee. "Now you can go call Smitty." A sly smile. "You already told him about this, didn't you?"

A hesitation. "He made me tell."

"How did he make you tell?"

"When I answered the phone he asked how I was doing," she confessed, sheepishly biting the tip of her index finger.

Tyler sighed while kissing her cheek. "I bet he's almost as excited as me."

"Almost," she giggled while patting his bottom. "Now go on…Daddy!"

———— ❦ ————

They spent the first few minutes of the call celebrating the news.

Tyler thanked Smitty for the influence he had been in his life, especially when it came to his marriage to Renee and his emerging faith.

"I lay this at your feet, too, you know," he said accusingly.

"Lay what at my feet?"

"This silly grin on my face," Tyler replied. "You remember. Last year at this time I would have thought my life was over if you told me I was about to become a father. Now it feels like my life has finally begun!"

"I hear you, my friend. Wait till you have a second. It just gets better."

"We'll see about that," said Tyler doubtfully. At fifty, even one child was more than he'd expected. Two was probably more than he should hope for.

A brief silence offered an opportunity to ease into the purpose behind Tyler's call.

"What should we do about Dimitri?"

"Nothing."

"But he—"

"It's out of our hands, Tyler. The Feds own the case from now on. I suspect they were at Dimitri's door with an arrest warrant before he had his first cup of coffee this morning."

Tyler felt a wave of relief. A dissonant chord that had kept him on edge for a year had finally resolved. But he also felt a twinge of disappointment. He had imagined himself making his first big arrest since rejoining the force. Still, he was grateful that, thanks to his partner turned boss and mentor, he was back in the game at all.

"But there *is* still the matter of this anonymous source," said Smitty. "Are you thinking Matthew Adams?"

"I am, sir," said Tyler, removing his friend hat to assume the role of subordinate. "Julia Simmons said she and the pastor got a bad feeling, like he might be preparing to harm himself. Or possibly someone else."

"Listen, Tyler, I hate to mess up such an exciting day for you and Renee, but I wonder if you might pull out the old file and see whether you can piece together a possible next step for Mr. Adams."

"No need to apologize, sir. I was thinking the same thing myself. I'll get right on it."

They ended the call.

Tyler walked back toward the kitchen. Renee stood facing the sink, still aglow over the big news. He approached, wrapping his arms around her from behind and resting the palm of one hand on her abdomen. She leaned into his presence to accept a kiss on her neck. Then he rubbed the protective cocoon, home to his forming little boy or girl, while whispering into her ear, "I love you, Mrs. Cain."

CHAPTER FORTY-TWO

Matthew approached the front of the classroom, where he placed one hand on the lectern, followed by the other. He relished the sense of dignified authority the pose evoked. Then he scanned the sea of vacant seats and naked desks he had often occupied while a student at the University of Colorado. His mind returned to lectures he had heard in this very room, delivered by his once-beloved professor, mentor, and, he had thought, friend.

It was Dr. Vincent who had enticed Matthew toward Manichean philosophy: Spirit good. Body bad.

It was Dr. Vincent who had encouraged Matthew's dream of earning a college degree, entering graduate school, and, eventually, becoming a professor himself. The same dream his mother had died to finance.

And it was Dr. Vincent, he now realized, who had caused much of the trouble. Not because he had identified Matthew as a potential assassin. That, he now understood, had been an unfortunate misunderstanding. Nor because of his absence during Matthew's dark days. College professors can't interrupt their writing sabbaticals every time a depressed former student requests a meeting.

The real reason Dr. Vincent was to blame had nothing to do with what had happened in the past twelve months. It was something he had said the year before.

"Remember, Mr. Adams, there's no such thing as a mortal sin. Just hard choices."

Fourteen words that had strengthened Matthew's hesitant resolve. Fourteen words that had changed everything.

They had convinced Matthew that Father Tomberlin was wrong to call volunteering a mortal sin.

They had convinced him that his mother's estate should fund a son's dream rather than sustain a decaying body.

And they had replaced Matthew's childhood dogma with a new, enlightened path. A path now strewn with five lifeless faces Matthew couldn't forget, haunting his sleep and fortifying his shame.

Matthew heard the heavy clank of an opening and closing door echo down the hall, followed by the click of shoes. He bent down to conceal himself behind the lectern. Then he breathed a sigh of relief. The steps were moving away from rather than toward his hideout.

He felt like a criminal on the run. A feeling he despised. A feeling he would end.

Matthew walked toward Dr. Vincent's desk, where he had placed two envelopes. Which to leave? The first contained a letter of thanks for all the professor had done to form his evolving beliefs. It represented Matthew's love for the world of academic scholarship. He had once aspired to an intellectual stature that, he had believed, might free him from the common duties of an ordinary life.

Clearing coffee mugs replaced by grading thesis papers.

Struggling to pay the rent replaced by proposals to obtain a grant.

Calming Mom's forgetful nerves replaced by receiving a department chairmanship.

The second envelope represented Matthew's angst. It held a note blaming Thomas Vincent for a descent into darkness the man's lectures, writings, and chats had propelled. Despite years of mental gymnastics, Matthew felt the gravitational weight of a reality his mutinous spirit had been trying to flee. A truth expressed in creeds he had recited as a boy yet rejected as a man.

There is a God. So all things are *not* permissible.

He held one envelope in each hand like a scale tilting between options. His former professor might have embodied Matthew's aspirations. But Father Tomberlin had been right. Just like Reverend Grandpa and, more recently, Pastor Ware.

They believed that every human being carried dignity as one made in the image of God. People are *not* debits.

They believed that God himself had taken on human flesh. The body is *not* bad.

They believed Christ had come to redeem what had been lost and restore what had been damaged. That he had come to conquer death, *not* embrace it.

Dueling envelopes awaited the decision. *What do you believe?*

He couldn't answer. He only knew what he had done.

Matthew placed the letter of blame on Dr. Vincent's desk while tossing the other in a nearby trash basket.

He slipped out of the classroom unseen before exiting the mostly vacant building. He took the long path to his car in order to take one last glimpse at his old place of employment, Campus Grinds. He peered discreetly through the window to see his former shift manager, Sarah, chatting with the only customer. She looked even lovelier than he remembered, her soft features defying rumors of a dreadful world. Then she turned. Matthew caught his breath. Pregnant? He smiled at the thought of Sarah becoming a mom. She'd be terrific, a nurturing presence throughout life for some lucky boy or girl. The kind his own mother had been before she left. Before he had insisted she go.

Five minutes later Matthew sat in the quiet solitude of his car trying to summon courage for what he was about to do.

No more hiding, he told himself.

No more guilt or shame or fear.

And, he could only hope, no more nightmares.

He looked at the passenger seat. It held the at-home transition kit originally intended for Congressman Tolbert's father. He paused while reaching for the object, the angry face of the elderly man invading his memory.

"Leave her alone!" he had shouted while swinging an old boot in Matthew's direction. That's when he had realized the Tolberts weren't doddering old debits eager to end their misery by supporting their son's cause. They had been targets, human beings he would have murdered had it not been for the old man's chivalrous courage.

Matthew thought of his first client, Brianna Jackson. She, too, had resisted his aid. She, too, had had a look of angry fear in her eyes.

"What have I done?" he whispered.

He lifted the lid. A small envelope printed with an elegant font greeted his eyes. "A Message from NEXT Transition Services." He broke the seal to read the note inside.

On behalf of NEXT Inc. we wish to express our deepest thanks to you for joining millions of other heroic Youth Initiative volunteers. As you are aware, your sacrifice will ease the financial burden on those you love and free desperately needed resources for the common good of a grateful nation. Please know that we admire your courage and feel honored to serve your needs as you carry out a simple, painless procedure.

Matthew froze. A surge of fear invaded the moment as the echo of laughter, the same sadistic, ravenous cackle that had haunted his dreams, overtook the silence. He dropped the page like a hot coal. But the laughter reverberated louder still, as if approaching from a shadowy darkness below.

He tried to open the car door. The handle was stuck.

He looked desperately out the windows, forward, right, and left. Then he peered through the rearview mirror. What had he expected to see, perhaps a crazed specter eager to pounce?

The laughter increased until it felt like a scream penetrating every fiber of Matthew's quivering form.

He tried whispering a prayer. But the impulse made him angry. Had he already descended too far? "When we reject the good that God is," Pastor Alex had warned, "all that remains is the evil he isn't."

Matthew looked at the box. It contained the same supplies he had used on three prior occasions. It seemed to be offering itself as an escape. From what? Insanity? Worse?

The noise rose louder still.

"Please, God!" Matthew shouted, pressing both fists over tightly clenched eyes. "Make it go away. Make it go away!"

Nothing happened. Matthew reached for the kit still resting on the seat beside him. A needle and vial of PotassiPass awaited its next willing volunteer.

Its next desperate soul.

CHAPTER FORTY-THREE

Alex searched his wife's eyes for any hint of doubt. Tamara had said three times that she supported his decision. But the moment of truth had arrived. In a few minutes he would exchange a steady paycheck for a clear conscience. Resignation, he agreed, was the best course of action. And, despite uncertainty over how he would provide for the family, an inexplicable sense of confidence had taken up residence where nagging timidity had lived for the past year.

He felt the change during Sunday's sermon. Alex delivered the kind of message he should have preached long before. Rather than indirect, vague references to respecting elders he told the congregation what they needed to hear.

Volunteering for the Youth Initiative is not heroic. It is suicide.

Coaxing parents to volunteer is not a prudent financial move. It's a violation of the fifth, sixth, and tenth commandments.

Remaining silent in the face of evil is not pastoral sensitivity. It's implicit consent.

Alex even told the congregation about the letter. "I don't want any of you to be surprised," he had said, "when you read in the news this week that I wrote an open letter to our elected officials challenging them to uphold human dignity rather than expand the transition industry."

The look on Phil Crawford's face during that message should have struck fear into Alex's heart. But it hadn't. Alex had already decided his next move. The church deserved to know the real reason he was leaving. It might, he hoped, prompt some to reconsider their own choices. Perhaps even their own worth.

"Are you ready?" asked Tamara, tightening her grasp.

He squeezed her soft hand. "I am. You?"

She nodded bravely.

"Then here we go."

They walked through the same office complex Alex had entered nearly every day since becoming pastor of Christ Community Church. He glanced at Mrs. Mayhew's empty desk.

"Well," he said with a chuckle, "I guess this is one way of getting rid of an incompetent assistant."

Tamara gently slapped his shoulder in rebuke.

"Truth is," he added, "I'm going to miss her. She can't keep a confidence, but she does care about people."

As they approached the conference room they noticed the lack of mingling camaraderie. It had been trumped by an awkward hush of tension. Phil Crawford, the lawyer, and five members of the board sat along with a gentleman Alex didn't recognize.

"I don't believe we've had the pleasure," he said while extending a hand toward the stranger.

The man ignored the offer.

"This is Freddy Baxter," said Phil tepidly. "He asked to join us for part of the meeting this evening in order to clear up the... um... misunderstanding that triggered a lawsuit against Christ Community Church."

"Not a misunderstanding," the man objected. "Your church caused a real mess for me and my—"

"Please, Mr. Baxter," interrupted the lawyer, "let's not jump to conclusions. We invited you here as a good-faith gesture to discuss what happened. I promise, we'll get to the bottom of this situation and, hopefully, avoid a prolonged ordeal in the courts."

Alex looked toward Tamara. She looked every bit as confused as he was. Both took seats at the conference table. "I was sorry to learn of your mother's diagnosis," he said to the man. "She's a delightful person."

The man huffed. "My mother is sick and, thanks to you, will probably suffer more than she needs to."

Alex looked toward the lawyer, who remained silent. Alex understood. Let the pastor, a man who has been asked to resign, take the fall.

"May I ask why you blame me for her illness?"

"Not for her illness. For her decision."

"Her decision to live?" asked Alex, prompting an agitated wriggle from Phil Crawford.

"Her decision not to volunteer."

"I see," said Alex. "So you think I'm to blame for your mother's view on suicide."

Freddy Baxter appeared to resent the statement. "There, you see," he said accusingly, his eyes shifting back to the lawyer. "He equates transitions with suicide."

"Now, Pastor," interjected the lawyer, "it would be best if we avoided moral judgments while discussing such a difficult, personal decision."

"Actually," said Alex, "difficult, personal decisions are exactly the time to discuss moral judgments."

A sudden sound summoned all eyes to look toward the door. Brandon Baxter was entering the room. "Sorry I'm late, everyone," he said. "I just learned of this meeting about an hour ago."

Phil Crawford flashed a false, puzzled expression. "Really?" he said with a lilt. "Sorry about that, Brandon. Must have been some sort of mix-up that—" Phil stopped short when he noticed an elderly woman following Brandon into the room.

"Hello, Freddy," she said in her son's direction. The man appeared alarmed, then ashamed.

Ellie Baxter winked in Alex's direction with the same spark for life she had displayed when they first met in the restaurant. The day she relayed the story of her husband, Freddy's late father.

Alex rose to his feet. "Hello, Mrs. Baxter. Please, sit here."

She accepted the offer gratefully. Alex moved two spaces, allowing room for the woman and her nephew.

Freddy Baxter made a single nod toward his estranged cousin. "Brandon," he said coldly.

"Freddy," came Brandon's chilly response.

Alex sensed a showdown was about to begin.

Phil Crawford spoke next. "Um, I'm afraid this is a closed-door board meeting."

"And I'm a member of the board," Brandon replied before Phil could continue, "who invited a long-term member of Christ Community to shed some light on a matter of pressing concern to the financial stability of this church."

Phil, for once, held his tongue.

"Please, Aunt Ellie, tell the board what you told me earlier today."

She fixed her gaze on her son's wilting eyes. "First, I'd like to correct a mistaken impression that I'm told prompted this evening's meeting."

"Mother," Freddy threatened.

Mrs. Baxter raised a single hand of maternal rebuke to silence her son.

"To begin, contrary to what my son may have assumed, he

does not stand to receive any portion of my estate when I die."

Freddy's eyes betrayed panic at the revelation.

She looked toward the lawyer. "Both my doctor and attorney were present when I made the decision. They will confirm that I was very much of sound mind and body at the time."

All color drained from Freddy Baxter's face.

"You should also know that my decision to reject the transition option had nothing to do with the activities of, sermons from, or conversations with this pastor. Although, I must say, I greatly appreciated what he had to say during Sunday's message."

She offered an affirming nod in Alex's direction before continuing.

"So any claim to damages my son has made can be ignored. Neither Christ Community Church nor Pastor Ware can be blamed for whatever financial problems Freddy and his wife may be experiencing."

The man's head fell into his hands.

The board seemed to breathe a collective sigh of relief at the disappearance of a threatening cloud.

"You should also know," Mrs. Baxter continued, "that I had my lawyer draft language for a revised will. In short, I intend to leave a sizable portion of my estate to Christ Community Church."

Phil Crawford slid his chair away from Freddy Baxter and toward the potential donation.

Brandon Baxter spoke next. "Aunt Ellie intends to give an initial contribution that is more than enough to pay off the remaining balance on the mortgage. With additional donations occurring on an annual basis until her passing, which, Lord willing, won't occur for many years."

The woman placed her hand sweetly on her nephew's arm.

"Now, Brandon dear, we don't know that." She turned toward Alex. "I only know what someone recently told me."

"What's that, ma'am?" asked Phil, as if suddenly enthralled.

"That God isn't finished with me yet," she said with an endearing grin.

"Well," said the chairman, "on behalf of the board I would like to extend my sincere thanks for your generosity. We believe the best days of Christ Community Church are ahead of us and—"

"There is one more thing," interrupted Brandon. He appeared to enjoy cutting Phil short. "My aunt has included a stipulation on the gifts."

The lawyer tapped a tablet and positioned himself to take official notes.

Brandon continued, "Alex must agree to continue serving as lead pastor."

The chairman's eyes shot in the pastor's direction. Alex shrugged to indicate he'd had no prior knowledge of the suggestion. "I would be honored," he said, "but I serve at the pleasure of the board and they've already asked me to resign."

"Then I move that the board annul the earlier severance package offer," said Brandon, "and instead offer Pastor Ware a ten percent raise if he agrees to continue on as pastor of Christ Community Church."

"I second the motion," said Roberto Wilson and Lydia Donovitz in unison.

"Now wait just a minute," Phil objected. "The chairman is supposed to call for a vote."

"The chairman wants to know who supports the motion," said Brandon.

Before Phil could react, Brandon received near-unanimous approval.

Alex looked toward his wife. She appeared to be forcing back tears of relief. Then he looked back toward Brandon, who was wearing a satisfied grin.

"Pastor and Mrs. Ware," Brandon said, "I think I speak for the entire board when I say we owe you an apology."

"For what?" Phil Crawford interjected.

"For ignoring his objections to the transition industry, among other things that have tied his hands."

"I appreciate that, Brandon," said Alex. "But I'm the one who owes you an apology. I should have taken a stand much sooner than I did. I was as much a frog in the kettle as anyone else. I figured evil was part of the world in which we live and that our job is just to do what we can to comfort the suffering."

"That is our job!" said Phil.

"It is, in part. But we must also do what we can to *prevent* the suffering." He paused, then released a determined sigh. "And so I need to make my own stipulation. I will stay on as lead pastor if the board agrees unanimously to sign a statement of belief."

"Already done," said Phil proudly. "I instituted that policy about five years back."

"Not the statement of doctrinal belief," Alex explained. "A statement affirming the dignity and worth of every human life, from conception to natural death. And"—he hesitated— "clarifying that it will be the official position of Christ Community Church to oppose the transition industry."

—⁓—

Before the meeting was adjourned, three monumental shifts had occurred.

First, Phil Crawford threatened to resign before storming out of the room. Mary Sanchez immediately recommended accepting the offer and nominated Brandon Baxter to replace Phil as chairman. The group approved by a vote of five to one. Alex finally had an ally in the chairman's seat. He also had an official invitation to craft a statement everyone would sign at the next meeting.

Second, Ellie Baxter wrote a check that would retire the church mortgage. With no monthly payment to cover, Alex could finally hire additional staff. Possibly even someone to "assist" Mrs. Mayhew.

And finally, Freddy Baxter slumped into the chair beside his mother like a boy who had, at last, seen the error of his ways. While closing the door behind him to offer the two a private moment, Alex watched them embrace: merciful mother forgiving a penitent child.

Alex now sat beside Tamara in the car, reflecting on all that had transpired. They prayed together, thanking God for invading dark moments with bright surprises.

That's when he heard the phone.

"Hmm," he said after glancing at the screen.

"Who is it?" asked Tamara.

"Just a second," he said while accepting the call.

"Pastor Ware?" A voice he didn't recognize. "My name is Tyler Cain, Denver Police. I hope you don't mind me calling so late."

"Not a problem, Officer," he said. It wasn't the first time the police had phoned after hours, usually to alert him to some tragedy that had befallen a parishioner.

"I have someone in custody who asked me to track down your number and give you a call."

"A member of Christ Community?" asked Alex.

"Couldn't say. He told me you would know him as Frank. He turned himself in about an hour ago. Seems pretty down. Can I give him the phone?"

"Yes, yes, of course," Alex replied.

A short silence on the other end of the line.

"Pastor?" he finally heard.

"Hello, Frank."

"It's Matthew, actually. Matthew Adams."

"Matthew, then." A pause. "How are you?"

"Not sure," he said. "OK, I guess. Scared. And a bit relieved."

"The officer told me you turned yourself in."

"That's right."

"For what?"

"I...I did something...bad."

Alex sensed a change in the man's voice. As Frank he had been elusive and frightened, a tortured soul. Now he sounded like someone beginning to locate his own humanity, calmly resolved despite anxiety over whatever might lie ahead.

"No," Matthew corrected himself, "I've sinned. And...I'm sorry."

Alex felt his heart warm at the sound of a soul moving toward the welcoming embrace of redemption. "I'm glad to hear you say that, Matthew. Very glad indeed."

"I was hoping you might, if you don't mind, visit me. I'd like to continue the conversation we started in your office."

"I'd be honored," Alex replied.

A brief silence.

"Ivan was wrong," Matthew said. "I know that now."

Alex recalled the atheistic mantra Frank had embraced. *If there is no God, all things are permissible.*

"Do you remember what I said about Ivan, Matthew?"

"You said he went mad."

"That's right."

Matthew sighed regretfully. "I nearly did the same."

"I know," said Alex. "But it sounds like you've taken a step back toward sanity, Matthew. I'll pray God gives you the grace to take another."

"Thank you, Pastor," the man said with moist emotion.

"I'll stop by in the morning," the pastor promised. "We'll talk more then."

Alex remained on the line for several minutes as Matthew Adams wept into the phone, a flood of regret watering a tiny seed of hope.

CHAPTER FORTY-FOUR

Julia winked reassuringly toward Amanda, who, having received Baby Leah gingerly into her arms, appeared paranoid about the possibility of dropping or squashing the girl.

"Here, let me help," Julia said before repositioning the child onto Amanda's lap. "There, now she can see everybody."

Baby Leah looked at Julia from her twelve-year-old perch. Then she waved her little hand thanks to coaxing from Amanda. Julia copied the gesture.

She returned to the greenroom sofa, where Kevin's parents sat with the other Tolbert kids and awaited the big moment.

"Where's Uncle Troy?" asked Tommy.

"He's with your mommy and daddy," Julia explained.

"He's gonna watch, too, isn't he?"

"Wouldn't miss it for anything," said Julia. "He said he wants to sit by you and watch the speech right over there." She pointed to a large screen mounted just above the refreshment table.

Tommy nodded approvingly before stuffing another truffle into his chocolate-rimmed mouth.

"My goodness, Tommy," came Mrs. Tolbert's distraught voice. "Look at that mess on your face. Come over here and let me clean you up."

The boy looked toward his grandpa in an apparent plea for rescue from one of Grandma's spit baths. Jim Tolbert raised both hands in a show of surrender.

"Sorry, Son," he said. "But you can't very well walk onto the stage with truffle stains, can you? It might create a scandal that lands you on the cover of the weekend journal."

The old man laughed at himself while Tommy sulked toward his grandmother's napkin.

"Do you really think they'll bring the kids onto the stage?" asked Mrs. Tolbert.

"Fifty-fifty chance," Julia guessed. "I imagine if the speech is well received they'll want to capture shots of Kevin's family hugging one another and waving to the crowd."

The door opened and a man poked his head inside. "Fifteen minutes," he said, the second of four countdown warnings they would receive. The next would occur ten minutes before the speech. At the five-minute mark someone would arrive to escort Angie to a special seat on the convention floor and direct Kevin to a staging area where he would await the moment of truth.

"I guess we should alert Kevin," said Julia as she walked toward a dressing room door.

Troy, Angie, and Kevin had huddled to discuss how to handle headlines that were less than an hour old. Evan Dimitri's arrest had led to several others, including that of a woman who had organized a series of supposed transitions and a man who had jammed the needle into Judge Santiago's neck. Most disruptive to the convention, however, was the revelation that Dimitri had been one of the largest donors to the prospective nominee, Joshua Franklin. The news had cast a dark cloud of uncertainty over the nomination process. Kevin had said he needed Troy's eyes on a few changes he wanted to make to his speech, including what he described as an unconventional conclusion.

Julia opened the door, interrupting the conversation. "Ready?" she asked.

"I think so," said Troy with an anxious sigh.

Angie looked adorably nervous for her husband.

"Hey there. You OK?" asked Julia.

A hesitant nod.

"You look amazing," Julia added after taking another admiring look up and down Angie's form-fitted elegance.

"Thanks, Julia," she said while accepting her friend's embrace.

"What about me?" said the man of the hour. "Don't I get a hug? I'm the one about to make a fool of myself."

"I very much doubt that," said Julia while offering her friend a squeeze of confidence.

They walked back into the greenroom just in time to hear another knock on the outer door. A man entered.

"Senator Franklin?" Kevin said at the sight of the surprise visitor. "I didn't expect—"

"Just wanted to wish you well," Franklin interrupted. "This is a big night for you, Congressman. A big night for all of us."

The senator appeared at a loss for words before clearing his throat.

"So," he continued, "I imagine you've seen the news about Dimitri?"

"I have," replied Kevin.

"A terrible shock."

"Yes, sir."

The men stood in awkward silence.

Franklin spoke next. "I was sorry to hear about what happened to your folks. I hope they're all right."

"They are." Kevin motioned toward where his parents were seated as if to introduce them. "In fact—"

The senator interrupted, ignoring the gesture. "I suppose it goes without saying that we see no reason to let any of this distract us from what needs to be done."

Kevin frowned, then grinned. "Of course."

Franklin began patting Kevin's shoulder. "Good. Good."

Another knock. "Ten minutes, Congressman," came a shout.

"Well, I'll get out of your way, Kevin. Like I said, this is a big night for you."

"Thank you, sir."

The prospective nominee turned to exit, only then noticing the presence of Kevin's clan. He appeared unsettled by the sight.

"My, my," he said with a tone of distant admiration, or perhaps condescension. "I haven't seen this many children in one place since I graduated from elementary school." He reached toward Tommy as if to pat the boy's head. Tommy managed to steer clear of the assault.

An embarrassed chuckle. "You certainly do have a big tribe, don't you? Too bad they can't vote," he said before walking out the door.

"Well," Troy announced after a moment, "I sure didn't see that coming."

"Me, neither," said Kevin.

Julia stole another glance toward the assembly of future voters waiting to cheer their father's on-screen appearance. No matter what happened, she thought, they could be proud of their daddy's efforts to make a difference. Just as she and Amanda took pride in all Troy had done to support his friend.

She accepted Troy's hand, savoring the security of his tender grip. Then she noticed Amanda watching them from the other side of the room as if relishing the sight of man and woman turned father and mother to an orphaned girl. An orphaned girl holding Baby Leah, a child many considered unworthy of life.

The sight brought Julia back to another moment. A prayer voiced in the middle of the night. "Please, God, protect Baby Leah." She remembered what her pastor had said. *Dreams sometimes have meaning tied to God's redemptive purposes.* He had likened them to movie trailers, glimpses of divine purposes.

Had Julia seen such a glimpse, she wondered? Had her dreams depicted mysteries beyond human comprehension? Had the sadistic laughter been a summons from an enemy seeking to drag Julia, all of them, into dehumanizing shadows? Had the mysterious man extending his hand been summoning a fatherless world back to his loving, paternal protection? Had the intense compulsion to pray been her most important assignment against an assault even more insidious than the expansive Youth Initiative?

Prayer for Amanda: the transition-orphan who now gave greater purpose to a childless couple's union.

Prayer for Baby Leah: a disabled child who was among those most vulnerable to the heartless reach of economic pragmatism.

Prayer for the Tolberts: a family that embodied the beauty and love at the heart of the God she had come to know.

A sound forced Julia back into the present moment. From Amanda's lap Baby Leah flashed an enormous grin while her arms and legs trembled in excited delight.

"What is it, girl?" asked Amanda while tightening her hold.

Every head turned in their direction.

"Did you hear that?" asked Kevin.

"We heard it," said Angie with a smile. "That's the fifth time in a week."

"Sixth," corrected Kevin proudly. "She's said, 'Daddy' six times!"

Another knock at the door. "Excuse me, Congressman. It's time."

"On my way," he replied while leaning down to kiss Baby Leah's cheek.

Troy placed a hand on his friend's shoulder. "Make us proud, Congressman," he said.

Then Kevin and Angie rushed out the door.

Julia and Troy joined the elder Tolberts on the sofa to watch Kevin deliver his speech.

"So, how did he decide to end?" Julia asked while squeezing the arm of her husband.

"Classic Tolbert," Troy replied. "He plans to flash pictures of his kids while inviting everyone to become a bright spot."

EPILOGUE

Teleprompt Script

Congressman Kevin Tolbert

Thank you, ladies and gentlemen, for the honor of appearing before you this evening. As Congresswoman Ortega just said in her gracious introduction, my wife Angie and I have four terrific kids. So you'll forgive me if I keep my comments brief this evening. [Glance at watch.] Bedtime is in thirty minutes! [Pause for laughter.]

In twenty-four hours you, the delegates, will decide who should succeed President Lowman as our party's nominee for the highest office in the land. I hope you take that assignment as seriously as our times demand. The future of this great nation depends upon strong leadership that understands the economic and social challenges before us; a leader who isn't afraid to make difficult decisions or tackle complex issues; and a leader who has demonstrated the kind of integrity and courage that will be required in coming days.

But before we nominate our candidate and finalize our party platform, it falls to me to say that there is an elephant in the room. And no, I'm not talking about our trunk-nosed mascot. I'm talking about a potential split over fundamental differences of opinion on how best to address the economic decline in which we find ourselves.

For decades every segment of the population, including the once-fertile immigrants, has fallen far below replacement levels. As a result the economic pyramid has flipped and now teeters under a top-heavy load. This year the youngest of the nearly sixty million baby boomers turned seventy-eight. The oldest, four million of them, turned ninety-five. So we find ourselves being squeezed from both directions. The cost to care for our oldest citizens continues to rise while the pool of working, taxpaying citizens continues to shrink. The combined GDP hit runs about five trillion per year.

This country has gone down the same path as every other developed nation in the world due to a combination of declining fertility and senior longevity. And based upon current trends, our pool of working-age adults will continue to shrink.

I'm sure you've heard countless pundits debate the merits of President Lowman's Youth Initiative. Many hoped these policies would help ease our economic decline. And it's true that we've managed to cut hundreds of billions of dollars in medical and entitlement expenses out of the federal budget. It's also true that millions of volunteers have chosen to transition much-needed assets to the younger generation. But we must ask ourselves, at what cost?

Is encouraging the old and vulnerable to die the best we can do to solve this problem? Have you, like me, felt a tiny fragment of your own dignity falling away with each and every volunteer appointment? Don't you, like me, believe there might be a better way, one that acknowledges the inherent value of every man, woman, and child?

Such questions caused us to look beneath the surface of the data to find a ray of sunlight in our overall cloudy picture. What we discovered, ladies and gentlemen, surprised all of the supposed experts. In short, the strongest areas of economic growth in this nation share two simple characteristics. First, they have much higher rates of fertility, more than twice the national average. Second, they have the lowest rates of transition volunteers. In other words, they run one hundred percent opposite to the priorities of Youth Initiative policies.

That's why we formed the Center for Economic Health, a coalition of public- and private-sector leaders seeking ways to make it easier for young people to marry and raise children. We are exploring ways our communities can welcome the wisdom and support of our elderly rather than pressure them to check out early. Many of you here tonight are part of that growing movement, and I thank you for your support. I'd especially like to express appreciation to a coalition of religious leaders who crafted the following open letter to elected officials such as myself.

An Open Letter to Our Elected Officials:

We, the undersigned, wish to express our gratitude for your service to this nation. You play a crucial role in the God-ordained institution of government and we pray that you will be given strength for the task and wisdom for the challenges that lie ahead. As members of the clergy from a variety of religious traditions we, like you, seek to ease the suffering of hurting people and to nurture health in an ailing society. The Hebrew Scriptures state that when the righteous rule, the people rejoice. As spokesmen and spokes-women for many of the people under your authority, we pledge our support and assistance in your effort to do what's right for this great nation. Toward that end we feel compelled to bring to your attention a growing concern over how some of the policies enacted in recent years are affecting the communities we serve.

First, difficult economic times have accelerated the already alarming decline in birthrates, further strangling off the only trickle of life capable of nourishing a rich garden of human thriv-ing. All of our religious traditions uphold the beauty and priority of parenthood. And despite the technological, social, and political pressures that make it increasingly difficult to do so, the most de-vout among us make the sacrifices necessary to bear and rear a new generation. We consider these families to be bright spots in an ever-darkening society. Will you join us in the effort to encourage and support those willing and able to shine the light of hope that radiates from the face of every newborn child?

Our second concern is directly related to the first. A shrinking pool of natural families has created an equally pressing crisis on the other end of the demographic continuum. Too few young and healthy bear the burden of a rapidly aging population. This state of affairs has created an economic strain on the entire society. Cultural elites derisively label the weak and vulnerable "debits" unworthy of life. The younger generation has come to resent rather than honor the old. But all of our faith traditions consider every human being worthy of dignity and protection, including those with graying hair and waning memories. Will you join us in the effort to defend the dignity of the aging and disabled among us?

I, for one, take these words to heart. I hope that the person we nominate tomorrow will do the same.

Take a long, hard look at the numbers, ladies and gen-tleman. You'll find that this nation's problem is not that we have too many old. Our problem is that we have too few young. We hope to see this nation back policies that will make it easier for families to thrive and to treat the old and disabled with dignity instead of like useless debits.

During this session of Congress I am sponsoring what has been labeled the Bright Spots proposal. If you can sort through all of the policy minutiae, budget projections, and legal-speak contained in the proposal, you will discover a very simple idea. It invites all of us to become bright spots in an increasingly dark world.

[Show picture of the family. Wait for audience reaction.]

These are the bright spots in my life.

Standing to my right is my lovely wife Angie. She is my best friend and life partner. But she's also the hope of our nation's future. Politicians talk about solutions. Business leaders produce innovative products. But only women like Angie can solve our most fundamental challenge. We need more people. And that means someone must accept the no-ble, sacrificial call to motherhood. Angie has done her share by bringing four children into the world: a world that has forgotten the urgent priority of bearing and nurturing the next generation. That makes Angie a bright spot; just like millions of other unsung heroes somebody calls Mommy.

The couple standing to my left are Gayle and Jim Tol-bert. I call them Mom and Dad. But the little ones standing in front of me call them Grandma and Grandpa. My kids relish every minute spent hanging around with their grand-parents. They love the tradition of eating chocolate chip pancakes whenever we visit almost as much as Mom and Dad love hanging crayon-drawn masterpieces on the refrig-erator.

[Show picture of refrigerator. Wait for audience sighs.]

Gayle and Jim Tolbert are, of course, bright spots in our lives. And yes, they contribute to the overall economy when they buy goods and services. But much more importantly, they represent a longstanding belief we would do well to reclaim: the value of human life shouldn't be charted on a spreadsheet. My parents, like millions of other elderly and disabled citizens, have resisted mounting pressure to volunteer. They refuse to chip another fragment away from our common sense of dignity, by reminding us that human worth is measured in hugs and kisses, not dollars and cents.

[Show picture of Baby Leah.]

This is my precious little girl, Leah. You can't tell by looking at her, but Baby Leah has a genetic disorder called fragile X syndrome that brings cognitive impairment. She is one who will always consume a higher share of resources than she will likely ever produce. Some have suggested people like Leah should be put out of their misery. But if we are honest with ourselves, it's not their misery we are trying to end. It's our inconvenience. Leah, like so many other disabled citizens, can't give back.

Or can she?

[Show picture of Tommy and Joy hugging Baby Leah.]

On the scale of hugs and kisses, she seems to be doing pretty well.

[Pause for sighs.]

Every developed nation on earth is asking what to do about those who cost more than they produce. But we are a nation founded upon a fundamental belief that all people are created equal and are endowed by the Creator with unalienable rights including life, liberty, and the pursuit of happiness. In that spirit, I challenge us to remember our past rather than fear our future. Yes, times are difficult. Yes, our challenge is great. But we must not forget that greatness is shown when we defend the weak and protect the vulnerable. Strength and growth are by-products of bearing and raising the young, not pillaging and sacrificing the old. We become a virtuous people when we give to the poor and treasure the weak.

So I invite you to join a growing movement lighting our nation's future.

Form a family and invest in the next generation. Every stable home becomes yet another foundation stone for rebuilding this great nation.

Elect leaders who recognize that government exists to defend the rights of the weak rather than indulge the appetites of the strong.

In short, become a bright spot!

God bless you. And may God bless the United States of America.

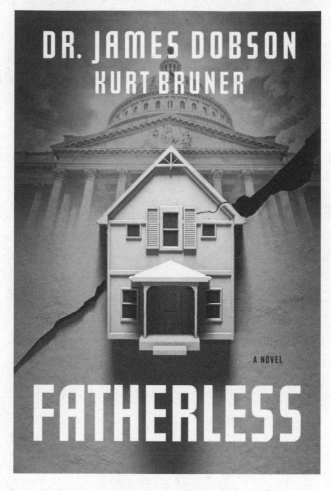

A NOVEL

FATHERLESS

Book One

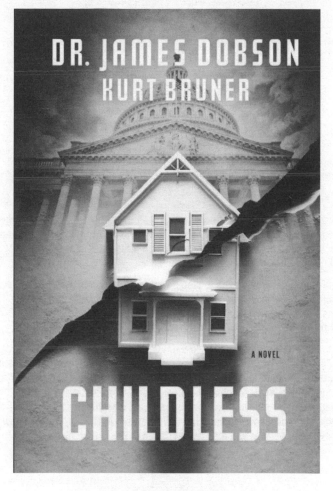

Book Two

DR. JAMES DOBSON

Dr. Dobson wasn't ready to retire when he left Focus on the Family in February 2010. He knew that God had given him a mission and a message many years ago, and that God had not yet lifted that assignment from him.

Dr. Dobson felt God directing him to start a a new ministry, which he did in March 2010, to continue the important work of strengthening families, speaking into the culture, and spreading the gospel of Jesus Christ. He called the new organization *Dr. James Dobson's Family Talk.*

Dr. Dobson has filmed a new series and documentary entitled respectively, *Building a Family Legacy* and *Your Legacy* that combines new and relevant material with some of the classic presentations from his original film series recording in 1978 and seen by over 80 million people worldwide. Lifeway Christian Resources is producing small group and personal study curriculum based on these timeless resourses and also sponsoring a nationwide simulcast that will premiere in October 2014. A new book by Dr. Dobson, *Your Legacy,* will also be published in the Fall of 2014.

The voice you trust
for the family you love

www.DrJamesDobson.org